JJ BLACKLOCKE

AFTERSHOCK

THE TRADEPOINT SAGA BOOK TWO

www.aethonbooks.com

AFTERSHOCK

www.aethonbooks.com

Print and eBook formatting, and cover design by Steve Beaulieu. Artwork provided by Tom Edwards Design.

Published by Aethon Books LLC.

ALSO IN THE SERIES

REFUGE

AFTERSHOCK

THE BEREFT

[1]
1868 OF 2000 ORBITS REMAINING

"Liar!"

The whispered accusation split the air of the dark reception hall.

Gredin froze, shocked. "Who is that?" she demanded. After the miserable night the Vennan delegation had just endured, she had assumed everyone would be lost in exhausted slumber.

Clearly, she was wrong.

"Traitor!"

This time, Gredin recognized the voice.

"Tetralanna," she said. Drawing a small luminth from her pocket, she fed energy into it. "I didn't expect to find you up."

"Up?" Tetralanna shrank from the sudden light, looking ill and shrunken, her hair a snarled cloud around her head. "Of course I'm up. I suppose *you* had no trouble sleeping!"

Selecting her words with care, Gredin said, "Given the news shared at the reception, this past night was difficult for all. I hope that most have finally found some measure of rest before they must rise to face the new day."

"I will never rest again!" Tetralanna proclaimed, her voice rising.

Gredin took a step closer. "You are grieving Venna's loss, as are we all. Come. Let me escort you to your bed. Sleep may yet come, if you allow it." She extended her hand.

But Tetralanna reared back as if the gesture had been a threat. "Do not presume to know my needs. You are only a foolish girl, scarcely old enough to be free of your Guides."

"I am young," Gredin conceded. "Nevertheless, the Power–"

"The Power! I am sick of your boasts concerning the Power."

But they were not boasts. According to Keegan's histories, it was long and long since any Vennan had heard the Power's voice. Nevertheless, on Gredin's first night on Tradepoint, the Power had informed her of the destruction of her world. The second night, after those in charge refused to believe her, it returned to mute Gredin's grief and instruct her to undertake leadership of the survivors. And last night, returning yet again, it ordered her to dispatch the surviving Travelers to find the world that would become their new home.

She felt utterly unequal to those tasks… but she couldn't refuse. She could only search within herself for new resources of wisdom and courage.

"Only the gullible believe your lies," Tetralanna persisted. "You call yourself First Speaker, but you and I both know that you stole the hlette from me!"

"Untrue. The hlette left you of its own accord. It was none of my doing."

A feral glint came into Tetralanna's eyes. "Where is it?" Her gaze darted to Gredin's jacketed arm. "Do you think to hide it from me? Or do you cover it out of shame for your theft? I have need of it. Return it now. It is the only one of my losses that you can remedy."

"No, Tetralanna. The hlette chose to come to me. It will remain with me until someone with a greater gyfte of Speech is born among us." Frustration warred with pity as she eyed her adversary. "You are exhausted and grieving. Emotion makes it difficult for you to think clearly."

"I have lost my Chosen. I have lost my world!" Tetralanna declared, her voice a wail.

"As have I," Gredin said, with more bite to her tone than she had intended. Dreff had been her dear Chosen. Now he was gone, his life ended, his essence returned to the Source along with all who had stayed behind on Venna. Learning of his death, she had wept a flood of bitter tears. But despair was a luxury she could no longer afford.

"It is not the same!" Tetralanna insisted, her tone contemptuous.

"No? How is it any different?"

"When we left Venna, *I* was First Speaker. *I* was the Voice of this delegation. You have taken it all and left me nothing." Tetralanna practically spat the words. "Nothing!"

Wearily, Gredin said, "We have all suffered terrible losses. Now a critical task lies before us as we strive to comfort our ravaged people. There is a vital role for you in that, if you would but see it. Get some rest, Tetralanna. You and I are the only two Speakers left alive. I would welcome your participation."

"So that you can take the credit when things go well?" Tetralanna's gaze grew cold. "No. I will *never* help you. You disgrace our House. You have pushed yourself to the forefront, claiming you alone can lead our people. But you will fail, and we will be all the worse for it."

The accusations stung. "I will not hold those hard words against you, for you Speak out of grief and exhaustion. Should you change your mind when you have had time to reflect, I will gladly accept your assistance." She crossed her palms and offered a brief bow. "I bid you farewell, now, for I have promised to meet with Tradepoint's Director."

"You leave us to plot with another race against your own people!"

"I go to ensure that we will have safe shelter here, now that our home is lost to us."

"You are a traitor," Tetralanna shrilled, "and too great a coward to stay and face me!"

Gredin walked on without replying. Left alone, Tetralanna might return to her chambers and rest, even if sleep evaded her. Gredin hoped so. In the former First Speaker's current state, she was of no use to anyone. What would it take, to calm her and soften her attitude?

One task at a time, Gredin counseled herself as she reached the antechamber. Keying the doors to open, she entered and let them close behind her, shutting away the sight and sound of Tetralanna. As the familiar mist filled the chamber, Gredin breathed it in deeply, grateful for its coolness against her hot cheeks.

She could not afford to be distracted by Tetralanna – not when her upcoming discussion with Wyve, Tradepoint's Director, held the key to their very survival.

[2]

1868 OF 2000 ORBITS REMAINING

"Good day's beginning to you, Director, Assistant Director."

Wyve smiled wearily at Pord's cheerful greeting, the traditional opening to each morning's holo-conference between himself, Figg, and their subordinate, the planet-bound Melding Mediator. Normally, he and Pord, the Melding Mediator, both entered the call with energy, newly risen to face their day, while Figg, as Assistant Director, was in the final hours of her night-shift duties.

But today he and Figg were weary and downhearted after a wakeful night unlike any Wyve could recall. Aware of Figg's sympathetic gaze, he prepared to update Pord.

"There is news," Wyve said by way of preamble.

"Yes, sir," Pord acknowledged, his tone instantly more subdued. "I listen."

"There has been…" *'An incident'* sounded far too minor. "There has been a disaster," he said, and waited for a moment, giving Pord time to absorb the weight of the word.

Pord would know, via remote telemetry, that no mechanical malfunction troubled Tradepoint. Read-outs appeared on Pord's consoles, with alarms if key parameters were violated.

Nor would Pord expect any unrest among the foreign tradeteams.

Security was equipped to stifle any disruption, and no serious challenge to Prett authority had ever been mounted. This was the Prett's station, orbiting their world. Tradeteams from nearly two dozen worlds came to exchange goods in the regulated neutrality the Prett provided. Harmony was in every race's best interest.

And so Pord must wonder what could possibly qualify as a 'disaster.'

Taking a breath, Wyve began to clarify. "It involves the Vennans."

Vennans were a calm, peaceful race, among the least contentious of Tradepoint's visitors. Currently, however, nearly a thousand Vennans were present on Tradepoint, so far exceeding normal numbers that it troubled the Vokastra, the governmental body of the Prett. Still, the Vennans were valued trading partners, and the size of the incursion had been tolerated.

"I understood that the Vennan delegation was departing today," Pord ventured. "Have they changed their plans?"

"Their plans have been changed for them," Wyve replied.

"By you, sir?"

"By circumstance." The terrible truth had to be stated. "The Vennan planet has been destroyed. They no longer have a home to which they can return."

Silence. Then, in a hushed voice, Pord asked, "War, sir?"

"They say not. A cosmic incident seems likelier. We aren't completely certain."

"What *do* we know, sir?"

"Initial word of the devastation reached us yesterday morning, through a member of their delegation. Corroboration was received last night."

With his characteristic political savvy, Pord plucked at one thread of the explanation. "Word reached you yesterday *morning*, sir? Before the Trisectoriana broadcast?"

The Vennans were currently present in such numbers because the Prett government was honoring the three-hundredth anniversary of Venna's initial visit to Tradepoint. Just yesterday, the elaborate commemoration ceremony had been broadcast planet-wide.

"Yes."

"You made no mention of the Vennans' current difficulty to the Vokastra beforehand?"

Wyve sighed. "At the time, the news was unsubstantiated. It seemed best to broadcast as planned. But now the news *has* been corroborated. I will, of course, inform the Vokastra."

"Awkward," Pord said, in what they all knew to be a massive understatement.

"Necessary. I expect the head of the Vennan delegation soon for a planning session."

"Head of the Vennan delegation," Pord echoed. "Would that be Cirin te K'lar?"

"No," Wyve said heavily. An unbidden memory arose of Cirin, the life-blood trickling from between his lips. "Cirin te K'lar died, last night."

"Died!" Pord sounded scandalized. Deaths on Tradepoint were nearly unprecedented.

Figg responded with her usual aplomb. "He arrived at last night's reception, already injured, and succumbed to those injuries shortly thereafter."

"Please extend my sympathies to the Vennans. Do they require specialized assistance?"

Wyve looked to Figg, who seemed equally nonplussed by the Melding Mediator's words. "Clarify," Wyve requested.

"If the Vennans intend to transport the body back to… Oh! If their home world is destroyed, as well… Well, then, how *do* they prefer to have the body dealt with? Cold storage is available on the station, of course, but if they prefer a planet-side interment, I can present a request to the Vokastra, although…" Pord floundered to a halt.

Taking pity on him, Wyve said, "There is no body to inter."

"No body?"

"When a Vennan dies, their body… evaporates."

"Evaporates?"

"When Cirin te K'lar's life ended, his body shimmered briefly, then simply ceased to be."

"Ceased to…?"

Figg cleared her throat. "No need to keep repeating the words, Pord. The Vennan died and his body vanished. I suppose we should be grateful. It spares us the regrettable necessity of respectfully disposing of a corpse."

"The Vokastra won't be happy to hear of this, especially so soon after Cirin te K'lar was honored. You're quite certain it was *that* Vennan?"

"Positive. But that's not the point, Pord. As unfortunate as his demise may be, the larger concern is the destruction of the Vennan planet."

"Of course." Pord sounded chastened. "What will they do? Where will they go?"

Wyve exchanged a glance with Figg. "For now, they will stay here."

"But they are on today's departure schedule."

"Then the schedule must change. Make the proper notations."

"Yes, sir. But…"

Wyve waited.

"How long a stay shall I indicate?"

"Through the current extremity of their need."

Pord hesitated. "And if that need extends beyond their allotted two thousand orbits…?"

Wyve frowned. Every visiting tradeteam had two thousand orbits during which to conduct its business. Past that, financial penalties were imposed for each additional orbit-long delay. At fifty orbits per day, it nudged laggards and opportunists like the Beng into making a prompt departure. Regulators had never anticipated the situation the Vennan delegation now faced.

He glanced at his desktop, where current orbital allotments displayed in a continuous scroll. The Vennan symbol and its current numbers, when they appeared, were all still a reassuring blue. "The Vennans have one thousand, eight hundred and sixty-eight orbits remaining – more than ninety percent of their allotment. That gives us time."

“Time for what, sir?”

“To discover how they plan to proceed.”

“Do the Vennans have off-world colonies? Those could provide a natural haven for them.”

“They’ve never spoken of such a colony. So far as I know, the nine hundred and thirty-seven delegates here on Tradepoint are all that remain of the Vennan population.”

Pord gasped. “Then they are doomed. Nine hundred and thirty-seven isn’t even a viable gene pool.”

The observation was factually accurate. Nevertheless, it angered Wyve. Controlling his tone, he said, “And yet those nine hundred and thirty-seven individuals are alive, and skilled, and in our care. They have a right to live out their individual lives, regardless of their species’ eventual fate. And Vennan lifespans appear to far exceed our own.”

“Do they? By how much? I don’t recall a specified range in their species profile.”

“No. But the evidence is right there in front of us. Yesterday’s Trisectoriana honored the three-hundredth anniversary of Cirin te K’lar’s arrival on Prettig as the first Vennan to establish a trading relationship with us. Historical records make it clear that Cirin was already a mature adult at that initial encounter, yet he showed no signs of advanced age when I spoke with him here, just a few days ago.”

“Well, he’s certainly dead now,” Pord pointed out, his tone acerbic.

Wyve scowled. “He died as a result of injuries, not infirmity.”

“Yes, sir. Your pardon. But a lengthy life expectancy makes the survivors’ situation more challenging. And much sadder. It might have been kinder if Vennans lived only a brief, vivid span of years. If your conjecture about longevity is correct, they will have a great many sectora in which to witness their remaining population dwindle to nothing.”

“You take a grim view,” Wyve objected. “There may be gains, as well as losses. Just last night, a Vennan trader took a bondmate. Children may result. Their lives can still bring them joy.”

“Will they? How joyful can life be, with their civilization

destroyed? What of the family members they lost? The entire Vennan delegation must be mourning their dead. Frankly, I wouldn't want to be one of those survivors. I would far prefer to have been among the vast majority whose lives are now at an end."

Wyve shook his head, repelled by the bleak vision Pord painted.

"But you are Prett," Figg pointed out. "And they are not."

"Obviously," Pord replied. "What point are you making?"

"That Vennans are not a rational, science-based culture. They are deeply religious, and capable of actions we can neither replicate nor explain. Their very presence on Tradepoint is proof of that. Before Cirin te K'lar's first arrival, we would have believed it impossible for a race to reach us without a navigable interstellar craft. But Vennans arrive without so much as a pressure suit, let alone a ship. They cross the vacuum of space with nothing but the clothes they wear and the trade goods they convey. When we ask how they manage it, they reply that some of their citizens have a 'gift' for traveling the river – and by 'the river' they mean the vast reaches of space itself. When we ask where they learned such a gift, they say only that each Vennan is born with certain gifts bestowed upon them by the power."

"The power?"

"Their term for a deity – an all-powerful supreme being."

Pord snorted.

"Just so. But that is their belief. So if you ask how the surviving Vennans will react to their fate, I cannot hypothesize. Nor should you. We can only wait and see."

"But 'wait and see' is not an approach that will appeal to the Vokastra."

That was true. The current governing officers were, in Wyve's opinion, a testy group of legislators, more given to action than reflection. That was the difficulty with elections. Every five sectora, the ruling body was subject to potential change, and the reverberations from the most recent election had not yet subsided. President Duv, newly appointed, was prideful. Dealing with him made Wyve nostalgic for the previous administration, stodgy but predictable. With Duv at the helm, matters were more volatile.

"It can't be helped," he countered. "The news only reached the full Vennan delegation last night. I'll know more after this morning's meeting. It may be lengthy, so I chose to speak with you first. Will you mention it in your morning briefing with the President or do you prefer to wait for more details?"

"A delicate question. Initial feedback from yesterday's Trisectoriana broadcast has been quite favorable. Duv won't want bad news on the heels of such a positive response... but how can it be helped? Things are as they are. Let me assess his mood, this morning. Then I'll decide. And you'll update me, once you and the Vennans have spoken again?"

"Depend upon it."

"Well then, for the moment, that leaves just one truly vital question."

"And what is that?"

"The fate of the geddel crystals, sir."

A pall settled over Wyve. The geddel crystals. Caught up in the Vennans' crisis, he had overlooked an issue of utmost concern to the people of his own home world, Prettig. Had he been Tradepoint Director too long? The priorities of the planet below sometimes seemed remote – even frivolous – compared to the challenges posed by the heady mélange of races whose concerns he dealt with on a daily basis.

Was that justifiable? He was Prettian. Tradepoint was the brainchild of the Prett. Early on, the station couldn't have survived without the massive infusion of money, equipment, and technicians supplied by the planet. Even now, financially self-sustaining as Tradepoint was, the planet below was its source of manpower, and the Vokastra provided the political gravitas and physical security force necessary to maintain the Pretts' position as the adjudicators and enforcers of Tradepoint's rules of conduct and the interspecies exchange of goods.

In orbit above Prettig, distanced from the bustle of daily life on the planet, Wyve ruled a hermetically sealed domain, but his importance and influence on the world below was miniscule. Tradepoint was far more dependent on the planet than the planet would ever be on Tradepoint. Losing sight of that fact guaranteed disaster. President Duv and the Vokastra ruled the world of Prettig. Wyve managed Tradepoint, a minor cog in Prettig's economy. Its solitary significance, in the Vokastra's view, was as a conduit for a regularized supply of geddel crystals.

Humbled by how far he had strayed from that awareness, Wyve said, "Of course, Pord. I'll inquire about the fate of the crystals as soon as the Vennan representative arrives."

"Inquire about…? You don't know whether the geddel crystals survived, sir?"

Figg said smoothly, "Of course not. Traders rarely divulge the source of their wares. Vennans travel widely. Their source of geddel crystals is likely off-planet."

"Likely?" Pord echoed. "Don't either of you understand? If the geddel crystals came from the Vennan home world, and that home world has now been destroyed, the result would be economic chaos. Geddel crystals are integral to our energy infrastructure. If our main source of supply falters, there will be an uproar. And if that supply fails altogether, it will mean retooling entire industries. Shortages. Business failures. Economic panic."

Figg pursed her mouth. "You exaggerate."

"I do not."

"We utilized geddel crystals long before the Vennans entered the equation," Wyve reminded the younger man. "There are other providers…"

But Pord cut him off. "None that supply the volume and quality of crystals brought by the Vennans. We are dependent on that supply to an alarming degree. You must contact the Vennan representative immediately and find out where matters stand."

It wasn't the sort of peremptory demand a Melding Mediator should ever make of the Tradepoint Director, but Wyve made a deliberate decision not to take offense. "That meeting is already arranged and will take place shortly. But, on reflection, I advise you not to raise the topic of Venna's demise with the President until we have more information in hand."

"No, sir," Pord said flatly. "I strongly disagree. Our only safety, in a situation as fraught as this may soon become, is to cleave to propriety and process."

"*Safety*?" Indignation heated Wyve's blood. "Melding Mediator, do as you see fit. But *my* primary consideration is the welfare of the Vennan survivors, not political expediency."

Silence.

When Pord spoke again, it was on a much milder note. "Sir, it was callous of me to reference 'safety' when the Vennans have suffered such a catastrophic loss. My apologies. We must of course see to the well-being of the refugees. Their situation is horrible. Unprecedented." He drew an audible breath. "I only ask you to consider how deeply interwoven their needs and the status of the geddel crystal situation may yet become, in the eyes of the Vokastra."

Politics and economics. The warning made Wyve want to grind his molars. But Pord was right to caution him. The Director and Assistant Director of Tradepoint were remote from the concerns of Prettig, literally and figuratively. As the junior-most member of their administrative triad, the Melding Mediator resided on Prettig, interacting daily with both the Directorship up on Tradepoint station and with the planet-bound government. As a result, Pord had the keenest sense of the mindset of the politicians in the Vokastra.

It also meant that the Melding Mediator was Prett-centric, learning about but never actually encountering the alien races that did business at Tradepoint. Wyve could still remember the disorienting shock he had experienced, nearly forty sectora past, when *he* was the Melding Mediator and had been precipitously promoted to the role of Assistant Director, conveyed into the heavens, and faced with his first contact with the Beng, the F'lala, the Chibi, the Hesch… He had longed to retreat to his quarters and hide beneath the bed.

Perhaps tradition was overrated, and the time had come for Melding Mediators to spend brief periods aloft during their tenure, the better to acclimate them to the job they were preparing one day to fill…

Wyve sighed. "I hear you, Pord, and I take your words seriously. Speak to the President when it seems wisest to you. Matters here will evolve rapidly. Be assured that I will update you as soon as we have more information concerning the geddel crystals."

"Thank you, Director. And, again, my apologies."

"And mine to you, for drenching you in such a torrent of unwelcome news."

"Even so, we three are having a better morning than the Vennans, I am certain."

It was a truth Wyve couldn't refute. "Indeed. For now, a good day's continuance to you, Pord," he said, and ended the call.

Beside him, Figg shook her head. "Troubling times."

"Indeed."

How long would he and Figg have to wait before Gredin te Balamont appeared? Informing Pord of Venna's destruction had set events in motion. Even now, Pord might be placing a call to the President's residence, despite the early hour. Wyve hoped not. But that decision, like so much else, had passed beyond his control.

"Figg…"

She turned her head, giving him her full attention.

Propriety warred against urgency… and lost. "You might take a stroll in the direction of the Vennan enclave," Wyve suggested in as idle a tone as he could manage… then hesitated as the mat beneath his feet pulsed briefly. "Never mind. She is here."

"An early riser," Figg noted dryly. "Or perhaps she has not been to bed at all."

With a whisper of slippered footsteps, their visitor appeared: Gredin te Balamont, First Speaker, Voice of the Vennan delegation, bearer of First Speaker's hlette. Tall and slender, she had been a commanding presence when she'd arrived at Wyve's door on the previous morning to break the news of her world's destruction. Garbed in a magnificent gown of scarlet, with her abundance of blond hair crafted high in an intricate crown of braids, her eyes bright, her color high, Gredin had been impossible to ignore.

This morning, she was a wraith. Her braids hung down in long, lank tails.

Her skin looked more sallow than golden. She was dressed in a simple jacket and pants such as Vennan travelers commonly wore, and the set of her shoulders was weary. "I promised to come," she said from the doorway, but made no move to enter, as if uncertain of her welcome.

Wyve waved her in. "Figg and I are glad you're here. Take a seat, please." He waited in silence while she did so, then asked, "Your people made it through the night without incident?"

She grimaced. "Each passed the night as best they could. Most are still asleep."

Wyve ordered his thoughts. "To begin, please accept my deep sorrow at the passing of Cirin te K'lar. A shocking event, and a shocking confirmation of the loss of your world."

Gredin inclined her head.

"Last night, when Cirin first appeared," Wyve continued, "I used my communication bracelet to alert our Clinic. They sent a team to help him… but he died before the team arrived."

Again, Gredin nodded mutely.

Determined to make his point, Wyve said, "In the past, your travelers and traders have declined our requests to undertake a medical study of Vennans. Now, with fewer than a thousand of your citizens left alive, I strongly urge you to reconsider that invitation."

Gredin blinked. "We have our Healers," she said, as if that ended the discussion.

Wyve persisted. "But do you have *enough* healers? And is their skill infinite? Clearly, they couldn't save Cirin's life, last night. I doubt that our clinicians could have saved him, either, given how little we know about your race, but we Prett aren't dependent on inborn gifts. When we encounter a difficulty we can't surmount, we make a study of it. We devise ways to resolve the problem. Let us undertake a study of Vennans and how their bodies work so that we can help you protect the survivors in your care. Agreed?"

Her expression was wary. "You go too fast," she said.

Wyve hesitated, unsure whether she meant that he had spoken too quickly or that he had requested her cooperation too precipitously. "Shall I say it more simply?"

"No. I understand. You talk of our safety. I will consider your offer… but I cannot yet agree to what you propose. I need time to think and to consult with others."

Wyve spread his hands in frustration. "You are the Voice, the leader of your delegation. You should be eager to agree. We want only to help."

Lines of stress and fatigue had gathered around Gredin's eyes. "You say you made this offer before, and our Travelers and Traders declined. I would confer with them and know why."

Because they are provincial and superstitious, Wyve wanted to snap. But Figg leaned forward slightly in her chair and said, "Of course. By all means, consult. Just know that we stand ready to help protect you, now that the risk to your people is so much greater."

Gredin recoiled. "Why should the risk be greater? Because I angered the Hesch and the Beng at the Traders' Market on my first day here?"

"Not at all," Wyve assured her. "The Hesch should be quite satisfied, since the Judgment was entirely in their favor. As to the Beng, they have a choice. If they don't wish to pay the fine, they can absent themselves for the next six sectora. I assure you, they are far more annoyed with me than with you. No, Figg means that there are now few Vennans remaining. Nine hundred is a population size that leaves your people acutely vulnerable to accident and disease. We wish to use every asset at our disposal to help safeguard your people. Our clinic's lack of knowledge about the Vennan body leaves you all in danger, but that can be mitigated with more research."

"I say again, I will consider it. But that is not what I came to discuss."

"My apologies." Wyve schooled himself to patience. The Vennans were a simple culture. It would take time and tact to educate them about matters that should be obvious priorities. As with any race, it was necessary to meet them where they were and coax them toward enlightened agreement. "We will return to the topic later, along with another urgent matter. For now, however, how can we best assist you? What do you need?"

"Space."

Cautiously, Wyve said, "Yes, we are in space, above Prettig…"

An impatient shake of Gredin's head. "No. Your pardon. I spoke the wrong word." She composed herself. "Room. Rooms. We need more places to be. We are…" She gestured at Wyve's desk, and the space behind it where he and Figg currently sat. "Last night, Ingarra and Beda and Keegan and I spread our bedmats on the floor in an area no larger than this. Many others did the same nearby, separated only by pieces of cloth that block sight but not sound. In the darkness, I listened long and long to the weeping of hundreds of my kinsmen."

Wyve stared at her, appalled by the image her words conveyed.

Gredin pressed the flat of her palm to her chest. "Please understand, I do not complain. We arrived on Tradepoint for a stay of three days only, for the Trisectoriana. Our people did not mind a few nights of sleeping closely. It was an adventure. But this is no longer an adventure. It is our new reality. We cannot go home. Everyone is sad and frightened. And I worry." She lifted her hand in a fluttering gesture that seemed to convey both uncertainty and apology. "If there is no additional room for us, tell me and we will find a way to manage. But Tradepoint seems so large, to my eyes, that I hope for a better answer."

Figg's fingers moved on the desktop, and a column of words took shape there.

connected enclave corridors

foam pads

cargo containers

consultation with bio-engineers

Grateful for her speedy grasp of practicalities, Wyve said, "Be assured, we have many better answers. To my regret, we cannot undo this disaster, but we can – and will – do much to ease the Vennan delegation's immediate discomforts."

It was the proper compassionate gesture. It also made practical sense. Overcrowding led easily to compromised hygiene and the spread of communicable diseases. Tradepoint routinely took precautions to avoid such difficulties, since the mere thought of an interspecies epidemic on the station filled Wyve with dread. But now, faced with such a large increase to the station's resident population, it was only wise to take additional preventative measures. And improved quarters would aid the morale of the Vennan survivors, as well…

Figg cleared her throat, and Wyve saw that the next item she had typed was flashing in a bid for his attention.

food supply

That was sobering. The Vennans had come equipped for a three-day stay, with their departure scheduled for 22purple today, shortly after their midday meal. It was 6green, now, which meant the Vennan kitchen staff would soon begin preparing a morning meal for the nine hundred residents of the enclave –

Oh no!

Wyve surged to his feet. "Come, Gredin. We must reach the Vennan kitchens without delay. Figg, leave your notes for my review and get some sleep. I will see you at 31purple."

"Of course, Director. I've sent for a transport pod to convey the two of you to the Vennan enclave. It should be in the corridor momentarily."

"My thanks," he said. "Gredin, if you're ready? I only hope we aren't already too late."

[3]
1868 OF 2000 ORBITS REMAINING

Miri te Kendar sat alone in the huge metal room created by the Prett for the kitchen Tenders' use.

Gredin had awakened her from a restless doze, requesting Miri to meet her and the Tradepoint Director in the kitchen. =*Touch nothing,*= Gredin had said. =*Let no one begin to prepare morning meal. I will explain when we arrive.*=

Miri had readily complied, glad to escape the muted sounds of misery in House Kendar's sleeping quarters. She felt numb, and she ached to be busy. When her hands were occupied, her mind quieted, concentrating solely on what dish to prepare next.

But Gredin had commanded her to guard the kitchen, not prepare dishes to soothe the ravaged hearts of her fellow Vennans.

None of Miri's fellow kitchen Tenders had yet made an appearance, nor were likely to, with the enclave still on its night cycle. Miri hadn't turned up the muted lights in the kitchen. There was enough illumination for her to see the evidence of hastily abandoned workstations. Last night, when news of Cirin te K'lar's death reached them, kitchen Tenders had hurried to the reception hall, where Gredin's words confirmed their worst fears.

Barred from constructive tasks, Miri sought the solace of a sweet memory:

"Enjoy your time away, my love. I leave now with the Kendar Tradeteam, but I will return before you complete your duties on Tradepoint." Zanther kissed her tenderly. "As always, I will place my homecoming gift on your pillow."

Miri swallowed hard, wishing for a hot cup of besk to cradle in her hands. The loss of her Chosen was one of hundreds of similar losses in the Vennan enclaves. Anguish was the new taste of life, bitter on the tongue, eradicating the savor of all that followed.

Like Cirin te K'lar, Zanther had returned to the Source. Miri prayed that his death had proven less painful than Cirin's.

"Your pardon…?"

Wiping her eyes, Miri turned to find Sill te Torr hovering in the doorway.

Sill took a hesitant step forward. Even in the dim light, Miri could see her red-rimmed eyes. "Sorry to intrude. I was hoping for a cup of besk."

"I wish I could make one for you," Miri said, "but Gredin commanded that nothing be prepared until she arrives with the Director."

Sill's brow furrowed. "But why? Surely a cup of besk can do no harm."

Miri's shoulders tightened. "I have no answer for you. Gredin made no mention of delaying food preparation when we put away the uneaten food, last evening."

"We?"

"Oh. Gredin, Keegan te Fliss, Ingarra te Balamont, her Chosen, Beda, and myself." Miri knew who Sill was, due to Sill's gyfte, but she realized it was unlikely Sill could say the same. "I am Miri, kitchen Tender from House Kendar." She crossed her palms and offered a bow.

"It pleases me to meet you, Miri te Kendar," Sill replied, returning the gesture.

Her manners heightened Miri's frustration. Why should a comforting cup of besk be forbidden? It seemed to underscore how completely the familiar rituals of Vennan life were being torn asunder. "Would you like to wait with me for Gredin's arrival? She was coming immediately." Miri offered a tentative smile. "Most of us in House Kendar start our day with a cup of besk. Is it the same in House Torr?"

"It was," Sill said, her expression sad. "I once Harvested a Memory for a Torr Trader who had visited the besk groves on Santelle's Holding. A beautiful place, misty and mountainous, the hillsides covered in besk trees, low and bushy, the blooms and berries ranging from pale green to deepest gold. After seeing that Holding, he said besk was worth whatever price House Santelle named." Sill shook free of the Memory, tears brightening her eyes. "And now all of it is gone. Still, our memories of Venna are precious and should be celebrated, not avoided." She sat down on the bench next to Miri. "We are Vennans. It is our duty and our joy to remember all we had and all we were, so as not to lose our way here."

Perhaps, in time, the Vennan survivors would agree. But today seemed far too soon. Miri hoped the food she prepared could act as her voice, offering familiarity and comfort. But eventually the supplies they had brought would run out… though not today, thanks to Gredin's foresight, last night.

"There are still besk berries in our kitchen stores," Miri said. "I'm sure Gredin will allow me to Make a pot, once she…"

Footsteps sounded, purposeful and brisk. "Miri? Are you here?" Gredin's voice reached the corners of the large room. Brilliant lights flared, and Miri blinked against the sudden brightness as Gredin and a much larger individual entered the safe world of her kitchen. "Oh, good." Gredin hurried forward. "When I saw that the lights were still off, I was afraid you might have fallen back to sleep. Oh! And you have Sill with you. Perfect, for I have need of you both.

"But I am being rude in my haste." She crossed her palms and bowed to them, the light glittering on her hair and hlao. "A fair morning to you both. I hope you found some rest, considering the early start we are having to this day."

The imposing figure at Gredin's side rumbled into speech before Miri could respond. "Good day to you, Sill te Torr. It pleases me to see you again," it startled her by saying in Vennan. It even crossed its broad palms and bowed its head, the gestures odd on so bulky a creature. Next, it turned to her. "Good day. I am Wyve, Director of Tradepoint."

Stunned at being addressed, Miri stared up at the creature. The rough, dark-skinned visage was a shocking contrast to Gredin's delicate beauty. Where she gleamed, the Director seemed to absorb light Only his large, dark eyes held any shine.

Flustered, Miri gathered her wits and manners. "Good day to you. I am Miri te Kendar."

The creature turned to Gredin, and a long string of incomprehensible sounds issued from it, like slow rolls of thunder on a wet day.

Gredin nodded and replied briskly before turning to Miri. "Wyve would like to begin, if you are ready. His morning has already been busy, and there is much yet to do."

"Begin? What is it that he wishes me to do? I am only a kitchen Tender – and now you say I must not do even that. Why? Sill came here in search of a hot cup of besk, and I had to refuse her request!"

"Your pardon, Miri. The Director wants to go through the kitchen stores with you. Show him everything we brought from Venna that might be cultivated for our future use, like sprouts or seeds or pots of herbs. I told him that you, of any of us, may know enough to answer his questions."

"But I cannot understand him." Miri stole a glance at the large individual. Where had Zanther found the courage to Trade with other races?

"I will translate, as the need arises," Gredin assured her. "Do not be afraid. Wyve is our friend. This inventory will help us. I won't leave the kitchens until you and he are done."

Reassured, Miri went to the storage unit that held their supply of besk berries, since besk was already on her mind. Gredin spoke to Wyve in the Prett's strange-sounding language, and he followed close behind, his movements oddly graceful for a creature so huge.

Miri pressed the control panel on the storage unit, and a large section of the metal front slid back to reveal shelves that were tall and deep and broad… and largely empty. The sight of them trailed cold fingers down Miri's spine as she surveyed the scant remains of their food stores. With nearly a thousand individuals to feed, it was a feeble bulwark against hunger, and she realized anew how sensible Gredin had been to save last night's uneaten reception food.

She reached up for one of the dozen remaining fine-cloth sacks bulging with besk berries, then froze as the Director approached and began to rumble above her head.

"Wyve will lift that down for you," Gredin said.

He hoisted the heavy bag effortlessly and carried it to a nearby counter. When he paused, appearing uncertain where to set it, Miri saw that the counter was still cluttered with cutting boards, knives, and other implements her fellow kitchen Tenders had abandoned when the shocking news of Cirin's return and death had spread throughout the enclave.

Blushing, she murmured, "Your pardon," and cleared the countertop in one large Sending, to Wyve's open-mouthed astonishment. Taking a quick moment to Cleanse the now-bare metal surface, she gestured for him to proceed.

Gredin spoke softly, and Wyve set the bag on the counter.

Miri untied the strings and scooped a small sample out of the bag. The pale gold berries seemed to glow on her palm. "These are besk berries from the Holdings of House Santelle," she explained. "We bake them and then grind them into powder. The powder dissolves in very hot water, and we drink it."

She worried that it might be too much information, but Gredin could edit or add as she saw fit when she translated. And indeed, Gredin immediately started an explanation in the Prett language, almost before Miri finished talking.

An incomprehensible dialogue ensued: rumbled words from the Director, a short response from Gredin, and a word in answer from the Director.

"Wyve asks if you can plant these berries to Grow the plants that produce them. He wants to know if they are still *semmini*. Alive."

Miri blinked. "I'm sorry, Gredin, but I don't know. You would need to ask someone with the gyfte of Growing. It is common knowledge that besk trees only Grow at the Holding of House Santelle. Sill might know more, for she holds a Harvested Memory of Santelle's Holding where the besk bushes grew." Miri turned to Sill and asked, "Would you be willing to share your Memory with Gredin?"

"Of course, but I'm not sure how helpful that will be."

Gredin grew thoughtful. "Perhaps you could share it with a Grower instead. They might glean more from it than I, and I could pass that information on to Wyve."

Miri sighed. "I am sorry to be of so little help."

Gredin shook her head. "I, too, find myself woefully unable to answer many of Wyve's questions. You've provided useful information. And Beda is a Grower. Between what he knows and the Memory Sill holds, perhaps we can piece together an answer." Then Gredin spoke to Wyve again, her words echoing in the quiet kitchen.

At the current rate, Miri realized that the process might take all morning. Poor Sill still waited patiently for her besk, and more than nine hundred enclave members would soon want their morning meal, assuming they had any appetite. Gredin herself no doubt had countless things to attend to, as well. Miri wished she spoke the Director's language; the inventory would go much more quickly. Perhaps one of the Traders would provide her with lessons, if she asked. Food would likely be an ongoing topic of concern between the Vennans and the Prett. In time, she might be able to ease some of Gredin's load, if she learned to converse in the language of their new home.

Gredin said, "Wyve is sending for storage and transportation units. He will take the besk berries and anything else the Prett might be able to Grow."

"Wait. Take the besk berries? All of them? What will people drink at morning meal?"

"Water. Hot, if they like. Cool, if they prefer."

"Water?" Miri echoed in dismay, the very idea outraging her gyfte.

"If having folks drink water for a time means we eventually have a healthy supply of besk berries to harvest, then we will all drink water and think ourselves well served."

"I suppose," Miri said dubiously. "But that will be thin comfort, this morning."

"Where food is concerned, we may have little comfort to offer for quite some time. Our goal for now is to see that no one goes completely empty."

Miri stared at her, stunned, then felt a flicker of shame. In her eagerness to offer Sill a simple cup of besk, she had lost sight of the larger cloud that hung above them. The food remaining in this kitchen was all that stood between their people and starvation.

This was Tradepoint, not Venna. With Venna gone, there would be no chance to replenish their stores. But whether any foodstuffs were available on Tradepoint right now was a question for which she lacked an answer.

Thank the Power that Gredin had been more clearheaded about the subject.

Grimly, Miri acknowledged the necessity of gathering everything from the kitchens that could be grown. Gredin was right. Far better to have items absent for a time than to lose them forever. If the Prett could salvage anything that had Grown on Venna, it would be a kindness beyond compare.

With brisk efficiency, Miri began opening cupboards. "Here are our seeds and spices," she said, indicating rows of cream-colored jars decorated with delicate, painted reproductions of their contents.

Gredin spoke to the Director, who opened each in turn. Some he collected, placing them next to the bag of besk berries. Others he rejected immediately. Miri soon realized that he wasn't interested in anything that had already been ground. Only seeds and dried berries that were still whole were deemed worthy of salvage.

"Thank you, Miri," Gredin said. "Are there any fresh berries left?"

"Quite a few," Miri said, her heart sinking. *What am I to serve at morning meal?*

"Show us, please."

The cooling units were immense, although many were now empty. Miri opened the correct door. Inside, baskets of fresh berries filled the shelved compartment, in colors from deepest purple to a pink so pale it looked nearly white.

The Director made a pleased noise deep in his throat, then rumbled a question to Gredin.

"The Director would like to know if this is all of the fresh fruit."

"Yes, all that's left," Miri said. "We ate most of it already or cooked it into the tarts for the reception." It was surprising how sad she felt, making that confession. Less than a day ago, she had been proud of the many exquisite items they had baked for the buffet tables. But now…

"You couldn't know what was coming," Gredin said. "Focus on the future."

"Just so," Sill concurred.

"If you wanted fresh berries, I suppose you're interested in the fresh vegetables, as well," Miri said briskly. "We have more vegetables than fruit left, almost two full units, not including the Growing racks."

Gredin turned to Wyve. Words flew back and forth between them, and Miri would have sworn that the Director's eyes gleamed brighter with each exchange.

Finally, Gredin said, "The Director is most eager to see. Please, continue, Miri."

It was easy to open the cooling unit doors, but harder to answer the questions that followed. Which items bore seeds within? What were their names? Which of them were easy to Grow? How long from planting to harvest? What nutrients did each provide?

By the time Gredin finished translating the Director's questions and Miri's best attempts at answers, Miri felt exhausted. She hadn't realized, until called upon to provide such a detailed account, how little she knew about the foods she prepared on a daily basis. She was a kitchen Tender, not a Grower.

The sudden arrival of half a dozen individuals who resembled the Director was a welcome distraction. They listened respectfully to a short speech from the Director, then brought rolling carts into the kitchen. Under the Director's supervision, they began to load the items the Director had set aside on the counter.

When that had been accomplished, Miri expected them to leave. Instead, some opened the cooling units Wyve pointed to and began stripping the shelves. Others placed sack after sack of besk berries gently on the carts. Another cart swallowed the baskets of fresh berries and a goodly supply of the vegetables.

"Gredin, please," Miri protested, near tears, "they're taking too much. I need to feed the delegation a morning meal soon." She tried to plan some sort of menu, based on what was left, but her thoughts scattered like skittish birds. "And more meals today, after that."

"I am sorry, Miri. Truly. But Wyve's actions are not a punishment, even though they make your work more difficult today. He is trying to help us preserve the foods we enjoy. Someday, we will pick fresh vegetables and berries again. But that won't ever happen unless Wyve plants the seeds we have on hand."

"Will you at least ask him to return the vegetables, once he has removed the seeds?"

"Of course," Gredin agreed promptly. She turned to the Director and spoke. The Director nodded and spoke, his words deep and solemn-sounding. "He assures me the food will be handled with great care, and anything they don't need will be returned here as soon as possible."

"Then I suppose he'll want to see the Growing racks next," Miri said dispiritedly. She crossed the kitchen to another wall of covered shelving. Pressing buttons, one after another, she opened the panels on five long shelves.

Light poured into the kitchen.

The Prett Director and his assistants halted in their work, their attention snagged by the sight of Miri's makeshift kitchen garden.

The shelves held a myriad of living plants. Row after narrow row of greens, of fresh herbs, of edible flowers survived happily under the tuned array of luminth shining down on them. The fresh smell of dirt and thriving plants drifted into the kitchen.

Wyve made a sound deep in his chest.

Gredin smiled, her eyes glistening. "It smells like home."

Miri swallowed the lump in her throat. "I wanted fresh things to decorate our plates and make us feel as if Venna wasn't so far away. And I brought plenty of House Kendar soil to place the plants in. Oh!" she said, remembering. "Beda's berry plants are in that one." She pointed to the last shelf. "He wanted them to have proper light so they wouldn't wilt and die."

Gredin hugged her. "You are a treasure beyond expectation, Miri. All of this will, in time, nurture and sustain us with the very tastes of home." Then she turned to Wyve, and Miri assumed she must be relaying, in that odd-sounding language, what Miri had just told her.

Whatever she was saying, it brought on a renewed flurry of activity. The assistants, so over-sized, nevertheless used deft, delicate motions as they removed the shelves that held the living plants, leaving gaping holes behind as they loaded them onto a cart of their own.

An urgent thought occurred to her. "The plants need the luminth light. And the luminth will need to be recharged from time to time."

"I will ask Beda about it," Gredin assured her. "I've already contacted him. He'll accompany the carts and help the Prett workers in any way he can."

The Director approached as his assistants finished loading the carts. Peering directly into Miri's eyes, he spoke.

"The Director is most appreciative," Gredin translated, her voice quiet and clear. "Especially for the soil. It will, he says, improve the chances of successfully Growing our Vennan seeds. He thanks you for your time this morning, and for the thoroughness of your efforts." She rested a hand on Miri's shoulder. "I must go, as the Director and I have not yet finished our meeting. But I will be back later."

"Wait! You need to eat something before you go."

"I cannot wait," Gredin said. "There is much I yet need to discuss with Wyve." She looked over at Sill, sitting quietly. "Sill, I am sorry there is no besk."

"I'll Make you a cup of roin tea, Sill," Miri said briskly. "I have enough leaves left to brew you a cup."

Gredin smiled. "Ah, Miri, see? You have begun to cope. Thank you for staying strong. I am sure other good ideas will occur to you, as the day wears on."

"We'll be eating a lot of porridge. Plain porridge, after the spices run out."

"I like porridge," Gredin said gravely.

"We had all best learn to like porridge," Miri replied, her mind already pursuing ideas for dishes based on the ground grain.

Gredin turned away. "Sill, I'll have need of you today, if you are willing. Could you meet with me and a few others at midday meal? I need advice as we plan for our survival here."

"I am honored to be included, if you think I have anything of value to offer."

"Definitely. Your gyfte, for one. Your experience, for another."

"Very well. Where shall we meet?"

"There is a space with a table and a few stools – though not enough – in the chambers I share with Tetralanna. Bring your meal there and we will talk while we eat."

"I look forward to our discussion."

"My thanks." Gredin turned back. "Miri, I would like you to attend, as well."

"Me?" Miri squeaked in surprise. "I am only a kitchen Tender."

"You are the head of the kitchens. And our food supply is a vital topic. If possible, I need you to report on the state of our food stores."

"I am more than willing. I prefer to stay busy."

"You may soon regret those words," Gredin said with another slight smile. She touched Miri's shoulder again. "Do your best, as shall I. It is all anyone can ask of us." She crossed her palms and bowed to both of them. "I wish you a good day," she said, and briskly departed.

A good day? As if that is any longer possible...

But Miri wouldn't let sadness stand in her way when someone needed the comfort her kitchen could provide. "A cup of steaming roin tea will be yours shortly, Sill," she promised, and set to work.

[4]
1867 OF 2000 ORBITS REMAINING

When Gredin stepped into the Director's office with Wyve at her heels, his desk was pulsing softly with light.

"Probably a final note from Figg before she headed to bed," Wyve said, walking to his chair. "She finds it difficult to let go of a problem, once her mind is engaged. Sit, please. Be comfortable. This will only take a..." His voice trailed off as he gazed down at the desktop.

Gredin sat, wondering how much uproar the lack of besk berries would prompt as people straggled out to start a day already destined to be bleak. Should she have compromised, splitting the stores so everyone could savor one last cup before...

"Well, *this* is awkward," Wyve said, his tone peculiar.

Gredin looked up in alarm. "What is it? A problem at the enclave?"

"No, not exactly," Wyve assured her, "but there appears to be some confusion about..." He straightened. "Our bio-engineering staff has a question about the enclaves your delegation have been occupying, and I don't know how to answer them without asking you some questions."

"Ask," Gredin said. "I will answer."

Her reassurance did not put Wyve at ease. Sinking into his chair, he said, "Before she went off-shift, Figg notified Bio that your delegation would be staying past the expected departure – a routine courtesy. Travel plans on Tradepoint often change on little notice. But since this alteration involved such a large number of individuals, the techs checked to ensure that the vaida-maki, maju-mako, and the toro-maka tanks wouldn't be overwhelmed."

The terms Wyve used were unfamiliar. And he had not yet posed a question. Concerned, Gredin asked, "What do you need to know?"

A gusty sigh. "When I say toro-maka, do you understand?"

"No," she admitted. "Can you use other words? Or say it in Vennan?"

Wyve's smile was thin. "I will try. When Miri gathers what she needs to make a meal, there are parts of her ingredients she cannot use. Bones, stalks, rinds, pits, yes?"

"Perhaps," Gredin said uncertainly. She had no gyfte for kitchen matters.

"Well, when Ingarra sewed your new dress from the Shodekekeen fabric, there must have been bits of fabric left over, too small to be of use. Such things – bones, stalks, rinds, pits, bits of fabric – all of those, when they are thrown away, are called toro-maka. 'Toro' because you can see them and touch them, 'maka' because they are no longer wanted or needed."

"*Toro-maka*," Gredin repeated dutifully, and waited for him to go on.

"When you sit down to a meal Miri has prepared, you eat and drink, and your body draws what it needs from the food. But your body cannot use everything you swallow, and so, later, anything you cannot use passes out of your body."

"Yes."

"We Prett refer to that as toro-maka, as well. It passes out of your body and is collected in storage tanks beneath each enclave. Eventually, our bio team collects the contents of those tanks for treatment. That's what they prepared to do, this morning, after receiving Figg's message, while you and I conferred with Miri. But they report a problem. They say the tanks beneath the Vennan enclaves are empty." He tilted his head. "For three days, your enclaves have housed nearly a thousand Vennans. Your traders provided an orientation for your delegates, explaining the hygiene facilities we provided. So what has happened, Gredin? How can the storage tanks beneath your enclaves be empty of toro-maka?"

She wished Burlon were with her. He might understand Wyve's distress. But she was the Speaker for the delegation, so she tried to puzzle out the source of his concern.

"I know nothing of these tanks," she said as a beginning. "What worries you the most?"

Wyve dropped his massive head into his hands and made a sound that might be laughter.

"Try," she urged. "Use simple words. We can manage this, you and I. Talk to me."

He nodded. "In simple words, Gredin, where is your maka? Where is the maka from the bodies of nearly a thousand Vennans?"

"Gone," she answered promptly.

"Gone where? It is supposed to be in the tanks, so that we can deal with it."

Gredin blinked. "We did not know you wanted it. From childhood, Vennans are taught to..." She had no Prettian for what she needed to describe. "...to Unmake it," she substituted.

"You haven't put it somewhere else, have you?"

Gredin frowned, puzzled by the peculiar nature of the question. "Somewhere else?"

Wyve flung his hands out in an extravagant gesture. "It isn't in the tanks. You haven't placed it outside of Tradepoint's walls, in space, have you? Or somewhere *inside* Tradepoint's walls? It should be in the tanks. It isn't in the tanks. When I ask you where it is, you say it is 'gone.' Gone where? Understand, please, the maka must be dealt with in a safe and healthy manner. I'm not angry. There will be no Judgment. I just need to know *where* the Vennan maka has been put so that–"

She held up her hand in supplication, overwhelmed by his burst of Prettian.

Wyve stopped and took a breath. "My apologies."

Striving for the proper words, Gredin said, "Do not worry. There is no... mess. No danger. We are not like rista, emptying ourselves wherever we happen to stand. We are Vennans, not animals. We understand the Cleansing chambers you provided and are grateful for them. But Vennans do not allow their *maka* to linger, nor do we place it in tanks. We..." *We Convert it,* she wanted to say, but had no Prettian word to explain. "We cause it to be gone."

"You send it somewhere else?"

"No. We... cause it not to be. We... take it apart."

For a moment, Wyve looked horrified, then thoughtful. "Like last night?" he asked. "When the Beng spilled cordial on your gown?"

"Yes... but no. Last night, I merely separated the cordial from the fabric and returned it to the glass. With *maka*, we..." She sighed. "It is simple to do. It is hard to tell. We return it to how it first began. Air. Water. The things that make the world."

Wyve's expression was intent. "You reduce it to its chemical elements?"

She shook her head. "More words I do not know. We take it apart. We make it simple again, and then it is gone."

"And that's why our tanks are empty?"

"I suppose. It is what every Vennan has been taught to do. Have we caused a difficulty?"

"Honestly, I'm not sure. At the very least, the problem isn't what I thought it was. Let me talk to the bioengineers and see what they say." Wyve rotated his head slowly, as if his neck pained him. "Tomorrow, you and I can discuss this anew. For now, you and I have more important matters to discuss. You raised the issue of needing more room for the delegation. I will begin work on an expansion plan. Can your people manage one more night as they are?"

"Of course," Gredin assured him. She had not expected to be taken so seriously. "We will wait as many nights as necessary. Just knowing that a change is being planned will comfort them."

"Thank you for your patience, and for the patience of your people." A decisive nod. "So, we will expand your living area, and explore the food you and your people need…" He hesitated. "We must be cautious about that."

"Cautious?"

Wyve frowned. "Vennans are used to eating food grown on Venna. Suddenly introducing crops from other worlds could cause problems."

Gredin waved away his concern. "Our Travelers have brought home many treats from Tradepoint in the past, and we have enjoyed them."

But Wyve didn't look mollified. "Those treats were likely things your traders had first sampled, themselves. There may have been items they tried that *didn't* agree with Vennans."

"Agree…?"

"Tasted bad, or made them ill. And what they imported may have been luxury items, eaten in small amounts. We must be far more careful introducing staples like meats and grains."

Gredin shook her head. "We do not eat meat."

"Not at all?"

"Well, our soups and stews sometimes contain bits of meat along with the vegetables. Or little pastries may have a bit of meat as part of the filling. And we enjoy fish."

Looking bleak, Wyve said, "We will begin by working to identify reliable sources of grain for you, along with a variety of vegetables and fruits." His fingers moved over the surface of his desk, and he made a sour face. "Your traders have purchased grain from the Wilra in the past, but not often, and not in great bulk. Other than that… nothing recent."

"We raise our own grain," Gredin told him, and then felt a jolt as memory corrected her. "We *raised* our own grain," she corrected. Now, Vennans raised nothing. The fields were gone. The Holdings were gone. Unless something was done, the tables would soon be bare. And Wyve was telling her that food from other worlds might taste terrible, or even harm them. "How do we know what to trust?" she asked, suddenly appreciating his concern.

"We test," he said. "We offer small samples of food to someone, then monitor how they react. The testing can be done in our Clinic, just down the corridor from here. And it should start today. But we need a Vennan willing to undergo the testing."

"I will do it."

"You will not."

She recoiled from his flat refusal. "Why? I am Vennan. I am willing."

"You are the Voice of your delegation, the one to whom your power chose to speak. Your people look to you for leadership and guidance. You should not undertake such a risk."

"The risk of an unpleasant taste in my mouth?"

"The risk of dying."

Gredin froze. "From food others have eaten without harm? How is that possible?"

Wyve closed his eyes. When he opened them again and spoke, his tone was gentle. "You are Vennan. Not Prett. Not Shodekekeen. Not Wilra. Not Hesch, or Beng, or Polpethtira. Not even Mamoran. Each race's body is different from the others. Different needs. Different vulnerabilities. Yes, there are likely many, many things that other races eat which can be eaten safely by Vennans. But it only takes one error for someone to die. So we are cautious. We conduct tests. We advise moderation when sampling any new food item. When one race decides to eat food from another, it is often only for convenience, or in hospitality. But your world is now gone, and the foods which sustained your people are gone, as well. We need to find safe, plentiful, affordable replacements. I advise beginning food testing today. We can begin with Prettian food. And I refuse to allow you to be the test subject. Find another. We will take every precaution to protect that individual. They will be as safe as we can make them. But I will not knowingly risk you."

"And I will not knowingly risk one of them."

"Then we are at an impasse."

"I do not know that word."

That drew a grim, rumbling chuckle from Wyve, "You may soon know it well. 'Impasse' means we have reached a point where we cannot agree. I will not risk you. You will not risk anyone else. It leaves us no path forward. But you cannot afford an impasse. Your people need safe food. Better to risk one than to risk all, is it not?"

Reluctantly, she nodded.

"A traveler or trader, perhaps. They are used to taking risks."

"No. We need them most of all."

Wyve tilted his head to the side. "Then choose someone else. Or ask for a volunteer. But you have very little time if Vennans are not to sit hungry at their tables." He shifted in his chair. "We will leave the topic, for now. I do not need an answer this moment, but I need one yet today. We cannot let time escape us on this matter, above all others. So think on it."

"I will," Gredin promised.

"In the meantime, there is another question to discuss – one brought to my attention before you arrived. You remember Pord?"

Gredin searched her memory and recalled a robed figure in a column of light. "A member of your Vokastra, perhaps, at the Trisectoriana?"

Wyve nodded, looking pleased. "Indeed, you saw him at the Trisectoriana, among those in the hologram from Prettig. But he is not a member of the government. Rather, he is part of Tradepoint's administrative team, our Melding Mediator. Figg and I work from here, he from the world below. When I retire – return to Prettig, that is – Figg will take my place as Director, Pord will become Assistant Director, and a new Melding Mediator will be appointed."

"And Melding Mediator is…?"

"Pord's official title."

Apprehension tightened Gredin's throat. She had begun to trust Wyve and Figg. The thought of Wyve leaving Tradepoint was frightening. "You do not return to Prettig soon, I hope."

Wyve's smile was kind. "No, not soon. But eventually. In the meantime, since Tradepoint is remote from Prettig itself, I rely on Pord to keep me in touch with my government's concerns. He raised just such a concern, this morning, when I informed him of Venna's loss, and I had no answer for it, so now I turn to you." The smile left his face. "It concerns geddel crystals."

Gredin shook her head. “Ask your question, but I know little about them. My House did not deal in them, other than purchasing them from time to time to use as ornamentation. You may recall that my dress was adorned with them, last night at the reception.”

“Indeed. A breath-taking display.”

She waved her hand in apologetic dismissal. “A pretty way to decorate a gown.”

Wyve’s expression became somber. “They are more than that to us. My government needs to know if Venna’s destruction means that the source of geddel crystals is also destroyed.”

It was clear to Gredin that her answer mattered a great deal to Wyve. With regret, she said, “I do not know. You must ask a Trader. I suspect Burlon will know the answer.”

“Then contact him and inquire, please.”

“Soon,” she said, taken aback by the peremptory demand.

“Now,” Wyve countered.

“I cannot. He is in his dydanin with his new-found Chosen, Chenna.”

“So I was told, last night. But you, or I, need to speak with him immediately.”

“Normally, he and Chenna would not emerge for twenty days.”

“I cannot wait twenty days for this answer.”

“Fortunately, you will not have to,” she said. “Burlon has promised to emerge later this morning to address the Travelers.” *This is the day we all planned to go home*, she wanted to say, but she swallowed the words, for Wyve knew it as well as she did. No Vennan would leave Tradepoint today, for any destination. And no Vennan could Travel home, ever again. “When he comes out, I will ask him the source of geddel crystals. Will that meet your need?”

“I suppose it will have to,” he said, slowly, still looking unhappy.

“Why is the answer so urgent?” she asked. Wyve was their friend and protector, but a dozen different concerns involving the welfare of the survivors needed to be explored. Why did Wyve choose to question her about baubles sewn on a party dress?

“Try to understand,” Wyve said. “Geddel crystals are used for serious purposes on Prettig. We are talking about the well-being of the Prettian economy."

"I do not know that word," Gredin said. "It is what, 'economy'?"

Wyve made a guttural sound, deep in his chest. "Never mind. We will set the issue aside until Burlon is available. You and I will focus on other concerns during the time left to us, this morning, shall we?" And he smiled. But it was the smile one would offer a small child, to divert them from a topic they were too young to understand.

Gredin shivered. What did she know of Tradepoint, or of the Prett and how they lived? Why had the Power selected her? She was unaware of how matters were managed beyond the walls of her own House, let alone beyond the boundaries of her world.

Yet she was alone here by choice. She could have intruded on Burlon and asked him to accompany her. She could have entreated Miri to turn the kitchens over to someone else and join her for the remainder of this meeting. She could even have thrown herself on Tetralanna's mercies. Despite her fury, Tetralanna might have been sufficiently flattered by the invitation to leave the shelter of the enclave and brave the journey to Wyve's office.

But Gredin had decided not to, because it was not the course of action the Power had decreed. She alone had experienced its visitations, these past three nights. And she had been told to ignore Tetralanna and undertake leadership of the surviving Vennans.

The Power could have spoken to any of the others. It could have addressed them all, if that had been its wish. Instead, it had singled her out.

And so here she sat.

Alone.

No, not alone.

Wyve was here. This member of an alien race who had been a stranger a few short days ago, this man who ruled Tradepoint, was someone she had come to trust. When she had stood in the custody of Prett security, weeping as she admitted her guilt over the injury to the Hesch trader, Wyve had still dealt with her calmly and kindly. Now, in the face of her planet's destruction, he stood as a bulwark between the homeless Vennans and the Prett Vokastra.

She owed him gratitude.

She owed him trust.

She owed him the truth.

"Gredin? Are you all right?"

She met Wyve's troubled gaze. "Yes," she said. "And I wish to tell you a thing."

He appeared to brace himself. "Is it about the geddel crystals?"

"No. I have already told you what little I know about them. This is something more important. Something no one else knows, yet. I imagine Burlon would urge caution and tell me to stay silent, but I believe you have a right to know."

"I am listening."

She felt very small, sitting on a bench in the Director's office. But she said, with resolve, "The Power came to me for a final time, last night. It said we were to seek New Venna."

Wyve leaned back slowly in his chair, watching her.

Gredin returned his gaze in silence.

At last, he said, "New Venna?"

She nodded. "Our new home."

"Where is it located?"

She shook her head. "I have no idea. That is why we must seek it."

"Viable planets that are uninhabited are not a common thing."

It was a statement. Gredin made no reply.

"But you believe New Venna exists, and that it's out there, waiting for you to find it?"

"Yes."

"And you'll risk your people's lives on that belief?"

"We have the Power's assurance that it is so. And we cannot stay on Tradepoint forever. We need a world. Our own world."

Wyve frowned. "Your 'power' couldn't be troubled to leave you instructions on how to get there? Coordinates? A star chart?"

His sour expression won a smile from her. "Such things would do our Travelers no good. They have their gyfte. They will journey upon the River until one of them finds New Venna."

"And then?"

"And then we will thank you deeply for your many kindnesses and pack our belongings, so that the Travelers can convey us to our new home."

"And all of this will come to pass… when?"

"Perhaps soon. Perhaps not for long and long. I do not know."

"And your Travelers will just keep searching because you tell them to?"

"In part because I tell them it is the Power's will. But they will also search because it brings them joy. Traveling the River is their gyfte. There is nothing they would rather do. So yes, they will search until New Venna is found, because it is what the Power directs them to do."

"What *you say* the power has directed them to do. Do they trust you so completely?"

"Most do not know me at all. Only a few know me well. But a Vennan would never falsely claim to know the Power's will. Look at me," she invited, gesturing at herself. "I am untested, not a person who wishes to order others about. I expected my life to be a small, sweet, quiet thing. But then I came here, and we lost our world, and the Power saw fit to inform me of that loss and instruct me to protect those of us who survived. So now my life cannot be small, or sweet, or quiet. I wish it could. But the Power has handed a precious burden to me, and I must carry it – perhaps for the rest of my days, or perhaps only until we reach New Venna. I do not know. There is no choice. There is only a task to be undertaken, as best I can. And so I will be steadfast, and learn all that I can, to make up for my inexperience. I am bound to make mistakes. I can only promise you – and my people – that my mistakes will never occur because I did not care, or because I failed to try."

Wyve drew breath as if to answer, then simply nodded. After another space of silence, he said, "I see why you are your people's Voice. Words are indeed your tools."

Gredin felt a trickle of relief. "You understand about the Power's promise? You believe me?"

His expression was wry. "I believe you, insofar as a scientist can."

"What does that mean?"

"I believe that *you* believe what you say about being visited by this power in your sleep, and being instructed to search for New Venna. We Prett are not Vennans. We are not born with such gifts. But I have seen enough unusual things in my dealings with races from other worlds to know that the Prett way is not the only way. So yes. Within the limited design of my own mind and the culture that shaped me, I believe you. And I will help you as best I can."

"My thanks," Gredin said, touched. "Is there advice you would offer, at the beginning of this difficult day?"

"Yes. For now, say nothing of your world's loss, except to other Vennans."

"But the guests who attended our reception already know," she protested.

"Not so. They know only that Cirin te K'lar died. His statement about the destruction of Venna and Palomar was spoken in Vennan, and was not understood by any of the guests but Figg and myself. The secret is still closely held. Say nothing of it, outside of your enclave, until you and Burlon have discussed the matter. There are those at the Traders' Market who would take advantage of your plight, if they learned of it."

It was a revelation that saddened and frightened her. She was confident the Shodekekeen would deal fairly with them, regardless of circumstance. But would the Beng? Or the Hesch?

Wearily, she nodded. "We will say nothing, for now."

"Just so you know, the Mamora and the Thalken departed, after last night's reception came to such an abrupt end. The Mamora were already scheduled to leave. The Thalken..." He tilted his head. "I rarely understand anything the Thalken do." He consulted his desktop. "And remember, the clause of the Judgment that prevents the Beng from approaching you expires tomorrow at 21green."

"21green?"

"Around midday meal. My best advice is to avoid the Beng entirely, if you can. Don't venture out of your enclave alone. Don't wander the Traders' Market."

"For how long?"

"For the next twenty sects or so. Then their orbital allotment will be up and they'll have to leave. But I expect them to be prickly for the remainder of their stay, looking for any situation where they can claim slight or injury, in the hope of a favorable Judgment to off-set the debt they incurred." He raised a hand and let it fall. "I'm sure you know, the Beng are not your friends."

"I am quite aware." Short and squat, the Beng were mischievous and annoying, even when they were in a good humor. During her recent run-in with them at the Traders' Market, they had crossed the line from mischief into harassment and attempted theft, and Wyve had passed a formal Judgment against both Gredin and the Beng, with most of the monetary penalty falling on the Beng. "Still, if the Judgment forbidding the Beng to approach me is still in effect today, it is safe for me to go to the Traders' Market if the need arises, is it not?"

"Technically. But I advise against it."

Frustration was a hot bubble in her chest. She rose. "Then what use is the Judgment?"

"I am not forbidding you to do so," Wyve said. "I am advising caution. Do you have a pressing need to go to the Market? If so, I will gladly provide a security escort."

"No. That is not the issue. I have a pressing need not to be controlled by the Beng. It is *they* who troubled *me*. Your Judgment should be all the protection I require."

Wyve asked gently, "May I say a thing to you in friendship, Gredin te Balamont?"

His mild request stole her indignation. "Of course."

"And will you sit to hear it?"

Gredin sank onto the bench again and folded her hands, giving Wyve her attention.

"This is a horrible day for your people – perhaps the worst in the history of your race. You have said that the power your people revere came in your sleep and spoke to you, not once, not twice, but three times. It spoke to no other, only to you. Do you not suppose, on this most terrible day for all surviving Vennans, that your loss might crush them beyond recovery?"

"They will not lose me."

Wyve's gaze was sad. "So you believe. But strange things can happen. Regrettable things. The loss of your world. The death of Cirin te K'lar." He placed his huge hands on the desktop. "If you have urgent need of something from the Traders' Market, permit me to send guards with you. If you have no such need, stay safely in your enclave until the Beng depart. Or, at least, do not venture out alone. Do this as a kindness to your people. It costs you nothing. Their peace of mind is more important than proving a point to the Beng, yes?"

The day had scarcely begun, and already she was weary. "Yes. You are right, of course."

"And one thing more. Accept this small device from me." Wyve turned to pluck an item from a shelf behind him. "Come and see."

Gredin rose and approached the desk.

The object Wyve held was an oval band, perhaps as wide as a finger. Its silver exterior matched the cool metal of Tradepoint itself. An oval jewel was embedded in its surface, and the jewel emitted a pulsing purple glow. Then, to Gredin's surprise, the color of the jewel turned to blue, and the glow steadied and became constant.

"What is it?"

Holding it out, he said, "A simple communication mechanism, designed to be worn around your wrist. It weighs very little, and we can adjust its size so that it will fit snugly. I don't think you'll find it annoying."

"Why would I wear such a thing?"

"To ease my mind. And for practicality, as well. Until we have identified and resolved the Vennan enclave's most urgent needs, you and I should meet often. Today, Figg and I were uncertain about when you might arrive. If you had been wearing this wristband, we could have agreed in advance on a time."

"I told you I would come in the morning. And I did."

Wyve sighed. “True. However, we Prett schedule our days more precisely than that.”

Gredin felt comprehension dawn. “The colored numbers over our door!” she exclaimed. “Burlon says they are a Prett contrivance involving time.”

“Just so,” Wyve said. “You know your color words, yes?”

“Yes,” Gredin assured him, “in Tradetalk and in Prettian.”

“Well then, memorize this color progression: purple, blue, green, yellow, orange.”

“Purple, blue, green, yellow, orange,” she repeated dutifully.

“And you know your numbers in Prettian?”

“I am more used to the words than the symbols,” she admitted, “but yes, I know both.”

“And how high can you count?”

“Through the hundreds.”

“Excellent. To use this wristband, you need only count to fifty.” He handed it to her. “Look at the oval. What number do you see there?”

The band felt insubstantial in her hand, far lighter than she had expected. Tilting it, she looked into the colored jewel and saw, swimming in its depths, a numeral. “Seven.”

“Yes. And what color do you see?”

“Blue. A few moments ago, it was purple, but then it turned blue.”

“Very good. You now know the time: 7blue. Before, it was 7purple. After, it will be…?”

She remembered the list he had recited. “Green. 7green.”

“If you were in your enclave, and your band showed 7green, and I had asked you to meet me here at 7orange, you would know to come to my office soon. But if we had agreed to meet at 10purple, you would have time to accomplish many other things before you left the enclave.”

It made Gredin feel itchy. “You slice the day into tiny pieces,” she objected.

“Precisely,” Wyve said, looking pleased. “Try it on. I will adjust it for you.”

She didn’t want a Prett *griimoni* on her wrist, counting and glowing. But it seemed reckless to refuse Wyve's offer, on this precarious day, and so she handed the wristband back to him and extended both her arms. "Where should it go?"

"On the wrist of the hand you use least."

"I don't understand. Do you not use both your hands?"

"Well, yes, of course, but… When you write things down, which hand holds your reed pen?"

She smiled. "You mistake me for Keegan. I have no call to write things down."

"Well then, when you brush your hair. Which hand holds the brush?"

"Are you teasing?" Gredin asked. When Wyve shook his head in denial, she answered, "I hold the brush with the hand on whichever side I am brushing."

"And when you pick up a glass to drink from?"

"Whichever hand is closest to the glass."

He regarded her, his air thoughtful. "Is that true only of you, or of all Vennans?"

"It is what everyone does."

"It is not what *I* do," Wyve objected.

"It is what every Vennan does," she clarified.

"Well. Your pardon. Clearly, I have much to learn about Vennans. With you and your delegation living among us, I hope to learn enough about your people to avoid asking such foolish questions. But, for now, let us focus on what needs to be done." He pointed at one of her hands. "We will put the wristband there, for now. When next I see you, tell me whether it has caused you any discomfort or inconvenience."

It took only moments for him to place the band around her wrist, and little more for him to reduce its size so that it rested snugly against her skin.

Gredin tilted her wrist, admiring the color-rich saturation of the jewel. "When will it be green?"

"All too soon. This morning is escaping me. Tomorrow, we will try meeting at 6yellow. That will give you and Figg time to confer before she ends her shift. Is that agreeable?"

"I will try," Gredin said, unwilling to promise blindly. "I do not know what may be happening in the enclave at 6yellow, but I will come here as closely to that time as I can."

"Well, if I need to talk with you sooner, the band will vibrate. Like this." He touched the desktop again, and Gredin jumped as the band around her wrist shivered briefly against her skin. "If you feel it vibrate like that, ask Burlon or one of the other travelers to bring you here to my office. I promise not to summon you unless something important requires your attention." He smiled. "I will use it later today, after midday meal, when the Clinic is ready to conduct the first food tests. When you feel it vibrate against your wrist, summon whoever you have chosen for the tests, and a security guard will accompany you both to the Clinic. And if some emergency arises and you need help, press down on the colored oval. It will send a signal to my office, and I will dispatch security to assist you."

"To the enclave?"

"To wherever you are. We can track the signal and pinpoint your location by…" He chuckled. "Never mind. Just remember to press it, at need."

Gredin nodded, feeling slightly overwhelmed by all Wyve had imparted. "I will make every effort to remember all your instructions," she promised.

"There is one more thing I wish to discuss before you leave."

"I am listening," Gredin assured him, wondering what additional request Wyve was about to make.

Wyve regarded her soberly. "I have not forgotten your historian's pressing need for paper, and both Figg and I will continue to seek a supply for him. However, since it is unlikely that will happen anytime soon, I would like to offer him the use of a crabe until a reliable source of paper and inks can be found."

"A *crabe*?" Gredin echoed, bewildered. The word was new to her, and strange-sounding.

"A griimoni that records information."

"You are kind but Vennans are unfamiliar with *griimoni.* And

Keegan has no Prettian words. He would not know how to use such a device."

Wyve gave a slight shrug. "The crabe could easily be programmed to use the Vennan language, and the operating instructions should pose no problems. If you agree, I will have it ready later today."

It was a distasteful solution… but a solution, nonetheless.

"My thanks. And Keegan's." Gredin smiled wearily. "Is there more you wish to say before I leave?"

"Nothing except that Figg and I both deem it wise to place a security guard near the entrances to the Vennan enclaves for the time being And I have requested one to escort you back now."

She opened her mouth to say it was unnecessary… then closed it without speaking.

"Thank you for indulging me." He looked up abruptly. "Ah. Your escort is here." Wyve rose from his chair. "This will be a hectic day, and a sad one. You have my sympathies. Remember to eat and take a quiet moment for yourself. I imagine we will have many new concerns to discuss, tomorrow morning. You remember the time for our meeting?"

"6yellow," she recited. "My thanks for your assistance and advice."

As Wyve had foretold, a member of Prett security waited outside the office door. "Transport pod?" the guard asked.

"My thanks," she said, "but I would rather walk, if that is permitted."

He nodded, and they set off together down the gleaming corridor, each step toward the enclave bringing Gredin one step closer to the resumption of her responsibilities…

A flash of blue light drew her gaze: the wristband. As she watched, the jewel changed from cool blue to the lush green of a Vennan hillside.

But there were no more hillsides. There was no more Venna. There was only this silver corridor, and the needs and sorrows of those who awaited her.

…Purple, blue, green, yellow, orange… However strange, she needed to be sensitive to how the Prett lived their day since the Prett

station was now the community's home for the foreseeable future. And yellow, the next color of this time-cycle and the color of tomorrow's early cycle meeting, was not far off.

Gredin felt the unnatural press of time, and sighed as a wave of homesickness rose to sting her eyes. The Vennan world, where days were measured in shades of sunshine and evening shadow, was gone. A new life, a different life, lay ahead of her, indifferent to her wishes and desires.

...Purple, blue, green, yellow, orange...

Time was suddenly a precious commodity.

[5]
1863 OF 2000 ORBITS REMAINING: 7YELLOW

Wyve pulled up the environmental reports. If he was correctly interpreting the information Gredin te Balamont provided, life-support data for the station was the likeliest place to begin. Scrolling through the menu, he selected *Environment*. Three options appeared: *Ambient Parameters*, *Atmosphere Parameters* and *Toro Maka.*

Toro Maka had identified the mystery, but their reports lacked meaningful data. Of the remaining two departments, *Atmosphere Parameters* seemed the most promising.

Wyve touched the appropriate key.

A dozen reports appeared. Scrolling, he found a likely title: *Atmospheric Deviations by Elapsed Time.* Selecting it, he considered what time period to use. *A sector should suffice*, he thought, and made the appropriate entries. Keying the report to generate, he was gratified by an almost immediate response. Opening the document, he studied the data.

Ah. There. Small but measurable increases in Oxygen, Nitrogen, Carbon Dioxide and Argon were apparent. He would alert the engineers and have them–

His desk signaled the call he had been awaiting… and dreading.

“Good day, President Duv,” Wyve said when the image was established.

The hologram of Duv, President of the Vokastra and Chairman of the Governing Ministers of Prett, grimaced. “Hardly that, if the Melding Mediator’s report is accurate. Indeed, I cannot recall another day that started this poorly.”

“I agree, sir.”

“Protocol is preparing a formal message of condolence. There should be enough time for you to deliver it to the Vennans, don’t you think?”

“Enough time, sir?” he echoed, and realized that he sounded like Pord.

“Before they depart.”

Wyve stared. Had Pord failed to make the Vennans’ plight clear? Or was this a particularly flagrant demonstration of Duv’s ability to ignore unwelcome information? In either case, it was better to leave Pord out of it, since the poor man had to deal with the President and the other members of the Vokastra on a daily basis.

“Sir… the Vennans won’t be leaving today.”

“Pardon?”

“They have nowhere to go, sir.”

Duv managed to look both angry and stubborn. “But there are a thousand of them.”

“Yes, sir. The sole survivors of their race.”

“Not our problem,” came the reflexive reply, fast and firm. “The continued presence of a thousand Vennans on Tradepoint would be an intolerable burden on the station – and an unconscionable risk.”

Wyve’s heart began to thunder. “Risk, sir? They are victims of a tragic loss. What possible risk could they represent?”

“Don’t be naïve, Director. The general population of the station averages roughly a thousand individuals on a daily basis, divided between Prett staff and security, and the various foreign traders and crewmembers. But now the Vennan delegation adds their *own* thousand individuals. *And you say they have no home.*” He shuddered visibly. “How do we defend ourselves if they attempt to claim the station?”

Wyve repressed a laugh at the notion of the mild-mannered Vennans mounting a coup.

"Sir," he said, regaining his composure, "I have never encountered a less scientific, less militaristic race than the Vennans. They have no wish to stay indefinitely on Tradepoint, nor the first notion of how to operate the station. I assure you, your fears are groundless."

"But we cannot be sure they are accurately representing their situation. Where is proof of their world's destruction? They could be at odds with their government, seeking a safe haven."

Wyve shook his head. "Sir, the Vennans are devastated. They believe their world is gone. I have alerted the appropriate departments to begin a scan but the chances are small that we'll find any corroboration since we have no idea where the Vennan home world was located. Nor do they. As I said, the Vennans are woefully unscientific."

"They travel here. They trade in geddel crystals of unparalleled purity. These are attributes of a technologically sophisticated race."

"They have evolved in ways we do yet understand, sir. Their abilities seem to be intrinsic, not the result of research."

President Duv's frown remained unchanged.

Wyve tried a different approach. One that had a better chance of penetrating Duv's stubbornness, despite the risk of upsetting him. "Our greater concern will be verifying that the Vennans' source of geddel crystals is still viable."

Duv's eyes widened. "Has the source of the geddel crystals been destroyed?"

"We don't yet know."

"Surely you had the sense to ask," Duv said acidly.

"Of course, sir. It was my highest priority when I learned of the Vennan news."

"And their response?"

Wyve sighed. "We should have an answer soon, sir. The Vennan enclave is still processing the loss of their planet and its population, and are deeply grieving."

Duv's eyes narrowed. "*We* will have suffered a devastating loss if the source of the crystals is gone. Loss of that resource, or even an interruption in supply, could cause significant difficulties for the Vokastra and myself, if it came down to a referendum."

"Pord updated me concerning Prettig's potential vulnerability on this matter during our morning conference," Wyve said. "And Figg and I identified actions to be taken, here on the station, to stabilize matters."

"Such as?"

"First, we lodged an immediate inquiry with the Vennan Voice regarding the source of the crystals."

"How can you be sure she'll speak truthfully on the matter? She seemed quite the hardened diplomat at the Trisectoriana ceremony."

Wyve felt his patience threatening to slip from his grasp.

"You may be referring to Tetralanna, sir, the Voice appointed for the Trisectoriana. Given the extent of this new disaster, a more appropriate individual has been selected to act as Voice for the Vennan delegation."

"Oh? And who might that be?"

"Gredin te Balamont, the Vennan interpreter. She now leads the delegation. Despite the early hour, I have already had a productive meeting with her. She is seeking information from the traders regarding geddel crystals, since she was personally unaware of their provenance."

Duv's expression brightened. "The one who can actually talk? She's in charge now?"

"The one who speaks Prett," Wyve clarified. "Yes, sir."

"Red dress. I remember. Well, *that* should move things along more quickly. No need to wait while everything is said twice over. When will she have answers for us?"

"Later today, sir. She is dealing with many critical issues, this morning."

"Not more critical than the geddel crystals."

Although appalled, Wyve said only, "Her focus is on maintaining a calm, safe situation within the Vennan enclave, in light of the shock and grief being experienced by the inhabitants."

A grudging sigh and a sour scowl. "That may be so. But hear me clearly, Director. We have no reason to assist the Vennans, now or in the future, if they can no longer supply geddel crystals."

It was the official Prett position, stripped to its basic components by Duv, sharp-edged and graceless.

"And the Melding Mediator informs me the Vennans have the bulk of their rotation allotment left. That gives them plenty of time to determine where to go from here."

"Mr. President–"

"Plenty of time," Duv asserted, overriding him. "I expect a more informative report from you, later today." With a smile that was all teeth and no warmth, Duv terminated the contact.

With the hologram gone, Wyve rolled his tension-stiffened shoulders. A discussion of what would ensue if the Vennans exceeded their rotation allotment had best wait until the situation around the geddel crystal source was clarified. If the response was positive, he would address the need for continued housing, as well as the year's grace from station fees which the Vokastra had gifted to them at the Trisectoriana ceremony. He would confer with Figg and Pord on how best to persuade the Vokastra to allow the Vennans to remain on Tradepoint without increasing their financial hardships. But the flow of geddel crystals would be a key element in any future plans.

For the sake of the Vennan delegation and his own peace of mind, he hoped Gredin te Balamont would have good news about that, when next they spoke.

[6]

1863 OF 2000 ORBITS REMAINING: 7YELLOW

"Burlon," someone whispered. Then, just as softly, "Burlon te Laith."

Chenna.

Recognition raced through his body. And with it came memories, some sweet, some harrowing. Reaching out, he pulled her against him.

She was his Chosen, new-found and cherished. They had spent half their first night in blissful discovery, learning the unique sensitivities of each other's bodies. The scent, the feel, the taste of her was imprinted deeply within him now, never to be forgotten. She was what he had hungered for, all his life. This was bliss.

But a point had come, deep in the night, when it fell to him to shatter her joy. Morning would force the entire enclave to learn the disastrous news, and he couldn't leave her unprepared. He might have to leave Chenna's side, later this morning, in the wake of Gredin's revelation to the delegation of their world's destruction. If that happened, he didn't want her stunned and bewildered, desperate for the comfort of his arms.

And so, with her in his arms, he had murmured the inescapable words: *Chenna, my dearest love, a terrible thing has happened. While we have been here on Tradepoint, our world was destroyed. We cannot go home. There is no home left. It is gone, and all who stayed behind are now dead, returned to the Source.*

First, she was bewildered, then frightened. Finally, as his words penetrated, she had wept in his arms until sleep reclaimed them both.

Now she was awake, and she whispered his name – his *new* name, for he had given up his House in order to take his rightful place as her Chosen. Never again would he be Burlon te Bentain. Laith was now his House…

"Burlon?" Chenna murmured, her tone one of faint reproach, and he realized he was holding her too tightly, with as much desperation as love.

He eased his embrace. "Chenna. My Chosen. My love." A new thought stirred, causing him to groan. "I must rise and go out to speak with the other Travelers."

He felt a shiver course through her. "To tell them about home and what happened there?"

"No. That will be Gredin's task. But I need to–" He stiffened. "Bleeding blisters, I forgot!"

Chenna recoiled and sat up, her eyes wide with shock and alarm.

"Your pardon," he said hastily. Now that he had a Chosen, he'd have to learn to watch his tongue. "There's someone I must contact. Will you give me a few moments?"

"Of course." She still looked unsettled, but she turned away and began to finger-comb her hair, giving him a semblance of privacy.

Grateful, Burlon undertook the calming ritual, slowing his breathing and willing his mind to a state of quiet. Then, resisting both worry and hope, he reached out with his private mind.

=Cirin?=

No response.

A gusty sigh of frustration escaped him.

Chenna turned back to look at him, her face soft with concern.

Burlon shook his head. "I was hoping to reach my friend, Cirin–"

"The one the Prett honored."

"Yes," Burlon confirmed, deciding not to launch into the complicated tale of how he had been forced to take Cirin's place at the official ceremony. It was a story for a less complicated day. "He and I are First Friends. I'm eager to share the joyful news that you are my Chosen. But he Traveled the River to see whether Gredin was mistaken, and it seems he's still not back."

"You are afraid for him?"

"No. Cirin is First Traveler of House K'lar. He'll be fine. But the delay… Well, I wish he'd hurry up and return."

Chenna took him in her arms, drawing him against the solace of her body. "How can I be so happy when I am so sad?"

"It is the same for me," he confided. The thought of rising and leaving Chenna ran counter to every instinct, but he had responsibilities to fulfill, and Gredin would need his help. "I must go," he said, more to convince himself than his Chosen.

She touched a fingertip lightly to his chin. "There. I have Freshened you." She stroked his arm. "Rise. Dress. You are needed."

Burlon stood up, comforted by this warm glow of love and acceptance intended solely for him. How could he not have realized what a precious, life-altering experience finding his Chosen would be? Had he not seen how finding Hayla had, overnight, transformed Cirin–

Cuts and slashes. Where are you, Cirin? I need you here!

Goaded by worry and guilt, Burlon Freshened yesterday's clothing – standard Trader's garb of pants, tunic, jacket, and ankle boots – and put it all back on.

Chenna suddenly grimaced as if he were a kamesta she had just found digging up her garden. "You can't go out like *that*!"

"Why not? What's wrong?"

She raised her fingertips to the golden hlao that encircled her own forehead. "You are Burlon te Laith now. But the knotting of your hlao still proclaims you to be Burlon te Bentain."

Embarrassment heated his face. "You are right, of course. But I must admit…" He gestured helplessly. "I have no idea how to tie House Laith's knot."

Chenna flowed to her feet, graceful in her nakedness. "This morning, I will tie it for you. But you must learn to do it for yourself." Her nearness and the intimate touch of her fingers were temptations as she retied his hlao. "You had better go," she said, her gaze warm with sympathy. "Go and help the others. But come back to me as soon as you can."

"Always," he vowed. Then, steeling himself, he turned and left her.

He had expected the reception hall to be fairly quiet. Instead, as soon as he stepped out into the little connecting hallway, he was assailed by the sound of people conversing in anguished tones, and weeping.

Ellis te Vell, a fellow Trader, leaned against the far wall of the passage, waiting for him.

"What's happened?" he asked sharply.

Ellis came and put her hand on his arm. "I am sorry to bring dark tidings on what should be such a happy morning for you, Burlon… but we have received terrible news. Unbelievable news." She drew a shaky breath. "Venna has been destroyed."

He already knew that. But *she* wasn't supposed to know it. Not yet. Who had let the secret slip? Tetralanna, out of spite? Or had one of the Travelers already attempted to leave Tradepoint this morning, forcing Gredin to reveal the truth?

Had the entire delegation been told?

"Help me find Gredin te Balamont," he instructed Ellis. "We'll be needed." And he started toward the reception hall.

But Ellis closed her fingers around his arm and dragged him to a stop.

Burlon turned back, astonished.

"There's more you need to know," she said. "Cirin te K'lar is dead."

"No. Cirin left to check on things. He's just not back yet."

"He returned," Ellis said. "Last night."

"No." It wasn't true. He wouldn't allow it to be true.

"After you and Chenna began your dydanin…"

"No." The little word kept escaping from his mouth.

"I'm sorry. I know he was your First Friend. But I saw him die. I saw him evanesce."

Burlon was sitting, suddenly, on the cool metal floor, one arm still held high in Ellis's tenacious grasp. He shook it free and stared up at her. "No."

She squatted in front of him. "Yes. I'm sorry, but yes. He returned in the midst of the reception and told us of the loss of Venna and of Palomar. And then he died."

Burlon shook his head stubbornly to refute her words, trying not to let his mind form the picture Ellis described. "I need to talk to Gredin," he said. Gredin would know what was happening.

I need Cirin.

But Cirin is dead.

No. Please, no.

"She is with the Tradepoint Director," Ellis said, her expression wary.

Well, of course her expression was wary. He was sitting on the floor, like a child. Bracing his hand against the wall, Burlon clambered to his feet. "Then I'll join her there." But he was supposed to meet with the Travelers, so none of them would attempt the journey home... But *that* was no longer a likelihood, was it, if everyone already knew of Venna's loss?

In the space of a single night, life had surged ahead, leaving him behind.

He forced himself to meet Ellis's gaze. "My thanks for coming here. For telling me. How does the delegation fare? How are matters in House Vell?"

Ellis's accustomed air of brisk capability faltered, and he saw the pain lurking just beneath. "Those of House Vell who are left do well enough, for so bleak a morning. But the delegation as a whole..." She grimaced. "People are Unbalanced. Scabs, Burlon, what do you expect? Most of them are homebodies, not adventurers like us. After three days here, they wanted to return to their Houses today. And now that is impossible. Forever." Ellis's eyes grew suspiciously bright, and she turned her face away. "It is the worst day any of us have ever faced."

"A truth," he agreed, and felt a trickle of guilt because, even now, a thread of joy wove through his anguish when he thought of Chenna.

Out in the reception hall, someone began to wail loudly. Burlon winced. “There is much to do,” he said, if only to block out the sound.

Ellis stared. “There is nothing to do except to mourn our dead. What purpose is left to us? We have lost our Houses and all of those we loved. There is no one to Trade for, no House to enrich. We are crowded together in this enclave like a pack of Beng. What is to become of us?”

“That,” Burlon said, “is what I intend to discover. First, I’ll go out and address the Travelers. Then I’ll find Gredin. Beyond that… well, I trust I’ll know what comes after that, once I’ve gotten that far.” He looked at Ellis. “Do you want to come with me?”

“I wish I could,” she said, “but my House awaits my return.”

“We will talk again soon,” he promised. “The delegation needs canny Traders like you. Stay strong. And, Ellis…” He willed his voice to steadiness. “Thank you, again, for coming to tell me.”

She nodded and walked away, her tread far heavier than usual.

Burlon waited until he saw her pass through the archway that opened into the reception hall. Then he doubled back to the door of the chamber he had just left, and opened it.

Chenna was huddled on the bedmat, her face wet with tears. She wiped hastily at her cheeks as he entered. “What has happened now?” she asked, looking alarmed. “Tell me.”

Burlon closed the door, securing their privacy. “The delegation already knows. It seems that Cirin…” He swallowed against the tightness in his throat. “Cirin returned, last night, after you and I came here. He told everyone of Venna’s loss. And then…” Another swallow. “Ellis says he died. She says she saw him evanesce.”

Chenna cried out.

He pushed on, intent on what he had come to say. “Shall I take you to be with your House? Are there those who could offer you comfort as you grieve?”

“Two or three. I am from the Holding, so I am only closely acquainted with a few folk from the House, and not many of them came here to Tradepoint.”

"Nevertheless, they are your kin. Our kin. Would you not be better off with them than here alone, since I must go find Gredin?"

"I suppose," Chenna said. "If I dress quickly, will you walk with me to find them?"

"Of course."

He watched her don her clothes, pleased that the knot in her hlao now matched the knot in his. He would feel odd, learning a new way to fasten his hlao. When he was young, his Guides had used a length of yarn to teach him the Bentain knot. He could still remember the glow of pride that warmed him, as a young man, tying that same knot for its proper purpose on the day his hlao first unfurled. But the Laith knot looked quite different. More intricate.

Perhaps he should ask Ingarra te Balamont for a length of yarn.

"I am ready," Chenna said, and took his hand. "Take me to Laith's sleeping area. I will reclaim my belongings." She tugged gently at his hand. "As you should, from Bentain."

Chenna was right. He was no longer a member of House Bentain. Removing his clothes and gear would free up space that the House could no doubt use. "I will. And, however difficult today proves, you and I will return here tonight and resume our dydanin. I swear it so."

"Then I am content for now."

They left the room together, but he felt her flinch when they reached the entry to the reception hall. Groups of people stood about, some conversing, some embracing, some comforting distraught individuals.

"Take me to Laith," he requested softly.

Chenna sighed. "It is across the corridor. We must go through the mist to get there."

And so he escorted her into the antechamber, inhaling deeply as the bio-mist descended. When it cleared, the outer door opened, and they stepped out into the harshly lit public corridor. Chenna pointed. "There. The second set of doors." She sighed. "And then the mist again."

And so he and Chenna went through it again, emerging at last into an area devoted to sleeping space for the various Houses. Ropes were strung from point to point, crisscrossing in intricate symmetry to support the cloth panels separating one small area from the next, offering only a flimsy pretense of privacy.

It hadn't mattered, when everyone was happy and excited. Now, with grief and despair haunting them, the arrangement was nearly unbearable.

Chenna tugged at his hand. "Laith is this way."

He followed her into the warren of cloth panels until at last she drew him to a halt. "Here," she said, and drew back a panel, gesturing for him to go inside.

Burlon looked around. The area seemed impossibly tiny in comparison with the chamber where they had just spent their first night together. There was only room for Chenna's unfurled bedmat and a small, weathered rucksack.

Chenna Fetched the rucksack to herself. "I'll deal with the mat later," she said. "But I'm glad to have my comb and a change of clothes."

A voice from behind them asked, "Chenna?"

Turning, Burlon saw a man and woman, not quite smiling but with a kindly air.

"Yes, I am Chenna. And this is my Chosen, Burlon. What service may we offer?"

The woman had violet eyes like Chenna's. A common trait in House Laith? "I am Ulin, and this is my Chosen, Payt. After last night's strange Choosing, we certainly know who both of you are. But why you are back? You should be getting on with your dydanin, uninterrupted."

Burlon crossed his palms to them. "Ulin. Payt. You are my first acquaintances within my new House. Chenna and I emerged because I must meet with the Travelers. Might I leave her in your company while I see to my duties? It is a poor morning for anyone to be alone."

"Certainly," Payt replied. "Ulin and I welcome you, Burlon. It is odd, this Choosing between two Houses but the Power would not deal falsely with such a fine young couple."

"My thanks. My Chosen is a kind and thoughtful person. I am honored to be hers."

A mischievous smile curved Chenna's lips. "We will see how honored you feel when I have you walk out with me to tend the hives." Then her smile vanished. "But no. The bees are gone now. Oh, Burlon! What will I do, without them to care for?" And she began to cry.

Ulin drew Chenna into her arms. Over Chenna's bowed head, she said to Burlon, "Get on with your day. Payt and I were going to rest for a while. We will take Chenna with us."

Rest? The day has scarcely begun, Burlon thought in surprise, and yet he felt it, too – a dragging lethargy, as if every direction were suddenly uphill, with no destination worth the effort. "Beloved, I will return to you as soon as I can," he pledged, and made himself walk away.

Exiting through the antechamber, he breathed mist for the third time, crossed the public corridor, and prepared to breathe it a fourth time on his way back to the reception hall. As he entered the antechamber, a crowd came with him. He failed to see a single familiar face, but their bleak expressions made it clear that they all knew there would be no homecoming.

The outer doors closed.

The bio-mist descended.

If all knew of Venna's loss, why gather the Travelers? No one would leave in the present situation, would they? And who was he to issue a summons, when Cirin was First Traveler?

No, Cirin *had been* First Traveler.

Like some belligerent Beng, he wanted to wail *Unfair! Unfair!* But it was too late. It hurt to know that Cirin had returned… and he had missed his last chance to see his friend. It was supposed to be safe! Cirin had a back-up plan. If Venna was gone, he was going to go on to –

Palomar. But hadn't Ellis just said something about Palomar?

Burlon searched his balky memory until he found Ellis's words: ... *told us of the loss of Venna and of Palomar…*

How could that be? Worlds didn't flicker out like luminth. Worlds remained constant. How could Venna and Palomar be gone?

He desperately wanted answers. But it was too late to question

Cirin, and only Gredin seemed to have the Power's ear. Beyond that, what source of information was left?

Perhaps the Prett. They prided themselves on their 'science' and their *griimoni*, as they called their various machines. He and Cirin had scoffed at such things. But if it enabled the Prett to explain the reason for Cirin's demise, he would not scoff. He needed to understand.

In the meantime, however, he needed to make a decision and stick to it. Was he summoning the Travelers or not? If he summoned them, what would he say? What *could* he say? It seemed only proper to acknowledge the loss of Cirin, who had been First Traveler of House K'lar, yet Burlon shrank from the prospect. What he and Cirin had shared went far beyond being favored with the same gyfte. He didn't want to offer some formal comment and then move on.

He didn't want to move on at all.

[7]
1862 OF 2000 ORBITS REMAINING: 8BLUE

"My thanks," Gredin said to her security escort when they reached the outer entrance to the Vennan enclave. "Please, feel free to go on about your day."

She didn't want the guard to accompany her into the reception hall. His presence might upset the people gathered there for morning meal. And it would be a relief to enter the bio-mist chamber and hear the outer doors close behind her, ensuring that she would have at least a brief moment of solitude before taking up her duties.

But the chamber, when she triggered the doors, wasn't empty. Two figures were already there. Gredin recognized Sill te Torr, but the man at Sill's side was unknown to her. As the bio-mist began its familiar cycle, Gredin said, "Sill? Is something new amiss?"

"No," Sill said. "Nothing more has gone awry, for which I suppose we should be grateful. Waiting for you here seemed like one of the few opportunities to catch you alone. Your kinsman wanted a moment of privacy with you, and I wasn't certain how else to manage it." She nodded toward the man at her side, and Gredin saw that the stranger's hlao was tied with House Balamont's knot. A kinsman, indeed.

"This is Vik te Balamont," Sill informed her. "Vik also bears gyfte of Memory. Before we came here to Tradepoint, he was charged to share a Memory with you during our stay. He is most anxious to do so now, given what has happened." Her smile of encouragement was gentle. "And now, if the two of you will permit, I am going to return to House Torr's enclave, across the corridor, and see if I can be of service there." And she left them.

Gredin turned her attention to the unfamiliar man, crossing her palms. "I am happy to become acquainted with you, although sorry it must happen on such a sorrowful day."

Vik looked solemn. "Indeed, it is a sad day. I hope that the Memory I bring will be some solace to you in this time of mourning." He gestured at the floor of the chamber. "Sit, if you will. We likely won't be disturbed here, since most everyone is at table for their morning meal."

Bewildered, Gredin sat down. "Whose Memory do you wish to share with me?"

"You will know, soon enough. Simply relax and open your mind to me."

Gredin leaned back against the chamber wall, rested her hands in her lap, and closed her eyes.

And the Memory unfurled, engulfing her utterly…

... Dreff's fingers trembled on the fine-jawed grippers. The deep pink stone tumbled free, bouncing twice on his worktable before coming to rest, glittering in the light of the luminth. "Desh!" he muttered.

A hand touched his shoulder, and Estin, his Tutor, said "That's enough for today."

"But I want to finish this dangle!"

"Your body is telling you to rest. Go," Estin urged, his tone kindly but implacable. "Fetch a cool drink for yourself, or take a walk in the gardens. Petron has given us a fine day to enjoy. That nelfi stone will prove far more amenable when you are refreshed."

Dreff bit back a protest. Estin was a talented Maker. The lessons he so generously provided consumed time he could have spent exercising his own gyfte. "Very well," Dreff said, masking his disappointment. He tucked the nelfi stone into a shallow niche, covered his work bench, and slid from his stool. "Tomorrow, I will begin anew." He crossed his palms and bowed to his Tutor. "My thanks for your efforts, Estin."

"And for yours, Dreff," the man said, bowing in return.

Which was how, after partaking of a glass of manzell juice and a buttered roll, Dreff found himself strolling through the children's garden. He could have walked in the garden outside his own chambers, but he wasn't ready to engage with others. The dangle design, an arc of stones in the colors of sunrise, still filled his thoughts.

A pair of younglings rushed by, chasing a flitter-flyer, and Dreff grinned at their energetic rush, glad there were no babies or toddlers present to be buffeted. The littlest ones would all be with their Guides, indoors or in the south gardens. But children who were steady on their feet and ready to explore a wider slice of the world found the west gardens a fine place to play with one another, and to begin to distance themselves from the constant, protective presence of their Guides. He could remember feeling quite daring, at their age, as he explored the paths and the mazes and the fountain, gradually becoming acquainted with the other younglings of the House.

As he strolled along the smooth path, he could see more children, some running and laughing like the pair who had just passed him, some playing formal games together, some simply chasing one another along the mossy paths. It was a particularly pleasant day, sunny and breezy, with a brilliant turquoise sky. He should thank Petron, First of Weather for House Balamont. Days like this were too fine to be taken for granted.

Feeling more relaxed, Dreff walked on through the gardens, drinking in the colors. Then he stopped, arrested by the sight of a very small pair of feet protruding from the edge of an elaborate flowerbed.

He sighed. The younglings were allowed to play on all of the paths, and in the little bush mazes, and even to dabble their toes in the shallow fountain, but they weren't to bother the formal flower borders. There were several other areas where, if they wished, they could pluck a blossom or two. But the formal beds were for the enjoyment of all, and there would be no enjoyment if the plants were trampled underfoot.

He approached the motionless pair of little pink feet, but he did so quietly. If this was some child who had been defeated at a game, or had their feelings hurt by a playmate, Dreff didn't wish to make matters worse by scolding them. Indeed, given the diminutive size of those feet, this child must be quite new to the wider freedom of the gardens. Perhaps they hadn't understood which areas to avoid.

Reaching the spot, he saw that the situation was less dire than it might have been: rather than sprawling belly-down on top of the plants, the youngling was at least on hands and knees. But this was still a child where no child should be.

"Good day to you," he said, hoping not to startle the little intruder into a careless move. "My name is Dreff. Who are you?"

"I'm Gredin. Go away now, please."

Dreff sighed. "If you come out of there carefully, I'll take you over to the bush maze, where you can play."

"My thanks but no," came the unanticipated reply.

He tried again. "You aren't supposed to play in the flowers. You'll crush them."

"I won't. I'm careful. Besides, Beda looks after this part of the garden. If I harmed anything, he'd put it right. But I won't."

Dreff felt a flicker of irritation, and Focused to calm himself. Younglings sometimes had strange notions, so he tried a different approach. "What are you doing?"

"Looking."

Well, that was less than informative. "Looking for what? Did your ball roll into the planting bed?"

"No."

"Then what are you after?"

"I don't know yet. Something called to me."

What did she mean, 'called to me'?

"An animal?" he asked. Creatures weren't normally tolerated in the garden. Still, occasionally, a kamesta managed to burrow undetected beneath the wall.

But Gredin said, "No. Not an animal."

Dreff was growing exasperated in spite of his better intentions, and he was tired of addressing this child's hindquarters. She wore a sky-colored felk trimmed in elegant embroidery, but the pretty garment already bore several smears of rich, brown soil. With a frown of concentration, he used a flick of Power to cause the dirt to fall away, leaving the blue fabric unsullied. "Looking for insects?" he persisted.

"No. Hush. I can't hear, if you keep talking."

"Can't hear what?"

With a rustle of leaves, the little girl knelt upright and pivoted to give him a cross look, her face flushed beneath the pale curls. "I told you, I don't know yet. And I never will, if you keep–" She stopped talking suddenly, a smile of breath-catching sweetness transforming her face. "There you are," she crooned and reached down to dig into the dirt with her fingers.

"What did you find?"

"A beautiful stone! Fetch me out and I'll show you."

He opened his mouth to tell her to Send herself out onto the moss, then realized she was too immature; for her own safety, her ability to Send from one location to another was Blocked, and would stay so until she was mature enough to use the gyfte prudently. Proud that most of his own Blocks had been removed, he Fetched her out of the planting bed and steadied her on her feet.

She barely came up to his waist, a wisp of a girl with blue eyes too big for her thin face. But she was radiant with excitement, unclasping her hand to show him what rested on her palm.

Dreff looked down with interest, and was disappointed to see nothing there but a dirt-encrusted pebble the size of his thumbnail. "That's just a dimbrel. You'll find a lot of them around here. It's pretty, though," he added, to humor her.

Her eyes narrowed. "It's not a dimbrel. And it's not pretty yet. The pretty part is inside."

Dreff looked with renewed curiosity. The true beauty of many stones wasn't apparent in their unpolished state. "If you give it to me, I can Craft it."

"No!" Her fingers closed protectively over the drab little pebble.

Dreff retreated a step. "The stone is yours. I would never take it from you. I just wanted to polish it and mount it, so you could wear it on a cord around your neck."

She shook her head. "I don't want it on a cord. I carry my stones in my pocket." Her expression softened. "Would you like to see them? I have two. Well, three, now."

"Certainly," he said, glad to calm matters.

She fished in the pocket of her felk – a particularly deep pocket, with a lacing to tie it closed – and produced a little cloth pouch. "Put out your hand."

Dreff bent down and obliged her, hoping the stones in her pouch weren't as dirty as the one clutched in her fist.

Gredin upended the pouch, and the two stones that tumbled out made Dreff catch his breath. The first was a semi-transparent piece of blue stretz that gave the impression of water and a horizon, with vertical streaks like trees reaching toward the sky. "That's the Ocean Holding," Gredin told him. And Dreff found that it did remind him of House Balamont's seaside estate.

The second stone was a rectangle of olivan. It was mostly clear, but its center held a stacked tower of pale green crystals. "I don't know where that is," Gredin confided, "but it's somewhere high." Her smile turned shy. "Do you like them?"

"Indeed," Dreff told her, bemused. Stretz was a semi-precious stone from House Avilar's lands. Olivan was a precious gem from Balamont's own Mountain Holding, prized for the fragile beauty of its inclusions. Neither belonged in a youngling's pocket. "Who gave these to you?"

She cast him a reproachful look. "Nobody. I found them."

It seemed highly unlikely, unless someone's necklace had broken, allowing a finished stone to tumble to the ground. But Gredin's proud air implied that she had plucked both stones from the earth, in all their present beauty. Ah well. The mystery wasn't his to solve. "They're quite beautiful," he told her simply, and straightened.

Her face fell. "Don't you want to see the new one?"

"You already showed it to me."

"That was the outside. Don't you want to see it again, now that it

has Become?"

Bewildered, he said, "I am happy to see whatever you'd like to show me."

Gredin opened her fisted fingers.

The dimbrel pebble was transformed. On her palm, amid the dirt, now lay a stone veined in shades of vivid green reminiscent of the garden in which they stood. He had never seen the like of it. "When you picked it up, it was grey."

"That was its shell. This stone wanted to Become, so I held it until it was ready."

"It's a stone, not an egg," he objected. "If I find another dimbrel–"

"I told you, it's not a dimbrel."

He had to agree. The stone on her palm was far from a common dimbrel. "If I find another stone, can you do that again?"

"It would depend," she said solemnly. "Not every stone wants to Become." With care, she placed all three stones in her pouch and placed the pouch in her pocket, tied the pocket closed, dusted her palms together, and looked up at him with a smile. "You said you can Craft. Do you like stones, too?"

Given all that he had just seen, he began to believe she had *found the other two stones on her own, after all. He smiled. "I like stones very much. I'm a Maker of jewelry. I study and Craft with my Tutor, and I get to use stones and jewels from every House on Venna."*

Gredin's eyes widened. "What do you Make with them?"

"I've studied many different sorts of Craftsmanship. So far, my favorite is working with gemstones. I like to design settings to display them in rings and pendants."

"Are they beautiful?"

"I think so. And so does my Tutor. And Alita, who is one of our House's Traders. Just a few days ago, she said she would offer my jewelry for barter at the other Houses." He smiled at her awed expression. "Someday, our Traders may even take my jewelry to Tradepoint."

"What's Tradepoint?"

Her question surprised him; he had forgotten how little she was. "Tradepoint is a special place, far away from here," he explained. "It's a place where Traders go, with the help of our Travelers. All manner of people go there to meet and exchange their goods."

"Why don't they just do their Trading here?"

"Because most of them aren't Vennan!"

Gredin took a step back, eyeing him. "Not of Balamont, you mean?"

"Not of any House. Not of Venna."

Gredin gave her head a vigorous shake of denial. "Everyone is Vennan."

Dreff reached down and tucked back a stray curl that had obscured Gredin's vision. "Not so, little one. Everyone on Venna is Vennan, yes. But there are worlds other than ours that have people of their own – people who do not talk or think or dress or even look like us."

"What do they look like?"

Dreff shook his head. "I have no idea, for it isn't my gyfte to Travel the River. But I've heard it said that the people who come to Tradepoint are very different. They do not share our ways, nor are one race's ways like those of the people from another world. Still, all people who wish to Trade in harmony are welcome at Tradepoint."

"It sounds like our Grand Market."

"Indeed, I think it is very like the Grand Market. Our House–"

"Balamont," Gredin said, pride shining in her eyes.

"Yes. Members of House Balamont take the surplus fish and fruit and vegetables from our Holdings, or the loaves that we bake, or the beads that we fashion and paint, and offer them to the other Houses in exchange for their goods – cheeses made from the milk of House Avilar's rista herds, or chairs carved by the artisans of House Kendar, or perhaps table runners or carpets woven at House Bentain, or for gems and stones from the other Houses' mines. Or for anything else that we desire."

"Then why do we need Tradepoint?"

"Well, some goods are not made by any of our Houses. Many items we enjoy don't come from Venna at all." He touched the material of her felk. "This cloth likely came from there."

"I want to go to Tradepoint!" Gredin exclaimed.

Dreff looked at her, perplexed. "Is Trading your gyfte? Or Traveling the River?"

"No. I have the gyfte of Speech. But I still want to go there."

Dreff hated to disappoint her, but she deserved the truth. "I doubt that will be possible."

Gredin looked crestfallen.

He placed his hand lightly on her head. "Going to a place like Tradepoint would mean time spent away from House and family. What sensible person would want that? Your place is here, as is mine. You are going to mature into a fine Speaker, and I into a Maker whose jewelry is highly prized. We will both serve House Balamont well, I am sure."

Gredin sighed deeply. "I suppose you're right... but I wish you weren't. Tradepoint sounds exciting!" She patted her pocket. "May we go play in the bush maze now?"

"Of course," he told her, and took her small hand in his own...

And reality returned. The bio-chamber was silent except for Vik's soft breathing and Gredin's own. Filled with wonder and sorrow, she looked at Vik. "Thank you," she said, her voice barely a whisper. "Oh, thank you, Vik."

His face was serene. "Your Chosen was known to me since he was a youngling. He came to see me, the day of our departure, and asked that I share this Memory of your first meeting with him, to show you that he remembered how very long the wish to visit Tradepoint had burned within you, and to let you know how happy he was that your ambition to do so was finally to be fulfilled. And remember, First Speaker, that this Memory is safely lodged within me. You are welcome to experience it whenever you wish, and each time it will seem as fresh and new to you as that morning's experience was to Dreff." He rose to her feet. "But now the day awaits us. We should go, before someone notices your absence and grows concerned." He moved toward the inner doors. "No doubt your path and mine will cross again in the days to come."

"May it be so," Gredin said, and stood up as Vik returned to the reception hall.

For a few moments more, she waited alone in the chamber, finally possessed of the solitude she had thought she wanted. But the sweet innocence of Dreff's Memory infused her with new energy and hope, as if she were a luminth and the Memory had filled her. With fresh resolve, she triggered the inner doors to open and walked out into the reception hall.

Before she had taken five steps, a man she did not recognize moved into her path. "First Speaker, I need an urgent word with–"

"I have been waiting longer!" a woman said, and grasped the sleeve of Gredin's jacket.

"First Speaker," someone said behind her, "I need only a moment, but I need that moment *now*."

In the space of a breath, one importuning individual had become three. As Gredin tried to frame a reply, the three doubled their number, then doubled that, as more and more people heard the voices and became aware of her return.

"Certainly," she said. "I will attend to what you have to say. Let us begin by–"

But the voices melded into a cacophony of sound, and Gredin realized that a crowd had formed and was swelling, closing about her from all sides, jostling her and each other as they vied with increasing desperation for her attention. Still dazzled and distracted by Dreff's Memory, she strove to steady herself, both physically and within her gyfte, but the chaos around her grew with each passing instant, taking on a feral edge altogether unlike anything she expected from her fellow Vennans, as if last night's disastrous news had torn them loose from the moorings of conventional behavior.

A woman blundered into her, nearly knocking her off her feet. Instead of apologizing, the woman clung to her, weeping. Gredin put a protective arm around her and said to those in front of her, with all the force she could muster, "Step back, please. All of you, just step back!"

Those nearest hesitated and then retreated slightly. But then the people behind them pressed forward in reaction, and the crowd closed in again, aggrieved, lamenting, distressed beyond reason, a seething mass of woe.

[8]

1862 OF 2000 ORBITS REMAINING: 8GREEN

The inner doors opened, but it was hard to leave the antechamber because a crowd of people clogged the area, raising their voices in a clamor, all trying to converge on a single point.

Burlon climbed onto a bench, then to a tabletop, to see over the heads of the crowd... and what he saw alarmed him. A single person formed the center of the commotion, surrounded by rings of people pressing inward with increasing agitation, voices clashing. Who...?

Burlon closed his eyes and took three slow breaths, composing himself. Then he reached out with his sense of private mind. =Gredin? Where are you? Are you all right?=

=Burlon?= The frayed contact carried an overlay of panic, then faded.

He let it go and turned his efforts back to physical action. Jumping down from the table, he moved away from the gathering group, maneuvering between tables and benches until he reached the steps that led up to the arrival dais. There he stopped, checking to be certain no one was nearby. Then he reached out to that mental contact again. =Gredin?=

=Burlon!=

He Fetched her out of the crowd as unceremoniously as if she were a sack of diller beans. One instant, she was trapped in the center of the crowd. The next, she was beside him, face white with distress, legs unsteady as she leaned against him.

Across the room, where she had been, a howl of protest and confusion filled the air. Then someone cried out, and someone pointed, and the group began to surge again toward Gredin.

Slinging one arm around her, Burlon dragged her up the steps and onto the dais, not stopping until they stood on the arrival medallion itself. As the Prett had designed it to do, the mechanism came to life, triggered by their weight on the medallion. A shimmering barrier sprang up, separating them from the room. and Burlon breathed mist for the fifth time that morning.

It wouldn't take long to cycle, as he knew from experience. But it kept them briefly separate from the crowd. He took Gredin by both arms and peered down at her. "Are you hurt?"

"No," she said, but he could feel her shaking in his grasp as she gasped for breath.

"What were they doing? What do they want?"

She shook her head. "Some had questions. Some wept. Some were angry with me, demanding to know why I hadn't told them about the dreams sooner. They all talked at once. I couldn't make anyone listen They kept drowning me out." She looked as if she might weep, herself. "It caught me unawares. I'm a Speaker. I'm the one they *should* come to with their questions. I should have been able to handle it. I just wasn't expecting so many people, all at once."

Her explanation sounded reasonable, but he had seen the wild energy of that group, and he was afraid for her. "You can't manage their questions all at the same time," he said. "You can address the group, certainly. But you can't answer everybody, individually, unless they stop shouting and wait their turn. They need to calm down and remember that or I'm taking you out of here."

"How can they be calm, on this of all mornings?"

"Well, crushing you isn't the answer!"

"No," she agreed. "But they won't, if I use my gyfte properly."

"I hope you're right, because the barrier will drop soon."

She touched his arm. "Burlon, there's something I must tell you. Last night..."

He steeled himself. "Cirin returned to the Source. Ellis told me."

Gredin tried to smile. "He did a brave thing, returning to warn us. Sill was there. She holds it in Memory. Someday, you may wish to view it, and see how courageous he was to the very end. And Hayla was with him." Her gaze was haunted. "It was like nothing I have ever seen, Burlon. He truly became one with the Power."

That wasn't something he was prepared to hear. Not yet. He nodded briskly and said, "You'd best prepare yourself to address these people. I don't think they'll be foolish enough to try to mount the dais, but there's no avoiding them now unless we Send."

The crowd had gathered at the foot of the steps, all waiting for Gredin to give them comfort, or answers, or simply as a target for their grief and fear and anger. They were strangely disheveled, some with rumpled teslans, others with their hair loose, or with strands escaping from braids that had apparently been slept on. Faces were drawn, eyes red-rimmed, mouths set in dour lines. The crowd gave off a febrile aura of anger and bewilderment, tension and pain.

Could Gredin maintain Control when the barrier shimmered out of existence? If so, he would offer his silent support. If not, he would make good on his threat and remove her from the enclave entirely. But he hoped she would be up to the task. That would be best for...

Ocean waves.

Burlon shook his head, but the image persisted, asserting itself irresistibly. He was standing barefoot on a sandy beach, gazing out over gentle waves as the sun rose. A cool breeze stirred his hair and caressed his face as the few clouds near the eastern horizon turned extravagant shades of gold and rose. Peace flowed into him with each breath...

And then the barrier retracted.

The ocean sunrise faded from his mind, leaving behind a relaxed sense of ease, and he realized, from the expressions of the people waiting below, that they had all experienced it, too.

He spotted Sill, First of Memory, smiling at him, satisfied with the aftereffects of what she had done.

On the instant, Gredin took a step toward the group. Spine straight, chin uplifted, she gazed out over them and spoke, her voice ringing with her gyfte. "Morning is upon us," she said. "We have withstood the night, and a difficult one it was. I have things to say to you, and words I would hear from you. Be assured, I will remain here until each who wish to do so has talked with me personally. But there are many of you, so that will take time. I invite you to seat yourselves for your better comfort." Her mouth curved in a rueful smile. "We startled each other just now, you and I, and matters became such that no one could be properly heard or answered. I would not have that happen again. So, please, on this morning of all mornings, look to your own comfort and care. Choose a table where you and your kinsmen can sit together in passable ease. Fetch morning meal from the kitchens, where Miri te Kendar and those who share her gyfte have worked to prepare food to strengthen us all. I will talk with you, one table at a time, until you all have had your chance to ask whatever is on your mind. I will get to all of you as quickly as I can, so please, find a place to sit, and we'll begin."

The girl did have a gyfte. At her final words, Burlon himself felt Compelled to go to a table and sit down. But he was forestalled by the touch of Gredin's fingers on his wrist. She said quietly, "I must stay here, for now, and deal with people's fears and questions. But I need to confer with you and Sill and Keegan and Miri, as well. Could you inform Keegan and bring him along at midday meal?"

"Of course. But where? You'll get no peace, out here."

"True. We'll be meeting in the chambers I share with Tetralanna. It is as private a place as I know, and she'll likely be absent, having her own midday meal with the House."

He glanced warily at the people settling at tables. "You'll be all right?"

She looked genuinely surprised. "These are our kinsmen, Burlon. They mean me no harm. What happened when I came in was unfortunate, but I can't see it happening again, now that I've addressed the group."

He raised a skeptical eyebrow. "People are still rattled, despite the Memory Sill shared. There's no telling what they might do. And you can't tell me you weren't frightened."

Gredin sighed. "I *was* frightened, and I'm grateful for your rescue. But the fault was partly mine. I was distracted. I didn't pay proper attention to my surroundings, and matters escalated. I won't be so foolish again. Go on. I'll be fine."

He supposed her words were sensible enough. Vennans didn't harm each other. The incident had been a result of high emotion and crowded conditions. Now that everyone had settled onto benches, the calm would likely persist. "Well, reach out to me at need," he said in parting, and left her to it, not envying her the morning that lay ahead.

His own morning was a bleak prospect, as well. He would seek out Keegan te Fliss and inform him of the midday meeting Gredin wanted. Then he would find Sill te Torr, knowing she held within her mind the Memory of Cirin's final moments – a Memory he needed to experience. Others in the enclave had witnessed Cirin's return. He could not remain ignorant of the details, not least for Hayla's sake.

Cirin had been his didana idia, his treasured First Friend, the person who knew him and understood him best. Now Cirin was gone, and he himself had felt no tremor of foreboding, no least inkling that anything terrible was happening. He had been too caught up in the joy of having found his Chosen, and the unparalleled bliss of joining with her.

Burlon groaned. Now that he knew the enormity of what finding his Chosen really meant, how could he face Hayla, who had lost Cirin even more profoundly than he had? The four of them – he and Chenna, with Cirin and Hayla – should have become each other's staunchest allies and most loving acquaintances. Now, instead, there was the inescapable awareness that the same night that brought Burlon and Chenna together had sundered Cirin and Hayla forever.

The loss of Cirin tore at him more intolerably than the loss of his multitude of kinsmen in House Bentain. And was that not, on the face of it, a shameful thing? He had lost his Guides, his parents, his sister, and score upon score upon score of others within House Bentain… and yet it was the loss of Cirin, not even of his House, which pierced him most viciously. Having Cirin as his didana idia had been the easiest, most natural, most like-minded relationship in his life. The loss of it felt wounding, as if he should urgently seek a Healer.

A short time later, he was hailed by Jentana te Bentain, who looked far more somber than at the previous night's reception. "You came out from your dydanin, then," Jentana observed, sounding astonished.

"I said that I would."

Jentana offered a wry smile. "It was one thing to say so before your dydanin began. I imagine it felt like quite another matter to follow through on your promise, this morning."

"I said that I would," Burlon repeated. His time with Chenna was precious, not a topic for banter, least of all this morning. "Your pardon. I need to speak with the Travelers."

The look Jentana cast him was sharp. "No time to chat with someone no longer of your House, I suppose?"

"That's not it at all," Burlon protested, disconcerted by Jentana's reaction. "Last night, I told the Travelers I would address them in the morning, so I need to do that. If you want to speak with me, I have no objection. It will just have to wait a bit."

"Oh, I wouldn't want to trouble you, Burlon te Laith," was Jentana's cool reply as he walked away.

Burlon watched him go, aggrieved. Had the man been looking for a quarrel? Last night's Choosing had been a public event, duly observed, duly approved. The fact that it involved two separate Houses was a bewilderment to everyone – to him and to Chenna first and foremost – but it made their Choosing no less true. Their hlaos had blended, which was the work of the Power, impossible for anyone to force or imitate.

Yes, but you volunteered to leave House Bentain.

Well, that was a truth. Faced with Gredin's pronouncement that they could not split their allegiance between two Houses, Burlon had felt moved to be the one to make that sacrifice. He was now Burlon te Laith. He would remain Burlon te Laith, even if, by some cruel fate, Chenna returned to the Source tomorrow.

Unimaginable, his heart protested. But Hayla would have said Cirin's death was unimaginable, less than a day ago. And now Cirin was gone.

Burlon shivered. He needed to get past it. Not over it; he would never get over it. It was a wall of glass, sleek and sheer, impossible to scale. But he needed to turn aside from the painful awareness of it, from the dominating immediacy of it, so that he could carry on with his duties for the day.

And yet he tarried, adrift.

It came to him, slowly, that what he felt was what he saw being played out by the others all around him. Everyone in the enclave was experiencing some dreadful variation on his pain. No one moved crisply, with purpose. No one smiled or laughed. Even people sitting in groups seemed encased in individual bubbles of unhappiness. From the look of them, no one had slept much, or slept well. The few folks who had Fetched morning meal were mostly just moving the food around on their plate. Any one of them, on a normal day, would have elicited concern from their House members, and the suggestion that a Healer be summoned.

Today, they all needed a Healing that could never come.

He should contact Keegan about the midday meeting Gredin wanted.

No, first he should contact the other Travelers. Why did that simple resolve keep sliding out of his mind?

Perhaps because it would confirm the terrible news. Perhaps because Cirin, who had been First Traveler of House K'lar for as long as he could remember, wouldn't be there. Or perhaps because there simply was no longer any point in gathering them.

But he had said that he would.

Like a rista tethered to a sapling, his mind raced in that circle of thought and returned yet again to where it had begun, with nothing accomplished.

Frustrated, he tried to recall the names of Travelers besides himself and Cirin. Bruise it, he knew these people. It was ludicrous to have to search his memory for something so obvious.

But he didn't want to talk directly with Travelers from House Bentain. Not this morning. And dealing with one from House Laith would be almost as embarrassing. House Fliss had sent no Travelers. House Balamont must be in more turmoil than most, given Gredin's dreams from the Power…

That still leaves nine Houses, he told himself sternly. *Pick one.*

House Kendar, he decided with a sigh. While recruiting individuals for the Trisectoriana, he had found Kendar to be a friendly House. If anyone was coping, it would be House Kendar. He would start there… if he could recall which Travelers from House Kendar had come.

His thoughts continued to balk and stray. Finally, after frustration awakened a dull pain behind his eyes, a name came to him: D'keen te Kendar, a gentle soul who rode the River with the ease of a bird soaring on an updraft.

Sitting at an empty table, Burlon quieted his mind and reached out to her. =D'keen?=

Instead of a crisp response, he sensed a vague upwelling of weary sadness.

=D'keen, I am sorry to trouble you, but I need to talk with you.=

=To me? Why? Has some further disaster befallen us?=

=No. But I need to make sure no Traveler leaves Tradepoint before we all meet.=

=Leave?= she echoed incredulously. =It will be many a day before one of us willingly contemplates Traveling the River, after what happened to Cirin.=

=What do you mean?=

Silence, as if the contact had ended. Then, =Cirin returned to the Source.=

=Yes, I know. But it is *all* that I know. Was there something about his death that…=

=Ask Sill,= D'keen interrupted, her thoughts shouldering his aside. =I don't wish to discuss it. I don't wish to *think* of it. Have Sill show you.= And with that she *did* withdraw.

Burlon blinked. Then, needing to distance himself from D'keen's reaction, he reached out deliberately to Sill te Torr. =Sill? Are you still in the reception hall?=

=No,= came the response. =I am with my House.=

=May I come to you?=

The sense of a sigh. =If you must,= she said, less than graciously, and was gone.

Burlon crossed the reception hall to the antechamber, waited through the mist for the sixth time that morning, and crossed the empty corridor to where House Torr members lodged, but he stopped short of their entrance, momentarily relieved not to be surrounded by mourning Vennans. In the far distance, he could see a retreating Prett security guard, patrolling, but no one else was in sight.

=Sill? I am outside your enclave. Do you know of somewhere private we could meet?=

=No. Do you?=

=Not really,= he told Sill reluctantly. =This stretch of hallway is as private a place as I know of, for now.=

=Then I will join you there,= Sill disconcerted him by saying. =Wait for me.=

It took longer than he expected for Sill to appear. When she came out into the hallway, her eyes were overly bright, and she seemed almost to vibrate. "Are you all right?"

"I have spent the morning preserving memories for my grieving kinsmen."

"You'll wear yourself out," he warned.

Sill made a dismissive noise. "What would you have me do – tell them their memories must wait? It would take a harder heart than mine to say such a thing. I've spoken with Vik te Balamont and he is doing the same, although it takes him longer to Harvest and then recover from the Harvesting." She came to a stop directly in front of him, trembling with intensity. "Our people are sick at heart, drowning in the realization that so much that we loved is gone. Lodging a Memory with us gives each of them a way to reclaim one small piece of what has been taken from them."

"But you will both exhaust yourselves."

"When we are tired, we will sleep, I assure you. But then we will arise and begin again."

"How many memories can you hold? More than Vik, because his gyfte is smaller than yours?"

"I do not know. So far as I am aware, no one with gyfte of Memory has ever found a limit."

"I suspect the gyfte has never been tested in circumstances as dire as these."

Sill shrugged. "We will do what we can, for as long as we can. If there is a limit, we will deal with that when we reach it. I told the members of my House that each of them should think carefully and select one vivid memory that they would like to preserve. Once I have finished with House Torr, I will approach the other Houses and make that offer to them. Vik will do the same."

"Nearly a thousand people," Burlon warned. "Can the two of you hold a thousand new memories?"

"We will try." She looked at him sharply. "So, what brings you to my door?"

"A gratitude and a request."

"Then let us begin with the gratitude."

He nodded toward the reception hall. "That Memory of waves and a sunrise…"

"People had become dangerously agitated. I thought it might calm matters."

"It did. You have my thanks, and Gredin's, as well."

"And the request?"

It was what he had come for. "I understand you were present when Cirin returned, last night… and that you witnessed his evanescence. I would have you share that Memory with me."

"The Memory is safe with me," she said, giving him a wary look, "and I will share it with you at a more appropriate time, be assured."

"I would see it now."

"Reconsider. This is a day of great sadness. Countless Vennan lives have ended, Cirin's among them. Select a happy memory of yourself and Cirin, and bring it to me for Harvesting."

"I will. But I also ask that you share the Memory of his passing."

"He was your First Friend. Why put yourself through such an ordeal?"

"He came back! He came back, and I wasn't there."

"Your presence wouldn't have saved him."

"But it might have comforted him. And so I owe it to Cirin to witness his passing."

"Would Cirin agree?" Sill asked gently. "Are you not miserable enough over the news?"

"That isn't the point. I need to know what happened because I must go to Hayla, Cirin's Chosen, to offer her what aid and comfort I can, and I can't do that if I don't know what I'm talking about. Please, Sill. Show me what happened."

For a bleak moment, he thought she would refuse. But, finally, she sighed and said, "Sit down."

"Let's walk down a bit, away from the doors."

And so they walked to a point midway between one enclave entrance and the next. Then Burlon dropped to the floor at Sill's feet, hating what was to come, yet determined to make it happen. Remaining ignorant of the details of Cirin's death was intolerable, as well as indefensible. He had to know. And so he calmed himself and flung his mind open to Sill's gyfte.

Music. Dancing.

Then a shimmer brightened the air.

And someone gasped.

And someone screamed...

The Memory was like a tapestry, oddly beautiful despite the grimness of its subject. When it released him, Burlon was shaking, which he suspected meant that Sill herself had been shaking when Cirin's body evanesced in a shower of golden sparks and vanished.

Wracked by sorrow and pity and a bone-deep horror that he knew would never leave him, he considered what he had just seen. It was not the relatively serene moment of passage he had envisioned. Instead, there had been blood and wounds and pain, a ravaging of Cirin's body that made clear why his spirit had been forced out, with no recourse but a return to the Source.

The state of Cirin's body when he passed put to shame every crude expletive Burlon had ever voiced. *Scabs*, he'd often cursed, or *Blisters,* or even, *Great gaping wounds.*

Well, Cirin had experienced great, gaping wounds. Burlon was haunted by the Memory of a glimpse of the pure white bone of Cirin's leg gleaming, visible through a gash in his thigh.

"Who was he talking about?"

Sill's question made no sense. "What do you mean?"

"Hayla asked who had done those terrible things to him, and he answered, *Zrach*, but I don't know who that is. Not a Vennan, surely."

A bubble of laughter welled up in Burlon's throat. He swallowed hard against it. There was nothing funny about the situation, and he might not be able to stop if he gave voice to that frantic laugh. Instead, he banged his fist against the wall, and the pain helped him to push the laughter deep and trap it there.

Sill stared down at him, clearly concerned.

That wouldn't do. She had only done what he'd begged her to do. And so, as levelly as he could, he said, "Zrach isn't a person. It's a place. Cirin tried to Travel the River to Venna, but Venna was gone, so he Traveled on to Palomar, only to find that Palomar had been destroyed, as well." He shuddered. "By then, he must have been exhausted, and shocked, and grieving. I suppose he could have tried to go on to Orifam, but that would have carried him even farther away from Tradepoint. If he was intent on getting back here quickly to warn us, he had few choices. Even Cirin couldn't manage coming all the way back here without a respite, depleted as he already was. Zrach was the next-best solution… or must have seemed so to him."

"I'd never heard the name until Cirin spoke it, last night."

"It isn't a place we go, except briefly as part of our training. No one lives there – well, no people. Just creatures."

"Ah. So Cirin was attacked by some animal, not by a person."

"An animal. Perhaps a bird."

"Like those bird creatures at the reception, last night?"

"No, no," Burlon assured her. "I'm not overly fond of the Hesch, but they're an intelligent, civilized race. No relation to any bird you'd find on Zrach." When she still looked uncertain, he said, "If the Hesch posed any danger to others, the Director wouldn't tolerate them on Tradepoint, and we would never have allowed them inside our enclave for last night's reception. They look peculiar but they're not violent. We're safe, Sill. I know you worry about our situation. We *all* worry about our situation. But don't fear the races we Trade with."

The glitter of alarm faded from Sill's eyes. "All right, if you say so. But you'll pardon me, I hope, if I'm not in any hurry to leave the enclave."

"Why?" Burlon asked, honor-bound to defend Tradepoint. "You came with us to the Director's office and attended the governmental presentation. Were you afraid then?"

"No," Sill admitted.

"Then why be reluctant to leave the enclave now?"

"Before, it was new and exciting – and temporary. Now…" She hunched her shoulders. "We have nowhere else to go." She reached down and touched his hair. "I am truly sorry for Cirin's loss. I know it is one more life out of so very many, but… Well, I am sorry."

He nodded mutely.

"Would you like to get up?" she asked, extending her hand.

But he shook his head. "I'll sit here for a bit."

"Well then, for now, I will leave you in peace. My House needs me," Sill said, and retreated to the Torr enclave's antechamber.

Burlon leaned his head back against the wall, then spotted a Prett security guard coming down the corridor toward him, perhaps concerned by the sight of a Trader sitting on the hallway floor. Burlon lifted a hand in reassurance. "All is well. I'm just thinking."

The guard hesitated, then nodded and went back the way he had come.

Burlon sighed. He'd needed to see the Memory of Cirin's death, to understand the impact it had doubtless made on the delegation. And it made him determined to take no chances with the safety of his fellow Travelers, particularly on a morning when everyone was shaken to their roots by the news of Venna's loss and the loss of the myriad kinsmen who had died with their world. No precaution was too extreme, no effort too great.

So decided, Burlon composed his private mind and reached out again. =D'keen?=

=Burlon,= the Traveler acknowledged with an air of weary patience.

=I need to meet with all of the Travelers immediately, in the corridor outside of Torr's enclave. Contact all of Kendar's Travelers, without exception, and bring them here as soon as they are all assembled. Can I depend upon you for this task?=

He thought she might refuse, or at least argue about it. Instead, she answered, =It will take a little time, but we will be there as soon as possible.=

=My thanks, D'keen. Truly.=

House Fliss and House Darius had sent no Travelers, and he had just spoken to House Kendar, so he worked his way through the other Houses – Avilar and Balamont, Bentain and Calidane, Indirin, K'lar, his own new House of Laith, then Shelahn and Torr and Vell – selecting one Traveler from each to receive his message: *Gather your Travelers and bring them to the corridor outside Torr's enclave.*

Soon, they began to arrive, individually and in clusters, gathering until there were nearly fifty Travelers standing with him in the hallway. He hoped the Prett security guard wouldn't ask questions; it might be difficult to explain.

He wished he had Sill's gyfte, or Gredin's, either of which would have enabled him to place his words within the private mind of everyone present without speaking aloud. But it was a skill he lacked, so he squared his shoulders and said, over the quiet undercurrent of conversation around him, "Listen, please."

The low hum drifted into silence. And then, to his shock, they all sat down and looked at him, as attentive as students in the presence of a Tutor.

"My thanks for coming," Burlon began, shaken by their combined attention. "Last night, while I was shut away in my dydanin, the rest of you were in the reception hall when Cirin returned, and pronounced our fate, and returned to the Source. I have now received the Memory of those moments from Sill te Torr. I have seen Cirin's wounds. I have watched him evanesce." His throat wanted to close, but he made himself continue. "Just as importantly, I heard his warning. Palomar is destroyed… and so is Venna. We have lost our Houses and most of those we love. We have lost our world itself. So I ask you for your promise, today, that none of you will attempt to Travel the River until we have had time to talk about our future and regain our Balance. This is no time for rash action. We who were many are now few. Our remaining kinsmen need us. We have no right to risk ourselves recklessly. Can we agree that none of us will leave Tradepoint until there is plan, and until the pain we feel today has begun to fade?"

A rough chorus rose, with some saying "Yes," while others said, "I agree."

"Is there anyone who disagrees? If so, state your reason. I will listen."

No one spoke.

"Very well. For this day and the days to come, we will all stay here, grateful for shelter on Tradepoint as we deal with our losses and spend time with our remaining kinsmen. My thanks for gathering so promptly. We will meet again, soon, I am certain," Burlon promised, and got to his feet.

Raggedly, they rose and began to disperse. Many turned away and filed solemnly into the various nearby antechambers, but more than a dozen approached him instead, their expressions doleful. He waited where he was, expecting them to ask questions. But no one said anything until Ravor te Vell said quietly, "To lose a First Friend is a heavy burden." The others murmured agreement.

Their unexpected sympathy rocked Burlon's Control. He tried to distance himself from the anguish he was feeling, making do with a nod in silent acknowledgment of Ravor's words.

It seemed to satisfy them. After another long moment, they turned and retreated to the antechambers, leaving Burlon alone again in the corridor.

For a time, he stood, tangled in the Memory of Cirin's demise, filled with horror, as well as grief. Again and again, the Memory played out in his head, from Cirin's first appearance within the dome to the instant his body vanished in a rising eddy of golden sparks…

Eventually, however, his conscience nudged, reminding him of tasks he was still honor-bound to accomplish. With a groan, he walked down the corridor to the access doors for the third of Venna's four enclaves, opened them, and stepped into the antechamber, where he underwent his seventh dose of bio-mist. It was getting ridiculous. Was there such a thing as an overdose? He should ask Wyve…

When the doors opened, he strode inside, asking neither direction nor permission. He knew where he was going. If someone wanted to object… well, that would be their misfortune.

A red-striped blanket marked the entrance he sought. He drew it aside and started down the cloth-lined maze, closing his ears to murmured conversations and anguished weeping. Such was the inevitable mood today, whatever enclave he chose to enter. He had a task to accomplish, and he needed to remain calm, in full Control his emotions.

At last, he reached the blue-patterned cloth of the sleep alcove that had belonged to Hayla and Cirin, and now was Hayla's alone. A luminth shone within. Not willing to risk being turned away, Burlon put his hand on the cloth barrier and drew it aside.

Hayla was there, curled in a tight ball on her bedmat, her eyes open but unfocused. She said, hoarsely, "We have lost him."

Burlon had rehearsed a dozen comforting things to say to her, but the honesty of her words, and her acknowledgment that they both suffered the loss, disarmed him. He replied, with equal candor, "I wasn't there for him, at the last. But you were, and I am beyond grateful for that."

She gestured. "Come here. I would tell you a thing."

And so he stepped inside and let the blue-patterned cloth fall into place, shielding them from intrusive gazes. He sat down, close enough for Hayla to reach out and touch his leg.

"You were with your Chosen," she told him, "just as Cirin was with his, and that was as it should be. There was no time for long goodbyes."

"Sill showed me," he acknowledged.

"Then you know. It was not a pretty end and yet, at the last, there was a moment's grace. We kissed, and I held him as he returned to the Source. But now I am here, and Cirin is gone forever, and what is the use of that?"

"I wish I knew," Burlon said. "Perhaps, in time, the Power will make it clear to us. But that is no comfort to us now. I can only say that I remain your friend, ready to aid you in any way I can. And I hope, in time, that you will become close to Chenna, as well."

At that, Hayla stilled. In something like her usual teasing tone, she said, "Indeed. Last night, you began your dydanin. I trust you acquitted yourself well?"

"I made every effort, and my Chosen seemed to find no fault with me."

"And you with her?"

"She is wonderous," Burlon said simply.

"A proper Chosen's answer," Hayla said, and began to weep. When Burlon made a sound of distress and concern, she patted his leg blindly. "For now, I would like you to go. I need this time alone. But talk to your Chenna about me. Tell her I am certain we will become good friends, once our days are less difficult." She rolled onto her other side, so that all he could see was the curve of her back. "Let me see if I can sleep now. I found little rest, last night."

Burlon stood up, feeling graceless and inadequate. "I will go because you ask me to. But I will come back soon. We understand each other's darkness, you and I." He took a step away, then hesitated. "Sill te Torr is storing memories for people. Think back over your times with Cirin and decide what recollection you would most like Sill to safeguard for you."

"I will think." Hayla's voice was muffled. "Be on your way now. I will see you later."

Heavy of heart, he left her and made his way out of House K'lar's area. But it occurred to him that another of his tasks lay close at hand. House Bentain's sleeping area was within this same enclave; he and Cirin had planned it that way. Having come so far, he might as well collect his belongings and take them back to the room set aside for his dydanin with Chenna. He kept his head down and his pace quick, wanting to gather his things and leave before anyone could –

"Burlon," someone said from behind him. "Burlon te *Laith*."

Bruises. He turned around and saw that it was Naria te Bentain, an imperious member of the House who had come to Tradepoint because of her gyfte as a sculptor. Many artisans had selected small, delicate examples of their art, but Naria had brought several wooden pillars, massive in size, elaborate in the intricacy of their carving.

The look she bestowed on Burlon now made him feel like an unwanted pile of sawdust at the base of her latest creation. Temper flared within him, and he offered her the barest courtesy of a nod. "Naria. You have something to say to me?"

"Only to ask your business, here within the House you have abandoned."

"My business is my own. Once I attend to it, be assured I will be on my way."

"Do so. This is a day of sorrow. Our House members deserve privacy from outsiders."

Outsiders? That was rather stretching the point. Burlon opened his mouth to retort –

"Burlon!" someone proclaimed. "Thank you for coming. Naria, if you'll excuse us…?"

Her gaze was not a friendly one. "Next time, show more sensitivity about who you invite into our area, Khest."

Khest's expression was mild, but his tone was quietly severe as he said, "Sensitivity? Burlon has been a member of our House for all of his life, until last night's strange events. These are unusual times. Why be so quick to cast him aside?"

"It is he who did the casting," Naria said, and stalked off.

In the wake of her departure, Burlon turned to his kinsman with a grateful smile. "I suspect her opinion is widely held, although few would choose to express it in such a manner on this unhappy day. I hope coming to my defense reaps you no bitter harvest from her."

Khest shrugged. "Let Naria think what she will. Shall we find a more private place to talk, before she thinks of a further rejoinder and returns to deliver it?"

"I'm headed for my former alcove. It's down this way. Will you accompany me?"

"Certainly."

It took a few twists and turns before they reached the space Burlon had set aside for himself. He drew back the cloth that curtained the entry and let Khest precede him.

It was one of the nicer alcoves, with a solid wall at its far end. Looking around it, he said, "I've come to take my things away. You could move your belongings here, if you like it better than where you are currently."

Khest looked surprised, then thoughtful. Finally, with a shy smile, he nodded. "I would like that, actually. Is there someone's permission I need?"

"That of the Trisectoriana organizer."

"And that would be…"

"Me. Just do it. It's not as if anyone's in charge of the House, at the moment."

"No," Khest agreed, his pleased expression fading. "This is all so wrong, so peculiar… How can we not be going home? How can we possibly stay in this strange place?" His breathing grew ragged. "How can Silandra simply be… gone? She nearly came with me to Tradepoint, but Vandi's child was due and she wanted to be there for the birth. Now Silandra and Vandi and the baby have all returned to the Source, and I don't know what's to become of me, without her."

His words touched Burlon. Cirin's death was a tragedy, one that pierced him deeply. But the thought of a newborn child dying – one too young even to have had its hlao created – was a level of horror he had not considered. And Khest, like Hayla, had lost his Chosen, who should have been his life partner, reliable as the rising sun.

No sun was visible from within Tradepoint's metal shell. And many Vennans faced this day knowing that, without their Chosen, they would henceforth make a solitary journey.

It was a grim prospect.

"We will find a path," Burlon said stubbornly. "In time, a new way will become clear. But, first, we must nurture our strength and mourn our losses."

The thought was daunting. Vennans were unaccustomed to death. Depending on your gyfte, you might regret a Trading deal gone wrong, or a rista kidlet that did not survive its birthing, or a plant blight that claimed part of a crop. But not people. Not kinsmen. Not loved ones.

Not a Chosen, unique in all the world, selected for you by the Power itself…

"Burlon? Are you all right?"

He jumped at the sound of Khest's voice. "I am well enough. Indeed, better than many. We are all beleaguered, but I have tasted joy while you were dining on loss and despair."

"And yet you taste loss, as well. You lost your First Friend. And you are leaving us."

The reference to Cirin's death was too painful to address. Instead Burlon said, "I am leaving House Bentain, but I am still part of the larger group, as are you. As are we all. Will you cease to know me simply because I sleep in a different part of the enclave?"

"No. Of course not."

"Good. I am less certain of Naria. She may not acknowledge me, once I move out."

"Naria is prideful. Your change of allegiance to House Laith shocked us, last night."

"It shocked *me*," Burlon admitted.

Khest's smile was gentle. "I imagine it did. Give Naria time to adjust."

Her sharp words still stung. "I expect to pay little attention to her opinions, now that we no longer share a House."

"And yet, Laith or Bentain, we are living more closely with one another than ever before. If matters between you and Naria can ease, that would be for the best."

Tradepoint was small indeed. Encountering different races was nearly unavoidable, and avoiding other Vennans was even harder, sharing a common meal with the community multiple times a day. He had no need of enemies, here or elsewhere. "Agreed," Burlon said. "I count on you not to be shy with me just because I am Laith now. If you have any need, or a question worries you, let me know. This is a time of adjustment for us all, and I am open to any suggestion that makes it go more smoothly."

Khest shook his head. "It is hard to know what to ask. This is a daunting place."

"It is different, but it need not be daunting. I know Tradepoint well and enjoy it."

"Enjoy?" Khest repeated on a note of incredulity.

"Enjoy," Burlon affirmed. "Once matters ease, come to the Traders' Market with me."

"You say that as if you are offering me a treat."

"I am. You'll see. If nothing else, the exercise would do you good."

Khest nodded. "I'll admit, we've been bottled up here more than is good for any of us."

"Then perhaps you would welcome a chance to use your gyfte," Burlon said. "My shoulders and neck are all in a knot. You could ease them for me, if you would."

The brightening of Khest's expression told him that he'd made a good suggestion. Khest was graced with gyfte of Touch. A legitimate chance to exercise his gyfte would steady him, on this day of sadness and upheaval. And Burlon would benefit, as well. The tensions of the morning had created a hot rope of discomfort from the base of his skull to an unreachable spot between his shoulder blades, and his temples had begun to throb.

"Sit," Khest directed.

Burlon did as he was told, surrendering himself to his friend's skilled hands.

At first, Khest's touch was gentle, almost tentative. But soon Burlon felt Khest's fingers become warmer, firmer, more authoritative, probing his shoulders and neck, even grasping his head and claiming the weight of it, rotating it. At some point, his mind surrendered, forming no new thoughts. The throbbing in his temples faded away, and the rope of tension unraveled. His head lolled, and only Khest's hand on his shoulder kept him upright. "Sleep," Khest urged, easing him onto the mat.

Burlon couldn't, of course. He had a dozen responsibilities to fulfill. He had…

"I'll wake you shortly," Khest promised, his words dim and distant.

And Burlon slept.

[9]

1850 OF 2000 ORBITS REMAINING: 23GREEN

Keegan te Fliss had spent the morning with members of House Balamont, asking those not too distraught to tell him their name and their main gyfte. There was no method to the order of his work; he simply moved from one willing individual to the next, entering the information he obtained in his notebook in as small a hand as he could manage and still maintain legibility.

Eventually, he would create a master list organized by gyfte, and another listing House members alphabetically, but the final versions of those would require even more of the precious paper he had brought from home. His existing supplies, intended for a four-day stay, were dwindling rapidly with the unexpected need to record information about the delegation.

Sleep, last night, had been difficult. To subdue his emotions in the cramped space of Beda and Ingarra's cubicle, he had concentrated on identifying the information Gredin would find most useful in the days to come.

He hoped to find a source of ink, or a way to create his own, or – at last resort – to dilute what he had. The Shodekekeen's fabric dyes might prove useable. But finding proper paper would be a far greater challenge. Races that visited the Traders' Market all seemed to use methods other than ink and paper to record their information.

The yellow paper the Shodekekeen had given him at the reception was intended for wrapping purchases. The yellow-speckled paper was lovely to look at, but it felt soft, and soft paper tended to be porous, causing ink to spread in fat, feathered lines. That was precisely what had occurred when he tested his ink upon it during morning meal. Therefore, it couldn't be used for creating written records; legibility was compromised, and it wasted precious ink.

He had questioned people all morning, but not everyone had been amenable. It was easy to avoid those who openly wept, but he had received a tongue lashing from several individuals who resented his inquiries. "Go bother your own House," one snapped, and Keegan had bowed in apology, unwilling to burden them with the news that his entire House had perished in Venna's destruction. People were in enough pain without adding his sorrow to their own.

Around him, some had begun sitting down to midday meal. Reluctantly, Keegan closed his vial of ink, secured his notebook, used a quick touch of Power to cleanse his reed pen and fingertips, and sought an empty table where he could eat in peace.

"Keegan!"

He looked around.

Burlon approached, moving with an air of purpose at odds with the room's inhabitants. "Come on," he said, reaching Keegan's side. "We're wanted."

"Who wants us? Where are we going?"

"Gredin wants to meet." Burlon grimaced. "I was supposed to tell you, but it's been quite a morning. Sorry."

Keegan nodded. Burlon and Chenna were likely the only two people in the enclave who had spent the past night happily. However, for a man who had spent the night with his new-found Chosen, Burlon didn't look very pleased with life.

"Are you sure this is where Gredin means for us to meet?" Keegan asked hesitantly when Burlon escorted him to the door of the private quarters originally assigned to the delegation's two Speakers. "Tetralanna ordered her out of these chambers, yesterday. Last night, Gredin and I slept with her Guides, in the Balamont portion of the enclave."

Burlon scowled. "That must have been a tight fit. But this is where she said to meet. And Tetralanna is no longer First Speaker. She shouldn't be ordering anyone around, least of all Gredin. I'll point that out to Tetralanna, if the need arises. But she's likely at midday meal."

Keegan hoped so. The day was bleak enough without another confrontation. He had already experienced the sharp edge of Tetralanna te Balamont's tongue, and he wasn't anxious to repeat the experience.

To his relief, Gredin was already there, with Sill seated next to her. Miri te Kendar, the kitchen Tender, was also present, looking sad and solemn.

There were five place settings on the small table, each centered by a steaming bowl and a glass of water, while a larger bowl in the center of the table sent its own plume of steam upward. Additional stools had been brought so that all five of them had a seat, and he and Burlon settled quickly at the remaining places, elbows and knees nearly touching those of their neighbors.

Gredin offered a small smile of welcome. "Much has happened since the five of us parted. To begin, the Power came to me for a final night-thought."

Keegan stared. He had slept in the same room with Gredin, crowded in with Beda and Ingarra. How had he slept through the Power's visitation?

"I will tell you about it shortly, but we should start by identifying the problems requiring immediate attention."

"Of course," Keegan said, and saw Burlon and the others nod in agreement.

"Please begin your meal, everyone. Keegan, could you please record the substance of our discussions and any decisions we reach? I want a clear record to consult, should the need arise."

"Yes," Keegan said, despite his worry over his dwindling supplies.

He placed his notebook, pens and ink bottle on the table above his place setting, then peered into his bowl, determined to eat quickly so that he could write unencumbered.

Burlon was also looking at the food offering. "What is this?" he asked dubiously, poking at the substance in the half-filled bowl.

"Coarse-ground porridge with aged huvvel cheese," Miri replied, her cheeks reddening. "The bowl in the center of the table is a vegetable chutney seasoned with herbs and spices. A spoonful or two on the porridge is a good complement to the cheese."

Burlon added a generous dollop of the colorful chutney to his porridge, spooned up a bite, and tasted it. "Quite good," he admitted.

Keegan's stomach growled at the savory smell, and he flushed. "Your pardon," he said, and saw that Miri was waiting for him to taste the concoction. The first spoonful was a revelation, a myriad of flavors and textures unfurling across his tongue. "However did you manage to make porridge so satisfying?"

Miri beamed.

Gredin, who had been making quick work of her bowl, paused to say, "Miri is deeply gyfted in the kitchen – something we'll be thankful for in the days to come."

Soon, spoons scraped the bottoms of bowls. When everyone had finished, Miri Sent the crockery back to the kitchen with a flick of her hand. "Brinlin te Calidane is overseeing the kitchen in my absence. She's expecting my Sending."

"Then allow me to Freshen the table," Keegan said, "as thanks for the fine meal." After doing so, he rearranged his tools and journal. Then, pen in hand, he waited for Gredin to begin.

"There is much to tell," Gredin began, "and many queries for which I need answers."

"You say you received another visit from the Power. Surely that is the place to start," Keegan urged, chagrined at having slept through the momentous event.

"Actually, the Power's message is not the most urgent issue for us to discuss."

Miri looked lost. Sill's brows pleated deeply. Burlon crossed his arms, watching her. "Then what *is* most urgent, in your opinion?" he asked.

Gredin said, "Early this morning, I went to Wyve's office to discuss our situation, as I promised him I would, last night. I had several pressing issues on which I wanted to hear his thoughts. And he identified several more." She sighed. "Burlon, he is desperate to know our source for geddel crystals."

"That's none of his business."

Gredin shook her head. "I explain badly. He is worried that they came from Venna or Palomar, and that our source for geddel crystals has been destroyed."

Burlon drew a weary breath. "Luckily for the Prett, and for us, Venna was never a source of geddel crystals."

"And Palomar?"

"No. Palomar was a simple world. We Traded with them primarily for the leaves and bark of a plant valued by the Prett and others for its healing properties. Wyve will be sorry for that loss, as I am sorry for the loss of the Palomari themselves, but it was only a small, steady Trade item. We went there as much because we found them congenial as for the profit."

Keegan found, to his own shame, that he had little sympathy to spare for the unknown Palomari. He was still grappling with the loss of his own House members, and the multitude of other Vennans destroyed in the space of a breath.

If the situations had been reversed, he supposed his House would scarcely have mourned for him at all. His parents and Guides, yes. But the others…?

Now he was here, and they were gone, and it finally seemed there might be a genuine call for his gyfte. There was irony in that, but he took no pleasure from it. And if, on Tradepoint, the tools required by his craft became unobtainable, that would be the cruelest irony of all…

"– the Vokastra demand to know. Wyve seems almost afraid of them."

Realizing his attention had wandered, Keegan attended again to the conversation at hand.

"As he should be," Burlon responded grimly. "As *we* should be."

"Why?" Gredin asked. "Wyve's explanation made little sense."

"Well, you're not a Trader."

"Nevertheless, I can learn," Gredin said stubbornly. "Explain it to me, since geddel crystals seemed to be the most pressing matter on Wyve's agenda."

Burlon considered. "The crystals facilitate the ways in which the Prett live and work. They are used in many Prett *griimoni* and they help to create such things as the lights here on Tradepoint and on the Prett world, below."

"How?"

Burlon grinned. "That is one question too many. In truth, I have no idea. But they have become essential to much of what the Prett do with their *griimoni.*"

"No wonder Wyve is so concerned about them," Gredin said. "What world *do* the crystals come from?"

"Sprygale. It is a longer journey from Tradepoint than from Venna or Palomar, but fairly straightforward." He shrugged. "I've taken Bentain Tradeteams there to Trade with the Sprygalians for long and long."

"But what if Sprygale was swallowed, along with Venna and Palomar?"

Sill and Miri looked shocked, but Burlon shrugged. "Why would it be? Sprygale lies along quite a different path of the River."

"Still," Sill mused, "if the crystals are that important to the Prett, Gredin cannot assure the Director that the crystals are safe without certain knowledge it is true."

"Then I will go to Sprygale," Burlon said, "as soon as we conclude this meeting."

"No!" Gredin's voice rang out in the small room.

Burlon blinked, looking taken aback by the force of her response. His gaze narrowed. "How else can we state with certainty that Sprygale is unharmed?"

Gredin's color heightened. "It is too soon to risk such a journey." Her blue eyes were earnest. "I will not lose anyone else, Burlon. And you are still in your dydanin time. You and Chenna should at least have the full number of your nights together."

Burlon scowled. "Wyve needs an answer for the Vokastra. They will expect the next load of geddel crystals to arrive on schedule."

"And when is that due to happen?" Gredin asked.

"Not for a while," he admitted. "but–"

"Well, then, there is no need to risk making the journey yet."

"Yet Sill is right," Burlon objected. "We must be truthful with Wyve. We can't afford to lose his protection and goodwill. He's all that stands between us and the Vokastra."

"I have no intention of being less than honest with Wyve," Gredin stated indignantly.

"Then what will you tell him about the crystals?"

"That we intend to honor our Trading schedule, once we are recovered enough to do so. If we must delay the journey to Sprygale, you may give some of the geddel crystals from my dress to the Prett instead." She turned Keegan's way. "Do you recall what Burlon said at the reception, when he first saw me in Trethen's dress?"

Keegan took a breath, calming his thoughts. The words welled up in his memory, accompanied by a vision of Gredin wearing the glittering dress with grace. "He said, 'We could feed the whole delegation for a year or more with what you have sewn on one panel of that skirt.'"

Gredin smiled. "Thank you. You see, Burlon? There is no need to Travel the River yet. Unless you were exaggerating about the value of the crystals on my dress?"

"Only slightly," he admitted, his tone grudging.

"I am happy to hear it. And I noticed some sizeable geddel crystals on the K'lar House sash you wore at the Trisectoriana. At need, we can utilize those, as well."

Burlon frowned heavily but remained silent.

Keegan made notes, documenting the problem and its proposed solution. If Burlon still saw himself as co-leader – now sole leader, with Cirin's passing – of the delegation, despite the Power having charged Gredin with leading the surviving Vennans, it seemed a situation ripe for contention.

Burlon said, "I suppose, apart from placating the Vokastra, providing the next allotment of geddel crystals gains us little."

"What do you mean?"

"We can't eat station credits. And, judging from today's midday meal, we are already running short of food."

Miri looked miserable. "I am sorry the offering disappointed you."

"No, you misunderstand me, Miri. I don't mean the food wasn't good. I ate every bite and was glad of it. But we must be low on food stores. We had planned to head home today, without further need to feed the delegation."

"Burlon's right," Gredin said briskly. "But Wyve and Figg took quick action."

"What does *that* mean?" Burlon demanded.

"I accompanied Wyve to the kitchen before preparations began for morning meal. He collected items he thinks are viable for planting and cultivation."

"Judging by the number of carts he filled," Sill said drily, "not much was left for Miri to work with." She smiled. "You did a wonderful job with midday meal, Miri. And this morning, too, when your kitchen was invaded. In your place, my wails of protest would have awakened the entire delegation."

"I wanted to," Miri admitted, her tone rueful.

Keegan joined in the brief laughter her reply elicited, then asked, "Is that why there was no besk, this morning?"

Miri nodded. "Nor will there be any for long and long, Gredin says."

Burlon rubbed his brow. "That won't be popular. But it's a good decision. If anyone can persuade our native produce to Grow, it will be the Prett scientists." He sighed. "Still, it will take time, and time is our scarcest resource. People must be fed."

"Can't we buy food? Sell my geddel crystals now, if you need the credits."

"We have plenty of credits, and the Prett awarded Cirin a station marker worth three thousand more at the Trisectoriana. He wouldn't want us to starve," Burlon said gruffly. "But it will be tricky, finding enough supplies on the station to feed us for any length of time."

"Tricky?" Gredin echoed. "Can't you simply purchase food for station credits?"

"Only when there is food to buy. Most races here trade other items, not food. They bring tech, or works of art, or cloth – things that can sit on a shelf for years without harm. The Hesch are an exception. They trade in dried fruits, nuts, and preserves. Wines and cordials, too. But fresh food? That's in short supply. The Wilra trade grain, but they aren't in port. The Beng trade grain, and they *are* in port, but..."

"...but they don't like us, because of the Judgment."

"Exactly. Still, they like profit. And their grain, and the Wilra's, is fine for us to eat. But I'd rather deal with Wilra than Beng, any day. Hesch goods are pricey but we've plenty of credits, for the moment. The problem there is that you can't make much of a meal from dried fruit and nuts."

"Why is fresh food so hard to obtain?" Keegan asked, bewildered. At home, the Market had sold fresh food of every kind.

"Most races rely on their home world for food. You never know who'll be in port to buy your goods when you come. It's easier and safer for them to bring things that won't spoil on the journey to Tradepoint. Even aboard their ships, they tend to stock preserved or dried foods since the trip here and back takes a long time for some of them. Fresh food is a luxury."

"I see a lot of porridge in our future," Keegan said, with deliberate lightness.

"There won't even be a lot of that, if the Beng get wind of our situation. They'll raise their prices, and I'll get far fewer bags of grain for my station credits."

Gredin said, "Wyve cautioned me to keep our situation a secret so as not to cause you difficulty at the Market."

"We need the Trade advantage on our side as long as possible. I'll check with Wyve about Wilra grain and notify the Hesch that I want to do business. Don't worry. I won't let us starve."

"But can't the Prett sell us fresh food from their world?" Miri asked.

"I don't know," Burlon said. "It's not something we've done, in the past."

What does Prettian food taste like? Keegan wondered, and made a note in his journal.

"In that case, we'll need samples before we buy any large amounts," Gredin cautioned. "Wyve says new foods might make us sick, even to the point of dying."

Miri looked appalled. "If I serve the delegation a porridge made from new grain, I certainly don't want to make them ill."

"Well, I already know we can eat Wilra grain," Burlon said. "It's what d'limten flour is made from."

Miri brightened. "D'limten flour bakes into a hearty loaf."

"And several Houses, including Bentain, tried Beng grain, long and long ago. A number of us made small purchases when the Beng first came, to establish a Trading relationship. We do that with everyone who has a maartza in the Traders' Market." He grimaced. "Beng grain is good-tasting and grinds into a fine flour much like our own lissanthel. But we soon decided it wasn't worth having to deal with the Beng to get it." He shook his head. "Time to reassess."

"Wyve suggests we undertake food tests in the Prett medical clinic," Gredin said, looking as weary as Burlon. "And studies of the Vennan body. He said our Traders and Travelers refused that, in the past." She sighed again. "I told him I would ask others to advise me. Burlon, do you know about this?"

Alarmed, Keegan asked, "Is there an issue of trust with the Prett? Might they wish us harm?"

"No," Gredin said firmly. "But what Wyve asks is apparently not without risk."

"What kind of risk?"

Burlon answered before she could. "The risk of returning to the Source."

Sill inhaled sharply at his blunt words, and Miri looked horrified.

But Gredin persisted. "Wyve asked me to seek a volunteer for the food testing. His medical team will be cautious, he promises, and he says they have an established process for the tests. It reduces the risk but cannot eliminate it entirely. If the volunteer reacts badly to a sample, there is little they can offer to mend matters. And so…"

"What Gredin isn't saying," Burlon said harshly, "is that the Director would like this volunteer to allow the Prett medical personnel to prod their body with Prett *griimoni*, in addition to being the food tester."

"But we have Healers," Miri and Sill protested, as one.

"So I informed him," Gredin confirmed. "But not *ample* Healers. He said, if they had known more about Vennans, the Prett might have been able to save Cirin. So I am torn. Why have we not cooperated with previous Prett requests?"

Burlon frowned. "There was no need. We came in small groups. We were careful to follow the Prett rules. Careful to put our personal safety first, as we have been taught from birth. All Tradeteam members act in this manner. It was decided by the Heads of House, long and long ago, that the risks of cooperating with such requests were too great, since Healers on Venna were never far away should injury or sickness occur. *And it never did.*"

"But dare we depend on that to continue? Nine hundred and thirty-seven of us are left, Burlon, with only a handful of unranked Healers and one ranked Healer among them. One! Our people are dispirited, caught up in sadness as they grieve their losses. Will caution and safety be frontmost in their minds? Should a need arise, dare we summon Salderon to manage it? What if there are two such needs, or three, in rapid succession? I do not intend to lose anyone else from this community. We need to view ourselves as a single House, with the safety of each individual as vital as the next. If the Prett become knowledgeable about us, is that not invaluable if it means the survival of a single Vennan who might otherwise be lost? I am determined that there be no cause for our kinsmen to grieve anew."

"Losing another Vennan is precisely what might happen if we agree to Wyve's request," Burlon snapped. "Surely you know what happens when the integrity of your vessel is violated."

"Of course she knows," Keegan said. "As do I, having observed Beda's Healing of her."

"What?" Burlon spun to squarely face Gredin. "When did you have occasion to call on Beda? Why were you in need of a Healer?"

"The Hesch injured my arm in the incident at the Traders' Market." As Burlon opened his mouth, Gredin added hastily, "I didn't realize until evening that his talons had pierced my skin."

A stormy scowl. "A pity you didn't realize it at the Judgement. You could have spared us much of the penalty we received! How could you not have realized?"

"I thought I felt so terrible because I was distressed. I didn't know that I had an injury that was making everything worse."

"And now, with it Healed, there is nothing left to show," Burlon groused, "so there's no hope of raising the point with Wyve."

"When the integrity of your vessel is breached," Sill said, "it is difficult to think clearly."

Keegan shook his head sadly. "It makes Cirin's struggle to return to us, so badly hurt, all the more heroic. I will add that to my account of his efforts. Everyone should know what he overcame in order to warn us."

Gredin looked around the table. "So, friends, what is our decision? Do we ask a volunteer to submit to the food tasting only, or both the tasting and the Prett's tests? I offered myself, but Wyve refused. He said the community should not risk losing me since, as First Speaker, I am the Voice."

Burlon snorted. "Obviously. Can you imagine what the delegation —"

"Community," Gredin corrected.

"...what the community would be like, with Tetralanna back as First Speaker?"

It was sobering. The entire situation was sobering, in Keegan's view. But there was only one reasonable testing candidate in the entire community of survivors.

"I'll do it," he said.

Every face turned toward him. Burlon dubious, Sill grave, Miri worried. Only Gredin was calm, her gaze steady, as if she had foreseen the likely outcome.

"Keegan, no!" Miri protested. "Oh, I wish I had never mentioned the idea of the Prett providing us with fresh food!"

"Scabs," Burlon cursed, "what makes you think you're the likeliest candidate? I'd rather risk Tetralanna's neck, if we go through with this at all."

Sill shook her head slowly. "Surely we are not in such dire need of food that we must ask you to take this risk!"

"But I am willing," Keegan said. "My gyfte is of limited value. The impact of my loss on the community would be small, should that happen. And my gyfte enables me to notice small details. That might prove helpful to the Prett medical team. Please don't distress yourselves. I am quite willing to aid the community in this manner."

"And if it results in your death?" Burlon's words were stark, but his tone was respectful.

"I am unafraid to return to the Source, having observed Gredin's visitation from the Power. And there is no one of my House left to bear the burden of mourning me."

"No one left? What do you mean?" Sill demanded, her tone sharp with shock.

Gredin answered for him. "Keegan is the last of his House. No other member of House Fliss undertook the trip to Tradepoint."

Miri gave a choked cry.

A single tear tracked down Sill's cheek.

"I am sorry for your loss," Burlon said gravely.

"As I am for all of our losses." Keegan assured them.

"Keegan, are you sure about volunteering?" Gredin asked.

"Yes." He gave her what he hoped was a reassuring smile. "I sincerely want to help."

"Very well. Are you willing to begin today? Wyve thinks it important to begin as soon as possible – today, if we can manage."

"The remainder of my day is yours," Keegan said.

"Then I will inform Wyve."

"Wait," Burlon said. "What did you mean about observing Gredin's visit from the Power?"

Keegan smiled. Little, it seemed, escaped Burlon's attention. "Two nights ago. She was hiding, you may recall, to avoid being forced back to Venna."

Burlon had the good grace to look abashed.

"I let her share my bedmat. In the night, I became aware of her encounter with the Power."

Burlon cast a glance at Gredin. "I thought the Power spoke to you in your sleep?"

"It did – although Tetralanna insisted on believing that I was only experiencing an unpleasant night-thought."

"Well, I knew better," Keegan stated. "Night-thoughts do not make you glow." He smiled when the group looked nonplussed. "Has no one in your Houses ever spoken of those who are touched by the Power? The House member who told me of it was Leel, who was one of the Sixty-Six. Otherwise, I suppose the tale would have been lost. Indeed, unless one of the Sixty-Six ventured here for the Trisectoriana celebration, we have now lost them all. I may be the only one left who knows the story of our beginning. Another time, I will tell you Leel's tale. For now, I will relay just one pertinent element of his story. When the Sixty-Six first awoke on Venna, and the Power spoke to them, they glowed – just as I saw Gredin glow, two nights ago, as brightly as the moon." He turned his gaze on Sill. "I would have you Harvest both that memory and my memory of Leel's tale, Sill, so as to keep them fresh for us all."

"Happily." Sill's smile was warm. "We may be deeply grateful for your stories in the days to come. I shall willingly Harvest any memories you deem important."

"Thank you." His face flushed with heat at the unexpected praise. No one in House Fliss had ever spoken to him as if he were rare or valued. "I will wait for you after the meeting is concluded, if I may. I want to lodge these memories with you before I go for the food test."

He did not add *in case something should befall me*. But awareness of that risk hung in the air between them.

Miri shifted in her seat. "Your pardon. Before we leave the topic of food, I am in need of some practical advice."

"Of course," Gredin said. "How can I help you?"

Keegan noticed that Miri gave Burlon a quick glance before looking to Gredin. So. She, too, had picked up on the tension between them.

"All my life, House Kendar has eaten five meals in a day: morning meal, a mid-morning snack, midday meal, a late-day snack, and evening meal. I believe this is true for every House. Our days are long, divided between lessons, physical activity, and the use of our gyftes."

Gredin nodded and gestured for her to continue.

"This morning," Miri said, "the community had a cold morning meal of leftover breads and preserves. Not many attended, and those who did ate sparsely, so there were few to comment on the poor offering. I had expected it to be an unsettled morning, so I decided to save the krouan to serve as mid-morning snack."

The krouan, hot pastries filled with cheese laced with bits of meat and vegetables, had been delicious, Keegan recalled, and very welcome. He had been particularly hungry after the light offering at morning meal and a busy morning collecting information on the survivors.

"For midday meal, the community ate what we five ate here. Since there was plenty of ground grain left, I experimented with this idea of savory porridge."

"It was delicious. And filling," Gredin assured her.

"My thanks, but I am worried. It will be time for late-day snack soon and, after that, evening meal. I set Brinlin and the others to Making a vegetable stew. Tonight, we'll serve it with hot loaves and whipped, herbed rista cheese."

Keegan's mouth watered as he listened to Miri recite the upcoming menu. "And what are you serving for late-day snack?"

"I don't know!" Miri wailed, catching them all up short. "I suppose

I can Make more porridge, plain or with a touch of kithris, this time. Or I could put out some of the reception food that we saved."

"Either of those would work," Burlon ventured cautiously.

"Yes. No. But…" Tears glistened in Miri's eyes.

"*Chee, chee, chee*," Gredin crooned, stroking Miri's arm. "What troubles you so?"

"We don't have enough food to go on serving everyone five full meals a day. We'll run out of supplies in no time if I try." Miri straightened her shoulders. "I'm sorry to be so emotional about it, but I surveyed what we have left, after the Director's visit, and it seems I must do one of two things." She looked around the table. "I can serve all five meals but reduce the portion size and water down the dishes where I can. Or I can skip the two snacks and offer three normal meals. But even that's not going to last if we don't get more supplies soon."

"Leave supplies to me," Burlon said. "Count on plenty of grain to work with. I should be able to get it delivered within the next day or two."

"We should be cautious," Gredin countered, "and not count on any food being available until it's actually in the kitchens."

"That isn't necessary," Burlon said, clearly annoyed.

"Actually, I think it is."

Keegan respected Gredin's caution. Tradepoint was a strange place. The Beng, upset over the recent Judgment, might choose not to do business with them. And he knew nothing about the Wilra. On the whole, he, too, would rather not count on supplies prematurely.

Gredin turned back to Miri. "Of the two, which option do you prefer?"

"Neither," Miri said glumly. "It discomfits my gyfte to imagine folk going hungry. I'm still unhappy I couldn't give Sill a cup of besk, this morning."

Sill smiled. "The roin tea was fine, Miri. Truly." She lifted her hands. "But why should Miri have to reach this decision alone? Can't we ask the community which option they prefer?"

"And achieve what?" Burlon asked. "You won't get everyone to agree on a choice, and those not on the prevailing side will be even more out of sorts than they already are."

"I suppose," Sill conceded. "Perhaps we should adopt Miri's first option and say nothing to the community. As upset as they are, they might not even notice for several days that the amount or quality has changed, and by then we may have more food to serve."

Now Miri was the one shaking her head. "Whichever option we choose, I'll have to explain it to the kitchen Tenders, and that leaves little chance of keeping it secret. My team includes kitchen Tenders from most of the remaining Houses. The news is apt to spread quickly, and people will be unhappy that we tried to fool them. I'd rather be honest and explain why we're acting as we are, rather than tell everyone an untruth."

"I agree," Gredin said promptly.

"As do I," Keegan said. But either alternative was going to be unpopular and upsetting.

Sill nodded.

"We're in agreement, then," Burlon said. "No untruths. Write that in your journal, Historian. Your account should reflect our desire to be honest with everyone."

Keegan began to write.

"However," Burlon continued, "if our choice is three meals a day, should we implement it now or wait until tomorrow to begin?"

"I propose we start serving three meals a day, as of tomorrow," Gredin stated firmly.

"And I will go with you to Wyve's office in the morning," Burlon said.

"That won't be necessary. Don't cut your dydanin any shorter than it already is. It isn't fair to you and Chenna."

Burlon hesitated, looking torn.

Keegan reflected that Gredin had just maneuvered Burlon into choosing between their subtle struggle for leadership and the rightful pleasures to be found with his new Chosen. Prideful assertions of duty were one thing; the joys of mating with one's Chosen were quite another.

"All right," Burlon capitulated. "But I need to know all that you discuss with Wyve."

"Of course. Indeed, I hope the five of us can meet daily to discuss issues affecting the community. May I count on the rest of you to continue to participate?"

"I am happy to be of help," Keegan assured her, and Miri and Sill quickly chimed in with their acceptance. After a moment, Burlon nodded, as well.

"We could meet here during morning meal, when I am freshly back from meeting with Wyve and Figg," Gredin proposed.

Miri's eyes widened. "How early do you meet with them? You need your rest."

"I'm fine, Miri. The overlap of Figg's and Wyve's schedules is quite early, but I want the benefit of advice from both of them."

Burlon nodded. "Their personalities differ. Together, they are a formidable team."

"I am glad you approve," Gredin said, with no trace of irony that Keegan could detect. "So, for the time being, I will arise, meet with Wyve and Figg, then join you four over morning meal. Afterward, I'll meet with individuals, then address the community at midday meal. And I will use the remainder of the day to be out among the community."

Hesitantly, Miri asked, "Can you make an exception to that plan, tomorrow, to tell everyone at morning meal what we've decided about the meal schedule?"

"Of course," Gredin agreed.

Miri toyed with the ends of her hlao. "Thank you. People will understand better, if you explain the decision to them. And if Burlon is able to Trade quickly for food, or buy it outright, the reduced meal schedule won't be for long."

"I have enough credits to purchase whatever's available," Burlon said, "but that doesn't necessarily translate into plenty of food. And our credits will be quickly depleted if we don't produce more items for Trade."

Miri looked alarmed. "Whatever's available? Are you saying that others may already have beaten us to those purchases?"

Burlon grimaced. "I don't mean to frighten you, but all of you need to understand our position. Tradepoint floats in space. Nothing Grows here that I am aware of. As I stated earlier, food offered for trade in the market is brought by others in their ships. Supply varies, depending on who's in port, and is limited in variety. There may be plenty of an individual item, like grain, in the Traders' Market or very little, especially if folk have been in port a while and sold off most of their cargo. I'll see what's available. And the Director will have a list of goods that races left behind for the Prett to sell on pre-agreed terms. I'll check that list, then begin requesting Trade conferences with anyone in port who's selling foods we know are safe."

"And if there is little to purchase?" Gredin asked, voicing the question Keegan supposed was uppermost in everyone's mind.

"Then we make do as best we can until someone with foodstuffs arrives in port. There's no schedule. Races come and go as they please. According to the board, the Mamora and the Thalken left port, this morning."

"No more kithris," Miri said mourned. "But we have what they gave us at the reception."

"And they may have left more with the Prett to sell on their behalf. If so, we can make that purchase, whether the terms are favorable or not. But until we have a way of producing new Trade items regularly, we should make every credit count. And unless we find some way to Make something out of nothing, our efforts will require the purchase of raw materials, which also eats up station credits." He looked around at them. "Tradepoint is our home now, assuming the Vokastra doesn't toss us out when our rotations are up, and assuming we can afford the continuing fines we'll start generating as soon as we exceed the orbital allotment."

"Stop it," Gredin demanded. "You're scaring them, Burlon."

"They *should* be scared," Burlon replied.

"Well, I'm not, and I refuse to become so. Fear won't serve us. The

Power has not abandoned us. Our problems are solvable, with time and attention. We will not starve today or tomorrow, or even the next day. Thanks to your lecture, we will use what food we still have wisely. We will be cautious and frugal, and trust that the Power has given us the necessary gyftes and intelligence to search out the answers we need."

She's using her gyfte, Keegan realized, *lacing her words with enough of it to chase away the terror Burlon's words were creating.*

"But you are wrong about one thing, Burlon," she said. "Tradepoint is not our home."

"Venna is gone, Gredin. Tradepoint is all that remains for us."

"No. Tradepoint is our temporary shelter. I am grateful. It keeps our people safe. But the Power does not intend this to be our home."

Burlon's stare was a challenge.

"At the start of this meeting," Gredin continued, "I said I had received another visitation from the Power."

"So you did," Burlon agreed cautiously.

"The Power charged me with guiding and protecting our people. It assured me we were on the proper path and said not to doubt my decisions. I am to help our people find the new thoughts and ways needed for our future." Gredin looked down at her clasped hands, then raised her head. "It also informed me that it will not Speak to me again, but it left one final directive. The Power instructed me to dispatch the Travelers."

"Dispatch us?" Burlon blurted. "Where?"

"Out onto the River to search for our new home."

Keegan took a breath, then another, and finally a third before the tightness eased in his chest. *What are we to take that to mean?* He saw bewilderment on Miri and Sill's faces, and narrow-eyed concentration on Burlon's.

"Everything I do," Gredin said, "every decision I make, must support that search. The Power says we cannot thrive without a natural world around us. Therefore, the Travelers are to seek New Venna."

"When?" Burlon asked.

"When will we find it? Or when will I inform the Travelers of their task and urge them to begin the search?"

"Either." Burlon stirred on his stool. "Both."

"I don't know."

"That's no answer! I will call the Travelers together and inform them of this news. The search needs to be carefully coordinated, and it needs to begin as soon as possible."

"No. If I'm not yet ready to have you Travel to a location as familiar as Sprygale, I'm certainly not going to risk our Travelers on a quest of this magnitude until they are restored to Balance. I need to be certain it is safe before I allow anyone to leave."

"Allow?" Burlon repeated.

To Keegan, the low growl of Burlon's voice carried a clear objection to the notion that a seasoned Traveler needed permission to exercise his gyfte.

But Gredin was the Power's selected vessel. If forced to take sides, Keegan would support Gredin. He had seen her glow. There was no higher imprimatur.

But Burlon pressed on. "Nothing is safer for a Traveler than the River."

"Cirin did not find it so."

Gredin's words hung in the air, glittering and painful. For a moment, Burlon looked stricken. Then he growled, "It was not the River that killed Cirin. It was Zrach."

"Who is Zrach? Why would he hurt Cirin?"

Sill bowed her head and said, "It is a place, not a person."

Burlon elaborated. "It's a Power-forsaken excuse for a world, inhabited by dangerous creatures. We rarely go there... but Cirin had no choice. Venna was gone, and Palomar. He would have been determined to return to us. Zrach was the only world along his path."

"Why not come straight back to Tradepoint?" Gredin asked. "Why stop anywhere?"

Burlon's face suffused with anger. "Cirin left here and journeyed to Venna – or tried to. When he found it gone, he had to continue on. Palomar was near. He would have headed there, knowing he could rest when he arrived. But Palomar was gone, as well. Two terrible shocks. Two chances gone. And the River flows without cease. He had to decide where to go, now that both havens had been denied him. But the only choice that would bring him back toward Tradepoint was Zrach."

Burlon grimaced. "Cirin knew he could not journey all the way back to Tradepoint without a rest. The effort would have overcome him. So he made the best decision he could. He went to Zrach. Knowing Cirin, he was as careful as he could be." He lowered his head. "It just wasn't enough. He was attacked. Injured. And even then, he made his way back to warn us. No one could have done better. No one."

Burlon's impassioned words were a stark reminder that everyone was dealing with deep wounds of loss. That they did not actually bleed and could not be Healed with an Intercession made their suffering no less real.

Gredin spoke gently. "Burlon, I am beyond grateful for Cirin's actions. No one has done more to keep us safe. No one. But the circumstances of his death underline our need for caution. Who knows what other unknown, threatening worlds our Travelers might encounter? Let us take the time to talk and plan. Consult with Wyve and Figg. Haste will not serve us well."

"But you say the Power instructs you to dispatch us to search for a new world."

"Yes," Gredin agreed, "but it didn't specify when that search was to begin. It did not command me to wake the Travelers from their sleep and order them to embark upon the River at that very instant. The Power expects me to protect our people. I cannot foolishly risk our Travelers when a short delay will ensure they are clear-headed while they search for New Venna. I will not lose anyone else, even at the cost of moving slowly as I follow the Power's instructions."

Burlon's eyes glittered. "And do you intend to tell the delegation?"

"Of course I will tell the community. It will gladden their spirits."

"When you do, the Travelers will clamor to depart. What will you do then?"

"Remind them that taking a short time to grieve together and adjust as a community is only right and proper. I will remind them that planning takes time. They will understand when I explain. I will do so tomorrow, at midday meal."

The tension between Burlon and Gredin was palpable. To diffuse it, Keegan asked, "Your pardon, but I am not certain we finished our discussion regarding Trade." He smiled apologetically. "I am trying to listen, write, and participate in the discussion. I do not wish to miss any important points."

Gredin nodded. "Thank you for keeping us on task, Keegan. Where were we?"

Keegan consulted his notes. "Burlon was explaining the need to generate credits on a regular basis."

"What have we brought to Trade in the past?" Sill asked. "I must confess, I have no idea what House Torr normally brought to the Traders' Market."

"Kendar carvers made chairs and such," Miri volunteered. "But I know little beyond that, nor whether any Kendar artisans attended the celebration. Even if they did, I don't know where they would find wood to use, in this place of metal. I am sorry, Burlon. I was thinking solely of kitchen matters."

"No need to apologize, Miri. Or you, Sill. No one at this table is a Trader, except for me."

"Do you have any suggestions?" Keegan asked, concerned. "I know you were jesting when you spoke of Making 'something out of nothing,' but…"

"I have no ideas," Burlon admitted, "but that comes of not knowing which Makers are here and what they brought with them. Once we have that information, the other Traders and I can scour the Traders' Market for materials our Makers can use in the exercise of their gyftes."

Lists, Keegan reflected. *I'm going to need all manner of lists. And that is a problem.*

"Burlon?" he ventured. "This morning, I started interviewing people about their name and gyfte. If their gyfte is Making, I can ask what materials they normally use."

Burlon looked pleased. "That would help. How long until you've talked with everyone?"

"I don't know. It takes people a while to warm to the notion of telling me about themselves. And there *are* nine hundred and thirty-seven of us"

Gredin nodded. "I'll inform the community of your efforts and ask for cooperation, especially from the Makers."

"Good. But I have a bigger problem – one you are aware of." He looked from Burlon to Sill to Miri. "I'm nearly out of paper. And my ink is running low."

Burlon scowled. "I thought you found paper at the Shodekekeen maartza."

"They brought a sheaf of it to the reception, and I've tried it. Sadly, it's too porous. The ink spreads, blurring the writing."

Burlon's scowl deepened. "Most races use devices to record information. Still, you found paper once when I thought there was none to find."

"Perhaps the Thalken. The paper of the painted scroll they gave us is very fine."

"As I already said, the Thalken left port yesterday." Burlon shook his head. "They're a strange lot. Arrogant. Easily offended. But they visit fairly regularly. When they return, I'll make inquiries on your behalf."

"My thanks, but what am I to do in the meantime? You and Gredin need information. I can gather it, but soon I'll have no way to record what I obtain."

Gredin touched his arm. "Don't despair. At this morning's meeting, Wyve offered to provide a *griimoni* for your use. He thinks you could learn to use it quite easily."

A griimoni? How... unsatisfying. "I prefer my pen and inks, so long as I can make them last."

"Of course. But you could accept his offer and learn to use the device. That way, if you do run out of paper or ink, your work needn't halt."

It made practical sense, even if the notion was unsettling. "Very well. Please tell Wyve that I accept and am grateful for his generosity."

"I have already done so," she said, and patted his arm.

"I have another item to raise regarding Trade," Burlon said.

"By all means, continue."

"While Keegan completes the lists of Makers, and the materials they'll need for producing Trade items, there are two projects that have already been requested, and that we have the means to produce."

"What might those be?" Miri asked.

"A highly ornamented coat, and a Sprygalian *timte* quilt. Majaya, Ruler of the Southern Seas, commissioned a *timte* quilt for her daughter, Q'iari, who will be joined soon with Jostan, the eldest son of Rangh, the Ruler of the North Reaches. And Rangh requests a coat for Q'iari, who is to be his son's *timte*."

"His what?" Keegan asked.

"His… Chosen, if Sprygalians *had* Chosens. He wants a coat of great beauty and warmth, something finer than any on Sprygale."

Keegan was intrigued. "Great warmth? Do they not Control their weather?"

"No. It's a beautiful world, rich in many things besides geddel crystals, but Sprygalians must live the days as they come. Rain or sunshine, heat or cold, they accept what they are given."

"Strange," Sill murmured.

"It makes Trading difficult at times. The North Reaches have chest-deep snow for weeks on end, making journeys by local means difficult."

"No wonder they want a coat and a warm quilt!" Miri exclaimed.

"Oh, Sprygalians have long mastered making things that are warm. Necessity compels them, in the North Reaches. But their workmanship cannot rival ours. Rangh wants *this* coat to be a wonder."

"And you want Ingarra to Make these items," Gredin said, smiling. "Well, seek her out, Burlon, and explain the projects to her in detail."

"The gown she made for you from the Shodekekeen fabric was outstanding. And her work with the geddel crystals on the dress you wore to the reception was beautiful, as well." His gaze roved over

Gredin's travel clothes. "Far more impressive than what you're wearing today."

"Burlon, don't be rude!" Sill admonished.

He shrugged. "A truth, if bluntly spoken. Gredin won't impress anyone, dressed this way. Consider Tetralanna. She's a canny woman who makes an impression by dressing the part. That's what you need to do, Gredin. Since you claim a leadership role, dress like a leader, here in the enclave and meeting with Wyve."

"But I have only the two dresses."

"Then you need more clothes."

"The Shodekekeen gave you fabric at the reception," Keegan reminded her. "Use that for another dress."

"It was given to the Vennan community!" Gredin protested.

"It was given to you, I strongly suspect," Burlon countered. "The head of the Shodekekeen trading delegation seems quite taken with you."

"And it favors your coloring," Sill volunteered.

Burlon grinned. "Even you can't claim there's enough fabric there for everyone in the enclave. Historian, your notes should reflect that Gredin is to have a new dress." Burlon's smile broadened, perhaps because the decision had gone his way. "And you'll need several more beyond that, Gredin. Your appearance needs to command respect."

"It sounds as if Ingarra will be busy."

"Can't be helped. And surely she isn't the only Needleworker who came. I hope not, for I want her to oversee the *timte* quilt and have it ready in time for the next Trade run to Sprygale." He rubbed his neck, looking suddenly downcast. "At home, Inthil te Bentain had nearly finished the quilt I originally requested. I told him I'd come, first thing upon our return, and claim it. But now he – and it – are gone, and we must begin again."

A hush fell over the group, and Keegan marveled yet again at how quickly they could move from light spirits to sadness.

"Ingarra will gladly Make the replacement quilt, if you ask her," Gredin said. "It may not be like the one Inthil created but it will be beautiful, I assure you. And she'll be glad of a project to occupy her days."

There was a larger message there, Keegan reflected. "Many in the community would benefit from something useful to do. But how are we to find meaningful tasks for everyone?"

"If we can locate suitable materials, our Makers can exercise their gyftes immediately, producing items to sell or barter in our maartza."

"And perhaps I should thaw the berry tarts we saved from the reception," Miri said. "You could sell them to the Beng. I'm sure the little gluttons would buy them."

The critical comment was so unexpected from mild-mannered Miri that Keegan chuckled. Burlon joined in, and even Sill and Gredin looked highly amused.

"Not a bad idea, Miri," Burlon said, "depending on how much they're willing to pay."

"I'd rather see our own people eat them," Gredin commented.

"As would I. But for a fine profit…"

"You can't eat profits!" Miri protested.

"Spoken like a devoted kitchen Tender," Burlon teased. "But a fine profit might buy you other edible goods."

"Now *you* sound like a typical Trader," she retorted, and they exchanged broad smiles.

Berry tarts… Keegan mused. *The Thalken seemed equally taken with our music and dancing…*

"Perhaps," he ventured, "we *can* Make something from nothing. Well, nothing tangible. Or not very tangible."

"What are you trying to say, Historian?"

Keegan flushed. "Miri's comment about the Beng and her berry tarts made me recall the Thalken at the reception. I'd hoped to see if they could provide paper suited to my needs, but they largely ignored me."

"You can count upon the Thalken," Burlon said, "to be intent upon themselves alone."

"No, they weren't intentionally ignoring me. At least, it didn't seem so."

"Your point, Historian?"

"They were caught up in the music and dancing. They moved as close as they could, watching and listening, until… until everyone had to leave. If those three Thalken enjoyed the music and dancing, might not others of their kind enjoy it, too? The Musicians already have their instruments. It would cost nothing for them to perform..."

"Something from nothing, indeed," Gredin murmured. "A clever notion!"

Burlon nodded. "I've never seen such things offered on Tradepoint, but it should be quite doable. And potentially profitable."

"Let us plan cautiously," Gredin said. "We should not invite outsiders into the enclave again too quickly. Our people are in no mood to tolerate strangers. And the Musicians may not feel ready to play until they have mastered their grief. Wyve may have helpful suggestions. I can discuss it with him tomorrow."

"Ask him for a performance space we could use," Burlon instructed. "And he might consider projecting a performance by hologram to the Prett world, as well." His face took on a sly look. "We would waive the fee, of course. It would earn us good will and remind the Vokastra that we are worth sheltering."

Worth sheltering? "Are they so uncaring of our plight?" Keegan asked.

Burlon shrugged. "The Vokastra don't think much about Tradepoint, except as a profit source. But our situation is different, stranded here for only the Power knows how long."

"That state of affairs upsets the Vokastra?"

"Yes."

"Because they want us to leave?"

"They want everyone to leave, Historian." Burlon sighed. "Let me explain. You've seen the lighted sign over the bio-mist antechamber, yes? Well, its numbers and colors are just another way to remind us that we have a limited amount of time in which to conclude our business and leave."

"But we have nowhere to go!" Miri exclaimed.

"Normally, our Tradeteams only stay for a small number of rotations, so it wasn't a problem for us. The color on the countback monitor starts at purple. I'm told it will change to blue, then green, then yellow, then orange. Finally, at two thousand rotations, it turns red."

"What happens then?" Keegan asked.

"It remains red but the number increases for every new rotation, with a penalty fee adjudged for each. The cost continues to rise, day by day by day."

"But we have two thousand days?"

"No." Burlon's answer was firm. "Tradepoint rotates around Prettig many times a day."

"How many?" Keegan asked, alarmed.

"Fifty. The Prett display the rotations in changing colors to keep everyone aware of where they stand in their rotation allowance."

Gredin made a face. "Then we must persuade the Vokastra that our situation lies outside of their normal rules."

"To do so, we have two ways to bargain." Burlon held up a finger. "The first is the geddel crystals. The Vokastra is anxious to discover whether crystals are still available. And *that*," he asserted, "is why I need to Travel the River to Sprygale soon. If all is well there, I'll inform Wyve that supply can remain normal so long as we don't have to worry about being asked to leave here by the Vokastra."

"And the other way to bargain?"

"At the Trisectoriana, the Vokastra granted a year's waiver of station and enclave fees. That will help, if the countback monitor turns red before we find New Venna."

"Wait," Gredin said, looking uneasy. "Wasn't the waiver intended for Trading visits?"

"I don't care what they may have intended. I will insist they honor it."

"But we shouldn't put Wyve in a difficult position. Or Figg. They are providing what assistance they can. When I requested more space for the community, Wyve said he would have new quarters ready in a few days."

"Extra space means extra station fees," Burlon objected.

"It can't be helped. The community needs better accommodations, now that our stay is extended. Wyve agrees. The current sleeping cubicles are cramped, with little privacy." She eyed Burlon boldly. "How would you and Chenna have felt, last night, if you had been in House Laith's quarters with nothing but a hanging screen to shield you from others?" She looked around the table. "Surely you all see how the community's mood will improve with better accommodations."

"My Chosen and I would be grateful for some privacy," Sill conceded. "How can we sustain the mood to mate, surrounded by the sounds of grieving House members? Doing so seems selfish, and yet mating with Marin keeps me in Balance for serving all those who need memories Harvested. What would the new quarters be like?"

"I don't know," Gredin admitted.

Remembering the little hologram of the Traders' Market from the Director's desktop, Keegan said, "Perhaps Wyve can provide a drawing to share at our next meeting."

"An excellent suggestion. I will ask."

"And will you include word of our new quarters in your announcements, tomorrow?"

"It is happy news, is it not? It will raise the spirits of the community."

"And give them more questions to ask. Did you satisfy all the supplicants, this morning?"

Unsure what Burlon meant, Keegan looked to Gredin.

"Not nearly." She looked around the table. "Burlon rescued me, this morning, when I was overwhelmed by the crowd. I had not expected so many to demand my attention." She smiled ruefully. "I went back later. I hope people took encouragement from that. But new folk kept joining tables I had already visited, and folks with whom I'd dealt returned with new concerns, and... Well, it was an endless process. I had to call a halt when midday meal was ready, so that I could come here. But I will try again, later today and tomorrow."

"Change your approach," Burlon asserted. "Sit and have them come to you. Then, if someone later thinks of a second question, they can weigh its urgency against waiting in line again. It may dissuade them."

"But I don't *want* to dissuade them. And the ones with the most urgent questions may be least able to muster the will and the strength to wait in line for their chance to ask."

"I'm concerned about your safety."

Looking astonished, Miri said, "Safety? What worry is that, within the enclave?"

Burlon shook his head. "You didn't see the mess Gredin got into, this morning, people pushing and shoving. Someone would have gotten injured if Sill hadn't intervened, calming us all with a Memory of the ocean."

Miri gaped. "Is *that* what that was? I was in the kitchens, tidying up, and suddenly my thoughts were far away. It was lovely. I could actually breathe." She blushed. "Thank you, Sill."

"Yes," Gredin said, "I am grateful, Sill. But there was no ill intent. People are confused and distraught. They feel insecure, and they are grieving. I need to meet with individuals and offer reassurance as well as information. Tensions will ease when they see that I will give them as many opportunities as they need."

Burlon snorted.

Sill said, "Still, you are one person, with many responsibilities. If you and Keegan compile a list of common questions, and your answers, the list could be read aloud to the community."

"But lists take time, as well." Gredin sighed. "For now, I will continue my efforts. It wouldn't be right to change my methods before everyone has an opportunity to talk with me individually."

"At least promise you will retire to your chamber when you become fatigued," Miri said. "We need you strong and well-rested."

"I fear no one will rest well until Wyve has our new quarters ready."

"Keegan claims Tetralanna turned you out of these quarters." Burlon scowled. "She had no authority to do that."

"She was First Speaker when she told me to leave."

"Well, you are First Speaker now," Burlon said. "Tetralanna will return to House Balamont's sleeping area. You and Keegan cannot continue to share your former Guides' alcove. There must hardly be room for four of you, much less your belongings."

Keegan said quietly, "I'm not concerned about my clothing, but I have no place to store my writing supplies and lists."

Burlon rubbed his jaw. "I didn't think about that when I accepted your offer for a private space to share with Chenna. I am sorry for ousting you without consideration for your needs."

Keegan flushed. "No need for apologies. I was happy to offer you the use of my chamber for the length of your dydanin. I don't mind seeking another space to sleep."

"Nor do I," Gredin said. "But we should make other arrangements. Ingarra and Beda were kind to share their chamber for a night, but we can't inconvenience them further."

Burlon tipped his head, indicating Tetralanna's sleeping chamber. "That space was set aside for First Speaker. That is now you. Tetralanna no longer has need of a private space," Burlon said bluntly

"She will not share your view. She will see it only as another blow to her pride."

"That's not my problem. What *is* my problem is ensuring that all members of the delegation are appropriately housed. If Gredin moves into the room Tetralanna has been occupying, and Keegan takes over Gredin's old chamber, everyone will have a proper place to sleep. And it gives us this outer room in which to meet, without worrying about Tetralanna intruding."

"It's logical," Gredin conceded, "but Tetralanna is already angry and defensive over losing First Speaker's hlette. And, like all of us, she is grieving. She won't view the matter sensibly, however you explain it to her."

"Can't be helped. Remember what I said about appearances? You are First Speaker. You should occupy the space designated for that purpose." He turned to Sill. "Tetralanna will respond best to you. Would you be willing to contact her private mind and ask her to join us here?"

Sill nodded and fell still. Then she said, looking grim. "Tetralanna is coming."

Burlon donned his 'Trader face,' the neutral expression Keegan had come to realize revealed nothing of the wearer's actual thoughts.

But, surprisingly, Gredin looked calm, despite the weariness visible on her face.

They didn't have to wait for long. All too soon, the door to the chambers whispered open.

"Sill, how may I be of service? I don't…" Tetralanna broke off at the sight of them, smug satisfaction blooming across her features. "Ah. You have need of me. Is there a problem your group cannot resolve? My advice on how to proceed in this Power-forsaken place?" Her eyes gleamed. "You provided little reassurance to the delegation this morning, Gredin. Give me your stool. This group requires an experienced Speaker."

Keegan listened, astonished by Tetralanna's overbearing pride, despite Gredin's warning.

Burlon said, "You were not summoned here to join us."

Tetralanna stiffened. "Then explain yourself – though why I should believe anything you say, after yesterday's dishonest spectacle, only the Power might know."

"Let me," Gredin said, laying a hand on Burlon's arm.

"You? You're even worse," Tetralanna spat. "I have no interest in your honeyed words."

"Nevertheless, hear them. As you are no longer First Speaker, you need to remove your belongings from this chamber. A space will be provided for you within the House. Do you require assistance packing?"

Keegan braced himself.

"Remove…? Absurd. How dare you? Sill, I am deeply wounded that you summoned me. I came to offer assistance, not to be insulted. As for the rest of you–"

Gredin said again, "You need to clear your chamber and join House Balamont's area of the enclave."

"Foolish, scheming girl. Occupying my chamber will not legitimize you as First Speaker."

"My claim became legitimate when the Speaker's hlette left your arm and came to mine."

Tetralanna's mouth tightened. "Then why hide it away beneath your clothing? Are you afraid it will leave you and return to me, where it belongs?"

Gredin shrugged free of her jacket. First Speaker's hlette encircled her upper arm, glittering under the harsh lights. But another object she wore caught Keegan's attention.

And Tetralanna's, as well. "What is that abomination?" she shrieked.

Gredin looked down. "That? A *griimoni* from the Director, for contacting me."

Tetralanna laughed harshly. "So, you are now the Director's creature. No one will trust you to act on their behalf."

Burlon stood up. "Tetralanna te Balamont. I, Burlon te Laith, am the authority for the housing and welfare of the Vennans who Traveled to Tradepoint for the Trisectoriana. These rooms do not belong to you. They are for First Speaker for the delegation. Since you are no longer First Speaker, you must cede them to the new First Speaker. I have already contacted Petron te Balamont to request a sleeping space for you."

Tetralanna was pale with rage. "It is *you* who needs to leave. All of you! Now!"

Burlon's voice was unyielding. "I will carry you out, if you wish to put on a foolish show for all to see. Or you can leave now, with your dignity intact. We will pack your things, and Petron will Fetch them to your new sleeping space."

"Tetralanna," Gredin said softly, "you will be among kinsmen, able to give and receive support as we grieve our losses. They will comfort you in ways that the solitary silence of this chamber cannot."

"Do not presume to know my needs," Tetralanna retorted.

Burlon surveyed her. "You do not look as if you weigh much," he said, and took a step toward her.

"Don't touch me!"

Burlon took a second step.

"Pack my belongings with care," Tetralanna snapped at Miri. "I will expect them straightaway." And, with a defiant swirl of her skirts, she swept from the room.

Burlon sat down, shaking his head.

"That woman is *horrible*," Miri said. "She had no right to talk to you that way, Gredin. I will gladly go and pack her things. Continue without me."

"Actually, we are finished for today," Gredin said, "unless one of you has another urgent matter to raise?"

"Just assure me you and Keegan can share these rooms amicably until my dydanin ends," Burlon said.

"Of course," Keegan said. "With this table and a space to sleep, I am well satisfied."

"As am I," Gredin added. "Take Tetralanna's room, Keegan. It is quite spacious. Your storage chest and metal table will fit nicely in there."

"No," Burlon objected. "Better that you take First Speaker's chamber, Gredin. I will talk to Wyve about enlarging your former space for Keegan."

"I can discuss the matter with Wyve," Gredin countered.

"Well then," Burlon said briskly, "I need to talk to Ingarra about the *timte* quilt."

Keegan put forth his own request. "Sill, could you Harvest those memories before you go? And I will inquire whether any of the Sixty-Six accompanied us here. They might have valuable advice. With only sixty-six individuals, they managed to create our society. What gyftes were most essential to that effort? I'd like to know, as we gather ourselves to begin again."

"And I will pack Tetralanna's belongings," Miri said, rising.

Sill got to her feet. "Gredin, may I use your old chamber to Harvest Keegan's memories?" She shook her head in wonder. "For such a small space, it has seen its share of startling events. Come along, Keegan."

"I'll be right there." He looked down at Gredin and Burlon. "I will await your contact about the food testing. Until then, I'll carry on with my lists, so long as my paper and ink last."

Gredin nodded. "Wyve says that he will make this band on my wrist vibrate, later today, when the Clinic is ready for you." She touched the device with a cautious fingertip. "I suppose even *griimoni* such as this one have their uses."

"Just so. A good day to you," Keegan said, and hurried to catch up with Sill.

[10]

1847 OF 2000 ORBITS REMAINING: 23PURPLE

"And so, what calls to you next?" Gredin asked Burlon, relieved that the meeting had finally ended. She already knew her own fate: meeting with more distressed community members to address their concerns and soothe their fears. She did not look forward to the task.

But that was ridiculous. These were her people. Not unreasonably, they were shaken by the loss of home, of House, of countless kinsmen returned without warning to the Source. Now, stranded in this place of metal, and *griimoni*, and races not their own, they needed her counsel and reassurance.

So why was she reluctant to rejoin them now?

"I'm off to check the warehouses," Burlon said.

"What warehouses?"

His look conveyed long-suffering patience. "*Our* warehouses, where each House stores items they've bought and those they're preparing to Trade."

"Don't the Tradeteams simply take it all home with them? Why leave things here?"

She thought her questions might annoy Burlon. Instead, he brightened, warming to his favorite subject: Trade.

"At times," he began, "we bring an item that someone – let's say the Wilra – wants, but they're not at Tradepoint when we arrive. Rather than take the item home again, we make arrangements with Wyve and lodge it with the Prett. If the Wilra dock while we are absent, they check with Wyve, agree to our terms, make payment, claim the item from the Prett, and load it onto their ship."

"And when it's something we've bought? Why would we leave *that* here?"

"It happens less often," he conceded, "but sometimes we Trade for something bulky or not yet needed. Rather than make the House store it, we keep it here until they're ready for it." His expression grew grim. "Well, we did. Before."

Before was becoming her least-favorite word.

"Still," Burlon continued, "we're in a funny position now. There will be items in the warehouses I've never seen. I know to a fine degree what's in the House Bentain warehouse, but the others were none of my business. Each House's area is shut off from the rest. But now…" He shook his head. "Thirteen Houses are left, counting poor Keegan as House Fliss. But there are warehouse areas for twenty more Houses that no longer exist." He cast her a speculative look. "Do you suppose House Santelle sold besk berries to other worlds? If they did, we might find sacks of them, waiting on the shelves. With goods from thirty-three Houses, we might find almost anything. Cheeses? Rugs? Or nothing, if they had no Trades pending. There's no way to know until we look…"

Gredin felt a glimmer of hope. Anything from Venna would be a treasure beyond price.

"…although getting into them presents a problem. In one sense, it's as you said – we're all one community now. That means common resources. No hoarding. No playing favorites. I'd already planned to explore House Laith's area, now that I'm one of them, but it goes beyond that. There's no reason why I shouldn't look at all of them, from Avilar to Vell." He cocked his head. "Some of the Houses may not like that notion, but I suspect they'll come around, once they see the others cooperating. The bigger challenge will be the lost Houses."

"I don't understand."

"Well, the doors are keyed to open only to someone of that House, wearing the proper hlao, or someone from that House's Triad. But we've lost twenty Houses. The other Traders and I will need to get clever about it."

"How?"

"I don't know yet. I'll begin with Laith, then figure out how to access the rest."

"I'm coming with you," Gredin said, filled with a sudden conviction that this was something she needed to witness.

"I'll let you know what I find," Burlon said, as if she hadn't spoken.

"No, I need to see the warehouses for myself," she told him, following.

"You can't."

"Why not?"

Burlon rolled his eyes. "Because you have people waiting for you. Did you forget or have you changed your mind?"

"Neither. I will talk to them as soon as we return."

"Oh, *that* will be a popular decision."

"It can't be helped. This is important."

"And they aren't? Because that's what they'll claim you mean."

"I am going for their sake – and for yours. You should have a witness, if you are going to make free of more than one warehouse."

That stopped him in his tracks. He thought, then nodded. "Fair enough. Come along."

Pleased at having convinced him against his will, she followed him out, but her satisfaction ebbed when they reached the reception hall. Several dozen people were clustered there, clearly awaiting her return.

Adopting a look of gravity, she Focused her gyfte and said, so everyone in the hall could hear. "Your attention. A matter involving our community's welfare requires my immediate attention. I will return to the enclave to continue answering your questions and concerns–" *As soon as I can*, she wanted to say, but substituted, "–once I have resolved this urgent matter." *Thank you for your patience and understanding*, she considered saying, but they weren't patient, and they wouldn't understand, and so she settled for a sober nod.

Taking the hint, Burlon strode purposefully toward the antechamber. She matched her pace to his. Numerous people clamored for her attention along the way but she simply kept her chin high and her steps rapid.

No one, at least, was bold enough to follow them into the antechamber itself. When the inner doors closed and the bio-mist descended, Gredin inhaled it gratefully.

Burlon offered a crooked smile. "Well! A Speech worthy of Tetralanna."

Horrified, Gredin opened her mouth to protest.

Burlon waved her to silence. "You misunderstand. I approve. You'll get nowhere by fawning and apologizing at every turn. You can't please a thousand people – at least, not *this* thousand. Whatever course you take, some will disagree. But they'll all sleep easier, knowing someone decisive is in charge."

She eyed him. "You were not so in favor of my being strong-minded, a short while ago."

He shrugged. "There's a time and a place. There are things you don't understand or haven't yet experienced. When those matters arise, listen to those better informed. But when you address the entire delegation–"

"Community."

"–community, you *need* to sound authoritative. That's what I meant about Tetralanna. Right or wrong, have you ever heard her sound uncertain?"

The mist cleared, and the doors to the public corridor slid open. Emerging, Burlon set off at a pace that was nearly a lope. Gredin considered asking him to slow down, then thought better of it. She had said she was coming along. Perhaps he was testing her resolve. Well, her legs were long. She could keep up with Burlon, and the exercise would be good for her.

When they reached an intersection of hallway, Burlon turned in a direction she had not gone before. At the next intersection, quite a distance farther on, he turned again, so that it seemed to Gredin they must be paralleling the course to Wyve's office. They passed door after closed door until Burlon suddenly halted. "This is ours," he said.

"How can you tell?"

He indicated a small panel displaying a series of marks and, below, a circle crossed by a pair of wavy horizontal lines. The circle was purple. The lines were green.

"What does the symbol mean?" Gredin asked.

"Us. Vennans. You've seen it before."

"I haven't."

"Then you haven't been paying attention. It's on the panel outside each of our enclaves, and it will light up on the big board at the Traders' Market when we finally have someone manning our maartza again – tomorrow or the next day, I hope."

"And the marks?"

He shrugged. "Prettian numbers for the inventory records on their *griimoni*."

"To what purpose?"

"Traders' business," he said shortly.

"To what purpose?" she persisted.

He sighed. "To assign station credits to us when we Trade goods to our advantage. To note the transaction when we make an even Trade. To take credits from us when we make a purchase or Trade to our disadvantage. New goods we bring are inspected by the Prett and noted in their records. A portion of every Trade goes to the Prett." His gaze bored into her. "And, because of the Judgment against you, a further portion of every Trade we make for the next six sectora will be credited to the Hesch."

Shame sent heat racing through her body. But the Judgment was a matter of official record. There was nothing she could do about it now… except apologize to Burlon, if she hadn't already. Surely she had. Surely, even in all of the upset and chaos…

But no. On reflection, she didn't remember doing so. When she'd left the Judgment, Burlon had stayed behind to talk to Shamka. And things had spiraled out of her Control…

"I am sorry," she said.

"For what?"

"For all that has gone on. When I went to the Market, I should have stayed with Ellis and the group. I shouldn't have taken Keegan into the Shodekekeen maartza. I should have called out to Shamka when I realized the Beng had come inside. And I never should have Sent, to get away from them. Tetralanna told me you'd forbidden it. If I hadn't panicked and Sent, I wouldn't have broken Nitikikani's foot, and he wouldn't have laid charges against me. You would never have been backed into having to Send in front of the Director. And we wouldn't owe Judgment money to the Hesch."

"Well," Burlon said. "That was quite a mouthful. Do you feel better now?"

Was that a hint of a smile at the corner of his mouth? Daring to hope so, Gredin said, "Not really. But I'm aware of what I've put you through, these past few days. And I'm sorry."

"These haven't been four days of my life that I'd care to repeat, except for finding Chenna. But I doubt they've been your favorite days, either. And the worst parts have been beyond anyone's Control. So I thank you for your apology, but it does us little good. We're still here. We're still without a home. We still have an enclave full of frantic people to calm. I don't know how this will all work out. But we've made a start at deciding what to do first. And Wyve will help, where he can. He's a good man. Just remember that he has his limits. The more problems we can solve for ourselves, the better."

She nodded, her gaze straying to the glowing purple numerals and the circle with its wavy lines. Curiosity awakened within her. "Can we go in? Do we need Wyve's permission?"

Burlon's look was withering. "I need no one's permission to enter my own warehouse, nor does any other Trader." Again, a muscle at the corner of his mouth twitched, and he added, "But *you* would need Wyve's permission, if you weren't with me. You're not a Trader."

Gredin was about to protest, then thought better of it. She'd wait until she saw what was inside. She might have neither need nor interest in coming here again. But if she did, she'd take the matter up with Wyve. The person whose permission she *wouldn't* ask was Burlon's. That was a path she didn't intend to tread. And so she watched with interest as he pressed a quick succession of buttons on the panel and pressed the palm of his hand firmly against the glossy surface below.

With a click, the door swung open.

As they crossed the threshold, lights in the ceiling came to life, illuminating the space.

Gredin noted that the ceiling was much lower than the lofty one in the reception hall. The lights were painfully bright, making her squint as they glared off the long line of metal doors.

"Thirty-three doors," Burlon said, "for thirty-three Houses."

She realized that the embossed emblem on the nearest door depicted a House knot, the unique identifier used on everything from a House's hlaos to its belts to the cords it tied around market bundles. "Which House is this?"

"K'lar," Burlon said. "Warehouse spaces were awarded in order of seniority on Tradepoint. Cirin..." His voice wavered, then steadied. "...was the first Vennan here, so K'lar has pride of place." He gestured to the other side. "Avilar was the next House to arrive. Then Santelle, Streth, and Gedd... but those three Houses are gone, now." He looked down at his feet. "Twenty Houses gone, in all..."

Determined to strike a lighter tone, Gredin said, "I wish we could start with Santelle's storage area. If there are besk berries in there, we will be very popular indeed."

"Unless you and I decided to keep them for ourselves," he teased, with a wicked smile.

Gredin didn't smile back. "That is a poor jest. You might as well talk of stealing from your Chosen." When his expression darkened, she said, "Oh, I know you would never do such a thing. But tell me, Burlon, are there those among us who might? I know little of folk beyond my own House, and not even many of those. You are a Trader and Traveler who has dealt widely with other Vennans, as well as other races. Advise me. How careful must we be? Should I summon Keegan te Fliss from his other labors and have him create a written account of all that is contained within this room? Would it be overly suspicious, or would I be naïve *not* to worry?"

There was misery in Burlon's gaze. "I don't know. There are many I would trust. Some I do not know well enough to judge. A few… In normal times, we Traders are an honest bunch. But normal times are over. People are frightened. Who knows how some may react?"

"Give me your best guess."

Burlon began to pace. "Some will assume that anything in their House's portion of the warehouse is theirs to dispense with as they see fit. They may also assert a claim over anything brought by a House in their Triad, if that House no longer exists. And what of goods brought here by entire triads that no longer exist? Convincing folk to view it all as common wares, to be used for the common good… That may take some powerful persuasion."

"Or a precautionary move. Can we ask Wyve to alter the door panel to respond only to the two of us, instead of opening to every Vennan Trader, until we can talk with the community?"

Burlon stared at her. "Did you enjoy nearly being crushed, this morning? Suggestions like that will stir everyone up again. People are already worried about shortages. If we lock the Traders out, keeping them from their own House's Trade goods, they will panic."

"It needn't be like that," Gredin said, waving aside his warning. "Our people aren't foolish. They will understand. The reasons will be obvious, once they look past what they're used to. We can't afford to act as separate Houses. Here on Tradepoint, the Prett see us as a single group – 'the Vennans.' We need to see ourselves that way, as well."

"I don't disagree. But people won't give up their Houses."

"They don't have to, not entirely," Gredin temporized. "Only where it concerns the community's well-being."

Burlon rubbed the back of his neck. "You say that as if it will be easy to accomplish."

"I'll explain it to them."

"You have a great deal of faith in your gyfte."

"Of course I do. It's why the Power chose me to lead."

That won a shake of Burlon's head. "You expect them to tamely accept that you're their designated leader? Your word against the Tetralannas of the world? They won't believe you."

"They don't have to believe *me*. They can believe Cirin," she said, then regretted her blunt words. "I'm sorry," she said, stricken. "I only meant–"

He waved her to silence and turned away. She watched his shoulders rise and fall, rise and fall. Then he turned back to her, looking grim but steady. "Most of them believe that Venna has been destroyed, because Ci… because he said so. But it's a big jump from there to believing that the Power spoke three times to you. You're unknown to most of them. You got yourself into serious trouble here, the second day of our residence, and the delegation lost privileges because of it. Most don't know you. They only know *about* you. And some have listened to Tetralanna, who has been all too eager to tell everyone why they shouldn't believe a word you say."

Gredin considered his words. Tetralanna's behavior, though regrettable, was not unexpected. And it was true that most in the community were strangers to her, though she had begun to mend that in her hours spent meeting personally with people. People would soon learn they could rely on her.

Now, however, she was dealing with things, not people. "Pick a House where we can start," she said, hoping to win Burlon's cooperation by ceding him the choice. When he said nothing, she prodded, "Shall we open Bentain, which is already familiar to you, or Laith, which is now your own? Or shall we start with what Balamont has stored here?"

His expression was bleak. "You say that lightly," he accused. "But it feels very different, now that I am here and the moment is upon me. Such a thing has never been done. Like any Trader, I have only ever entered my own House's storage area, or one of our triad Houses. Now, some would say I have lost my right to enter Bentain as a kinsman. If I venture into Laith's area, as is now my right, I do it knowing that Traders from Laith may resent my presence there, too." He shook his head. "I know it is what we came here to do, but the training of a lifetime is not easily overturned. I would rather we settle for Balamont alone today."

Coming to the warehouse had been entirely Burlon's idea, and now he seemed to wish he were anywhere else. But his sudden change of attitude was no more extreme than the repeated shifts in her own mood. This was the first day of a strange, new life. Everyone was shaken by loss, frightened by exile, nervous about what might happen next. Burlon's words identified the problem: *the training of a lifetime is not easily overturned.* They were feeling their way forward as if engulfed in darkness. There were no landmarks to guide them.

Gredin nodded. "Do nothing against your conscience. But I am here, and I agree that I should explore what resources Balamont may offer, since that is my House. You need not accompany me, but you are welcome, if you wish to."

Burlon didn't reply but he raised no objection when she walked slowly down the row, examining the embossed emblem on each door she passed.

It became clear, as she walked, that Balamont had not been quick to join the flow of Travelers to Tradepoint after Cirin te K'lar first came across it in his long-ago explorations. She supposed that should not surprise her; Balamont was a cautious, conservative House, slow to deviate from accustomed ways. In time, however, every House on Venna had seen the advantage of conveying their goods to Tradepoint, and Balamont would not have wanted to be left out.

And so it was, at the very back of the room, that she found the door for Balamont, its familiar House knot gleaming from the raised metal medallion. "How do I open it?" she called over her shoulder to Burlon.

"Place your hand upon the knot."

She rested her palm against the cool metal.

A little thrill danced through her, not unlike the sensation when she touched her hlao or First Speaker's hlette. So. The emblem on the door was an object of Power. With a faint click, the door slid to one side, vanishing into the wall. Lights blossomed, revealing rows of shelving.

She hesitated. "The door won't close and shut me in, will it?"

“Only if you want it to. If you close it, there is a knot on the interior of the door, as well.

Or you can stand aside and I will see what Balamont’s shelves hold.” He did not add *if you’re afraid*, but she heard it in his tone.

That stiffened her resolve. Taking a deep breath, she stepped inside.

As promised, the door remained open, leaving a line of retreat and a clear view of Burlon, standing just inside the entrance from the public corridor.

Gredin turned her attention to the nearest shelves.

The first thing she saw was a luminth of pale pink stone, no bigger than her fist. It wasn’t empowered, and therefore gave off no light, but its presence reassured her, all the same. At home, spare luminth were often left in spots where they might be needed. Here in this warehouse, despite the bright overhead lights, the shelving units were wide and deep, casting their recessed areas into heavy shadow. A small luminth such as this one would be handy.

It made the area seem less intimidating. Picking up the luminth, she transferred energy into it. Then, when it was glowing rosily, she knelt down to begin her inspection.

Groupings of table linens covered the bottom-most shelf on her left. Matching sets of napkins and table runners in a variety of colors, their edges intricately embroidered. Table coverings in a variety of sizes and shapes, some dyed in softly subtle patterns, others a single hue, from pure white to rich green. Individual mats, some thickly quilted, some delicately thin.

The second shelf was waist-high. Straightening, Gredin viewed pottery bowls and platters, pitchers and plates, serving tureens and borkins – half bowl, half divided plate. The bowl of a borkin could hold a serving of soup or chowder, or sauce for whatever tidbits were offered on the plate’s surface. Decorative bowls and vases occupied the next section of the shelf, formed in shapes from the natural world, from leaves to flowers to birds to flames.

The final shelf, chin-high, was stacked with blankets, as well as the sort of caps and capes and scarves worn in wintertime at a mountain Holding, or at sea. Made from rista shearings spun into yarn and then woven on a loom or knit by hand, these objects were known for their warmth and their ability to repel rain and snow. For all that, rista wool had a soft hand that made its touch welcome against the skin. When she was a small child, Gredin's favorite toy had been a tiny rista figure made of felted wool. She had dragged it everywhere, and it had held up well against everything from the dirt in Beda's garden to Gredin's attempts to 'feed' it at table…

Nikbik. She had called it Nikbik.

Somewhere along her path from toddler to child to woman, she had lost track of Nikbik. Perhaps he had gone on to entertain some other child within the House. Whatever his fate, he had not made the journey with her to Tradepoint, and so was now truly gone. Destroyed.

Ridiculous, to feel a stab of grief over a child's lost toy when she was responsible for the well-being of her entire race. Nevertheless, she rested her fingertips against one of the blankets, remembering the touch of felted rista wool beneath her chin as she drifted to sleep.

"Something wrong?" Burlon called.

"No." She moved on, embarrassed.

The bottom of the next set of shelves was filled with stacked lengths of glinn wood, some carved, some shorn of bark, some still in the natural state in which they had been cut. Their scent was subtle; the wood was prized for its durability and the beauty of its grain, not for its aromatic properties. Nevertheless, it spoke to her. Much of House Balamont's furniture had been carved from glinn. It took oil or polish prettily, and many Vennan carvers were partial to it.

Above that shelf, to her bafflement, were racks and racks of seashells. Along with the more common shells, she found bowls of tiny lavender tinka shells, a collection of the finely wrought bunkles commonly known as 'lady's ears,' a tray of multi-colored patsina shells that looked like butterflies, and a pair of krenks, each as broad as a dining platter. The outside of each closed krenk was grey and crusted, but she knew the inner surface would be as pink as her tongue, and sleek to the touch. Krenks were good eating, but she had never considered what might become of their massive shells, afterward. Apparently, someone on Tradepoint had an interest in them.

The top shelf held bolts and bolts of the sort of gauzy panels commonly hung at windows and archways to soften the light on a too-sunny day or subtly tame a strengthening breeze. Sometimes, they were even used to gently separate one portion of a room from another. Most of these bolts held plain gauze in white, cream, or pastels, but farther along the shelf she saw finished panels that sported embroidery depicting twined ildarian vines along the edges, and Gredin recognized Ingarra's handiwork.

Across the aisle, she bent and saw row upon row of ingots from the Balamont mines, each kind of ore melted and cast into a different shape. She only knew them from the use Dreff made of them when he crafted his jewelry; he had kept an ingot of each in his work area.

The waist-high shelf above the ingots made her catch her breath. It held hundreds of small, flat-topped containers, each with a design depicting a berry, or a flower, or a plant.

Jam.

Honey.

Pickled relish.

Miri was going to weep with happiness.

"Burlon, come and see!"

She thought he might refuse, but he came at once, perhaps worried by her urgency.

"Look," she commanded, and gestured at the shelf. "Isn't it wonderful?"

"Wonderful," he agreed with enthusiasm. "These will command a fine price at the Market."

Gredin spun to stare at him in horror. "No!"

"What do you mean, no?"

"These are for the community."

"The community can't live on honey and jam."

She squared off against him. "Perhaps not, but Miri says we may be eating a great deal of porridge in the days to come. Honey and jam would make that far more palatable. And this is Vennan honey. Vennan jam. Vennan preserves. They should be eaten by Vennan mouths, not by any greedy Beng who flings a station credit our way!"

Burlon looked grim. “These are luxury items. A dozen jars would buy enough grain to feed your House a nourishing, hot breakfast for several days.”

She was trembling inside, but she kept her voice level. “Clearly, you and I do not agree on this matter. Leave it for now. We can discuss it again in a few days’ time, when we have a better notion of how things stand. But until we talk again and come to an agreement, I want it understood that these jars do not go to the maartza.”

“Or to the kitchens.”

“Or to the kitchens,” she conceded. There would be no speedy end to their stay on Tradepoint, and no easy resolution to their troubles. A few days’ delay would do the community no harm, even if it meant eating unsweetened porridge while she won her point with Burlon.

The final four shelves were empty. “Is it unusual for storage space to go unused?” she asked, to shift the conversation onto less contentious ground.

“Not at all,” Burlon said. “Any purchased goods from other races likely went home with Balamont’s most recent Tradeteam. But there would be a slow, steady call for items like those ingots, so it makes sense to have left a supply here, where they could be moved to the maartza on demand. As to the rest…” His gaze strayed assessingly over the other items, from glinn wood to pottery to table linens, and he shrugged. “I will talk to your Traders. Some of this may have been brought with a particular buyer in mind, while the rest was intended to keep your portion of the maartza well stocked.”

“A good idea,” Gredin agreed. “So, will you inspect anything else while you’re here?”

Looking unhappy, Burlon said, “No. It doesn’t feel right. I’ll wait until you make your announcements, tomorrow. If there’s an uproar over goods being treated as communal, better to know that before I act. I don’t want other Traders to feel I was less than open about the matter.” He cast a hard look her way, as if daring her to tease him about his change of view.

But Gredin only wanted peace. “What about access through the outer door?” she asked. “Will you leave it open to all the Traders?”

Burlon grimaced. "I suppose not. Overnight, at least, we'll lock things up tight. It may annoy some but it will do no real harm."

Retreating to the door of Balamont's area, Gredin drained the little pink luminth and set it back on the shelf by the door, ready for whoever visited next. "What about the overhead lights?"

"They'll shut off when the door closes, if no one is inside. More Prett *griimoni.*"

And so Gredin closed the Balamont door and followed Burlon past the closed doors of the other Houses, and out into the public corridor again.

Burlon fussed with the panel there, which made little chirps and beeps. Then a light flashed, an illuminated number appeared, and the panel went dark.

"There. For now, no one can get in without me except Ellis te Vell. I trust her, and it is wise to have two people to count on, rather than just one," he said. "Now, let's get you back to the enclave. People will wonder where you've gotten to."

They walked in silence until they reached the entrance to the Vennan antechamber. There, Burlon hesitated, gesturing for her to step inside. "I have an errand to run," he said, "but I wanted to see you back safely first."

"What errand?" Gredin asked.

Burlon bristled.

She raised her hand. "I mean no offense. I'm just curious."

"I'm going down to talk to Wyve."

It wasn't the answer she'd expected, nor one she cared for. "I would rather you didn't."

"Why not? I've dealt with Wyve for long and long. Are you telling me I'm to stay away from him now, just when we need him most?"

"I'm telling you that Wyve and I have matters in hand, and I think it best if we have a single spokesman deal with him, to avoid confusion."

"There needn't be any confusion," Burlon said, with a sardonic smile. "Wyve has Figg. And you have me."

"It isn't the same."

"Actually, it is, more or less. We each have our strengths. You can deal with the community as you see fit. But I'm the one who understands Tradepoint."

"Then I'm coming with you to Wyve's office. How else will I learn?"

"You don't need to learn." He sounded exasperated. "You're not a Trader. What you *need* to do is to delegate."

"But–"

"Listen," he said with quiet intensity, placing his hands on her shoulder. "I'm going to ask Wyve whether any races not currently in dock left anything useful behind that we might Trade for – grain from the Wilra, if there is any, and anything else that might buy us a little time while we get our food supply sorted out. I don't need your help for that. Do you know a fair price for Wilra grain? Or what of our goods might interest them? No. You don't. And today isn't the day for you to learn." He tightened his grip. "Be sensible, Gredin. You can't be everywhere at once. And that crowd in the enclave is waiting for you to sit down with them, as you promised." He released her. "Go. Listen to them. Trust me to deal with Trade matters. Or tell me you *don't* trust me, and count me out of your daily meetings. I'm not Tetralanna. If you can't see that distinction, I don't know how to help you."

She could read the strain in the lines around Burlon's eyes. Since yesterday, he had gained a Chosen, changed Houses, lost his First Friend, and rescued her from a mob. Like the rest of the community, he was coping as best he could. This was no time for a full-fledged argument about who was in charge, not if she wanted to retain his advice and assistance in the troubled days ahead.

"Talk to Wyve," she said, surrendering. "I'll go meet with people. And I'll see you tomorrow over morning meal, if not before."

"Tomorrow morning, if not before," he agreed, and strode down the corridor.

Gredin watched wistfully until he was out of sight, then entered the antechamber alone, to keep her promise to the community.

[11]

1835 OF 2000 ORBITS REMAINING: 35YELLOW

Walking the metal corridor, Keegan realized that Gredin looked even wearier than she had at their meeting.

He had glimpsed her in the reception hall while he sought folks to engage with his questions, and had been surprised to see that she, despite her earlier objections, had adopted Burlon's suggestion and was seated at a table, with people queueing up to speak with her there. Keegan sympathized. Everyone was unsettled, and he hated to disturb them, but Gredin and Burlon desperately needed the information he was charged with obtaining, so he gently introduced himself and made his inquiries.

Some refused to answer, their gaze wandering. Some cursed him. Some wept. But a few attempted to return his smile, however unsteadily. For those who answered his questions, he offered sincere thanks when he finished, heartened by their courage.

The line of individuals waiting to talk with Gredin never seemed to shorten. Eventually, he had simply walked to a table near the winding line and taken a seat, coaxing people into answering his questions while they waited their turn.

"What do they ask?" Keegan inquired of Gredin, curious to know what folks found important enough to endure the long, slow-moving line.

She sighed. "Mostly the same few things. Is Venna really gone? What will happen to us? Why did the Power allow our world to be destroyed? Are we safe on Tradepoint? Their words vary, but the grief in their eyes is all the same."

Walking on Keegan's other side, Ellis said, "Understandable. Most had never left their House until they Traveled here. Being a Trader, I have a better understanding of our situation than most, but I've been tempted to join the line, just to have you tell me all will eventually be well."

Keegan shook his head. "We need a more efficient way for Gredin to reassure the community. That line stayed long the entire time I was there asking question."

Gredin sighed. "Now you sound like Burlon. I hope, once everyone has spoken with me and had their fears addressed, the line will abate." She offered him a tired smile. "But it won't be today or tomorrow. It will take time for them to feel heard, and longer to begin to feel safe."

"Take care not to become exhausted. Tetralanna will be watching for any weakness."

"I know," Gredin conceded. "It's partly why I am taking this break to accompany you and Ellis to the Prett Clinic. And I want to be at your side as you begin this process." Her blue gaze was direct. "You are my friend, the first to believe when I spoke of Venna's destruction. I want to be certain this food-testing procedure goes well for you."

"I will keep a close eye on things," Ellis said grimly, "if only to redeem myself for losing track of you both at the Traders' Market."

"That was my fault, not yours," Gredin said.

"And mine," Keegan added, quickly.

Gredin offered Ellis a reassuring smile. "I am not so naïve and emotional as I was then, Ellis. The changes the Power wrought in me are real. I know better than to act rashly."

"Well and good. But Burlon asked me to look after Keegan, and I intend to. You can't be everywhere, Gredin. Why do you think we have Tradeteams instead of single Traders?"

Ellis's practical words made sense to Keegan, but he doubted Gredin would agree. Today's meeting had shown her tendency to take all problems and issues resulting from Venna's destruction onto her own shoulders. Perhaps, as her confidence in her fellow meeting members increased, she would modify that behavior. For now, however…

"Here we are." Ellis stopped in front of a wide door bearing an emblem: a green circle with yellow lines radiating from it. "That's the Prett symbol for a place of healing." Next, she pointed at a large disk in the same shade of green. "Pressing that makes the door open." Suiting her words to action, Ellis pressed the disk with the heel of her hand.

The door slid swiftly open, releasing bright light and a strange odor into the corridor.

Ellis entered and spoke to the Prett seated at the desk near the door. Keegan caught what he thought was a greeting in Tradetalk, and hastened to enter, with Gredin following.

Inside, the odd smell was stronger. Wide doors flanked each side of the desk. When Gredin stopped alongside Ellis at the desk and said something in Prettian, the Prett replied, nodding.

"I informed this person the Director sent us, and we are expected. This person assures me someone will come shortly."

"Your Prettian is good," Ellis said. "Better than mine. My Trading duties are mostly carried out in Tradetalk."

Gredin smiled. "Languages are part of my gyfte. I wish I could stay and translate for Keegan, but I still have people waiting to meet with me." Her smile dimmed. "Testing Prettian food is critical to obtaining a supply we can count on. Today, I am here to see Keegan safely into competent hands. After today, it will be just the two of you."

"I will be fine," Keegan said promptly. "Ellis is accustomed to dealing with the Prett and will make a fine translator."

The door to the right opened before Gredin could respond, and a new Prett emerged, dressed in flowing green pants and a tailored green smock. A symbol identical to the one on the outer door adorned the smock's left shoulder, except for the lines radiating from the dark green circle, which alternated between yellow and deep orange.

"Welcome," the Prett said in hesitant Vennan, bowing slightly and offering them crossed palms. "I am Binn, a Third Level dariiseri."

"*Dariiseri* is Prettian for 'healer,'" Ellis murmured.

Keegan repeated the name and title several times in his mind, determined to remember them, politely bowing and offering Binn his crossed palms in return.

Gredin bowed in greeting, as well. When she straightened, she spoke a few sentences in Prettian to the healer, then waited patiently through the response. When the rumbling words halted, Gredin turned to Keegan. "Binn is female. 'Third level' is her status as a healer – quite advanced. She is fluent in Tradetalk and knows a little Vennan."

"That's good news," Ellis enthused, brightening. "I'm curious… Would you ask her about the smell?"

Keegan repressed an amused smile. Curiosity seemed to be a common trait among Traders, one he himself shared.

"Of course," Gredin said.

The only word Keegan understood in the exchange that followed was the healer's name.

When Gredin turned back to them, she looked faintly troubled. "Binn says it is like the mist in the antechambers but invisible. It penetrates the air everywhere inside the clinic, to kill anything that might enter our bodies and make us ill."

"Oh," Ellis said. "Another Prett safety measure. That's fine. They wouldn't subject us to anything that would harm us."

Not knowingly, Keegan thought.

Binn motioned for them to follow her through the open door.

Keegan let Ellis and Gredin walk ahead of him while he observed more details for later entry into his histories.

The wide corridor was made of metal but it was matte, not polished, and paler in color than the public halls. Closed doors punctuated the hallway, blending almost seamlessly with the walls, the doors' control panels the only spots of color in the long corridor. Every panel contained a large symbol in bright red, each different from the last, with lit squares of various colors below. Keegan wondered whether the red symbols were the Pretts' method of distinguishing one door from another. He would ask Ellis to ask Binn, when there was time.

Binn stopped at a door near the end of the hallway and spoke.

Gredin nodded but allowed Ellis to translate the Tradetalk for Keegan's benefit. "Binn says you should go here. Everything is ready for the test."

"Good you come," Binn said then in Vennan as she keyed them into the room beyond.

The pale metal walls of the room were burnished to a soft shine. Keegan had expected tables and counters of odd-looking equipment. Instead, there was a solitary chair.

"Binn?" Gredin began an exchange in Prettian.

When she and Binn finally fell silent, Keegan asked, "What did you discover?"

"We are in the right place, despite the room's emptiness. She says the Director instructed her to take great caution in her work with you. You will try just one variety of Prett grain today, something called *miichli*, which is very common on Prettig." Gredin's lips quirked in amusement. "The chair is apparently for Ellis. Binn wishes your companion translator to be comfortable while she waits."

"Am I to stand then?" Keegan looked around the room. "And where is the grain?"

Before Gredin could answer, Binn touched the metal wall.

A chest-high section of it began to extend. The motion, smooth and silent, continued until the slab reached a third of the way across the room. At a further touch, the top peeled back, receding into the side of the rectangular slab, revealing a thick cushion the color of sand.

A sleeping surface, Keegan realized. *Some sort of Prettian bed.*

Binn pointed at him and patted the smooth surface.

Keegan felt a thrill of panic awaken. "Does she want me to lie down on that?" He walked slowly to the strange bed. "I'll need your chair, Ellis, to use as a stool."

But he had spoken too soon. At another touch from Binn, the slab sank to the height of the benches in Wyve's office.

Keegan swallowed the urge to laugh, since his mirth might reveal the growing nervousness he was feeling. And, if it did, Gredin might call a halt to the testing. These tests were important work that needed to happen quickly if the community was to gain a much-needed food source.

"I will not need your chair after all, Ellis." He walked to the bed and sat down. The thick cushion gave beneath his weight, deliciously soft, and he instinctively relaxed.

Binn spoke, and Gredin said, "She would like you to lie down, Keegan."

Keegan thought it an odd position to expect him to eat from, but he complied, swinging his legs up and lying back. The surface welcomed his body.

Binn spoke two words of Vennan. "Good. Wait." She adjusted controls and the bed rose to the height of Binn's waist. Its surface pushed upward in places so that he was sitting up comfortably, his knees slightly bent. Then Binn turned to the wall and pressed it several times in quick succession.

Ellis gasped, wide-eyed, and even Gredin looked startled. Following their gazes, Keegan looked over his shoulder… and felt his own jaw drop in amazement.

The wall above his headboard shimmered like water, then coalesced into colorful lines and symbols. Near Binn, a section of wall opened, revealing a tray that held a spoon and plate.

Keegan nearly laughed to see such mundane objects dramatically reveal themselves.

The plate was oval, with a series of smaller oval depressions around the edge. Like most things on Tradepoint, it was metal. The substance filling the little wells looked like pale-yellow mush, but the amounts differed from barely enough to taste, to twice that amount, to a double of that in the next, and so on. *A progression,* Keegan realized.

Ellis moved her chair to the far side of his bed. "Good?" she asked Binn in Vennan.

"Good," Binn replied, and offered the spoon to him, handle first.

He took the spoon and waited for her to hand him the plate.

Instead, Binn touched the side of the bed. A broad band of metal curved up and over his lap, then flattened. Binn set the plate on it, squarely in front of him and spoke, with Ellis translating.

"You eat." Binn tapped the well with the tiniest helping. "Eat slow. Say if feel bad."

With a silent prayer to the Power, he spooned up the mush. It barely filled the bowl of the spoon. Raising it to his nose, he sniffed.

It smelled… earthy, the aroma not unpleasant.

Encouraged, Keegan put the spoon in his mouth, emptying it but allowing the food to remain on his tongue.

The mush tasted of… nothing.

He rolled the bite around in his mouth. It remained unobjectionable, so he swallowed.

"How did it taste?" Ellis asked eagerly. "Did you like it?"

"There was nothing to like or dislike. It's just… bland."

"Perhaps that's good," Gredin offered. "Wilra grain is strongly flavored. Miri might appreciate a grain that blends more easily with other flavors."

"This certainly won't compete with anything. It could have been mashed benroot, for all the taste it had. Or perhaps there wasn't enough on the spoon to taste," he said, and moved his spoon to the next oval.

"No, no, no!" Binn's voice boomed, and she hastily plucked the spoon from his grasp. A torrent of Prettian followed.

"What is she saying?" Keegan asked in alarm. "What did I do wrong?"

Gredin held up a hand to forestall his questions, intent on Binn.

At last, she spoke. "Binn says you must wait a specified time before trying more. There is a strict procedure. She is recording your body's reactions. If all is well when the observation time ends, you may eat again. She will inform you when that time arrives."

Binn's dark eyes watched him closely as he absorbed Gredin's words.

"Fine. Yes," he said directly to Binn, nodding his understanding. "Your pardon." He looked to Gredin. "I'm curious, though. Recording my body's reactions? How is she doing that?"

"A moment, please, while I inquire."

Binn replied promptly to Gredin's Prettian query, and another flood of mysterious words flew past him as they conversed. Finally, both fell silent.

"The terminology Binn uses is very specific, and I can't easily translate it. But it seems that the screen of numbers and symbols above your bed tells her things like the temperature of your body, and how often you take a breath of air."

"But nothing is touching me!"

"The bed you rest on relays the information." She held up a hand. "I, too, am perplexed as to how it can do such things. But I suspect we will never understand Prett *griimoni*."

More time slid past with no change. Keegan said, "You should return to the enclave, Gredin. It seems this process will mostly be spent waiting for the next spoonful of mush. I have Ellis to talk with, and the folks waiting for you must be impatient."

"You're content to have me leave? You have but to ask, and I will stay."

"Go. I hope to hear at tomorrow's meeting that you decreased the waiting line by half."

"May your words prove true," Gredin said, a thread of seriousness in her teasing rejoinder. "Ellis, contact my private mind when Keegan is safely back in the enclave."

"Assuredly. Good luck with the questioners."

"My thanks." Gredin turned to Binn and spoke, apparently taking her leave of the healer. Binn nodded vigorously, and Gredin bowed to her with crossed palms. Binn copied the gesture and watched Gredin closely until she exited.

Ellis said quietly, "Gredin te Balamont values you, Keegan. If I understood her correctly, she just told Binn that if any harm befell you, she would seek Judgment from the Director."

Keegan didn't know whether to laugh or worry. "It is just Gredin trying to be all places at once," he assured Ellis, deciding to treat the matter lightly. "Please apologize to Binn for Gredin's warning and tell her that Gredin is being overly cautious because she is tired."

"I think I'll just leave things as they are," Ellis replied. "It's like a good Trader's bluff. If needed, it might turn the Trade in your favor. And, if not, no harm is done."

Time passed even more slowly after Ellis's pronouncement. Keegan wished he had brought his journal and writing implements with him. Reviewing his lists would have given him something to do. Finally, however, Binn approached the bed.

"Good," she said in Vennan, and tapped on the plate to indicate the next well of food. The oval depression contained twice the amount of the first.

Keegan spooned up the mush, gave it a few token chews, and swallowed.

The larger amount left a gritty taste behind, and he turned to Ellis. "Would you tell Binn I would like some water?"

Ellis translated the request to Binn, who nodded. Keegan watched, curious to see where she would obtain a glass and the water to fill it.

Taking a few steps farther along the wall, Binn pressed her finger to an area that, to Keegan's eye, looked no different than any other. A panel rose on a whisper of sound, and Binn reached in and withdrew a long, thin object, then closed the panel before carrying the object over to the bed.

It was a translucent pouch filled with liquid. A small, round projection the size of his thumbnail extruded from one end. From the Vennan point of view, it looked nothing like a glass. Keegan looked at Binn inquiringly. "Is this water?" he asked. "How do I open it?"

Behind him, Ellis rendered his questions into Tradetalk.

"Here," Binn replied in Vennan. She pointed to the round projection and mimed turning it between her fingers, then offered the pouch to Keegan.

He took it gingerly and was pleasantly surprised by how stable it felt. The translucent material had a nubby texture, easy to grip. He shook it and felt the shift of liquid inside. Carefully, he turned the cylindrical projection.

It rotated smoothly and made a small *click* when it stopped.

Aware of Ellis and Binn watching, he brought the pouch to his mouth and closed his lips around the projection, at the same time raising the bottom to encourage the water to flow out.

Nothing.

Bewildered, Keegan withdrew the pouch and regarded it.

Binn made a sound, drawing his attention, and spoke a few words of Tradetalk.

Ellis translated, "Binn says the contents will not spill out of the opening. You must suck and swallow, to obtain the water."

Enlightened, Keegan lifted the pouch to his mouth once more, sealed his lips around the projection, and drew on it.

Fresh, cool water rushed from the opening, filling his mouth, and he swallowed hastily to keep it from spilling from between his lips onto the bed cushion.

Experimenting, he applied less suction the second time, and obtained a manageable sip. After several more, he offered the pouch back to Binn.

"No," she said in Vennan. She mimed turning the projection the opposite way, then tapped the table next to his plate.

Keegan twisted the projection until it clicked again, then laid it on the table.

Binn nodded. Touching a thick finger to Keegan's arm, she rumbled into speech.

Keegan grinned. The vibrations from Binn's deep voice traveled through her body and the finger touching his arm, creating a tickling sensation.

"Binn says you are doing well. She will continue to observe you, and asks that you tell her immediately if you feel unwell."

Keegan met Binn's dark, solicitous gaze. "Yes," he said in Vennan.

Binn removed her finger from his arm and shifted her scrutiny to the lines and symbols glowing on the wall behind his head.

A soft chime sounded. "What was that?" Keegan asked Ellis.

"I'm not sure. Perhaps Binn can explain–"

But Binn hurried past them both, the hem of her smock rippling. Reaching the door, she keyed it open just far enough to see the individual on the other side, blocking that person's view of the room. A rapid flood of Prettian ensued, the tone making it clear that Binn was displeased by the interruption.

"They're talking too fast," Ellis said. "But the person in the hall mentioned the Director."

Silence fell. Binn thrust her hand through the narrow opening. A moment later, she pulled it back within the room and keyed the door closed. Only when she approached the bed again, nostrils flaring, did Keegan notice the device in her hand.

He looked anxiously at Ellis, wishing again that he understood and spoke the Prettian language. He'd even settle for being conversant in Tradetalk. It was one more shortfall at a time when he needed to be an aid, not a hinderance, to Gredin's efforts.

"Please ask Binn what is wrong," Keegan urged Ellis. "Why is she upset?"

Their talk went on for longer than he liked, but finally Binn said, "Good?" in Vennan.

"Good," Ellis confirmed.

"Are we in trouble?" Keegan asked.

Ellis shook her head. "Not at all. But the same can't be said for the Prett who came to the door. Apparently Binn left strict instructions that your food testing – which Binn refers to in Tradetalk as a 'contest' – not be interrupted. The person at the door claimed to be there on the Director's orders. Under questioning, they admitted they were late in arriving, but were adamant that the Director wanted you to have the *griimoni* tablet immediately."

Binn, who had waited while Ellis spoke, held the object out to him.

Keegan accepted it gingerly. "My thanks," he said, and set it on the table.

Binn walked back to her customary place, her expression clearing.

"So she's fine?" Keegan asked Ellis softly.

"She is, now that the Director's messenger has departed, his task complete. That reestablishes her authority here," Ellis said dryly. "But why is the Director giving you a *griimoni* tablet?"

"Because I'm running out of paper," he responded glumly. "And ink. And my pens won't last forever, either. Gredin and Burlon need information, and my supplies will be gone before I can create all the lists they require. Gredin said the Director thought a tablet would be helpful. And here it is, already causing problems."

Ellis shrugged. "Well, you can't insult the Director by giving it back. See what you can do with it. It will help pass the time, at least."

"I suppose you're right," Keegan admitted, and picked up the device.

Oddly, the tablet wasn't made of metal. Instead, the two-toned outer covering seemed more like the polished dishes House Darius produced, with the top paler than the bottom. The tablet was light, and Keegan wondered how it could possibly aid him. How did one write on it, and with what? And what happened when its small writing surface was filled?

Keegan turned the *griimoni* idly in his hands. If he could just find a supply of paper…

Binn took his hand with a grunt that sounded exasperated. Isolating his index finger, she used it like a crude reed pen to swipe across the paler side of the tablet.

The surface shimmered and resolved into lines and symbols not dissimilar to those on the wall monitor. Then the tablet said, "Welcome. Please listen. The following demonstration will teach you how to use this *crabe*."

It was talking in Vennan!

Keegan shivered, repressing the urge to fling the device away. "It's not… alive, is it?"

"Of course not," Ellis said impatiently. "It's a *griimoni*. The Prett are good at making them. This one must be specially for you, though, or it would use Tradetalk or Prettian. No wonder the Director wanted to be sure you received it safely."

When the Shodekekeen paper had proven nearly useless, and with the Thalken's departure from Tradepoint, his frail hope of finding a supply of paper had seemed doomed. Faced with those twin defeats, Keegan knew that his personal dislike for the tablet meant little. If this machine enabled him to be useful to Gredin and the community, he needed to learn what it could do.

Unsure how breakable it might be, Keegan set it down carefully.

The screen shimmered into a blur of colors, then went solid.

Steeling himself, he reached for the tablet again.

This time, he swiped his finger along its surface on his own. The face of the device shimmered obediently. Lines and symbols reappeared. The strange Vennan voice welcomed him.

"...use this *crabe*. First, we will review the main directory, here on the screen you are currently viewing. There are nine boxes, each containing a symbol–"

Binn's finger tapped twice on the screen, and the voice stopped in mid-sentence. Then she tapped beside the next well of mush on the plate.

Keegan set the *crabe* aside and picked up his spoon.

This round's serving of mush was larger, requiring several applications of his spoon before the well was empty. As before, he chased away the grittiness with sips of water, but a chalky coating remained on his tongue.

His stomach gurgled and clenched.

"Binn," he croaked.

A wave of queasiness swept through him, followed by a second. He swallowed against them, his insides roiling. A third, stronger cramp built, low in his belly.

Then Binn was there, pressing an oval half-mask over his mouth. He tried to recoil from it, but it clung to the skin above and below his lips, extruding a long pouch, as the newest spasm began to empty his insides.

Waves of vomiting followed, continuing long after he felt hollow. When they finally eased, he was relieved to find that the reservoir of the pouch had contained all that he had spewed. Shivering, he removed the mask from his mouth with a shaky hand, almost afraid to trust that the ordeal was over.

"...chee, chee, chee..."

Binn wiped his face with a cool cloth.

Breath by breath, the shakiness receded, leaving exhaustion in its wake.

Binn tugged gently at the hand holding the pouch, and he let it go obediently. With care, she pinched the top of the pouch closed. Then, as Keegan watched in relief, she carried the noxious mess away and disposed of it.

Embarrassed at feeling too weak to Convert it, he fell back against the bed. Its soft surface welcomed him, producing an enveloping warmth. He sighed and closed his eyes against the bright sting of the lights.

"Good?" Binn's oddly accented Vennan asked from nearby.

"Good," he murmured, if only to reassure her, hoping that some shred of useful knowledge had resulted from the bewildering misery he had just endured. For now, however, he could only surrender to the pad's supportive embrace and wait for the last of his body's outraged reaction to subside.

The *crabe* would have to wait.

[12]

1811 OF 2000 ORBITS REMAINING: 10PURPLE

Seated in the reception hall, the community members pivoted on their benches to face the arrival dais as Gredin mounted the steps to address them.

"A fair day to you all," she said, drawing on her gyfte to be certain everyone in the vast room could hear. "Many of you feel unwell and would gladly have stayed abed, so my thanks to you for rising to attend morning meal so that I might address you as a group."

She had risen in darkness, long before anyone else in the enclave was stirring, to prepare for her second day of morning meetings with Wyve and Figg. Dressing had been easier than the day before, since she now had a sleep chamber to herself, but Gredin chafed over her meager choices, remembering Burlon's admonishment about her clothing. What was she to do – wear an elaborate scarlet gown to morning meal? No. If her clothes needed attention, it would have to wait. More serious matters were afoot.

"After today, I will address you instead at midday meal, so you needn't rise so early. But it is important, this morning, for everyone to hear several pieces of news that will affect today and the days to come."

Her meeting with Wyve and Figg had been lengthy, although not as arduous as their first. Wyve told her of his arrangements with Burlon for the purchase and delivery of the last of the cargo of Wilra grain, which could be ground into d'limten flour...

"You may have noticed that our repast today includes fresh-baked d'limten rolls. For that, you can thank Trader Burlon te Laith, who negotiated the purchase with the Tradepoint Director. Thanks also to our kitchen Tenders, who are working tirelessly on our behalf. But our food supply is still sparse and so we are discontinuing the mid-morning and late-day snacks." A buzz of comment began, but she spoke on, overriding it. "As soon as we replenish our food stores, one or both of those small meals will be reinstated. For now, we take this precaution to assure everyone a full meal at morning, midday, and evening."

Several knots of people still murmured agitatedly, including a group from Balamont.

Gredin continued. "With that in mind, I encourage everyone to do their best to finish all they have been served, this morning. If you cannot, perhaps a kinsman would be glad of it. Or you might tuck your unfinished roll into your pocket, to tide you over until midday meal. In the meantime, on a happier note," she said, pushing new energy into her tone, "the Tradepoint Director says that plans are in process to provide less crowded conditions for our bedmats, and cushioning to place beneath them."

The discussion had become complicated when Wyve used the hologram on his desktop to display the enlarged living quarters he planned for the Vennans. A Prettian word she didn't understand kept recurring, and she asked Wyve to find a different way to say it. He attempted to do so, and Gredin stared at him in consternation. "Boxes?" she repeated, certain she had misunderstood. "You would place us in boxes?"

Wyve chuckled. "Yes. Large, strong boxes." He gestured at the office where they sat. "Any room is a box, yes? It has a top, a bottom, and sides. What we will bring together for you and your people are many, many boxes. Placed against each other, and on top of each other, they will make..." He gestured. "...a Vennan... place. A Vennan... nook. A Vennan... hive. Many small places gathered to form bigger places. Groups. Clusters."

Figg said, "Like a Vennan House. Many people, each with their own space, but with those spaces gathered together."

Now, addressing the community, Gredin made no attempt at a detailed explanation. Better to offer people the basic facts – *more room, more comfort*. The Prett would do what the Prett would do, and the community had best accept it with gratitude. Doubtless it would look strange, but that mattered little. In time, they would adjust.

Again, she gathered her energies to steer them to the next new reality.

"We came here as a delegation from Venna, to celebrate the Trisectoriana," she reminded them. "But the celebration is over, and circumstances have taken a dark turn. Now, we are the entirety of Venna and so we will forego the term 'delegation' and address ourselves as what we now are – a community."

Some, distressed by her reference to Venna's loss, turned away. Others listened passively, not fully appreciating the distinction she drew.

She tightened her Focus.

"Here on Tradepoint, others view us a single entity. They know nothing – and care nothing – about Balamont or Indirin or Torr. They only know of Vennans. That is how they will treat us, so it is how we must treat ourselves. I Speak of how we behave outside of this enclave, venturing abroad in Tradepoint to the Traders' Market and beyond. But I Speak, as well, of how we deal with matters *within* the enclave. Some Houses sent many members here. Some sent few. Some Houses journeyed with members from their triad, while others did not. Some Houses sent no one – and those Houses are now gone. House Fliss sent one member – the historian, Keegan te Fliss, with whom many of you have spoken. Sadly, he is now the only survivor of his House."

A low sound, between a gasp and a moan, ran through the group.

Gredin gave it a moment to be voiced and felt. Then, relentless, she pressed on. "As a result, nothing is as it was. Some large Houses are suddenly small. Some Houses, now deprived completely of their other triad members, stand alone. Many of the old alliances have been ripped asunder. It is our new truth. All of us combined are far, far smaller than even the smallest House was on Venna. We cannot afford to split into even tinier divisions. Instead, we will combine our strengths, nurturing every individual, regardless of House."

"You would have us abandon House? Never!"

The interruption was shocking, but its source was not.

Tetralanna.

All morning, whether hurrying along corridors or sitting in meetings, Gredin had felt a persistent chill that made her grateful for the travel jacket she wore. Now, faced with Tetralanna's gyfte-laced objection, she shrugged the jacket away and let it fall, revealing her sleeveless tunic and the golden gleam of First Speaker's hlette, twined around her upper arm.

"Do not twist my meaning," Gredin commanded, making icy blades of her words. "I tell you, and everyone in this room, that we will become *more* than just our House. As small children, our Guides and parents were everything to us. We clung to them for protection, instruction, nurture. Our little world seemed complete. But we grew and realized we were part of something larger – our House. Again, our little world seemed complete. But our minds and gyftes continued to develop, and we were introduced to the disciplines of study, placing ourselves under the direction of Tutors and Mentors. Again, our little world seemed complete. But later, as we matured, the Power gave us opportunities to grow again. In some cases, we found our Chosen. Others, by Traveling the River, found new worlds and new races they could not have imagined in their childhood, and rejoiced in their gyfte. And our world grew and again seemed complete."

She held the delegation's attention in the hollow of her hand. No one, not even Tetralanna, stirred. Gredin let the words flow from her lips, trusting the Power to guide her.

"Now, the Power gives us a new opportunity to grow, the most challenging opportunity we have yet faced. It bids us to look beyond the love of Guides and parents, the structure and loyalty of House, the instruction of Tutors and Mentors, the blissful fulfillment of Chosens, the blessing of our gyftes, the sobering awareness that other races fill the skies and wish to interact with us. Now, the Power asks us to transcend the limits and expectations we placed upon ourselves when the Sixty-Six first began. Our old home, our safe haven, our beloved Venna has been stripped from us, and we few who remain must emulate the Sixty-Six. We will rise to that challenge. We will craft a new way of life and bring it into being. But not here."

She paused, drawing deeply on the hlette's support, aware that every person in the reception hall sat unmoving, not even seeming to breathe.

"Not here," she repeated. "Tradepoint is a place of metal and *griimoni.* It floats high in the sky, circling the home of the Prett. But Tradepoint is only our temporary haven. We are grateful for the shelter it provides, but it can never be our home."

Under the bright lights, Dreff's flamestone pendant glowed like an ember against her skin, and she drew courage from it, touching it tenderly before she forged ahead.

"For three nights in a row, the Power came to me, and on the last of those nights, it said, *Our people cannot stay on Tradepoint forever,* it told me, *separated from sea and sky and the good green earth. Dispatch the Travelers so that, in turn, they can find New Venna.*"

A ripple of reaction ran through the room.

"It used that name – 'New Venna.' A world to take the place of what we have lost."

Many in the room began to weep, but Gredin sensed that these were tears of hope, signaling a release from the crushing worry and sadness that had overwhelmed everyone when Cirin te K'lar delivered the shattering news of Venna's destruction.

"New Venna is not a world yet known to us, but the Power promises it is ours for the seeking. Never have our Travelers been so sorely needed… which is why we cannot yet have them begin the search."

Heads snapped up. Mouths opened in silent protest.

"Think on it," Gredin urged, softening her tone. "Who among us feels well, this morning? Yesterday was an ordeal. Our nights echo with thoughts of lost loved ones. Balance evades us. Focus and Control are elusive. We struggle to deal with the blow of Venna's destruction.

The community has suffered loss upon loss. Chosens, children, parents, Guides, kinsmen, friends – all ripped away. Sill te Torr and Vik te Balamont push themselves to the limits of their endurance to safeguard memories of those who have returned to the Source. We reel beneath the blow."

No one tried to deny it. They could not. It was the truth they lived.

"And that is why these next days must be spent together, mourning, strengthening one another, the better to regain our footing and move forward in safety. No one can say how long it will take to locate our new home. Each Traveler who embarks on the search may be the one to find New Venna. It could happen at any time. But we must proceed as if the effort will take long and long. We must give our Travelers time to think of well-reasoned plans for how best to search. We must guard our health and rally our spirits. We must find ways to endure on Tradepoint while our new home is sought. Better, we must find ways to prosper. And, to do that, we must help one another – not just within our House, but throughout our community."

"Again, you Speak against House!" Tetralanna objected.

Anger simmered within Gredin, but she kept her expression serene. "I Speak on behalf of all. If a Balamont Traveler is fortunate enough to locate New Venna, should only the members of House Balamont be entitled to live there?"

Tetralanna colored. "No. That is a ridiculous example, and you know it."

"Then what of our kitchen Tenders? If Miri te Kendar prepares a certain dish, should it be served only at the Kendar table?"

"No, I–"

"Burlon te Laith arranged the purchase of Wilra grain for our use. It sits before you as the fresh rolls gracing your plate. Should that grain have been saved for Laith's meal alone?"

"No. Let me–"

"What of the Balamont warehouse, here on Tradepoint? When I examined it yesterday, I found jars containing jam and honey and pickled relish. Do we serve them throughout the community or reserve them for Balamont's members alone?"

And Tetralanna hesitated. It was only for a moment, but it was telling. "We share them," she said, but she spoke the words flatly, without force or conviction.

Gredin drove the point home. "Your agreement heartens me. You see why the Vennan warehouse is now without House distinctions. All that is stored there will be used to benefit the entire community, and deals struck by our Traders will benefit us all, not just a single House."

That raised a rumbling grumble of shock from several people – the Traders themselves, no doubt. Well, Burlon would have to help them see the sense of this new approach.

"Wait."

Tetralanna.

Again.

Gredin had hoped the logic of her argument would sweep even Tetralanna up in its flow. But that, apparently, was too much to be hoped for. "You have an objection?"

"A point you seem not to have considered."

Gredin gestured for Tetralanna to continue.

"You mentioned different Houses supporting the Trisectoriana to differing degrees. Our Head of House sent a substantial contingent of Balamont's members here. Some of the other large Houses, like Indirin, were less supportive. Now that we are stranded here, Balamont's contributions will be far more substantial. Should we receive no consideration for that?"

The members of House Indirin glared at Tetralanna with open enmity, and the atmosphere in the room seemed on the verge of curdling.

Gredin stepped into the silence. "Let us take your point to its logical conclusion," she said. "Is it your stance that Keegan te Fliss should be left to starve?"

"What?!" Tetralanna squawked like a water hen startled off her nest. "I said no such thing. No one spoke of Fliss. What nonsense is this?"

Gredin shrugged. "You feel that House Balamont deserves more consideration than House Indirin because of the difference in their size. Correct?"

"Well, I only… Houses that give more should receive more, in all fairness."

"Keegan, the sole survivor from House Fliss, is now a House of one. You can get no smaller than that and still exist. So he would fare very poorly, under your plan."

"Well, we certainly wouldn't let him starve. Keegan te Fliss is a special case."

"No," Gredin countered sharply. "He is *not* a special case! Keegan te Fliss is any one of us, if matters had fallen out differently. Keegan te Fliss is precisely why we must concentrate on ensuring the wellbeing of each individual, instead of clinging to our old considerations of House. If each individual contributes their best to the welfare of the community, then each individual is equally deserving of the benefits the community receives, regardless of their House's size."

Tetralanna looked away, jaw set, lips compressed.

"And there is a matter for our Travelers and Traders to consider, along with any other Vennan who leaves this enclave," Gredin said, pushing her advantage. "We will not speak publicly of Venna's destruction. The other-world guests who attended our reception do not understand Vennan, and therefore know only that Cirin te K'lar met his end. They did not understand his words about the fate of Venna and of Palomar. The Tradepoint Director agrees that our Trade negotiations will best benefit by keeping the loss of Venna secret, for the time being. Someone will eventually discover that we are all still here, and ask why. For now, however, no one is to inform outsiders about Venna's demise."

That request garnered scattered nods and an absence of audible complaint; the Traders and Travelers no doubt saw the sense of Wyve's advice, as Burlon had.

But Tetralanna, it seemed, was not yet done. "Who is 'we,' if I may inquire?"

Gredin looked at her, nonplussed. "What do you mean?"

"You keep saying 'we.' 'We will not speak publicly of Venna's destruction.' And you claim the Power appointed you to lead our delegation. Have you now begun appointing others, as well? If so, what are their names? How have they been selected? This is not how Vennans make decisions, as I think the delegation will agree."

Tetralanna knew the answers to the questions she asked. Summoned to retrieve her belongings, she had seen the group seated around the table, and she now seemed determined to single them out for attention from the community.

Well, Gredin had no problem with that, and no apologies to make.

"As you state, I was visited by the Power and charged with safeguarding the members of this community. But Tradepoint is a new way of life for me, with rules and dangers I do not know well. Therefore, I turned for advice to Burlon te Laith, the surviving official coordinator from the Trisectoriana. He is both a Trader and a Traveler, and long acquainted with Wyve, the Tradepoint Director, and the Assistant Director, Figg.

"My next most vital concern, beyond our physical safety, involved ensuring that our community members are fed, so I asked Miri te Kendar to confer with us, in her role as head kitchen Tender. Her knowledge and willingness to cooperate with the efforts of the Prett have already proven invaluable.

"The third individual whose counsel I sought is Sill te Torr, in her role as First of Memory. Sill possesses a vast array of Memories from the world that lies behind us, and she is helping to guide us toward a future that does sufficient honor to our past.

"And, finally, I have found the services and insights of Keegan te Fliss to be of great use. Many of you have already cooperated with Keegan as he circulates within the community. He is listing all of our names and gyftes, the better to identify what resources we have at our disposal, and what gyftes we have now lost altogether. Indeed, information gathering has been our most important task in these first hours and days. Unless we know what we have, it is hard to determine how to better our condition." She swung a stern look Tetralanna's way, then surveyed the rest of the room. "And, to enlarge our resources, Keegan is sampling unfamiliar foods every day at the Prett clinic, risking–"

"Gredin!" Keegan protested.

But she continued. "–risking his health to keep the rest of us safe and well fed." She spread her hands. "So. Individuals from four different Houses, for the reasons I have just explained, constitute my 'we.' They are giving generously of their time and gyftes, and they deserve your gratitude."

"That's as may be," Tetralanna said, "but we had no voice in their selection. You shut yourselves away behind closed doors, making decisions that affect the entire delegation."

"Not 'delegation.' Community. Words matter, as any Speaker knows. Our days as a delegation came to a tragic end. We are now the community. Indeed, we are Venna."

Sober silence.

Gredin decided she was guardedly pleased with how the talk had gone. Thanks to Tetralanna's flamboyant interjections about the sacred importance of House, the mention of a reduction in the number of daily meals had become a mere afterthought. That might relieve Miri. And the initial mention of thorny topics like communal goods and the delay in seeking New Venna had been weathered. All in all, it could have gone far worse.

Quite intentionally, Gredin looked away from Tetralanna, settling her gaze on the farthest reaches of the vast room. "I am grateful for your attention, all of you. Finish your meal or rise to begin your day, whichever suits you. I will take my place in a few moments, ready to–" Her spirits sank a little as she saw that people were already beginning to crowd forward. "–address any additional concerns you may have," she finished, and came down the steps to seek a sip of water before settling to another endless round of questions.

[13]

1792 OF 2000 ORBITS REMAINING: 28YELLOW

Burlon stood beside the departure dais steps, scanning the people meandering through the reception hall. Shoulders slumped, gazes downcast, they were a sorry sight, although not as alarming as those who sat at the tables, hands empty, staring into the middle distance.

Some wept openly, but fewer than yesterday.

Was that a good sign or a bad one? The half-filled room had a gloomy atmosphere. No one moved purposefully, and there was little buzz of conversation.

At the other end of the room, a long line of people waited for their turn with Gredin. Watching, Burlon saw three more join the tail of the line as she dispatched one. The girl could take root in her chair and folks *still* wouldn't be satisfied.

He supposed people needed someone to listen to their troubles. Just not Gredin. And not like this. If Tetralanna would just rise from her pit of misery and lend a hand…

A figure moving energetically caught his attention: Keegan te Fliss, leaving a seated group and heading Burlon's way. If Keegan, the sole survivor of his House, could manage a smile, what right did Tetralanna have to weep and wail?

"Good midday," Keegan called, the vigor of his voice a welcome antidote to the room's torpor. "I have been making progress, seeking out the Makers."

Burlon said, "There's another way you can help. Are you willing to leave the enclave?"

Keegan nodded. "I'll help any way that I can."

"Good. Then let's be off. The walk will do us good."

Just leaving the reception hall made Burlon feel better. It troubled him that Chenna was confined there all day, but last night had been blissful for them, and she had seemed in good spirits at midday meal. Ulin and Payt had clearly taken a liking to her – as who wouldn't? – and spent the morning with her.

"Where are we going?" Keegan asked as they entered the antechamber.

"Somewhere you haven't been before."

Keegan's eyes brightened. "So… not the Traders' Market and not the Director's office."

"Correct." Burlon glanced at him through the bio-mist. "You have settled into your new quarters without further harangues from Tetralanna?"

Keegan smiled. "Yes. I am avoiding her until her memory of the eviction is less fresh. If she draws comfort from being with her House, the move may cease to irk her so badly."

"Good fortune with that hope. And have your hands fallen off yet from overuse?"

Keegan wiggled his fingers. "Still attached. Still working."

"And you are sleeping?"

His smile faded. "Tolerably," he said. "And you?" Then he blushed.

Burlon grinned. "My Chosen and I sleep soundly when we sleep at all. Despite the distressing days, our dydanin progresses well."

"I am glad of it," Keegan assured him, his cheeks still red.

The mist dissipated, and the outer doors opened. They emerged into the public corridor, with Burlon leading. "We're going to where the Houses store their Tradegoods. Eventually, we'll need an inventory of everything on the shelves, but that will be tricky with twenty Houses lost. For today, I'll settle for cataloguing House Laith, House Bentain, and House Fliss. I had a brief look at House Balamont's goods, yesterday with Gredin, and I'll summarize them for you as best I can." Seeing Keegan's daunted look, he said, "I hope to reopen the Vennan maartza tomorrow. I'll select an assortment of merchandise to transfer, and you and I will tally those things up."

"Certainly," Keegan said.

When they reached Door 739, Burlon tapped in his access code and pressed his palm to the panel. The outer door swung open.

He brooded about the twenty doors belonging to Houses lost in Venna's destruction. The embossed knots sealing each House's inner door had been wrought before his lifetime. Burlon had no idea how the knots had been crafted. They were Vennan work, activated by the Power, while the outer door to the warehouse was typical Prett *griimoni*. As matters stood, each House door opened to the touch of an individual from that House, or to someone from that House's affiliated triad, and to no one else.

It was why he had hopes of accessing the chambers for both Laith and Bentain today. This morning, Chenna had tied his hlao for him, so Laith's door should respond. After he was done examining their goods, he would retie his hlao in the Bentain knot he had worn until his Choosing with Chenna, two short nights ago. He couldn't reason with the doors. He could only do his best to meet their requirements.

"Let's get started," he said to Keegan, and closed the outer door.

"Astonishing." Keegan looked around. "Thirty-three. A door for every House…"

"Everyone Traded," Burlon said, striding to Laith's door. "Now, watch what I do. You'll do the same to open Fliss's door."

Keegan came close, wide-eyed.

"There's no trick to it. You simply place your hand upon the knot, like this." Burlon suited the action to his words, pressing his palm to the cool surface of the embossed knot.

Nothing happened.

"And then what?" Keegan asked after a moment.

Burlon withdrew his hand, then placed it upon the Laith knot again.

Nothing.

Scrapes and bruises! Did I get it wrong at the Choosing? Should I have stayed with Bentain? Or is it Gredin who got things wrong, making us Choose a single House? Perhaps there's no way to change the House you were born into. Perhaps...

"Burlon? Is something wrong?"

He backed away from the door, shaken. "I'm not sure."

"How can I help?"

The question steadied him. Keegan te Fliss was a kind man, well versed in the ways of Venna. Slowing his breathing, Burlon said, "The door should have opened to me. It didn't. I'm trying to figure out why. I am only newly of Laith. I don't yet know how to tie the Laith knot. But Chenna knotted my hlao for me, so I'm confident it's tied properly. Perhaps the door senses that I didn't tie it myself. Perhaps I don't 'feel' properly Laith yet, where the door is concerned." His insides shifted uneasily. "It's possible I never *will* feel properly Laith, to the door's perception. Perhaps it can only sense those born to the House."

Keegan nodded thoughtfully. "Has a door ever refused to open to someone before?"

"Not to my knowledge." Reaching up, Burlon slid the hlao from his head and unfastened the Laith knot, allowing the ends of the hlao to dangle free. Then, grimly, he raised it and allowed habit to assert itself as he tied the long-accustomed knot for Bentain. Finishing, he knew he had tied it properly. Then why did it feel peculiar against his temple? Gritting his teeth against the sensation, he walked to Bentain's door, which he had opened hundreds of times, and set his palm against the door's knot.

Nothing happened.

He felt sick, betrayed by his own gyfte. Or had the gyfte been betrayed by him? Aligning with a different House, had he somehow broken faith with whatever instinctive connection existed? What kind of Trader was he, if his own warehouse refused to acknowledge him?

"Perhaps something is wrong with the door itself," Keegan suggested. "Perhaps all of the doors are affected. Has anything changed recently?"

"Our planet died," Burlon said sourly, then felt a pang of shame when he saw the pain in Keegan's eyes. "Your pardon, Historian. I am rattled, but that's no excuse for dealing sharply with you." He tried to concentrate on the problem at hand. "Yesterday, I changed the setting of the lock on the outer door, but that's Prettian. It should have no effect on these inner doors."

"And the inner doors worked properly, yesterday?"

"I didn't try to open any. The only door we opened yesterday was Balamont's, and that was done by Gredin." Burlon brightened. "You can test the matter, Historian. Let us see if House Fliss's storage area opens to your touch."

"But I am not a Trader."

"Neither is Gredin. Come. It does no harm to try." He guided Keegan down the row to Fliss's door. "Just place your hand on the knot," he urged.

"Will you hold my notebook while I try?"

"Of course." Burlon grasped it carefully, knowing how much it meant to the historian.

Hesitantly, Keegan stretched out his hand and pressed it against the embossed knot.

The door slid silently aside.

Keegan looked from his hand to the open doorway to Burlon, his eyes wide with shock. "It opened," he said, a fragile smile blossoming on his face.

Burlon felt a stab of jealousy, quickly outweighed by relief. The fact that Fliss's door had opened promptly to Keegan was encouraging. Whatever was causing his own difficulties with Laith and Bentain, he would reason through the problem and find a way to set it right. Or, if his change of House allegiance caused some permanent impediment, he would do as he kept urging Gredin: delegate. An inability to open warehouse doors was embarrassing but wouldn't prevent him from exercising his gyfte at the Traders' Market. Having Chenna as his Chosen was worth *any* price the Power might exact.

"May I go in?" Keegan asked.

"By all means. No one has a better right than you."

At first glance, the lower shelves in the Fliss warehouse looked bare. When Burlon came closer, he saw that they actually held tray upon tray of carved pins and pendants depicting feathers, flowers, and leaves. Some were carved from wood, but most were incised rocks and gemstones in a wondrous array of colors, detailed to a fine degree that nearly fooled the eye.

"The workmanship is exquisite," Burlon murmured, impressed.

"Many in my House were gyfted Makers, clever with their hands."

"Then why did none come for the Trisectoriana?" Burlon asked, genuinely curious.

"I don't know for certain. It wasn't discussed in my hearing."

Something in his tone caught Burlon's attention. "But you have a guess?"

Keegan sighed. "What does it matter now? They stayed behind, and so they perished."

"Did you urge them to come?"

A brief exhalation that might have been a laugh. "They would not have listened to me. My House members were firm in their opinions, unlikely to be swayed, least of all by me."

"So they had a reason for not attending?"

A sigh. "House Fliss and House K'lar did not deal willingly with one another. My Head of House tried to discourage me from attending to commemorate the Trisectoriana."

"Ah. Because Cirin was also to be honored."

Keegan nodded. "It was an ungenerous attitude for them to take. We benefitted from Tradepoint like all Houses. None of that would have been possible without Cirin. I thought it only right to come so that I could add an account of the Trisectoriana to my Histories."

"But your House disapproved."

A shrug. "My Head of House disapproved of much of how I spent my time," Keegan said, his tone more sad than bitter. Abruptly, he gestured at the shelves. "Examine what you will. I'll wait out there." And he walked back into the central aisle of the warehouse, leaving Burlon alone with what little was left of House Fliss.

Burlon was tempted to follow, but he resisted. Balked as he was from entering both Bentain and Laith, he couldn't afford to ignore this warehouse area. So resolved, he looked for the customary luminth, found it near the entry, and fueled it to brightness.

The nearest upper shelf held an array of pots and jars, some fashioned from stone, others from clay that had then been glazed and fired in a variety of colors, one color per jar. The effect was more workmanlike than decorative. The front-most jars were small enough to fit on the palm of his hand, while the pots at the back of the shelf were three or four handspans tall and considerably wider. All were fitted with lids.

Burlon gazed at them, puzzled. Were they empty, intended for general storage to be determined by the purchaser? Or did their value lie in their contents?

Picking up one of the littlest jars, he pinched the knob of its lid between thumb and forefinger and lifted it. The neck of the jar was too narrow to admit more than a trickle of light, preventing him from seeing within. He raised it to his nose and sniffed.

A sneeze instantly overtook him.

He had the presence of mind to clamp his thumb over the opening of the little jar and to clutch the jar tightly as his body convulsed in half a dozen violent sneezes. Finally, eyes watering, body trembling in the aftermath, he became aware of Keegan patting his back.

"Are you all right, Burlon? Should I take you out of here?"

"No," he rasped, and tried to draw a measured breath without reawakening the need to sneeze. When he managed it, he held up the little jar. "What the seeping sores is *in* this?"

"I don't... Oh! Is that what made you sneeze?"

Feeling a little foolish, Burlon confessed, "Yes. I sniffed it, to see if it was empty."

"Well then, I suspect it's powdered blayn. A spice. Kitchen Tenders use it."

"Carefully, I trust," Burlon growled, then relented. "A foolish move on my part. Traders are taught to be more cautious. But I didn't expect something in our own warehouses to be so…"

"Volatile?" Keegan ventured, and smiled.

"Precisely." With respectful caution, Burlon sealed the little jar and placed it back on the shelf. "So then, what do you make of the rest of these jars? More sneezing powder?"

Keegan appeared to take the jest in stride. Burlon had feared the little historian would retreat again to the central aisle, but he stayed, examining the shelf Burlon indicated.

Keegan lifted his shoulders. "I don't know. Nothing is labeled. Judging by the blayn, the rest might be other spices and herbs, but that's only a guess. The colors may signify the contents. There are thirteen blue pots, at the back, and twenty-five yellow, but only one each of red and brown, and four green. Or the colors might just be whatever glaze was handy when the pots were made. But all of the jars and pots are lidded. I doubt they're empty."

"How good is your knowledge of kitchen spices?"

"Fair. But Miri's would be better."

It was true. And Miri would have time on her hands, with midday meal over and no late-day snack to prepare. She was already part of their little group. If he asked, she would likely come. But she wouldn't like walking the corridors alone, nor would she know the way...

It was all the excuse he needed. Focusing, Burlon reached out to Gredin's private mind. =Where are you?= he asked, though he already knew. Where was Gredin ever, of late, but sitting in the reception hall, listening to an unending litany of people's woes?

=In the enclave,= came the clipped answer.

=Well, I need you here at the warehouses, and Miri along with you.=

The sense of a sigh. =When?=

=Now would suit.=

=I can't.=

=You can. And should. It will benefit the community far more than what you're doing. Tell them you'll be back, if you must. Are you at your usual table?=

=Yes.=

=I'll have Miri join you there,= he said, and let the contact lapse before Gredin could do more than sputter.

Miri was easy to persuade. =Kitchen spices?= Excitement colored her thoughts.

=We have reason to hope so. Can you help us identify them?=

=Of course.=

=Collect Gredin from the reception hall. She knows the way. We'll let you in when you get here. And, Miri… my thanks.=

=Oh, desh. I'm happy to have something to do.=

Burlon withdrew from her thoughts, blinking himself back to an awareness of his surroundings. "Miri and Gredin are coming," he told Keegan. "Let's examine the rest of this while we wait."

Aside from the jewelry and what Burlon hoped were spices, Fliss's stores were utilitarian: finger sticks and other eating implements in a variety of styles and levels of decoration, woven floor mats, two shelves of rolled carpets, and an enormous pair of kettles.

"Those may already be spoken for," Burlon mused. "They're a hefty thing to have brought unless your Traders already had a customer lined up." A new thought creased his brow. "Many things in our warehouses may already be on order, awaiting the buyers' return to Tradepoint."

"And if they are?"

"Then we have two choices – let the deals go through as arranged and pocket the payments, or cancel the contracts, if we no longer want to part with the goods. That's not often done since it can lead to hard feelings, but we'd be within our rights." He grimaced. "Except we aren't admitting to Venna's destruction yet. That would mean cancelling Trades without an honest explanation and running the risk of angering Trading partners we'll need in future."

"What should we do?"

Burlon gave a mirthless laugh. "Hope that no pending Trades come due until enough time has passed. I'll talk to Wyve and find out what arrangements are currently on the books."

"It all sounds complicated."

"Normally, it's straightforward. But I was only concerned with one House's promises, then, not thirty-three. The simple days are gone. These are going to be–"

Gredin's voice sounded in his mind. =Burlon? Miri and I are here.=

"–stranger times," Burlon concluded, and gestured for Keegan to accompany him to the main warehouse door.

Upon entering, Miri seemed awed by the long warehouse aisle and its array of doors, and by the realization that a House's unseen treasures lay behind each door. But she soon steadied, drawn by the possibility of kitchen spices in House Fliss's area.

"Take Miri in and show her," Burlon instructed Keegan. "I need to talk with Gredin."

As soon as Keegan and Miri were out of sight, Gredin asked, "What's so urgent?"

"The doors may be malfunctioning. See if you can open Balamont's door again."

She drew back. "You called me down here for that?"

"Of course. These warehouses are our lifeline. Besides, we needed Miri, and she needed someone to show her the way."

"Prett security could have escorted her. Several hundred people are waiting for me!"

"They just want someone to share their misery. Sitting them in groups to talk to one another would do just as much good – perhaps more, if it reminds them that others have woes, too. It's ridiculous to spend your time that way."

Her jaw tightened. "You should be pleased. You want me out of your way, don't you?"

Her accusation was more bluntly honest than Burlon had expected. He opened and closed his mouth twice before finally admitting, "I want you to recognize your limits, before you end up in trouble again. You know little of Tradepoint and the races here. Speaking Tradetalk isn't enough. In fact, it may be too much, since it enables you to embroil yourself in matters better left alone. Attend to the community and leave Tradepoint matters to me."

"And yet," she observed, her tone cool, "you just made me leave the community to come down here and aid you in a matter concerning Trade."

Slice it, she was right. That was exactly what he'd done. What had possessed him?

Burlon fought the impulse to sit down and put his head in his hands. At a loss, he fell back upon what he needed from her. "Open the Balamont door," he said.

She eyed him.

"If you would be so kind," he added.

With a curt nod, she walked to the end of the aisle and placed her palm against the embossed Balamont knot.

The door slid open.

Gredin took a few steps inside, then came out again.

Checking to be sure her jams and honey are still there, Burlon thought crossly.

"Now what?" she asked. "Shall I close it?"

"No. Leave it, if you will. Keegan is here. He will write out an accounting."

"Then are you done with me? If so, I should get back. Bring Miri when you're done."

He didn't want to speak the next words, but curiosity drove him. "House Laith is part of Balamont's triad, along with House Torr, is it not?" he asked, knowing full well that it was.

"Yes," she said stiffly. "What of it?"

"You should be able to open the doors to all of the Houses in your triad. Often, when a triad's Tradeteam comes here, the team brings goods from all three Houses of the triad, but with Traders from only two of the Houses, or even just one. Regardless, the goods need to be stowed in the proper areas, so each lock recognizes every House within its triad." He blew out a sigh. "You realize, these locks were created before my life began. But learning about Tradepoint, and about the warehouse and the locks is part of every Trader's training. Any Trader you ask would tell you the same, unless they were among the very earliest ones to come in the days just after Cirin's first arrival here. And so, while you are here, I would have you open Torr and Laith."

"I can try to open Torr, I suppose," she said. "You can open Laith yourself now, remember?"

He'd hoped to avoid explaining to her, but that hope was gone. He walked forward and confessed, "I did not forget. I tried. It would not open to me."

She looked at him, the harshness draining from her expression, replaced by a pensive regard. Then her eyebrows rose. "Silly man. Your hlao is tied for Bentain."

Burlon sighed. "I wish the solution were that simple. Chenna tied my hlao in a proper Laith knot, this morning, but the Laith door would not answer to my touch. When it refused, I retied my hlao for Bentain, thinking… I'm not certain what I was thinking. Perhaps that a door could only respond to someone born into that House, and that Bentain would still open to me. But it refused, as well. At that point, I didn't know whether the difficulty lay with the doors or with me, so I had Keegan approach the Fliss door." He gestured in frustration. "It opened to him. Balamont has opened to you. And I am left not knowing what to try next."

He had thought she might mock his dilemma, but she shook her head slowly. "A frightening thing, to be at odds with your gyfte. Let me think."

"Wait. There is more for you to consider."

"Another difficulty?"

"A different one. What are we to do about the doors where a complete triad has been lost?"

She shook her head. "Stop. One trouble at a time. We will reason this through as we go. Take me to Laith's door, since you say it should open to me." Gredin looked at him pensively. "Who is in Bentain's triad?"

"It is – was – Fliss and Tetarrin. But when Bentain's door refused me, there seemed little point in trying Fliss, since I had Keegan here to open it. And he should be able to open House Tetarrin and Bentain, as well. But there are other Houses where we have no such solution at hand. We'll need to list the Houses we have lost," he said, "and see which of them have surviving Houses from their triads. Some may not, but for those that do…"

Gredin raised her hand. "I say again, one trouble at a time. Take me to Laith's door."

He walked her there, frowning at the portal. *I have pledged myself to your House for all time. Why will you not yield to me?*

Gredin approached the door without hesitation and placed her hand upon the knot.

Equally without hesitation, the door slid open at her touch.

It was supposed to do so. Laith was part of Balamont's triad. He should be entirely pleased. But a part of him was disappointed to find the door perfectly capable of opening, when it wanted to. Why had it adjudged him unworthy?

"Burlon? Did you want to go in?"

Perversely, he didn't. Not like this, under someone else's auspices. Under Gredin's auspices.

"Not just now," he said, "but we'll want Keegan te create an account of the Laith goods, as well as Balamont and Fliss."

"And Torr?"

Laith had opened to Gredin. There was no reason to doubt that Torr would do the same. "Perhaps not today. There is a limit to what we can expect Keegan te accomplish."

Since he had announced his willingness to postpone opening House Torr's area, he expected Gredin to renew her intention of returning to the enclave. Instead, she came to stand close beside him. "What did you feel when you put your hand upon the Laith door's knot?"

Reluctantly, he thought back. "Nothing. No least flicker of connection."

"And when you retied your hlao and approached the Bentain door?"

"Equally nothing, as if it had never opened to me."

"Oh, Burlon, I am sorry. Perhaps…" she began, but her voice trailed away into silence.

"Perhaps?" he prodded.

Gredin shook her head. "Truly, I do not know. Your Choosing with Chenna was a true act of the Power. Your hlao blended with hers. But it is utterly new, this Choosing between separate Houses. And I still believe that a Chosen pair cannot be divided in allegiance. You two had to select a single House to which you and your children belong. But I didn't foresee a difficulty such as you faced today, with neither House's door opening to your touch."

"The Power failed to whisper in your ear about it?" he asked, amazed that he could offer even a small jest about such a weighty matter.

"The Power does not appear to trouble itself with details," she responded, and Burlon found himself sharing a small, wry smile with Gredin as they reflected on the complications surrounding them.

Dimly, they heard Keegan and Miri conversing, Keegan's voice steady while Miri's swooped high with what sounded like excitement.

"Perhaps our guess of kitchen spices was correct," Burlon ventured.

"I am grateful for anything that can lift Miri's spirits," Gredin confided. "She says her Chosen was a Trader. Did you know him? Zanther te Kendar."

A memory of Zanther's face formed in Burlon's mind – a cheerful, kindly Trader who always wore a smile. They would have been an amiable couple, Miri and Zanther. Burlon bowed his head. "I knew him. He was liked by all." Cirin was gone, and Zanther, and how many more Travelers and Traders he hadn't yet realized were lost from his life?

It hurt in a way that was different from the loss of his kinsmen. These others, Cirin and Zanther, were his gyfte kin, understanding the thrill of the River and the satisfaction of a well-turned negotiation. They were gone, and he was much the poorer for their loss.

Desperate for distraction, he looked beyond Gredin. "That door there, beside Laith, is House Pilain. It formed its triad with Anthelmin and Hetemar. All three of those Houses are lost to us. No member of that triad survives. Are we forever barred from knowing what lies behind their doors? These doors, these knots, are the Power's work. My Trader's mind yearns to know what lies within. They may hold nothing… or they may contain goods that would aid us in these early, difficult days of–"

"Burlon?" Keegan's voice, from the Fliss warehouse. "Can you come and look at this?"

He was grateful to hear excitement in someone's voice. "I'll return in a moment," he said. And when he reached the open doorway to Fliss's warehouse, he had to smile at the sight of Keegan and Miri sitting on the floor, surrounded by groupings of pots and jars. Miri's hand rested protectively on the lid of the largest pot. Keegan was writing in his notebook.

"You called for me?" Burlon prompted when neither turned his way.

Miri offered him a smile like sunrise. "Do you realize what we have here?"

"No. That is why I asked you to come. Tell me."

"Treasures. Nearly every spice and herb I have ever used, as well as curls of jelimar bark, an entire pot of dried kuma leaves, and sitka peel, and crystalized sap from the trees in Fliss's ombiri grove. And do you see that wooden chest? It is filled with sea salt." She shook her head. "These supplies won't last us forever, but they will be an immense help as we work to make what little food we have as tasty as possible. May we take these back to the kitchens now? Keegan has no objection, and it would benefit the entire community. Please, Burlon?"

Caution rose within him. "They may already be spoken for," he said. "Fliss Traders brought them here to sell. Orders may have been placed in advance."

Miri shrank back. "But these are Vennan spices. You won't let some other race take them, will you? We *need* them."

"No, you *want* them," Burlon said, feeling unkind. "If Fliss Traders made a promise–"

"No." Keegan looked up, unusually resolute. "I am House Fliss, all that remains of it. Check with Wyve. If contracts were made, cancel them. These spices are for the community."

Burlon shook his head. "That isn't for you to say."

They stared up at him.

In the silence that ensued, Burlon heard a light clatter from the central aisle where Gredin waited. Had she become impatient? It couldn't be helped. This matter had to be dealt with.

"Listen to yourselves," he ordered, his voice gruff. "Have you understood nothing I've said in our meetings, yesterday and today? Gredin and I had this same wrangle yesterday over Balamont's jams and honey and relishes. Yes, these things are a taste of home. Yes, they would enhance the food on our tables. But I tell you now what I told Gredin – we can't live on them. A plate that holds nothing but jam and spices won't sustain us. Our first concern *has* to be obtaining the food itself, in sufficient quantities to put meals in the empty bellies of a thousand people a day, three times a day, for as long as we're here – not necessarily to fill those bellies tastily, or abundantly, but at least so no one goes to bed hungry. If some race will pay an exotic price for crystallized ombiri sap, or jelimar bark, or has developed a weird fancy for inhaling powdered blayn and sneezing their fool heads off, the profit from one little jar may buy enough food to fill our empty pantry for a week of meals. What would you have me do?"

Miri wilted and began to weep.

Keegan held his gaze for a long, tense moment, then looked away.

Again, a skittering clatter sounded in the central aisle.

Ignoring it, Burlon leaned down to pat Miri's shoulder. "It doesn't mean they're gone for certain, Miri. But we have to wait and see, and be clear-headed about the choice we make."

Her head bobbed in acknowledgment, though her face was still hidden in her hands.

Groping for a crumb of comfort to offer, Burlon said, "The hungrier people are, the more they'll appreciate the food that's put before them."

"We've made a start on *that* today," she choked, "taking away their mid-morning and late-day snacks. We may not need to Cleanse tonight's plates – people may lick them clean." Her tone steadied. "I am sorry, Burlon. I grew excited and didn't think matters through. You are right. But it hurts my gyfte to think of all we could do with these, given the chance."

If she had railed at him, or pouted, or continued to weep, he could have remained sensible. But she was Miri, gentle and kind, and he suddenly heard himself saying, "If you could choose one thing from this room for the kitchens, Miri, what would it be?"

He had thought the choice would be difficult, given the variety of goods spread around them, but Miri didn't hesitate. "The kuma leaves. They're dried, so they'll stay strong nearly forever if their pot is tight-closed. We can break off just what we need, none wasted. They'd put a fine savor in a stew or soup, or even in a pot of hot water, with some vegetables chopped fine."

"Then take them with you and put them to good use," he said, "if Keegan agrees."

"I have no say in the matter," Keegan replied. "We are one community or we are not. I was wrong to say what I did."

"Still, what you said was kindly intended," Burlon pointed out, feeling that recognition was due. Keegan's assertion of House rights had been short-sighted, but it had been devoted to the entire community's needs. That was a vital line of distinction, for they might yet see Houses act from motives less pure, where their warehouse goods were concerned. "I have been less than consistent myself in how I refer to the goods in these warehouses. This is new to all of us. It will take time and effort to adjust our thoughts." He nodded at Miri. "Sometimes, we find a place between, when both arguments have merit. Take the kuma leaves, Miri. The fate of the other jars and pots will be decided later, but this much is for the community. I am sorry I spoke harshly."

"And I for shedding tears. We struggle to learn how to manage our worry and grief." With reverent care, she picked up a tall, slender pot and cradled it in her arms.

Burlon heard the clatter behind him yet again. What had Gredin gotten into? He should find out. Looking from Miri and Keegan te the pots and jars, he asked, "Do you need help, putting these back on the shelf?"

"No, we are tallying what's here, and organizing like with like."

"Then I will leave you to it," he said, and turned to go.

As he did, something small skittered past on the metal floor of the central aisle.

Burlon jumped, then shook his head, annoyed with himself. The Prett used complicated tech to ensure that no pests survived on the station, especially in the warehouses. Whatever had just gone by wasn't alive. But what *was* it?

Reaching the threshold, he leaned past the doorframe, looking to his right, where the mysterious thing had been headed.

A dark object, roughly rounded and smaller than his thumb, sat at rest in front of one of the closed doors – House Relling, perhaps. Or was it Deldora? He couldn't recall.

Still perplexed, he looked to his left… and saw Gredin.

She sat in the middle of the aisle, peering down with great concentration at something she poured from hand to hand, back and forth. Then she clasped both hands together and abruptly pulled them apart. The objects fell to the floor, creating the little clatter Burlon had heard.

Most of the objects landed in a neat heap in front of her.

One did not. Instead, it caromed off at an angle, sliding on the floor until it bumped to a halt in front of another closed door.

Burlon stepped out into the aisle. "Gredin?"

She looked up at the sound of his voice but her gaze failed to fix on him, as if he were part of the warehouse's architecture.

"Gredin," he said again, walking slowly toward her. "What's that you're doing?"

At least she seemed to see him now, her gaze tracking his motion as he neared her. But her expression was slack, and she offered no answer.

Stopping in front of her, he hunkered down. Close at hand, he saw that the little heap in front of her was made up of stones. "What are these for?" he asked in honest curiosity, and reached out, intending to stir the pile with his fingertip.

"Mine," Gredin whispered. She put her hand down, and suddenly the stones were all on her palm, although he hadn't seen her grasp any of them. She closed her fingers over them and said again, still whispering, "Mine."

Unsettled, Burlon stood up and backed a pace away. "Yours. But what are you doing?"

"Asking."

"Asking… what?" he said, although the better question might have been *Asking who?*

"Which doors to open."

Turning, Burlon saw that four warehouse doors now had a stone sitting directly in front of it. His breath came quicker as he realized that all four doors belonged to lost Houses.

Which doors to open…

"Well then," he said, as if he wasn't requesting the impossible, "open them."

She produced a little pouch and secured the stones from her hand within it, then got to her feet. Sliding the pouch into her pocket, she walked to the nearest stone-marked door.

"House Streth." Her voice was strong and firm as she placed her palm on the embossed knot.

The door slid open.

Burlon's knees wavered.

Gredin was unfazed. Bending, she scooped up the stone, pulled out her pouch again, dropped the stone in, put the pouch away, and walked to the next stone-marked door.

"House Pilain," she announced, and placed her palm.

The door slid open.

Again, she bent for her stone and put it carefully away before moving on.

"House Relling."

Her palm.

The door slid open.

Collect the stone. Stow it in the pouch. Move on.

"House Jothell."

Palm.

Door.

Stone.

Pouch.

Gredin turned as if to continue, then hesitated, blinking, looking like a child who had just awakened. Her gaze sought his. "Burlon?" She began to tremble.

He hurried to her on weak knees, trembling himself from what he had just witnessed.

She reached out toward him. Did he only imagine that her hand emitted an eerie glow?

"Do you need to sit down?" he demanded, alarmed.

"That would be… nice," she said, her voice a wisp again.

He helped her to sit on the floor with the solid wall at her back.

Gredin's head lolled. "I was waiting for you," she said, the words like a question.

"You did more than wait," Burlon replied.

"Tell me," came the soft request.

"You threw rocks at the doors," he said irreverently, to win back a bit of his nerve. Seeing her startled look, he said, "When I came out, you were fiddling with the stones from your pocket. When I asked what you were doing, you said you were asking which doors to open."

That answer seemed to strike a spark with her. She closed her eyes for a moment, then opened them and said, "I thought I dreamed that."

"No. You dropped the stones, and some of them landed in front of warehouse doors. Doors which you then opened."

"Balamont?"

"No. You had already opened Balamont. The doors you opened were Streth, Pilain, Relling, and Jothell – all Houses that headed their respective triads. All Houses that are lost, and their triads with them. All Houses whose doors I feared would remain closed forever."

Slowly, she looked around the room. Seven doors stood open: Balamont, Laith, and Fliss, joined now by Streth, Pilain, Relling, and Jothell.

"Go look inside," she suggested. "You know you want to."

It was true; he was aquiver with anticipation. But something held him back. "Come with me," he said. "I think you're meant to. Those doors opened to you, not me."

She nodded. "Can you help me up?"

It was his turn to hesitate, but Gredin's color had improved, and her eyes seemed to fix on him properly. He stood and reached down to her.

As her fingers neared his, he felt a little snap of energy leap the gap between them.

Gredin seemed to feel it, too. Her eyes widened, and she rose with renewed vigor. As Burlon steered her toward the closest open door, she asked, "Which House is this?"

He looked at her in surprise. "You announced it when you opened it, moments ago. Have you forgotten so soon?"

Gredin sighed. "Well, I do not know it now, and I do not remember knowing it then. So tell me, if you will, what House's wares we are about to view."

"House Jothell."

She shook her head sadly. "I never made the acquaintance of one from that House."

"Then this is the closest you will ever come to such a meeting," he observed, and drew her with him over the threshold.

The luminth that awaited them was pale blue stone veined with white, cleverly carved into the shape of a little bird. When Burlon lifted it to add his energy to it, it flared quickly to a painful brightness. Hastily, he damped it down, softening the glow. "Your pardon," he apologized. Then he turned with Gredin to see what goods had been placed there, brought by Vennans who would never again tread the corridors of Tradepoint.

[14]
1761 OF 2000 ORBITS REMAINING: 10BLUE

Gredin looked around the little table, pleased to see everyone.

It was a relief that the disagreements of the past two meetings – mostly between herself and Burlon – had not driven any of them away. She was beginning to rely on them and view them as her allies. Even when opinions differed, their words were honest and well intentioned.

"A good morning to you all," she said.

"You sound far too cheerful for a woman who spent yesterday listening to complaints," Burlon grumbled.

"They weren't *all* complaints," Gredin said. But, in truth, most had ranged from whining to fright to anger to accusation to pleading. And few were satisfied with the limited information she could offer.

"Morning meal is horrible without besk. Tetralanna agrees."

"The meals have become so repetitive."

"Is this place in danger of being destroyed as Venna was?"

"...can't breathe here! I need to see the sun..."

"The portions seem to grow smaller by the meal. Are we going to starve?"

. . .

"Don't you care? Tetralanna shares her tears, but you are cold and calm."

"I can't bear what has happened. My Chosen is gone..."

"What does the Director say? A Trader in my House says we won't be allowed to stay here for long. Where will we go?"

"When will the besk return? I can't believe you let the Prett take it from us..."

"Why did the Power choose you rather than Tetralanna? I have known her for long and long, while you are only..."

"...the Power spoke to you in the voice of your Chosen, so it must be true. Please, Gredin, ask the Power to let me hear the voice of my Chosen again."

"...Gredin?"

She blinked and found four pairs of eyes regarding her with concern.

"Your pardon." She forced a reassuring smile. "Shall we begin? Sill, I believe you are first to report, today."

"Yes. Many more people have sought me out to Harvest memories of their loved ones. Vik te Balamont says the same is true for him. I take that as a good sign."

"Why do you think so?" Keegan inquired, his reed pen poised.

"For a successful Harvest, the giver must Focus on the memory they wish me to collect. A measure of Control is required as the two of us relive it together. The grief we are experiencing makes Harvesting impossible for some. But the increase in requests suggests that people are beginning to come to grips with their losses."

"Starting to recover their Balance," Keegan said softly.

"Yes. I Harvest memories, I eat, I join with my Chosen, I sleep. That is now the shape of my days." Sill smiled. "And, of course, I meet with all of you. Keegan, you may begin your report. I am done."

He laid his pen aside. "I can support Sill's observation. More people are lingering at table after a meal. More are willing to be interviewed for the lists. Only one wept today, and they were quickly comforted by others nearby. Like Sill, I believe the strongest among us are starting to awaken from these darkest of times."

"That is good news," Gredin said. "But as the community more fully awakens, we must help them find ways to exercise their gyftes."

"Save that topic for when it's your turn, Gredin," Burlon said.

The rebuke stung. Burlon was correct, but she wished it had been one of the others who reminded her. Using the procedure they had agreed upon kept the meetings orderly and made it easier for Keegan te take his notes, but need Burlon have been so brusque?

"My thanks for the reminder, Burlon," she said, keeping her tone level. "Keegan, please continue."

"Just one thing more," he said on a note of reluctance. "Tomorrow or the day after will see an end to my paper."

He removed a folded square of yellow from his journal, and Gredin recognized it as a piece of Shodekekeen paper.

"I've tried all of my inks on this, in the hope that one would prove successful. But, as you can see–" Keegan unfolded the paper "–they were all absorbed too readily to remain legible."

"I'm so sorry," she said. It was another piece of home lost to them all. Forever.

"I'll keep my eyes sharp when I'm at the Traders' Market," Burlon promised. "Even if no one has paper, there may be some acceptable substitute."

But it won't be the Vennan paper that Keegan treasures.

"How do you fare with the Prettian *crabe*?" Gredin asked. "Can you use it, once your paper is gone?"

"I believe so. I'm making good progress with the teaching voice. It's easier to understand than I first feared," he admitted.

"Anything would be difficult to learn while emptying your insides," Burlon asserted. "You're tougher than you look, Historian, if you plan to return today for yet another test."

"Someone must. And Binn and I have grown used to one another."

"We are deeply grateful for your efforts, Keegan," Gredin said. "While the first two attempts made you ill, perhaps today's Prett food will agree with you."

"With the Power's blessing." He smiled ruefully. "At least yesterday's mush showed us to be ill-suited partners on the first mouthful. I was not nearly as sick as on the first day."

Gredin looked at him askance, and he laughed.

How long has it been since I heard someone laugh? she wondered. Rewarding him with a smile, she asked, "Do you have more to tell us?"

"Just that I continue to work on completing the lists of names and Houses and gyftes."

"Our thanks, Keegan, for all of your efforts."

"I am happy to do all that I can."

Gredin looked across the table at Burlon, the next in order to share his news. "Burlon, it is your turn. Please proceed."

"With so few races currently present on the station, our opportunities for Trade are less than ideal. Still, each new day brings a chance of new arrivals, and so we…"

Why did she find him so annoying? Maybe it was his unflagging energy, the nearly visible glow from being so in Balance from his dydanin with Chenna. She didn't begrudge him time with his Chosen. How could she, when his days were spent ensuring the safety of the community? But she wished she could absorb the excess hlinga he seemed to shed. She found the long days ever more taxing. Lately, she crawled onto her mat soon after evening meal, falling deeply asleep almost before she could pull the pouch of stones from her pocket and place it beneath her pillow…

"Gredin? Are you listening?

Chagrined, Gredin shook her head. "Apologies, Burlon. I *am* listening now. Please continue."

"Very well." He gave her a searching look. "I will save my concerns for the end of my account. But be warned, I intend to talk to you bluntly about them."

His words lay like sacks of besk berries across her shoulders, weighing her down. It was barely past morning meal, yet she was so tired that she dreaded facing the line of questioners who gathered while she sat here, making the best plans she could for the community.

Burlon cleared his throat. "I've sent another request to the Hesch enclave, to set a time to initiate a Trading session."

"How many requests is that?" Keegan inquired, pen at the ready.

"Three," Burlon replied sourly, "and I'm still awaiting a response."

Gredin's anxiety sharpened. "Why do you suppose they haven't replied? Is it because of what happened at the Market with Nitikikani?"

Burlon shrugged. "I don't see why it would be. The Judgment went their way. It's hard to believe they would pass up the opportunity to trade with us, given the profit they stand to make. I wouldn't, if our positions were reversed." He shook his head. "It's annoying… but Trading with the Hesch often is."

Miri and Sill seemed to accept Burlon's words without concern, but the explanation rang hollow to her. "And what if this third message goes unanswered? Contact them with a fourth?"

"No," Burlon said, looking cross. "If I don't receive a response soon, I'll seek them out at the Traders' Market."

"Is that wise?"

Burlon's expression morphed into the one Gredin disliked the most: his unreadable Trader's face. "By the time our Historian finds a Prett grain our bellies can tolerate," he said, "I'll have obtained plenty of Hesch food stuffs to accompany our porridge. No need to worry."

"I have been charged by the Power to worry," Gredin said tartly, rubbing her brow.

"Well, the food situation is in hand, although it may not seem so to you. And I have good news on a different matter. Ingarra has made a start on the Sprygalian *timte* quilt."

Just hearing Ingarra's name made Gredin feel better. It had been days since she had talked to her former Guide. Perhaps she could join Ingarra and Beda for evening meal.

"She's recruited several other Needleworkers to aid her," Burlon continued, "and she seems confident they can complete it soon."

Gredin smiled. "Ingarra is a marvel. I am eager to see the finished quilt."

"But she is concerned," Burlon added, "that she has so little material in her workbag that is appropriate for the project."

"Ingarra has high standards. It is what makes her work exceptional."

"Oh, I've come to appreciate Ingarra's talent, and her kindness. She wasn't complaining. She was only making certain I understood that she would need more material to create a quilt as elaborate as I require."

"She'll want to make her own selections." Gredin was certain of that.

"I'll take her to the Shodekekeen maartza and buy her whatever she needs."

"Tetralanna said the red fabric the Shodekekeen gave to me was expensive. Can we afford the supplies you'll need?"

"Whatever we spend, we'll profit many times over when I take the quilt to Sprygale." Burlon leaned back in his chair. "You realize, Gredin, that I must Travel the River to deliver it?"

A sweet-faced woman, her red-rimmed eyes dark with grief, clutched her hands. "Let me leave, I beg you, Gredin te Balamont. My little ones await me at home. They'll be missing me, as will my Chosen. You're the one the Power talks to. Please, Gredin, ask the Power to see me safely home."

Gredin's heart ached. "Tell me your name."

"I am Jallaina. Jallaina te Shelahn."

"Jallaina, hear me. Venna is no more. Your loved ones have returned to the Source."

"No. You're wrong," Jallaina whispered. "Let me go home." She began to weep in earnest, her dark-gold hair unkempt. "Just let me go..."

"And if I'll be Traveling the River when the quilt is finished, there's no reason why I and the rest of the Travelers can't begin the search for New Venna immediately. Today even. Keegan and Sill affirm that many have passed through the worst of their grief. What task could be more uplifting for a Traveler than the search for our new home? Let us go, Gredin."

"Let me go..."

"No," Gredin said, cold inside. "It's still too soon for you and the other Travelers. Most of the people I talk with are not in Balance. And the few who seem steadier are fixated on having their questions answered. Based on the hundreds I have talked with, the community is still shaken. In fact, some seem more distressed than ever."

Keegan looked up from his writing. "Perhaps it seems so because you are dealing with those most mired in grief and shock."

"Nevertheless, we will wait a bit longer."

"I'm glad you brought up the folks in line," Burlon countered, his jaw taut. "How can you not see that you're wasting your time, meeting with people one by one?"

"The people need to know that I value their concerns. It gives me a chance to meet the individuals of our community, and to learn their names and Houses."

"Keegan is gathering that information."

Gredin lifted her chin. "They need to know that *I* hear them. It builds trust."

Fine words, Gredin thought, *but how many times have I wanted to scream at them to go away, or to stop whining over minor inconveniences? Can't they see how tired I am? Don't they know it hurts when they compare me to Tetralanna, and find me lacking, or berate me for not weeping as they do? Who are they to judge me? Who are they to judge the Power's actions?*

Burlon snorted. "It's not effective. Look at the length of the line. I've seen people finish talking with you and walk straight to the end again, instead of going about their business."

Does he sense how much I want to rebuke individuals who think they can receive the answer they desire, simply by asking again? "Stopping now would only upset people more."

"I'd rather deal with indignant individuals than have you collapse from exhaustion, Gredin. How can you lead effectively if you don't have the time and energy? You're wasting most of every day on this endeavor."

"It's not a waste." She held up a hand as he started to talk again. "I'll see what progress I make today, then reevaluate."

"If you must. But be sure to eat. And stand and walk around, from time to time. You are more than a mind and a gyfte. Don't ignore your vessel."

"You should make them all sit down and eat their meals like decent folk," Miri added.

Burlon stared, incredulous. "Are you saying that people skip meals to stand in line? I would have thought they'd be too hungry for such foolishness."

"They're not going hungry," Gredin explained. "They eat their food in line."

It sounded benign. But she knew that the reality was altogether different…

People were finally starting to gather for midday meal. Relieved that a break was at hand, Gredin stretched her sore back after bidding Neeth te Darius goodbye, and decided she would talk with one more person before rising to seek her own meal.

Movement, and the scent of food, caught her attention.

It took her several moments to understand what she was seeing. In twos and threes, people were leaving the line – but only to claim food from nearby tables. Everyone who left returned with two bowls and passed the extra bowl to the person who had held their spot in line.

And then they began to eat, standing up, rather than cede their place.

Such behavior would never have occurred on Venna. The shock of their world's loss was eroding core habits and civilities. Fighting discouraged tears, Gredin Fetched her own bowl and motioned for the person next in line to come forward…

"That's ridiculous," Burlon stated emphatically.

"It isn't ideal," she admitted, remembering how difficult it had been for her to snatch quick bites while an individual framed their question. She'd had to rewarm the food in her bowl repeatedly, since it chilled while she gave her responses.

"I'm going to hold you to your word, Gredin. See how matters progress today, and we'll discuss this again at tomorrow's meeting."

How could that sound like a threat, when she herself had proposed the idea?

"Is there anything else you wish to put forward, Burlon?" Gredin asked, longing to insist that he had no such authority over her.

"No. I'm done, for the moment."

Relieved, she said, "My thanks for your patience, Miri. We're ready for your food update."

"The Wilra grain is a blessing. I'm grateful, Burlon, that you obtained it so quickly from the Prett, while we can still intersperse it with some of our remaining lissanthel flour. It should tide us over for a good twenty days or more."

"Everything so far has been quite tasty," Burlon admitted.

"I hold a meeting with the other kitchen Tenders, after the dishes from evening meal are put to rest. We plan a tentative menu for the following day. And we experiment, the next day, trying out new ideas and flavor combinations."

"What happens if your experiments are less than successful?" Sill asked.

"We eat them for our own meal." Her hazel eyes sparkled. "That was the first rule I put in place, to keep everyone firmly grounded."

That drew smiles around the table.

"It will be wonderful when Burlon obtains more foods for us to work with. Until he does, you'll see a lot of porridge and bread."

"Do you have other concerns to share?"

"That's everything for now, Gredin."

"Then it's my turn." She smiled. "The first section of new quarters will be ready soon, perhaps by late tomorrow. I think the community will be pleased by the amount of space and privacy the Prett are providing. Since we plan to move House Balamont first, I'd like to announce it today so the House members can prepare."

"Once Balamont moves out of the reception hall, we'll have more space for dining and Making," Burlon said. "Maybe even for dances."

"Dances?" Keegan repeated.

"Don't sound so shocked, Historian. People need exercise, and dancing provides a pleasant opportunity for that."

"As long as no one is pressed to participate, I could see it raising spirits," Sill said, looking thoughtful. "I'll inquire among the Musicians if you like, Gredin."

"Thank you, Sill. That would be helpful."

"Anything else we should know?" Burlon asked, a hint of challenge in his voice.

"One more thing. Today, Wyve is sending cushions to be used under our bedmats, enough for everyone to have their own."

"If they're anything like the cushion on my bed in the Clinic," Keegan said, "Miri may need to delay tomorrow's morning meal. Everyone will still be sleeping!"

Miri wagged her finger at him. "We'll see what wins out – hungry stomachs or comfortable bones." But she smiled at his jest, nonetheless.

Gredin wished she could prolong the moment of camaraderie. These four people were the foundation beneath her Power-appointed role as leader of the community.

Why, then, did everything feel so impossible at times?

"I believe we are finished." She rose and offered them her crossed palms and a bow. "My thanks to you all. May the Power bless this day's tasks."

But she wished, as she left the table, that she was going anywhere but back to her place on that hard bench, to face the endless line of anguished survivors.

[15]
1742 OF 2000 ORBITS REMAINING: 29ORANGE

Eleven Traders. Punctures and pus! How can there be just eleven Traders left alive?

Burlon strode down the public corridor, unsure whether the knot in his middle came from fury or fear. Preparing for the Trisectoriana, he and Cirin had recruited kitchen Tenders, a major Healer, a fistful of minor Healers, Speakers, Assessors, a First of Memory, a writer of Histories, Growers, more than a dozen kinds of Makers, and enough Travelers to make him wonder if it was possible to overcrowd the River… and they'd only brought eleven Traders? To *Tradepoint*?

Rashes and hives. What had they been thinking?

Better not to ask. They hadn't *been* thinking, not clearly, or they never would have journeyed here with fewer than a dozen of the people who understood Tradepoint best.

Of course, no one knew they'd be stranded here, dependent on Traders for the very food on their plates. It was supposed to be a four-day trip.

Now, instead, Venna was destroyed.

He himself had gained a Chosen and lost his House.

And Cirin was dead. What was he supposed to do with *that*? Every time he remembered, he felt as if he'd swallowed a bag of hefty, jagged rocks.

Bubbling with anger and grief, Burlon swung around the corner–

–and nearly barreled into three portly F'lala. They recoiled, their white hair puffing up. Startled, Burlon took three quick steps backward in reaction.

For a frozen moment, the tableau held: three frightened F'lala facing a lanky, panting Vennan. Well, that wouldn't do. Burlon dropped to one knee and said, in hasty Tradetalk, "Much pardon ask. Make hurry, go careless. Much regret." He looked at the floor, letting his averted gaze underscore his apology.

The F'lala murmured amongst themselves in their native tongue, an incomprehensible language that sounded to Burlon as if they spoke underwater. He held his position, letting them determine whether to let the matter drop or prolong the encounter. He owed them that much.

One of them made a burbling sound, then said, in Tradetalk, "F'lala talk Thalken."

What was *that* supposed to mean? The Thalken had left port. And what did they have to do with the current situation? Bewildered, Burlon straightened, silent.

"Thalken go Vennan enclave, other night."

Ah. They were talking about the reception. "Yes," Burlon agreed, although he and Chenna had left for the heady solitude of their dydanin before the foreign guests arrived.

"After, Thalken talk F'lala. Say night stop much quick. Say Vennan kirntaykla end."

Vennan kirntaykla? Burlon looked at them, confused. Then understanding struck him. *Vennan Cirin te K'lar.* The Thalken had told the F'lala of Cirin's death.

Slowly, he nodded.

"F'lala know this Vennan kirntaykla. F'lala sorry hear make end."

"I thank," Burlon said, his voice gone to gravel.

"Speak other matter?" the F'lala asked, its tone brightening. "Trade question?"

And, just that quickly, they're back to business, Burlon thought sadly. But what did he expect? Did he really wish to prolong a discussion of Cirin's death, here in the public corridors?

"Trade question," he affirmed. "You ask."

The lead F'lala looked pleased. "Thalken say Vennan make music." Seeing Burlon's puzzled look, it clarified, "At enclave."

The Musicians. The dance, where he had found Chenna… Afterwards, when he and she had left the hall, the Musicians and dancers performed for the guests. "Yes," he affirmed.

"Thalken say much good."

The Thalken rarely condescended to acknowledge that anything not crafted by the Thalken themselves could be 'much good.' But he remembered Keegan's words, the day after the reception, about the Thalken being caught up in the music…

Something for nothing, Burlon thought, and his Trader's gyfte came alert. "Yes," he said, and added, "Sorry no F'lala come, that night."

"Thalken go home."

It was a fact. What point was the F'lala trying to make by stating it? Burlon just nodded.

The F'lala shifted its stance slightly. "F'lala still here."

Ah. "F'lala still here," Burlon agreed.

The F'lala patted a wayward poof of white hair, smoothing it into conformance. "Vennans make more music?"

Burlon tried to look bewildered by the question. "More?" he echoed.

The F'lala hesitated, and Burlon wondered if he should have offered a more encouraging response. It was a sort of game between traders, neither side wanting to express too much desire when a new deal was contemplated. But the F'lala had already come a certain distance down that path by bringing up the topic of music in the first place.

After a moment, the F'lala drew itself up and asked, "Vennan make music for F'lala?"

There it was: a request.

Burlon adopted a thoughtful look, then let it warm into a smile. "Maybe so. Will ask Vennan who make music. Is hurry?"

The F'lala wobbled its head in negation. "F'lala green."

Green. So the F'lala were only midway through their current rotations. Plenty of time.

"Good," Burlon said. "I talk music Vennan tonight, tomorrow. See if say yes." And he took a tentative step forward, as if to continue on his way.

The F'lala's hand moved – a small gesture, but one for which Burlon had been watching.

Obligingly, he stopped.

"What trade?" the F'lala asked.

It was a fair question. To the best of Burlon's knowledge, musical performances were a new concept on Tradepoint. There was no precedent for price. The F'lala were interested, which could mean a lucrative exchange. On the other hand, presenting a musical performance cost the Vennans nothing, so anything the F'lala paid would be pure profit. And if they were pleased with the performance, and considered it worth the price, they might return for more, or recommend Vennan musical performances to other races, as the Thalken had made the recommendation to them. There was the length of performance to consider, and whether to present only instrumental music or include vocal performances. No one had sung, at the reception, so far as he knew, so perhaps that novelty was best reserved for some future date…

But should the price be set in station credits or in goods?

"Depend," he said – a Tradetalk word central to every deal. "What F'lala have?"

"Vennan come Trader Market, our maartza, see F'lala goods."

Burlon didn't have to feign his reluctance. The F'lala dealt mostly in tech. He was hoping for something out of the ordinary – preferably edible. "Music not maartza goods," he pointed out. "F'lala maybe offer something not maartza goods."

The F'lala looked flustered. "What Vennan want?"

The most casual of shrugs. "Not know. Maybe… something eat?

"Vennan want F'lala food?"

"Maybe. Not know. Look. Taste. Like new. Like surprise." He

thought back over the tales he had heard about the reception. "Music night, Beng come Venna enclave. Bring flagle. F'lala know flagle?"

The F'lala's eyes opened wide. "Not know this word."

"Flagle new. Vennan like eat new. Like eat surprise."

"F'lala not know flagle."

"No matter. Maybe have F'lala food Vennan never try. Trade new music, new food." When the F'lala hesitated, Burlon changed tactics. He didn't want the F'lala to disengage from the entire transaction because they were embarrassed not to have anything desirable to offer. "Or you trade station credits for Vennan music. We find some good deal make, you, me."

It was a commitment. Now he had to work out some acceptable compromise, even if it meant underpricing the music on this first occasion. The F'lala's continued good will was worth it. And who knew what opportunities such a Trade might awaken?

"I go Traders' Market now," he said. "Look F'lala maartza. Later, I talk Vennan make music. Message F'lala later."

All three F'lala nodded, and one said, "I ask F'lala food. Message Vennan later."

Burlon crossed his upturned palms to them and bowed his head briefly. "Have good day."

"Good day. Again, sorry hear Vennan kirntaykla end."

"I thank," Burlon said, and moved past them, continuing on his way.

But his spirits sank. The Thalken had clearly spent time on idle gossip before they left Tradepoint. Was his visit to the Traders' Market going to be filled with people's reactions to Cirin's death? The temptation to return to the enclave and Chenna was strong.

He hardened his resolve. It was important to reopen the Vennan maartza soon, and he wanted to survey the Traders' Market first, see what was being offered in the other maartzas, in order to select the best array of goods from the warehouse. New and different always brought better prices.

And he had another motive for visiting the Market. Three times in two days, he had dispatched a message to the Hesch to open a dialogue about available edible goods in the current Hesch cargo. It was a step that saved time if the desired items had already sold or were in short supply. He often forwarded such inquiries, and received prompt answers, to help plan which purchases to complete and which maartzas to approach first.

But he had received no reply from the Hesch.

Well, no matter. He would approach them at their maartza and see for himself what was available. Trades always came down to a face-to-face meeting, in the end.

It felt good to be walking the corridors, not huddled at that too-small table with Gredin and the others, or sitting on a crowded bench in the reception hall for meals. As a Trader, he enjoyed people, drawing energy from his interactions with them. But he was also a Traveler, and Travelers liked their privacy. *Needed* their privacy. If it weren't so, they could not so happily undertake solitary journeys upon the River.

With his twin gyftes, Burlon was a walking contradiction, not quite content in either state.

It's no kindness to have too many gyftes, Cirin had asserted. *It leaves you unsettled, divided in your attentions. I'd rather be what I am, through and through – a Traveler, never happier than when I am launched upon the River.*

But Cirin had evanesced. Having returned to the Source, was he now part of the River he so loved?

"Don't think about it," Burlon said aloud.

When he reached the entrance to the Market, he examined the light board to see which maartzas were open for trade. Only five maartzas were open: the Beng, the F'lala, the Hesch, the Polpethtira, and the Shodekekeen. An unusually scanty count. Just his luck.

Well, tomorrow the Vennans would bring that total to six. And Wyve talked as if the Rodorno were expected soon. Happily, there was no sign of the Chibi. Having the Chibi and the Beng in port at the same time was enough to try everyone's patience. And the Anamandasit and the Kikaradd were both absent, so he was spared their endless feud and the bickering that accompanied it. It was anyone's guess when the

Wilra would glide into port, but he privately hoped they would manage it before long. He had bought up every sack of Wilra grain available, and he wasn't sure what he would do when those stores were gone.

Wouldn't it be grand if some heretofore unknown race arrived, their cargo hold loaded with fresh fruits and vegetables? But that was unlikely. Fresh fruits and vegetables were a touchy, time-sensitive cargo. The Vennans had always been able to get away with bringing fresh fruits and vegetables because the River journey between Venna and Tradepoint was a relatively short one. But the other races who frequented Tradepoint journeyed in metal ships, and it took them long and long to make the voyage – far too long for most fruits and vegetables to tolerate the trip.

Apparently, flagle was an exception.

The thought brought a faint smile to Burlon's lips. The Beng were nasty little toe-stubbers. But if their ill-intentioned offering became a legitimate food source for the Vennan community, he might even forgive some of their past annoyances.

Still smiling wryly, he pressed his palm to the lighted plate, waited while the door completed its scan, and watched the immense doors to the Traders' Market slide open.

People moving. Traders talking. Lights gleaming on offered wares. A distant glint of blue fur – some Shodekekeen returning to its maartza. An elusive scent of spice that made his nose twitch. High overhead, blue-white lights glared, harsh and revealing, their muted reflections appearing on the scuffed metal floor plates like cloud-covered moons.

The Traders' Market.

Something deep within him relaxed in a recognition that went far beyond the visual. This place was crafted to gratify his Trader's gyfte. It felt like a second home to him.

Or – now and for the immediate future – his first and only home.

The striding gait that helped him traverse Tradepoint's corridors with quick efficiency served little purpose in the Market. This was a place to meander from maartza to maartza with the calm air of disinterest that served Traders well. Only his gaze betrayed him, keen and canny as he examined each new display.

His scale of interest had recalibrated between his last visit and today. All his senses were open, all prejudgments suspended. The filter by which he had long judged an item's desirability for import to House Bentain was nearly useless now, for it differed widely from his current awareness of the new community's needs.

Before, he had Traded to enrich his House, to bring its members pleasure. Now he Traded to ensure the survival of his people.

Burlon took his time, allowing the ambience of the Market to soothe his worries. The roomy, free-standing structures that housed the maartzas were each identical in size and construction – high-ceilinged, deep, and formed from metal, as everything on Tradepoint was metal. They were arranged in rows, with a broad aisle separating each row from the next, and an equally spacious area between each maartza and its nearest neighbor. Crowding bred quarrels, and so the Prett provided plenty of space for all.

Each trading race brought its own unique goods to the Traders' Market, displaying those goods and decorating their maartza in accordance with their own race's aesthetic. Some maartzas were familiar to him from his many past visits to them. For others, he barely spared a glance, already knowing that their shelves held nothing that appealed to a Vennan.

And so he began by simply walking the aisles, glancing from side to side, seeing which maartzas were busy and which were idle. The Hesch, he saw, were dealing with a group of flossy-haired F'lala, while a slender Polpethtira lingered a few steps from the Hesch entrance, clearly intending to visit once the F'lala departed.

Fine. He would deal with the Hesch later, when no one was waiting.

As he started to turn away, the purple-skinned Polpethtira turned her head and, spotting him, gave a little jump, looking pleased. A moment later, abandoning her vigil, she stepped lithely to Burlon's side.

"Vennan?" she asked, as if to confirm his identity, and Burlon hid a smile as he nodded. It was hard to imagine her confusing him with any other race currently in the maartza. Shodekekeen were blue-furred, bear-like creatures who sometimes moved about on all six legs but could also stand upright on their back two. Hesch, who resembled birds, including their long beaks, were tall and almost skeletally thin, black from head to clawed feet. Beng were short and squatty, always dressed in green coveralls, with identically cut brown hair. They walked about in packs, largely indistinguishable from one another. F'lala, with whom he had just dealt in the corridor, were taller than Beng but plump, topped by clouds of white hair.

Of all the races present, he supposed Polpethtira and Vennans were most alike, physically, but that wasn't saying much. Both races were slender. Both walked upright on two feet. Their facial features were similarly cast. But Vennans were tall, with fair skin and hair. Vennan Traders could be male or female, but in the Traders' Market, their clothing was the same: jackets and pants in sober shades of blue or brown or green. Polpethtira were much shorter, with deep purple skin and no hair at all. Amongst themselves, they communicated through hand gestures, and their traders were exclusively female. Polpethtira wore no clothing, preferring to adorn themselves with intricate white designs painted onto their bodies.

And so Burlon was amused by the Polpethtira's wish to be assured that he was Vennan. But he had no wish to offend, so he kept his expression sober. "Yes. Vennan."

"Polpethtira orange," she said. "Go soon."

Again, Burlon had to bite back a smile. The purple-skinned Polpethtira was not actually orange, but he understood her meaning: her Tradeteam was down to its final segment of orbits. Soon, they would leave Tradepoint.

"Before go, want make trade Vennan."

Burlon attempted to hide his surprise. After an early Trade that Cirin had made with them purely for diplomacy's sake, several sectoria ago, the tech-producing Polpethtira had not been customers of theirs. "What want?" he asked, genuinely curious.

"Trip home long. Ship food..." She made an eloquent face that made it clear how little she thought of Polpethtiran shipboard cuisine. "Want Vennan food like other night."

Yes, well, don't we all? Burlon thought, reflecting on the many delicacies served at the reception, and the nourishing but unexciting fare currently gracing the enclave's tables. With regret, he said, "Vennan maartza no sell food."

The Polpethtira's fingers fluttered as if in distress, but she didn't retreat. "No maartza. Small food. Small crew." She held up five fingers. "Please you ask basket girl?"

Basket girl? "Much sorry, but–"

The Polpethtiran trader touched her own chest, then reached out her fingers stopping just short of Burlon. "We pay good. Know what Vennan like. Baskets. Credits. You pick."

It was a calculated suggestion. The Polpethtira sold all manner of high tech *griimoni* in their maartza – things that were of no use to Vennans. But this little trader seemed to know that. And what was this mention of a *basket girl*?

A glance showed him that the Hesch were still dickering with the F'lala. With a philosophical shrug, Burlon said, "You show." And he followed the little trader down the aisle.

At the Polpethtira maartza, no customers were present, so he and the trader went inside immediately. The trader on duty looked up as they entered, her expression sharpening to interest as Burlon's companion commenced a flurry of hand gestures. One of them ushered him to a seat while the other vanished into the back room of the maartza, returning soon with a metal tray loaded down with three tiny cups, an intricately woven basket, its design consisting of white strands and other strands that were the same dark blue as the wafers it contained, and a tall, lidded pitcher from which a curl of steam emerged.

Burlon watched, fascinated. He had passed the Polpethtira maartza hundreds of times but had never seen them offer hospitality to anyone. Every instinct of his gyfte urged him to relax into the situation. Hospitality once spurned would likely never be offered again. For the foreseeable future, now that the Vennans were forced into full-time residency on Tradepoint, it was more important than ever to cultivate good relations with other Tradeteams.

The decision carried with it a degree of danger. Keegan te Fliss underwent daily, supervised food tests at the Prett Clinic because not everything edible was acceptable to a Vennan body. And here *he* was, in the middle of the Traders' Market, preparing to sip an unidentified hot beverage and nibble on wafers offered to him by the Polpethtira.

But he would be cautious. And he trusted his gyfte.

The beverage, when they poured it into the little cups, was pale pink and smelled faintly of flowers. Imitating the actions of the Polpethtiran traders, he lifted the cup between the fingers of both hands, blew briefly across its steaming surface, and took a small sip.

Flavor uncoiled in his mouth in a potent cloud of spice, with a delicately sweet aftertaste.

Delighted by it, Burlon fought down the urge to take another swallow immediately. Instead, he nodded and smiled to indicate his pleasure, then set the cup carefully aside and accepted a wafer from the basket.

From its appearance, he expected the blue wafer to be crisp. Instead, it was chewy, with a texture more like the edible skin of a fruit than like any baked good he had ever eaten. When he bit down on it, it resisted a bit, giving off a fresh burst of flavor each time his teeth compressed it. As to what the flavor was… he was at a loss to identify it, or even think of a fair comparison. It was primarily moist in the mouth, with a faint, pleasant taste that wavered between savory and sweet.

He had bitten off only a small corner of the wafer, yet it kept him chewing for quite some time. The flavor, though subtle, didn't fade; the final chewed bit was as pleasing as the first bite.

And suddenly the Polpethtira's wish to purchase a small amount of left-over food from the reception seemed far more acceptable to him. He would have said that the *last* thing he needed to do was sell any of the little food they had, especially party treats made from Vennan ingredients – and for what? *Griimoni*? Or even baskets? The baskets were eye-catching, as was the carpet he was sitting on, but you couldn't eat them.

But this tea and these wafers were something new. How much

supply did the Polpethtira have here with them? How available was it, on their home world? How willing might they be to accept an order today and bring more with them on their return? People in the community sorely missed their besk. But if Miri could offer people a steaming cup of *this* tea…

Or, in his desperation, was he making it out to be better than it was?

He set the rest of the wafer aside and picked up the tiny cup. Being small, its contents cooled quickly, and Burlon was able to take a sip directly, without blowing on it to cool it.

Again, a complex cloud of spice, with a faint tickle of sweetness at the end. Wonderful.

The Polpethtiran traders were watching him. When he met their gaze, the one who had brought him to the maartza asked, "I show baskets now?"

Burlon offered them a slow smile. "Baskets good. Drink *very* good. We talk Trade maybe, very good Polpethtiran drink for very good Vennan food?"

They looked bewildered. "This drink?" the spokeswoman asked on a note of disbelief.

He gave a slight shrug. "Is nice change from Vennan drink," he said, belatedly wary of showing too much enthusiasm. But the Polpethtira had let their guard down, too, allowing him to see that they didn't consider the tea anything noteworthy.

He set the cup down and lifted the wafer. "This good, too. Maybe Trade both?"

The Polpethtira fluttered their fingers at each other, disconcerted, then turned back to him. "Polpethtira trade tech. Know Vennan not like tech. Basket girl say basket beautiful. We take same to her at Vennan reception. Now we ask trade Vennan food, make trip home happy time. We ask what want. You say trade Vennan food for tharaman, maybe chingee." Their expressions were sober, their eyes wide. "You make joke Polpethtira?"

Burlon felt a twinge deep within – not from the food and drink, he was sure, but from his gyfte's awareness that matters were going awry. Did the Polpethtira think he was mocking them?

Quickly, he raised one hand, fingertips to the ceiling, palm to the Polpethtira – a Tradetalk gesture asking for a pause, usually as part of a request for clarification.

They nodded their permission for him to proceed.

With care, he pointed into his cup at the remaining liquid. "Is *tharaman*?"

An affirmative nod.

Holding the wafer between thumb and forefinger, he tilted it. "Is *chingee*?"

Again, a nod.

He set the wafer down beside the cup, crossed his palms to the Polpethtira, and briefly bowed his head. "Vennan no laugh. Vennan no make joke. Vennan much like *tharaman*, much like *chingee*. Want serve *tharaman, chingee* to many Vennan. Many, many Vennan. Want make Trade. Polpethtira want small Vennan food for small crew go home. Vennan want big *tharaman, chingee* for many, many Vennan. Offer you small Vennan food, offer station credit. Is possible? We talk this thing?"

A shy nod. "We talk."

He pointed at the pitcher. "Polpethtira have *tharaman* here? In maartza? In warehouse?"

One of the traders waggled her hand. So, they had… some. More, at least, than the single pitcher sitting before him, but not as much as he sought. If he understood the situation properly, they brought *tharaman* to Tradepoint for themselves and the occasional favored customer.

He was eager to change that.

"Polpethtira go home soon, yes?"

A nod.

"*Tharaman* come from Polpethtira home?"

A nod.

"Vennan want make deal. Vennan want Polpethtira come back Tradepoint, bring much *tharaman* for Vennan."

He was being precipitous. He should approach the whole matter slowly, not least because he was basing his current belief in the safety of *tharaman* and *chingee* on two sips and a nibble.

But sometimes Trade was like that. You simply trusted your gyfte and took action when the opportunity arose. The Polpethtira were leaving soon, and he wanted this deal. At worst, he was committing the community to today's Trade and one additional shipment. That was survivable, even if his judgment turned out to be misplaced.

And that could happen. There might yet be a problem with Vennans ingesting *tharaman* and *chingee*. Or the taste might not be as universally popular as he assumed it would be.

But he didn't believe it. This was going to work. It was going to boost morale. People could drink *tharaman* in place of their beloved besk. And a single *chingee* wafer would last a goodly while, as a snack or as an accompaniment to morning meal. If he and the Polpethtira could come to an agreement on the terms of the Trade, this would be a good day's work.

But he was making assumptions, based on food and drink which were unfamiliar. "You show me *tharaman*?" he requested.

They blinked, then gestured toward his cup.

He smiled and shook his head. "No." He gestured at the peculiar pitcher. "You show how Polpethtira make *tharaman*?" He needed to know what he would be asking Miri and the kitchen Tenders to undertake. Was *tharaman* like besk, the result of baking berries, then grinding them into a fine powder that dissolved in hot water? Or was it more like roin tea, where leaves of roin plants were harvested and dried, after which they could be stored almost indefinitely before being steeped in a pot or individual cup to the desired strength.

One of the Polpethtiran traders still looked puzzled, but the other nodded decisively and walked to the back room again. When she returned, she was carrying another tray on which rested a second tall, metal pitcher, a stoppered bottle, and a small metal box.

"You watch," she said, setting down the tray.

"I watch," Burlon assured her.

She grasped the empty pitcher with both hands, one hand low on its base, the other just beneath its spout, and twisted. It came apart in two pieces, and the Polpethtiran trader set the top portion aside.

In the lower portion, nestled at the bottom, was a small ball of perforated metal, with a metal button on its top. When the trader pressed the button, the tiny ball sprang open like a flower with four petals, revealing a hollow center.

Burlon watched closely, mystified.

Next, the trader opened the metal box, and Burlon recognized the box's contents: small balls of formed sugar. Several races on Tradepoint, including the Polpethtira, loved sweet things, and it was not uncommon for such traders to carry a few sugar balls in a protective case in their pocket, and pop one into their mouth when the mood struck. But he had never seen an entire box of the sugar balls.

The Polpethtiran trader plucked one from the box and placed it in the hollow center of the 'flower' at the base of the pitcher, then lifted the small bottle from the tray. She twisted the cap and drew it slowly upward, revealing a slender glass rod attached to the cap. When the rod was lifted clear of the bottle, he caught a whiff of the flower scent, and saw a pale pink drop of thick liquid form on the rounded tip of the rod.

"Tharaman," the trader said, slid the rod back down into the bottle, and refastened the cap. Next, in pantomime, she touched the bottle to the sugar ball once, twice, three times, and folded the four petals of the metal ball up around it until they clicked into place. The top and bottom halves of the tall pitcher were reunited, fitting together securely. Removing the pitcher's lid, she said, "Water. Much hot," and indicated a point near the top of the pitcher. "Then wait."

"How much wait?"

She gestured at the pouring lip. "No smell, no pour. Smell tharaman, drink good."

Burlon sat back, considering what he had just seen. The tharaman in the bottle must be a syrup or extract. Three drops went onto the sugar ball in its little perforated cage. Then hot water was poured in. Once the steam took on the fragrance of the tharaman, the tea was ready to serve.

At least, that was how Polpethtira prepared it. Vennan kitchen

Tenders would likely explore other methods since they'd be preparing it for a thousand people, not three.

He picked up his cup and swallowed the last of its contents, now entirely cool.

Even tepid, it was pleasing. And it would likely taste just as good without the sugar ball.

"We make two Trade, one small, one big?" he ventured, emboldened by the knowledge that the Polpethtira were down to the final days of their current stay. The closer to departure a Tradeteam came, the more direct their transactions became.

They gestured for him to continue.

Well, somebody had to go first.

"Small Trade now. We give Vennan food for journey, you give two bottle *tharaman*. Big trade, you bring many, many bottle *tharaman*, many, many basket *chingee*, we sit down together, agree on station credit price. Yes?"

Fingers flew in silent communication that left him in ignorance while the two traders conferred. At last, their hands settled into their laps, and one said, "Small trade, you give Vennan food for journey, we give one bottle tharaman, two basket chingee, one box kilam." Her gesture indicated the box of sugar rounds. She patted her chest twice in what appeared to be a gesture of apology, and said, "One bottle tharaman all we bring."

Burlon nodded. "Yes. Understand." He plunged ahead. "And big Trade?"

A nervous look. "Talk home. Ask. See. Want say yes but… talk home first."

It wasn't what he wanted to hear but it made sense. He was pushing them beyond their trading authority. They needed to consult before making a firm commitment.

"Understand," he said. "Trust Vennan. You bring, I buy. We find price make Polpethtira happy, make Vennan happy."

And there he had to leave it; his gyfte told him so. Burlon waited patiently while they produced a large cloth bag and placed within it the bottle of *tharaman*, two packets of the chewy blue *chingee*, and the metal box of *kilam* sugar rounds.

Then, to his consternation, they added the metal tray and the empty pitcher which had been used for the demonstration.

He opened his mouth to protest… but it was a tricky moment. The tray and pitcher could be a friend-boon, commemorating a new trading relationship. Or the objects could be a bribe. The Polpethtira were giving him their half of the trade goods now, unsecured, showing good faith that the Vennans would uphold their half of the deal by delivering the food packet. Enhancing their share with the tray and pitcher could also be an unspoken prompting for the Vennans to be equally openhanded.

What the Polpethtira didn't realize was that he, like they, was engaging in a Trade of unauthorized goods. He had no one's permission to barter away leftover Vennan delicacies from the reception. But food for five Polpethtira was a tiny thing, weighed against a thousand Vennans. What the Vennans stood to gain in good will and future Trades for *tharaman* and *chingee* was more than worth it.

He just had to persuade Miri of that. And Gredin.

Well, he would. He would make them see that this was a good Trade.

When Burlon left the Polpethtiran maartza, he made a conscious effort to dim his elated smile to an expression of casual affability. Showing excitement in the Traders' Market was unwise. Better to be calm and turn his thoughts toward the next Trade.

But, between the F'lala's interest in Vennan music and the Polpethtira's interest in Vennan food, this first trip to the Traders' Market was going unexpectedly well.

Holding to the discipline of his gyfte, he went next to the F'lala maartza, since he had promised to do so, and surveyed the goods offered there. But it was as he expected: shelf after shelf of *griimoni* and tech, none of which were of use or interest to him. If the F'lala to whom he'd spoken in the corridor didn't respond with an offer to sample some F'lala food, Burlon would simply set a price in station credits.

With his F'lala visit done, Burlon checked again on the status of the Hesch maartza and was pleased to find it empty of customers. He had Traded often with the Hesch, and he was eager to strike a deal today. The Hesch were known for luxury items, from wines and cordials to dried fruits and nuts. None of those goods would be a complete meal, but they could provide a touch of variety when Miri and her kitchen Tenders had to serve the same basic food at multiple meals.

And there was still the embarrassing matter of the Judgment to be gotten past. Now that the Vennans were constrained to stay on Tradepoint for the foreseeable future, it was important to regain a congenial footing. It unsettled him that the Hesch hadn't responded to his messages on the two previous days, but matters were easier to settle, face-to-face. And the Hesch had no reason to be dissatisfied. Yes, Gredin had accidentally injured the Hesch Tradeteam leader, Nitikikani, but every aspect of the Hesch's demand for compensation had been granted, including the out-sized monetary fine. Now he was coming in person to soothe their injured pride so that relations between Hesch and Vennans could return to normal.

From his vantage across the aisle, he glanced again to be sure the Hesch maartza was available. Yes. Two Hesch were inside, but no customers. The doorway's perimeter was unlit.

Taking his time, Burlon crossed the aisle and stepped through the sensor at the entrance to the Hesch maartza. His passage triggered a brief flash of light from the ceiling. Hesch had keen eyesight, and preferred visual cues to sounds or vibrations, which were the additional maartza-entrance options offered by the Prett.

The two Hesch moving amongst the shelves didn't acknowledge his presence.

"Good day to you," Burlon said, and set his bag of Polpethtira tradegoods just inside the door, to free his hands and avoid any potential confusion.

The Hesch continued working as if he wasn't there.

So, they wanted to be coaxed, did they? Normally, he would have left them to stew in their own self-importance. But that was another luxury he could no longer afford. He wanted no enemies or lingering grudges…with the exception of the Beng. The Beng were always in a snit about something, and would be as cross as a nest of merjins for sectora to come, given the debt assigned to them. But they deserved it. The whole thing had been their fault.

Nitikikani, on the other hand, hadn't even been in the Traders' Market when Gredin blundered into him and injured him, in her hurry to escape the Beng. And so Burlon would set aside his pride and be the one to mend matters. Gredin could thank him later.

Walking forward, he said, "Sorry for interrupt. Vennan want–"

"Stop talk. Leave."

He halted and, for good measure, retreated a pace. Crossing his palms, he inclined his head and said, "Two message I send. No reply. I come now just–"

"No talk. No trade. Go!"

Burlon's temper flared to life. This was not how traders dealt with one another. Still, he was in the Hesch's maartza as a supplicant, so he swallowed his annoyance. "I come bad time? Sorry. If want, I–"

One of the Hesch advanced on him, beak clacking. The other said, "Still talk? Maybe need Prett security, help find maartza door?"

"Hey!" Burlon objected and stood his ground. "Simple question! Hesch get my two message, no get my two message? Say. Then I go."

The first Hesch now towered over him, and Burlon's field of vision was dominated by gleaming black feathers and the rough-textured black and green gauze from which all Hesch clothing seemed to be fashioned. There was no actual contact between himself and the Hesch, but it was a near thing. He had never been so physically close to one.

The Hesch clacked its beak, and the sound was loud enough to make Burlon flinch.

Overhead lights flashed, indicating that someone else had entered the maartza. More Hesch? Not a happy thought.

Instead, a rumbling Prett voice announced, "Security."

"You take this Vennan out," the second Hesch said loudly. "Not welcome. Told go. He stay. Told again go. He stay. We no trade

Vennan. We no talk Vennan. You take Vennan out Hesch maartza, tell no come back."

Anger was rarely a Trader's friend. Burlon spread his arms at his side and eased back a step, taking great care not to brush against the confrontational Hesch looming over him. "I go," he said in Tradetalk, and added in Prett, for the benefit of the security guard, "I don't want an incident. Just help me leave. And I have a bag on the floor, near the door. I need to take that with me, if you can lift it carefully for me."

"Too much talk," the far Hesch objected. "Go now!"

Step by cautious step, Burlon retreated toward the doorway. The overhead lights flashed, most likely marking the Prett security guard's exit. When Burlon reached the threshold, his bag was gone – hopefully, into the custody of the guard. In any event, he couldn't pause to investigate. The first Hesch advanced as Burlon retreated, as if to force him from the maartza.

The lights flashed again as he moved backward into the public aisle. The Hesch stopped at the threshold, its bead-like eyes glimmering in the light.

The security guard said softly, in Prett, "Come away, trader. Let them cool."

It wasn't bad advice. After two more backward steps, Burlon dared to turn his head and look away from the Hesch's glare. The security guard was already heading down the aisle, carrying the bag containing the Polpethtiran tradegoods. Burlon started after him.

"You go, Vennan!" came a harsh shout from the Hesch maartza. "Hesch no want you here. Tell all Vennan trader stay away! No make Hesch call Security new time."

It was mortifying. Traders strolling the aisle swiveled to stare. Someone in the F'lala maartza came to its entrance, no doubt to see what the commotion was about. Burlon could feel his cheeks flaming. But a shouting match would resolve nothing. He straightened his spine and followed the Prett security guard.

For the first time in his life, Burlon was glad to leave the Traders' Market behind.

[16]
1709 OF 2000 ORBITS REMAINING: 10GREEN

Gredin had no appetite.

She watched the others tuck into their morning meal eagerly, but all she felt was a bone-deep weariness. Using her finger sticks, she placed a dumpling in her mouth and chewed listlessly.

"Is it not to your liking?" Miri inquired.

Gredin quickly swallowed the dumpling. "It's good, Miri. Truly. I just don't seem to be hungry." She dredged up a reassuring smile. "But I continue to marvel at your ingenuity."

Rather than accepting the compliment with her customary wide smile, Miri said glumly, "It was Brinlin's idea to fill the dumplings with a mixture made from the vegetables the Prett returned after harvesting the seeds. I had her lead the preparations for morning meal. I just couldn't stay organized. I was more of a hindrance than a help, I'm afraid."

Gredin groped for something comforting to say to bolster her friend's spirits.

Burlon, as had become his habit, spoke first. He seemed to be in fine form, fresh from a night with Chenna. "You've worked hard ever since we arrived on Tradepoint," he told Miri, "rising early and not retiring until late. You're overly tired."

“We’ve all worked hard,” Miri protested.

Sill set her finger sticks aside. “True, but in different ways. I exercise my gyfte a great deal during the day, but it requires far less physical effort than your gyfte.”

“And you’ve helped me with the warehouse inventory,” Keegan added, “when you should be resting.”

“I’d rather stay busy,” Miri assured him.

“Perhaps an early night would help,” Sill advised. “It isn’t wise to use your gyfte without adequate rest and nourishment.”

Their concern seemed to embarrass Miri. “Pay no attention to my grumbling. We have more important matters to discuss,” she protested, and cast a beseeching look at Gredin.

“Several,” Gredin said, to rescue her. “I will share them as soon as we have gone around the table. Sill?”

The First of Memory sipped broth from her bowl, then said, “The improvement I saw in the community seems to have slowed. Vik is troubled by this as well. Oh, and I spoke to Sarson te Vell, who coordinated the Musicians for the reception. He will consult those with gyfte of Music. He seems to think most will be eager for a chance to exercise their gyfte. He promised to seek me out once he has spoken with them all.”

“Contact me as soon as you have news,” Burlon directed. Gredin experienced a flare of irritation at his assertive manner, then felt foolish when he added, “I am eager to get back to the F’lala while they are still interested, to make the most profitable arrangement I can.”

“Of course, Burlon.”

“Well done, Sill,” Gredin said. “Keegan? How did you fare with the Prett food yesterday?”

“I wish I had better news. The Prett grain has all proven to be unacceptable. But Binn and I have not lost hope. We will try a fruit or vegetable today.”

Gredin grimaced. “I am sorry that your willingness to aid the community has caused you such unpleasantness.”

“It will not continue indefinitely,” he assured her, and grinned. “At some point, Binn will simply run out of new foods to outrage my insides."

The kind-natured historian, last of his House, was proving to be a true friend and staunch ally. And how did she reward his unflagging support? By having him go daily to the Clinic to ingest strange foods that caused him to become miserably sick.

Perhaps her thoughts showed, for Keegan said, "Do not blame yourself, Gredin. Binn is determined to prevent any serious harm from befalling me." Keegan smiled. "And her refusal to leave my bedside has had an unforeseen benefit. She assists me with the *crabe* while we wait between bites of food. I am making good progress, thanks to her help and the *crabe*'s tutorial. I've even learned a few words of Tradetalk in the process."

"I could ask a Trader to sit with you at meals and converse in Tradetalk, if you want to improve your ease with that language," Burlon offered.

"I am perfectly capable of assisting Keegan with that," Gredin objected, then exclaimed in annoyance as her grasp on her finger sticks slipped. The slender implements fell to the floor, taking the last dumpling she had been nibbling with them, leaving messy blotches on the Shodekekeen fabric she wore. "Desh," she muttered, vexed by her lack of coordination.

"I see them," Keegan announced, peering beneath the small table. The finger sticks reappeared next to her bowl. The dumpling appeared a scant moment later. "Don't worry, Gredin. I've Cleansed it all."

"My, thanks." Cheeks aflame, Gredin turned her attention to the spots on her clothing, applying her Focus and Control. But nothing happened. The spots remained, taunting her.

Stunned, she concentrated, pushing her fatigue aside. With grim effort, she cleansed the rich Shodekekeen fabric spot by spot, returning it to its former pristine state. By the time she completed the task, sweat beaded her hairline, and her hands were trembling.

"… wrong? Gredin?"

She blinked, slowly coming back to awareness. Which of her companions had spoken? She tried to recall the voice, but it was a blur.

Licking dry lips, she said, “Your pardon. I… I allowed my mind to wander.” She offered a shaky smile. “It appears you are not the only one with wayward thoughts this morning, Miri.”

Burlon nudged her glass of water closer, his gaze searching. “I told you, meeting with folks one by one is too taxing, Gredin. Take a drink. You’re far too pale.”

“And eat,” Sill urged.

Gredin wanted to do neither. She felt queasy, but if she admitted she was in difficulty, Burlon would bundle her off to her sleeping mat and take over. She had no intention of leaving the remainder of the meeting – and any subsequent decisions – in his hands. The Power only knew what he might convince the others to do in her absence.

Carefully, she lifted the glass and took a sip, forcing her hands to remain steady as she set the glass aside. Then, mimicking Sill, she picked up her bowl with both hands and sipped at the broth, rather than risk the finger sticks again.

When she had safely set the bowl aside, she took another small sip of water to clear her mouth. “I am fine,” she said firmly, “although I thank you all for your concern. Was there anything else you wished to tell us, Keegan, before I move on to Burlon’s report?”

“Only that I continue working on the lists. I have talked with nearly half the community and recorded their details.”

“That’s good progress,” Burlon said approvingly, then grinned. “A pity Gredin doesn’t have a *crabe.* She’s spoken to so many people, these past few days, we might be nearly finished. She could have collected a few details after she finished answering *their* questions.”

With Burlon’s teasing scraping at her temper, Gredin shifted restlessly on her stool.

“Actually, there is no need for Gredin to use the *crabe*,” Keegan said, smiling. “I have set up a table near the line that awaits her daily, close enough that members of the community are willing to talk with me while they wait their turn.”

“Very resourceful, Historian.”

Gredin cleared her throat, more than ready to move on. “Your turn,

Burlon. Have you been equally resourceful in your negotiations with the Hesch?"

Burlon sobered. "No. I was unable to meet with the Hesch about a trade."

"Were they absent from the Market?"

"Oh, they were there," Burlon admitted. "But they refused to talk to me. When I persisted, they called security and had me escorted from their maartza."

Silence filled the room.

"Don't worry," Burlon said. "I'll try again. I'm sure it will be fine, once a little more time has gone by."

"Nitikikani's foot is still broken," Gredin pointed out. "I know it pains him. He had to sit at the reception. They are likely still angry with me."

"Even so, you're not a Trader. It makes no sense for them to act this way. Vennan Tradeteams have long done business with the Hesch. They won't want to give that up indefinitely."

It sounded logical, Gredin supposed. Calming even. And yet…

Burlon spoke again, scattering her thoughts. "I do have some encouraging news, however. Despite how few maartzas are open at present, I made a small Trade with the Polpethtira – one I think Miri will agree has potential, once I show her what I purchased."

"Food?" Miri asked, eagerly.

"Partly. A new drink, as well, that might make up for our lack of besk."

Miri beamed. "That sounds wonderful, Burlon."

"Well done," Sill said, smiling.

"Tell us the details," Keegan urged. "For my records."

"The Polpethtira sold me a bottle of *tharaman*, a flavoring that makes a sort of hot tea. I also bought two packets of *chingee* – a pleasant-tasting chewy wafer – and a supply of *kilam,* the sugar rounds the Polpethtira use to sweeten *tharaman* tea." A moment later, five tiny cups appeared, the kind usually reserved for condiments, along with a plate of dark blue wafers. "Taste them and tell me whether you find them enjoyable."

"Wait!" Gredin said. "How do we know this is safe?"

Burlon smiled. "I drank the *tharaman* and ate the *chingee*, and I'm just fine."

"That was reckless of you," Gredin snapped. She picked up the tiny cup and peered into it, ignored the murmurs of pleasure sounding around the table, intent on tasting the pale pink liquid and making her own judgement.

The faint scent of flowers was misleading, for the warm tea tasted of spices and left a pleasant taste in her mouth. "It's quite good," she admitted.

Burlon smiled, obviously pleased. "Try the chingee," he urged.

Gredin reached for a wafer. The dark blue rectangle felt smooth in her fingers. She sniffed it but could smell nothing. Taking a bite, she was intrigued by the dense chewiness of the wafer and the burst of flavor that resulted.

"It's a strange taste," Keegan said, "but I like it."

"I agree," Sill said.

Gredin continued to chew, extracting all of the flavor she could before swallowing.

Miri spoke, her hazel eyes gleaming. "It reminds me a bit of manzell that has been dried, but with a coating of crissinth instead of honey."

"And a touch of darderry, perhaps?" Gredin mused.

"Yes!" Miri exclaimed. "It *does* remind me of darderry." She smiled. "It's unusual. I wouldn't mind one of these with a cup of the tea, as a substitute for midday snack."

"How many station credits did this cost?" Gredin asked. "Were you able to negotiate a fair Trade for these items?"

"The Polpethtira didn't have enough for everyone currently, but I made it clear I was interested in a much larger order. Unfortunately, the current traders didn't have the authority to agree to the larger Trade. They need to consult with their superiors when they reach home. But I presented our request as persuasively as I could. With any luck, we should receive a sizeable shipment of the new items when they return to Tradepoint."

"I'm still curious about the cost," Gredin stated. "You've cautioned us to be careful with our credits. Are these items expensive?"

"Minimal, for this first Trade," Burlon said. "Just a packet of left-over reception food for their journey home."

"Just?" Gredin exclaimed.

"But that food is for us!" Miri protested. "For when spirits are low in the community."

Burlon held up his hands. "Wait. I'll explain."

Gredin gave him a cool stare. "Proceed."

"The Polpethtira approached me in the Traders' Market. Once I got them past the idea that we would accept baskets as payment, our negotiations proceeded smoothly. It became clear they were quite taken with the reception food and wanted to make a trade for it. They offered me refreshment while we talked, which is how I discovered the *tharaman* and *chingee*."

"I don't see how tea and crackers is a worthwhile exchange for our Vennan food," Gredin said crossly.

Burlon sighed. "Listen, all of you. There are only five Polpethtira here. A basket of food to feed them will scarcely make a difference to our stores, compared to feeding a thousand Vennans. This is a new Trade I am proposing with the Polpethtira. We are learning about each other, and about how much we can trust each other. If I give them a generous basket of food in payment for the tea and wafers they have currently offered, it's all the likelier they will present our proposal enthusiastically. If they return with a cargo that includes the wafers and tea, we have a new Trading partner, one who might take a chance and bring other food items, in addition to *tharaman* and *chingee*. Because that's what traders do."

It made sense, Gredin thought. And although it hurt to think of Vennan food going anywhere but to Vennan tables, Burlon was right that provisions for five individuals would make no significant impact on their reserves.

"When do you need the promised packet?" Gredin asked.

"They requested we bring it to them three days from now."

"Very well. Miri, will you take responsibility for preparing the packet? You'll know best which items to include. And use a generous hand. I prefer to make a good impression on the Polpethtiran traders, even if a bigger Trade never materializes."

"Of course, Gredin," Miri said, but she did not look happy at the prospect.

"My thanks. Burlon, is there more to report?"

"Just that few races are currently in port, which makes finding food items, or paper, or ink difficult. With luck, more races will dock soon That's all the news I have, but I do want to discuss your dealings with the community, as you promised at our last meeting."

"The subject is on my agenda," Gredin responded. "But it is Miri's turn, and I have another food issue to discuss, as well. One that requires a decision."

Burlon frowned but said only, "By all means, let us hear Miri's report."

Miri looked nervously around the table. "Our food supplies are holding up, for the moment. We are in no danger for the next few weeks, except for the dullness of repetition in the foods being offered at table. The Wilra grain was most welcome. It allows us to stretch our existing food much farther. The trick is to come up with offerings that *seem* different, despite containing the same basic ingredients." She offered Burlon a smile. "The kuma leaves will help a great deal. Everyone working in the kitchens was thrilled when I brought them in. Thank you."

Why is Miri thanking Burlon? He is only one individual, not the sole decision-maker. "I am glad you find them helpful, Miri. Is there more you would say?" Gredin inquired.

"No," Miri said quietly.

"Then I would like to discuss the fate of the other food items we found in the warehouses, particularly the jams and honey and pickled relish in House Balamont's area." Gredin turned her gaze to Burlon. "Did Wyve's records show any Trades in progress for those items?"

"No," Burlon admitted.

"Then we can turn them over to the kitchen Tenders."

"No," Burlon said forcefully. "At least, not all of them. I intend to open the Venna maartza soon. We need items for the shelves, to draw traders in. Luxury items like those are always popular. We should see if anyone is interested in making a good Trade for them before we consider handing them over to our kitchen Tenders."

You're wrong, Gredin thought, annoyed at his peremptory manner. She intended to woo the opinions of the others to her side, no matter what Burlon said. "Burlon, you are a Trader. You would keep all of the warehouse goods for Trade, simply because that is what they were used for in the past. But our situation has changed, and the manner in which things were always done can no longer apply. Our home is gone. Those warehouse items are the last of their kind."

"True. But that will make them all the more valuable, when – if – we sell them."

"Right now, no one but Wyve and Figg know that Venna has been destroyed. Are you saying we should make our situation known to all? Are we so short of credits that we must share our dark news and set new prices for our goods based on their limited numbers?"

"No. But a generous account balance is never a bad thing. It allows us the freedom to Trade for whatever we need, from any race in port. And the balance will dwindle quickly, since we must constantly Trade for food."

Heads nodded around the table.

Gredin spoke before Burlon could press his point further. "Then I propose a compromise. Take the relishes for Trade in the Vennan maartza and leave the jars of jam and honey for Miri to use as she thinks best."

Burlon regarded her. "You feel strongly about this."

"I do. Even a small taste of home would lift spirits."

"And when it's gone? Won't folks grieve all over again for what they've lost?"

"Yes, but with regret, not despair."

Burlon contemplated her words. "Depending on what the others think, I could agree to giving the jam and honey to Miri and taking the relishes for the maartza."

Gredin exhaled. “Keegan, Sill, Miri, do you have any objections to that proposal?”

“No,” Keegan and Sill said in unison.

Miri said only, “Honey? Vennan honey? And jam from Vennan berries?” Her eyes shone with joy.

“Then we are in agreement,” Gredin said. Fatigue pulled at her. “Keegan, please record our decision.”

“Of course,” he said, already tapping at the *crabe*.

“If Miri shares her plans for the jam and honey before she uses it,” Burlon said, “Gredin can make certain the community is properly appreciative, prior to their tasting it.”

Miri nodded. “Of course. Once we have the jars, the other kitchen Tenders and I will discuss how they can best be used. We’ll want to make the occasion a sort of happy ceremony.”

“If that is settled,” Gredin said. “I have several more topics to cover. First, an update on the new housing. Thanks to your comments and suggestions, stairs have been eliminated, along with Prettian lights and plumbing in each cubicle, since we have no need for such things. There will be a block of private areas on the ground level where individuals can attend to their bodily needs and convert the waste. We will ask those with gyfte of Tending to care for the areas, as they do in the current enclaves.”

“How soon will everyone be moved?” Keegan asked.

“Within a day or two. With no need for the Prett to supply light and water to each cubicle, construction is progressing quickly. As each new block is ready, we will move people. And everyone should have the foam bed cushions now.”

“They’re a big improvement,” Burlon said. “No one should be complaining of stiff backs or sore muscles.”

“They are a marvel,” Sill agreed, smiling.

Gredin smiled, too. “And there is one more bit of pleasing news. The Prett are reworking the expanded section of corridor we will inhabit. They plan to seal one end so no one can enter or exit there, and place an antechamber at the other, where it will exit to the public corridoors. As a result, there will be no more need to undergo the bio-mist anywhere within the enclaves."

"A small thing," Keegan said, "but thoughtful on the Director's part. The change will improve the community's spirits and make us feel more united."

Burlon nodded. "I'll give Wyve my thanks when next I talk with him."

Gredin bit back a reproof at his presumptuousness and said, instead, "Wyve also reports progress with the seeds and plants he removed from our kitchen stores. All of the items have been catalogued and, with Beda's help, the ideal Growing environment for each has been identified." Gredin smiled, this time without effort. "They were quite taken with your shelf garden, Miri. Beda said their excitement hadn't faded by the time he left the Growing area. Apparently, they don't often see plants Growing in dirt, here on the station. And they used all manner of *griimoni* to examine the luminth providing light for the plants."

"Why?" Keegan asked.

"Beda said they were anxious to duplicate the proper lighting, since the Prett are unable to recharge luminth. They've asked that someone from our community take on that task, if the Prett cannot duplicate the output from the luminth before they dim."

"The scientists will worry at the problem until they resolve it," Burlon said "It's their nature. But if you need someone…"

"My thanks, but I've already asked Beda. He was pleased to be of help."

"And he is a Grower," Miri reminded them. "He must be happy for an opportunity to exercise his gyfte."

Gredin nodded. "He finds the Prett scientists odd, but he is intrigued by their methods and excited by what they are doing with the *flagle*, which is new to him. The Prett scientists believe it will yield a fine crop in the future, enough to feed the entire delegation a good meal."

Burlon's lips quirked. "So the Beng may have given us more than they intended."

"Time will tell," Gredin said. Her first interaction with the Beng in the Shodekekeen's maartza had been unsettling. As a result, she doubted whether she would ever feel kindly toward the greedy-natured beings. "That covers everything except my last topic – the time I spend answering questions for our kinsmen."

"I hope you're finished with that fruitless endeavor," Burlon said bluntly.

"Not fruitless," Gredin protested. "Just time-consuming."

"It drains you. It would drain any of us, if we had taken on that duty."

Heads nodded in agreement, giving Gredin hope that her next announcement would be greeted with equal understanding and support.

"My thanks for your concern on my behalf. I admit, the time I spent didn't produce the results I'd hoped for, and so I've decided to end the process. But I want the community to feel their concerns are heard, so I will ask each House to select a volunteer to hear their House members' problems and questions. I'll meet with those volunteers each day, to hear an overview of the concerns and answer any new questions that arise. It should improve communication, and be less taxing for me, as well."

Silence. A silence which quickly grew uncomfortable.

Finally, Keegan spoke. "Are you certain this is the best solution?"

His quiet question seemed to unfreeze the others' tongues.

"It seems to me," Burlon said, "that you are going from one extreme to another."

Sill moved restively on her stool. "It has been only a few days since we learned of Venna's destruction. Our people are coping with hard changes, and many individuals in any given House are virtual strangers to each other. Moreover, we're in the midst of moving everyone to new quarters. Is it wise to make another significant change just now?"

Gredin looked from one to another of them in disappointed astonishment. Fighting for calm, she said, "I believe my plan has merit. It will increase the time I have at my disposal to meet with key people – just twelve people daily, since Keegan already has my ear – rather than dealing with an endless line of individuals. Isn't that what you were all urging?"

"It *would* give you more time to rest during the day," Miri conceded.

"Yes," Gredin agreed. "And more time to *think*. I can scarcely find a moment of quiet, once the day begins, much less respond to urgencies without leaving everyone else waiting for me, or a task abandoned, unfinished."

"So you go from trying to talk with everybody to only meeting with a dozen?" Burlon challenged. "These days, it's hard to find two people who agree, in or out of the Houses. How do you know the individual from a House will present a fair sampling of their House's concerns?"

She looked around the table. "I want to try this. If it doesn't work, I'll devise a different plan, and another after that, if needed, until I find one that works for me and the community. But I believe this plan has a good chance for success, and that we will all feel its benefits."

"So you're determined to go forward with this idea?" Burlon asked.

"I am," Gredin said, with a lift of her chin.

"Well, I suppose putting it into practice for a few days can't do much damage. We can reevaluate and make changes, if necessary, to keep any problems you create small."

Burlon's words felt more like a threat than an endorsement. Would he try to take over leadership of the community, if she failed? "And you are so certain that I'll create problems?"

"Gredin *is* First Speaker," Miri interjected. "She can handle most problems."

Unwilling to waver, Gredin said, "My thanks for your support, Miri. And, with that, we are done for today. I will inform the community of the changes at midday meal."

"I look forward to hearing you Speak," Keegan said quietly, though his gaze still brimmed with concern.

"We all do," Burlon said, and rose. "Give my thanks to Brinlin for a fine meal, Miri."

"I will," Miri said, standing with the others. "She will be pleased you enjoyed her food."

"It is my turn to clear the table," Sill said and, with an elegant gesture, Sent the remains of morning meal back to the kitchens before exiting on the heels of the rest of the group.

Abruptly, Gredin found herself alone at the pristine table. Trying to ignore her aching head, she braced herself to face the reception hall. One more morning of sitting out there. One more morning of finding the patience to listen attentively to each new individual. Knowing that she would soon be free of the ordeal gave her the willpower to face the coming line of anxious individuals with equanimity. *After all*, she reminded herself sharply, *they are my community. They deserve nothing less.*

She forced herself to rise from her stool and, straightening her shoulders, carefully schooled her features to an expression of calm interest before following the others. The sooner she began, the more opportunities she would have to provide the reassurance the community so desperately needed.

She was still reminding herself of that, hours later, when she rose to address the community. As Gredin mounted the steps and turned to the sea of faces, she caught a glimpse of ildarian blue: Tetralanna, sitting in a group of House Balamont's members. Despite the difficulties that existed between them, Gredin was relieved to see that Tetralanna had rejoined their kinsmen.

Grateful to the Power, Gredin took a breath, touched the hlette on her arm, and reached for her gyfte. "Good day to you all. I have news to share." Her Power-enhanced voice resulted in a sea of upturned faces as everyone attended to her words.

"First, I hope you are all enjoying the new cushions for our bedmats. If you have not yet received one, please make your need known to me. As for our new accommodations…" Gredin let her words flow smoothly over the crowd, observing the reactions of the community.

"…and lastly, I present a new way for those with questions, suggestions, and concerns to bring them to my attention without standing in a long line, awaiting your turn. Instead, each House should select a volunteer willing to listen to their House members, then meet with me daily to pass the information along and receive a response that can be relayed back in a timely manner. I suggest each House spend the rest of today discussing who among you might be best for this important duty. Once you decide, please make it known to Keegan te Fliss. He will record your selections and I will announce those names when I Speak with you tomorrow."

A buzz of conversation began to build among the community members, and Gredin hastened to finish before her increasing fatigue could cause her gyfte to falter.

"My thanks to all for your willingness to try this new way of voicing your concerns, and to those of you who will become your House's volunteer." She dredged up a reassuring smile. "Hopefully, this will make the days less stressful for you all. Your welfare is my most important concern. Now, please finish enjoying the meal before you. I appreciate your attention."

Gredin released her gyfte and descended the dais steps, anxious to seek her room. She felt dizzy. Chilled. Weak.

And profoundly grateful not to be facing an endless line of anxious individuals.

[17]

1677 OF 2000 ORBITS REMAINING: 42YELLOW

Keegan caught himself nodding over his lists.

The day had been long. Back home, everyone in the House took a lengthy rest after midday meal. Here on Tradepoint, that custom had fallen away. On the first three days, they had been far too busy preparing for the Trisectoriana reception. And in the days since, with the knowledge of Venna's loss laying heavily upon them, normal schedules were wildly awry. People lingered in the reception hall, wandering about or engaged in sad conversation with their kinsmen, instead of retiring and trying to sleep.

Keegan stayed active, as well, gathering information from the other survivors. Late in the day, he attended his daily session at the Clinic with Binn, undergoing food challenges. As a result, he was full of yawns, now that evening meal had concluded.

He usually devoted a final span of time to organizing the information he had gathered, since it was only useful if it could be located. But his heavy eyelids warned that he had nearly reached his limit. Sleep threatened to overwhelm him.

=Keegan te Fliss.=

His name resounded within his private mind, and the demanding tone informed him of precisely who had just addressed him.

Tetralanna.

Composing himself, he replied. =Tetralanna te Balamont. A fair evening to you. What service may I offer?=

=We require your presence on behalf of House Fliss. Come to the reception hall and join us.= And the contact melted away, ending the conversation.

Keegan stared at the wall. What had Tetralanna meant by *on behalf of House Fliss*? And what did she mean by *require*?

If nothing else, she had roused him back to wakefulness.

On instinct, he reached for his notebook and the roll of pens and ink. But no. He had only half a sheet of unsullied paper left. Instead, with a sigh, he picked up the Prett *crabe,* tucked it beneath his arm, and headed out to the reception hall, leaving his luminth glowing softly on the table to welcome him when he returned.

The lights in the reception hall had not yet been dimmed for the night, although the hour was quite late. Nearly a hundred people were scattered around the room, walking alone or sitting in clusters of three or four. And one larger group had staked out a corner. As Keegan watched, a solitary walker straying toward the group was intercepted and shooed away by Tetralanna.

Starting toward her, Keegan looked more closely at the people behind her. There were more than a dozen, mostly unknown to him, but he recognized Naria te Bentain, a sculptor. Yesterday, he had interviewed her briefly, and learned a bit about her gyfte. Her Chosen had stayed behind on Venna while Naria came to Tradepoint for the Trisectoriana, so she was now without her life partner. Unlike many who shared her situation, however, she had remained coolly self-possessed while he interviewed her, polite but brisk.

What cause did Naria te Bentain and Tetralanna te Balamont share? And who were the others, conversing with such animation? Prodded by curiosity, he quickened his step.

"And here is House Fliss," a man in the group called out in greeting as Keegan reached them. "We are complete."

"As complete as we can ever be," a woman said, her tone a tart admonishment.

"Now, now," a different man said. "We have all suffered great losses. But we are here tonight for our new beginning."

The woman rolled her eyes and turned her back on him.

Tetralanna spoke, and Keegan felt the soothing ripple of gyfte that laced her words. "It is late and we are weary, but we are prepared to sacrifice for the good of our Houses. I honor you all for that. This gathering need not take long, but it seemed fitting to greet one another privately and discuss any concerns we might have, before we are formally introduced tomorrow."

Keegan looked around in surprise at the group. These, apparently, were the volunteers Gredin had asked each House to select. Thirteen surviving Houses should mean thirteen volunteers, and he currently saw fifteen individuals.

"Your pardon," he said into the silence that followed Tetralanna's words. "As some of you already know, I am Keegan te Fliss. My role at the Trisectoriana was as historian, and I continue to serve the community in that capacity. Could each of you provide your name and House to me, so that I might make a written account of this first gathering of House volunteers?"

There was a general murmur of approval, although some remained silent, and a few cast wary looks his way.

"My thanks. I'll take a seat and call each of you over by House so that I can–"

"Take a seat, by all means," Tetralanna interjected, "but we are already joined in conversation. When one of us is free, they will come to you. Now, Ovek, you were saying…?"

Keegan sighed. These individuals would be donating a great deal of time, listening to the concerns of their House members and bringing those concerns to Gredin. It would do him no great harm to wait. There would be no House members for *him* to listen to. He was all that remained of House Fliss, and his daily meeting with Gredin, Burlon, Sill, and Miri gave him all the opportunity he required to discuss his concerns.

He settled at the nearest table, drew his *crabe* from under his arm, and turned it on, adjusting it to accept tactile input rather than spoken commands. He had worked through the tutorial again and again until he mastered the operating instructions. With that accomplished, he had begun to replicate some of his handwritten lists on the *crabe*.

It was painstaking. The tablet was learning him while he learned the tablet. Vennan was not its original language, but it adapted quickly and remembered. His first step had been to teach it the name and appearance of each individual letter needed to form Vennan words. Next, he had taught it the proper way to write the thirteen House names, and the names of all the gyftes, a small Vennan vocabulary, and to recognize those names and words when they were spoken aloud.

Alone in his room, he sometimes spoke aloud the information he needed the *crabe* to assemble and retain. In public, he caused a keyboard of light to appear on the table and touched each letter in turn. It was effective but tedious, and it brought him none of the joy of using pen on paper. Nevertheless, he was impressed by the *crabe*'s versatility. He could draw on its screen with his fingertip, then use its tools to refine what he had drawn, and the machine could retain the image. In that way, he had reproduced the knot pattern for each House, and taught the *crabe* to insert either the House name or the House symbol, depending on the given list. And the 'page' on which he typed or drew was essentially endless. A list or document or History entry could be as lengthy as its contents required, without ever exceeding–

"Keegan te Fliss? Am I intruding?"

He realized that he recognized the woman who stood before him. "Nunellin te Vell! I am gladdened to see you." When he had first begun to gather information on the survivors, House Vell was the first House he approached, and Nunellin had been the final member of her House to be interviewed. Five difficult days had passed since that encounter, and he was relieved that she seemed to be bearing up well under the sorrows that burdened the community.

She smiled and sat on the bench across from him. "Whenever we meet," she said, her tone teasing, "you seem determined to question me."

"As a historian, it is my lot," he said, smiling in return. "So, you are the volunteer for House Vell?"

"Yes, although many were willing."

"Vell is a willing House," Keegan affirmed.

"I will gladly converse with my kinsmen and note matters that trouble them."

"My thanks on Gredin's behalf. It is important assistance."

Nunellin shook her head. "Others like yourself do far more. And I was deeply saddened to learn of the loss of your House." She folded her hands on the tabletop. "Is there information you need, beyond my name and House?"

"No, that is all, at least for the moment. Thank you."

"Then I will go so that someone else can talk with you."

When she left, two men and a woman approached. "I am Sulian te Avilar," one man said. "My companions are Lillig te Kendar and, at her side, Mallar te Calidane."

"Ah! You are members of a triad," Keegan acknowledged. House Avilar, House Kendar, and House Calidane had been united as a triad in Trading and other endeavors for as long as he could remember.

They looked pleased. "Indeed," Lillig said, her voice soft. "And my kinswoman Miri thinks highly of you. Should you wish companionship at evening meal, there will always be a place for you at Kendar's table."

"And Calidane's," Mallar echoed.

"And Avilar's," Sulian stated. "We three and our Houses nearly always agree, in matters large and small. If there is anything you need, please make it known to us."

They were friendly and kind, speaking tactfully around the edges of his loss. With House Fliss gone, he had no kin to join at mealtime, and lacked the resources offered automatically by House members. Theirs was an uncommonly kind set of offers, in these days of scarcity and uncertainty. Keegan crossed his palms to them and offered a sincere bow of his head. "It would be a privilege to dine with you," he said. "And, should I require anything, I will remember your generous words." He hesitated, then admitted, "In truth, there is one thing I need, although I doubt whether anyone within the community can help."

"And what might that be?" Sulien asked.

"Paper to write upon. My supply is nearly at an end, and it is an unexpectedly scarce commodity, here on Tradepoint."

Their faces fell.

He waved a reassuring hand. "I hardly expected you to know of a source, but it costs me nothing to ask. In the days ahead, perhaps you might ask others on my behalf. I would be grateful."

"So it shall be," Lillig assured him, and he believed her.

The three of them left him then, engaging in animated conversation with one another.

When no one else approached, he woke his *crabe* and began the list, having relied on his gyfte to retain the information he had so far obtained. The screen lit, creating a fresh page on which he inscribed the Houses and individual names of the four volunteers who had just–

"What is *that*?" a voice demanded from behind him.

Reflexively, Keegan stroked the *crabe* back into slumber, then looked over his shoulder. "Your pardon?" he asked, his startled tone sharper than he had intended.

A muscular man pointed a finger at the *crabe*, while his companion waited in silence at his side. "I asked you what that was."

Keegan was tempted to reply, *No concern of yours.* But these were troubled times. People were on edge, their tempers frayed, their manners misplaced. There was little to gain by taking offense. He said, "I am recording people's names and Houses, as I was asked to do."

"Well, I see no sign of it. Where are the words?" Reaching down, he poked the *crabe* with an incautious finger.

Keegan hugged the *crabe* to his chest protectively. "It was given to me by the Prett. My supply of paper and ink has run out, yet there are more lists that Gredin and Burlon – and now Tetralanna – wish me to create. This enables me to do so without the need for paper."

Looking disgusted, the man turned and stalked away.

Astonished, Keegan looked to the man's companion. "Who was that?" Keegan asked.

"Palla te Laith."

"And you?"

"I am Ovek te Torr." He took a cautious step closer. "Is that really a

Prettian *griimoni*?"

"Yes. It is called a *crabe*."

"Oh, yes! Sill has mentioned it."

"Would you like to see how your name appears, when I enter it on the list of new House volunteers?" Keegan invited.

Ovek, seeming curious, took another step.

"Ovek?" Tetralanna called. "We have need of you."

"Your pardon," Ovek murmured, and hurried off to join Tetralanna and Palla te Laith. Another triad: House Balamont, aligned with House Laith and House Torr. Keegan spared a sympathetic sigh for Burlon, the newest member of House Laith, if Palla's cross manner was typical of the welcome Burlon received there.

After Ovek's departure, Keegan sat alone for a time, wishing he were in his bed. Six members of the group had yet to approach him – seven, if he counted Tetralanna – and they seemed in no great hurry to do so. Or, more precisely, seven Houses remained on his list... but there were ten people mingling and mixing, for reasons that were still unclear to him.

When more time crept past, he reached out to Tetralanna's private mind. =Do the others wish to be listed? If not, I will return to my room.=

The look she gave him was black with annoyance, but she spoke to those around her, and four came his way, looking impatient. When they reached his table, they stood side by side and announced their names and Houses as if dispensing with a tiresome duty.

"Edin te K'lar," said the first woman.

"Rig te Indirin," said the man beside her.

"Fennin te Shelahn," said the next man.

"Naria te Bentain," said the final member of their party, the woman's features a cool mask of disdain, an expression with which he was already well-acquainted. "Does that suffice?"

"Yes." Keegan pitied the House members destined to approach those four with their problems and concerns.

The quartet turned as one and walked away.

With an increasing sense of misgiving, Keegan activated his *crabe* and entered their names and Houses. He sensed little sympathy or patience in the cold faces that had just confronted him. Yet they had, for whatever reason, volunteered. And Gredin would meet daily with the twelve volunteers. If there was a problem, she would soon notice.

And do what? Go back to meeting daily with nearly a thousand individuals?

Keegan was more than physically tired. His spirit was weary. Countless others shared his situation. Many in the community were too centered on their own losses and difficulties to reach out with compassion to their kinsmen. What would happen if the few effective helpers exhausted themselves and withdrew?

"Keegan te Fliss?"

A shy voice tiptoed into his ear. Looking up, he saw a woman's face, open and sympathetic in ways the faces of the previous four had not been.

"Yes," he affirmed. "A good evening to you."

That won a small smile. "I am Amata te Darius. I will be representing my House."

"Thank you, Amata te Darius. I will add your name to my list. And may I ask you one additional question?"

"Of course. What would you know?"

Keegan nodded toward the people still clustered around Tetralanna. "My list is now complete for every House but Balamont, and yet I see three more individuals who are unknown to me. Can you identify any of them?"

Amata nodded. "They are the contenders for Balamont. Tetralanna te Balamont came to help them resolve the impasse and make a final selection, but that has not yet happened. We others will return to our Houses for the night soon, while those from Balamont continue their debate, with First Speaker guiding their efforts."

"Tetralanna is not First Speaker," Keegan corrected. "That title, and First Speaker's hlette, now belong to Gredin te Balamont. Nevertheless, Tetralanna is still a Speaker. I'm certain her assistance will aid the contenders."

Amata looked chastened. "Your pardon."

"None needed. I only felt the need to clarify their respective positions to avoid confusion. Tetralanna was the Voice at the Trisectoriana, but the Trisectoriana is past. With Venna lost, the Power itself appointed Gredin te Balamont as First Speaker, to guide us safely forward."

"And she truly meant what she said?" Amata asked.

"In what regard?"

"That we are to have a new home? A new world?"

"Indeed. We have the Power's word that New Venna awaits us."

The tension in Amata's face eased. "I am grateful to hear you confirm it."

He could have replied, *Gredin already told you so.* But it was enough, for now, to have Amata go on her way in a less worried frame of mind.

That left only the three individuals from Balamont to be listed. Again, he reached out to Tetralanna's private mind. =I have completed the list, except for your kinsmen. Do you wish me to list them all or to leave Balamont unlisted until they agree on a House volunteer?=

=I wish to be left uninterrupted so that I may counsel them in peace,= she snapped.

The day had been long. For the fourth consecutive session, his appointment at the Clinic had ended with him spewing up everything he had ingested. He was drained, as was his patience.

=Then I will complete the Balamont entry in the morning,= he informed her. Picking up his *crabe*, he rose from the table and began the journey back to his chamber.

=Keegan? Keegan te Fliss!=

No. Why should he treat her any better than she treated him?

But he knew the answers to that question. Because she had lost her Chosen. Because she had lost First Speaker's hlette. Because she was no longer the Voice, and was to be pitied.

He stopped walking, giving her a final chance. =Yes?=

=I have not yet dismissed you!=

His sympathy vanished. =I will see you in the morning,= he replied curtly, and walked away.

[18]

1645 OF 2000 ORBITS REMAINING: 26ORANGE

Gredin felt that her life had become a series of repeating patterns.

That would be fine, she supposed, if she could get the patterns *right*. But she hadn't managed to – not yet – and so she kept announcing and implementing plans, only to later uproot them. It made her look foolish to the community. Indecisive. Confused. Unreliable…

But that was preferable to perpetuating a pattern she knew to be wrong, and so here she was, preparing to address the community and change the pattern yet again.

At morning meeting, Keegan's account of the behavior of the new House volunteers had filled her with foreboding. This should have been simple. How had it gotten so complicated? Desh! Were her four fellow meeting members' misgivings proving true already?

Bracing herself to rise, she contacted Keegan's private mind. =Has Balamont settled their difficulty?= she asked, embarrassed for her House.

=Nearly,= Keegan replied. =Tetralanna asks that you leave Balamont to the end of your announcements. Last night, the position was contested by Marakett, Crovek, and Ibbin. Crovek now steps aside, and Tetralanna assures me that Marakett and Ibbin will resolve the matter by the time you have announced the other Houses.=

Gredin fought the unexpected urge to weep. =Very well,= she acknowledged, and mounted the steps of the arrival dais so that everyone could see her from where they sat.

For today's announcement, she wore the scarlet Shodekekeen gown. She felt over-dressed and slightly ridiculous, but Burlon had given her a subtle nod of approval, which both annoyed and reassured her. Somehow, she would have to make time to visit Shamka's maartza and purchase more fabric, then beg Ingarra to create a few new outfits for her. She had packed for a short visit, and her few clothing choices were now woefully inadequate…

As she reached the top step, the entire reception hall fell silent. There was no need for her to request their attention. Was she training them, or were they training her?

Smile, she prompted herself as she faced them. *They are tired and sad, and you ask them to embrace yet another change – one you are making largely for your own sake.*

"Good day to you all," she began. "My thanks for–"

Someone at the back shouted, "We can't hear you!"

Shocked, Gredin faltered. Not hear First Speaker? How was that possible?

She crossed her arms over her chest, the fingertips of one hand seeking contact with First Speaker's hlette while her other hand reached up to grasp her flamestone pendant between thumb and fore-finger. Warmth coursed through her in a strengthening wave. She made herself smile more broadly. "Your pardon. The good meal our kitchen Tenders provided distracted me."

She saw a scatter of answering smiles.

"Over the past few days, many have endured a long line, waiting to bring their concerns to me. The process permitted me to converse with many people I had not yet met, but it forced individuals to wait in line for a lengthy time in exchange for a few short minutes spent actually talking with me. That is why, yesterday, I asked you to confer within your Houses and select a member to whom you could entrust your questions. Now that those individuals have been selected by each House, I will meet with each of them, daily, to learn of your concerns.

You will deal with your House member, who dwells in your portion of the enclave, and any line of questioners that still exists will be much shorter, consisting only of your kinsmen."

As far as she could sense, her words awoke no great excitement or anticipation, but neither did people seem angered by the change. It only remained to introduce the House volunteers to the community, not least to honor them for their selflessness in pledging a part of every day to the service of their House.

"As I name each new House volunteer, I ask that they come to the front of the hall and assemble in a line on the step below me, so that all might see their faces and learn their names." Feeling steadier, she released the hlette and pendant, and dropped her hands to her sides.

Within her private mind, Keegan prompted her. =Avilar. Sulian.=

"For House Avilar, Sulian," she announced.

A murmur of comment from the large Avilar contingent as Sulien came forward.

=Bentain. Naria.=

"For House Bentain, Naria."

She noted a sour expression on Burlon's face as Naria te Bentain made her way between the tables, and wondered what tale lay behind his look.

=Calidane. Mallar.=

"For House Calidane, Mallar."

The members of House Calidane were seated near the front of the hall, so it took little time for Mallar to reach the steps.

=Darius. Amata.=

"For House Darius, Amata."

Amata te Darius wore a teslan of the same rosy gold as a slice of ripe placrim. Gredin wondered whether the Shodekekeen might have fabric in that particular shade.

=Indirin,= Keegan prompted. =Rig.=

This time, she ignored him. "For House Fliss," she announced, her words ringing forth strongly, "Keegan."

She and Keegan had disagreed over whether his name should be announced, but Gredin was resolved. *You represent House Fliss. Being its only surviving member makes no difference.*

And so, with an embarrassed air, and his ever-present crabe tucked in the crook of his arm, Keegan took his place beside Amata te Darius.

=Indirin,= he prompted again. =Rig.=

"For House Indirin, Rig."

Rig stalked to the steps as if he had a more important engagement elsewhere – not a promising attitude for a man who was agreeing to listen to the concerns of others. Still, he had volunteered. Perhaps his air was deceiving.

=Kendar. Lillig.=

"For House Kendar, Lillig."

Of her own accord, Lillig te Kendar crossed to the far end of the assembled group and began a second line on the next step below. As she did so, she looked over her shoulder and smiled up at Sulian te Avilar. The warmth of her smile reminded Gredin that the Houses of Kendar and Avilar belonged to the same triad. She knew little of such things, but she was grateful for any sign of friendship that transcended House boundaries.

=K'lar. Edin.=

"For House K'lar, Edin."

The woman who answered that summons wore no smile and met no one's eye as she mounted the steps and took her place.

=Laith. Palla.=

"For House Laith, Palla."

Palla te Laith was a strong-shouldered man, and the scowl he aimed at Keegan awoke a shiver of alarm in Gredin. Keegan was the most congenial of men. What prompted Palla te Laith to give him such a scathing look?

=Shelahn. Fennin.=

"For House Shelahn, Fennin."

The man who approached looked, if anything, slightly bored by the entire proceeding. But that was preferable to the open animosity on Palla te Laith's face.

=Torr. Ovek.=

"For House Torr, Ovek."

Ovek had a kinder bearing, his eyes bright, his gait energetic as he came from the rear portion of the reception hall to stand beside Fennin te Shelahn.

The list was nearly at an end, with only Vell yet to come. Had Balamont reached a decision between Marakett and Ibbin, or was the ceremony going to limp to an awkward halt after her next announcement?

=Vell. Nunellin,= came Keegan's prompt.

=For House Vell, Nunellin.=

Nunellin te Vell was bright-eyed as she took her place on the lower step.

Gredin held her breath, waiting.

=Balamont,= Keegan began, and Gredin smiled in relief. But he hesitated, the message only half-delivered. Then he began again. =Balamont. Tetralanna.=

The smile melted from Gredin's lips, and she almost asked him whether he had misspoken. He had told her it would be Marakett or Ibbin, had he not? But Keegan's words were unmistakably clear in her mind. And so Gredin straightened her back and said, with firm emphasis, "And for House Balamont, Tetralanna."

Tetralanna was at the very back of the reception hall, and she came forward with slow deliberation, nodding to acquaintances in many different Houses as she walked to the steps. She wore the sleeveless, full-skirted gown she had worn to Wyve's office on their first day. It was an impressive garment of cobalt, sapphire, and ildarian blue. The only addition was an openwork shawl draped around her shoulders. Perhaps she, like Gredin, found the room a bit cool for comfort… or perhaps it was meant to distract observers' eyes from the absence of First Speaker's hlette on her upper arm.

When Tetralanna reached the step and took her place beside Nunellin te Vell, she glanced briefly down the dual row of House volunteers, then smiled at the assembled community and said, in a voice shimmering with gyfte, "On behalf of those who stand here with me, allow me to say how proud we are to have been selected. And let us all offer proper gratitude to Gredin te Balamont. In the first confused days after the destruction of our beloved Venna, she labored diligently to establish communication with our Prett hosts, and has done her best to cope with the myriad decisions that needed to be made. But now we are rallying from our devastating losses, and it is only fair that the burden be lifted from her inexperienced shoulders and distributed properly among the Houses that remain. And so, as she requested, the Houses have conferred, and we thirteen stand before you now, selected by our kinsmen, ready to undertake our duties as the newly appointed Heads of House, representing your concerns and accepting our unified role as High Council."

Gredin struggled to draw breath, realizing that the force underlying Tetralanna's Speech had gradually built, lulling her into a sort of numbed receptivity. But the terms *newly appointed Heads of House* and *High Council* shocked her back to alarmed awareness as the hlette pulsed around her arm and her entire body began to vibrate.

With an effort, Gredin shook off the web of Tetralanna's words and fought to gather the Focus she would need to address the entire community and refute the brazen assertions. But as she opened her mouth to begin, she saw Burlon scramble to his feet, wide-eyed, staring past her shoulder. The double line of House volunteers below her began to shout and scatter, and Gredin realized that the vibration was real, emanating from the step on which she stood.

Whirling, she saw that the dome had risen to cover the arrival dais. And within its curve stood five unfamiliar Vennans who stared back with a shock and confusion equal to her own as the bio-mist descended to obscure her view.

[19]

1643 OF 2000 ORBITS REMAINING: 27BLUE

Burlon had already braced to leap to his feet in protest when he heard the outrageous claims Tetralanna was making about her new status and that of the people standing with her at the front of the reception hall with her. When the dome triggered, and a Tradeteam appeared on the arrival dais, he rose instinctively, trying to identify… There! Just before the bio-mist obscured his view, he spotted a face he knew: Yohn te Avilar.

That face made a certain sense. Yohn was the head of House Avilar's main Tradeteam, a Traveler of no small repute. But where had he and his team come from?

There were only two possibilities. The first, which Burlon longed to believe but largely discounted, was that Gredin and Cirin were both mistaken, and Venna still existed, safe and undisturbed, with everyone's Houses anxiously awaiting their return.

The second possibility was that Yohn and his Tradeteam had been on some other world, carrying out a Trade mission, and had come directly from there to Tradepoint to drop off their cargo before heading… home. Which no longer existed.

Anxious conversations were buzzing, but people had largely stayed seated. That wouldn't last, once the dome retracted. Burlon addressed

Gredin's private mind. =Can you make everyone stay where they are, until I can inform the newcomers of what's happened?=

=I'll try. Who are they? Where did they come from?=

=It's a Tradeteam from House Avilar. I recognize their Head. I think I can reach his private mind, but it's going to take more than a moment or two to explain. I want to keep them from being mobbed when the dome retracts. I'll be as quick as I can.=

=I understand. Did you hear what Tetralanna said?=

=We'll address it later. Right now, Focus on the community. Do your best. I'll see if I can contact the Tradeteam.=

She nodded, and he saw her cross her arms again, one hand to her flamestone, the other to First Speaker's hlette. Then she opened her mouth to Speak.

He ignored her words as best he could, Focusing all of his attention on reaching out with his private mind. =Yohn? Yohn te Avilar! This is Burlon. If you can hear me…=

=Of course I hear you, silly man,= came the jovial reply. =What sort of a party *was* that Trisectoriana? Are you all still too wine-dazed to Travel home?=

=Hush. Listen, Yohn. We have a serious problem. Answer two questions for me, and then I will explain. Where did you and your Tradeteam just come from? And do your Tradegoods include anything edible?=

=I don't see why that's any business of House Bentain's.=

Burlon didn't know whether to laugh or groan. =Just answer. Please. It is more important than you can possibly imagine.=

=So you claim. Well, we've just left a world that calls itself Odoro, but they won't trade with you. Our triad is handling their needs quite well, thank you. We Traded with them for several different things, none of which can be eaten. Now, what is all this about?=

Yohn's answer was a double disappointment. He and his Tradeteam had come from a foreign world, not from a Venna that had somehow been spared. And their baggage held no trove of food to ease the kitchen Tenders' worries. Still, Yohn had answered him and was owed answers in return, despite the shocking nature of the news.

=I will tell you,= Burlon assured him. =But know, first, that I am in absolute earnest. This is no jest or made-up tale, nor an attempt to get around you in matters of Trade. This is the saddest truth I have ever spoken in my life, and it will take us days to explain it to you fully, but here is the worst of it. Venna has been destroyed.=

=What?=

= Venna is no more.=

=What are you saying? How can that be?=

=We don't know. But Cirin te K'lar lost his life, trying to prove it was not so.=

=Cirin has returned to the Source?=

=Yes, as has everyone we left behind on Venna when we came here.=

A wave of anguish flowed from Yohn's mind into Burlon's.

=The crowd you see here in the enclave are the survivors. We are here because, although the Trisectoriana is over, we have nowhere to go. When Venna was destroyed, twenty Houses met their end, and only one member of House Fliss is still alive.=

On the dais, beneath the dome, the mist began to thin.

=You and your Tradeteam are a blessing from the Power. Your House's survivors believed you to be dead. Take what heart you can from knowing that Avilar sent more individuals to attend the Trisectoriana than any other House. But your losses are still vast, as are ours. Tell me quickly, what individuals are with you?=

He could sense the effort it took for Yohn to reply. =Myself and four others from our triad.=

=Their names? Their Houses? Their gyftes?=

=Shoal te Avilar. A Trader. Mistilan te Avilar, also a Trader and Shoal's Chosen. Trafin te Calidane. A Trader. Plithik te Kendar. A Traveler. And you know me, Yohn te Avilar, Traveler.=

=We have only moments before the dome opens. Your House will tell you much of what has happened here. I have just a few more facts for you.=

=Tell me.=

=We learned of Venna's loss because the Power spoke to Gredin te

Balamont. That is her, just outside the dome, in the red gown. And I am no longer Burlon te Bentain. I found my Chosen, but she is of another House. I have joined her there and am now Burlon te Laith. Oh, and the Hesch are currently refusing to deal with us.=

=The Power? A Chosen from a different House? The Hesch? Burlon, each thing you say awakens a hundred other questions!= Yohn protested.

=It is the way of things, since Venna's loss. We are in troubled times. No Travelers are leaving Tradepoint, while we adjust to our grief. That may change, any day now. For the moment, however, we are asked to remain where we are, and to do all we can to regain our Balance.= He prepared to withdraw his thoughts. =Gredin is First Speaker,= he said in conclusion, =and is doing what she can to keep your return orderly, but it may not be possible for long. You and your Team should prepare yourselves. Your kinsmen will be frantic to greet you. And, Yohn…=

=Yes?=

=Contact me later if you have questions that your House cannot answer. And welcome. We are deeply thankful to have you and your Tradeteam here among us.=

Mind speech had always been challenging for Burlon. He could converse with someone's private mind or he could observe his actual surroundings, but it was largely impossible for him to do both at once. And so, having ended his conversation with Yohn te Avilar, he found the moments that followed were like waking from a night thought. He had to blink to clear his sight, and it took a few moments before what he saw truly coalesced in his mind.

The dome was down.

Yohn and his Tradeteam were leaving the arrival dais, loaded with bundles.

And the room was utterly silent.

Struck by how unlikely that seemed, Burlon looked to Gredin.

She stood as he had last seen her, arms crossed, pendant clasped in one hand while the fingers of her other hand pressed hard against First

Speaker's hlette. She looked like a stone carving, beautiful to behold but too motionless to be real.

Alarmed, Burlon looked to his left, then to his right, then craned his head around to look at the people seated behind him.

They, too, seemed carved from stone, frozen in place.

A prickle of heat ran over Burlon's skin at the unnatural sight. Rising on unsteady legs, he hurried forward, gesturing for Yohn and his Tradeteam to stop at the bottom of the steps. "A moment," he said, his voice a hoarse croak. "Wait just a moment."

Yohn did as he asked, turning to answer the low, urgent questions of his companions.

"Gredin?" Burlon approached her, unsure what had transpired, but quite certain she was the source of it. "Gredin, it's all right. You can release them now."

Nothing changed.

Burlon reached out and pried Gredin's fingertips away from the hlette.

A violent shiver coursed through her, and her eyes widened. "No!" she whispered. "Don't! Without the hlette, I cannot–"

Behind him, people began to stir and murmur.

Burlon enveloped Gredin's chill hand in his warm one. "It's all right. You've done what was needed. It's over. You can let go now."

He had intended to ask her to announce the names of the new arrivals, but she looked ghastly, her lips tinged with blue, her breath coming in gasps, her whole body trembling. Slipping an arm around her, he guided her to the steps and helped her to sit. And when that seemed to bring her only marginal relief, he eased his hold on her hand and pressed her fingertips against the gleaming hlette again.

A sigh eased out of her. "Are they well?" she asked, her words scarcely audible.

"Who? The new Tradeteam?"

"No. The community."

He stared. "Why wouldn't they be?"

She shook her head. "I didn't mean to… I only intended…" She lifted her head and looked at him, her gaze troubled. "I didn't know I could hold them, like that. I just meant to win you time to explain. But everyone was upset, some afraid of the dome, some uncertain what was happening, and… and… I just wanted everyone to stay seated and still for a minute."

"Well, you certainly managed that."

"But there were so many, and they were already so agitated. I kept remembering the morning they pressed in on me, and I didn't want that to happen to the Travelers, and so I… I…" She shook her head again. "In truth, I don't know what I did, or how."

"You won the new arrivals the time they needed. You need do no more."

"But Tetralanna–"

"No. Leave it, for now. We have regained five of our people, five we thought were lost forever. That is wonder enough for one day. We'll sort the rest tomorrow."

The reception hall was filling with the robust sound of voices, some uplifted in joy, some in excitement, some in grief, some in question. The community, in all its complexity and contradiction, seemed none the worse for the momentary stillness that had been forced upon them.

Burlon stood and reached a hand down to Gredin. "You need your bed."

She looked up at him, her face still pale. "In a bit, when I feel stronger."

"Now. You have only to stand. I will take you there."

"No. Please. I have no wish to look ill in front of the entire community by having you carry me to my chamber."

"And you think huddling here is any better? Well, be at peace. I don't intend to please Tetralanna by parading you through the reception hall. Rise to your feet, for the benefit of anyone who might be watching, and I will Send both of us to your rooms."

"But we aren't supposed to Send."

That surprised him into a laugh. "And who laid down that rule? I did. It was meant for those unused to Tradepoint, not for me." Again, he extended his hand. "Come. Make one effort. Stand, and I will do the rest."

She hesitated.

"Stubborn woman. Trust me."

Gredin's hand lifted to his.

He gripped it.

With a grimace of effort, she rose. Swaying on her feet, she said, "Perhaps I should…"

"No."

Placing himself between Gredin and the community, Burlon took hold of her and Sent.

[20]
1558 OF 2000 ORBITS REMAINING: 13PURPLE

Ingarra clung to Gredin's arm. "Oh, nifflin, you're certain this is safe?"

"I would never knowingly put you in danger," Gredin replied.

And that, Ingarra knew, was absolutely true. "Well, then, I'll stop worrying," she said, and settled the strap of the carrybag containing the *timte* quilt top more comfortably on her shoulder.

On her other side, Miri said, "Excellent. I'll do the same."

Ingarra smiled approvingly, trying not to let her pity show. Two days had passed since the astonishing arrival of the Avilar Tradeteam, a Tradeteam which included a member of House Kendar... but not the member Miri longed to see. Why had the Power spared Plithik te Kendar but not Miri's Chosen, Zanther?

It was one of many questions that held sleep at bay, each night. Only the comfort of Beda's arms allowed Ingarra to slip at last into slumber. But a Chosen's embrace was a comfort now denied to Miri, who had lost Zanther, and to Gredin, who had lost Dreff, and to...

"Hayla?" she asked, looking over her shoulder.

"Here," Hayla said, behind them.

Poor Hayla. Her Chosen, Cirin, had died in her arms and evanesced, leaving nothing behind but his empty clothing and First Traveler's hlette.

Compared to these three women, Ingarra knew she shouldn't complain. But she and Beda had a different pain to bear – the loss of their sons, Refik and Julen. Out of all the kinsmen so abruptly gone from their lives, it was their faces she missed the most…

No, no. Dark thoughts wouldn't do. Leaving the enclave for the first time since their arrival on Tradepoint was intended to be an adventure and a reward.

Releasing Gredin's arm, she said, "I'll step back and walk with Hayla, if you and Miri don't mind. I'm hoping for her help at the Shodekekeen maartza."

"A fine idea," Gredin said. "Burlon says Hayla has an excellent eye for color and design. Burlon has her on the lookout, today, for… Well, I'll let her explain it to you."

Ingarra fell into step with Hayla. "So, Burlon has recruited you, too, has he? That gives us something in common. What is it he's asked of you?"

The delicate skin beneath Hayla's eyes had darkened as if she, too, found sleep elusive. "Burlon is skilled at pulling others in on his schemes. He and Gredin want simple ways to make our new quarters more welcoming."

That seemed a tall order. The larger living quarters provided by the Prett were no cozier than the rest of Tradepoint. Linking several new enclaves to the original four, the Prett were equipping them with large metal boxes, open on one end, one box for each Vennan.

The metal boxes were tall; no worry of bumping your head. And each was deep enough for a generous sleeping area at the back, where it was private, and a sitting area toward the open front. Two people standing with their arms outstretched might just be able to bridge the width. And Chosen couples like herself and Beda were assigned a box twice that width, with low dividers to indicate separate 'rooms.' The foam sleeping mats donated by the Prett were thick and comfortable, but were the only furnishings most people had, aside from the bedding they'd brought from home.

Home…

Ingarra forced her attention back to Hayla. "Welcoming boxes? A challenge."

Hayla shrugged. "When you live in a metal box, any addition will improve it."

"True," Ingarra conceded. "So then, you're seeking…?"

"Things that are colorful and cost little, to make the rooms seem… softer. And fabric."

"Fabric is much of my errand, as well," Ingarra said, pleased. "We can explore the Shodekekeen maartza together. Gredin says they have fabric in all colors and textures. What will you use it for?"

"Privacy panels to hang at the entrance to each…" She grimaced. "I can't go on calling them 'boxes.' No one can be happy, thinking they live in a box. What shall we call them?"

Ingarra pondered the question. "Nests?"

That won a smile from Hayla. "The Prett would approve, since they think we fly up to them like birds. They first planned to build staircases to each level. Can you imagine?"

"Poor Prett, unable to Send."

"The entry openings need a curtain. If they're different colors and patterns, people can spot their own entry more easily. We can close them when we'd rather be on our own, and leave them pulled back when we're open to a visit."

"A fine idea. But with almost a thousand of us, you'll need a great deal of fabric," Ingarra said.

Hayla didn't look troubled. "We'll start with the draping panels we used to section off the communal sleep areas. I won't need much extra beyond that. The real trick will be sorting it all by color and pattern to prevent confusion over who lives where. You won't want six green panels all in a row."

"Definitely not. Once I finish my project for Burlon, I'll help you sort. We can chat while we work."

"I'd like that," Hayla said. "So, what does Burlon have *you* doing?"

"He calls it a *timte* quilt, and he says I am to purchase whatever I need for its completion, when we go to the Shodekekeen maartza. It's for the daughter of some Head of House on another world, to celebrate finding her Chosen. And I'm planning a magnificent coat to go with it. The girl and her Chosen will be settling in the Middle Realm, where the winters are colder than she is accustomed to, and her new Chosen's father, and her own mother, want her to have these gifts to keep her warm."

"Did Burlon say what world they are on?"

"I believe he called it Sprygale," Ingarra said, pleased that she remembered, and was gratified to see Hayla nod sagely. "Ah, you know of it?"

"Indeed. It's the source of our geddel-crystal Trades with the Prett. That explains why Burlon is so eager for matters to go well, whatever the cost. He would do nearly anything to please the Prett, and the simplest way to please the Prett is to collect a big supply of geddel crystals on his next Trading trip to Sprygale. If you do a handsome job on this quilt and coat, it will help keep us safe, here on Tradepoint."

The thought was intimidating. "I'm just a Needleworker."

"And Burlon is just a Trader and Traveler. But the two of you, by combining your gyftes, can do much to sweeten the mood of the Sprygalians. And that, in turn, will do much to sweeten the mood of the Prett. And sweetening the mood of the Prett will do much to keep us safe."

Ingarra wasn't sure she wanted that responsibility resting on her shoulders. How much worse, then, must Gredin feel, responsible for the safety of the entire community? And that nonsense Tetralanna had stirred up, claiming to be Head of House! She might preen and strut and attempt to lay claim to the title, but words didn't make it so. How hurtful for Gredin, working so hard to do what the Power asked of her, to have Tetralanna and the other House volunteers attempt to brush her aside…

"I haven't upset you, have I?" Hayla asked. "My words were meant as praise."

"No, no," Ingarra assured her. "I only hope my work will be good enough."

Gredin said, over her shoulder, "Needlework is the Power's gyfte to you, and you serve it well. Of course it will be good enough."

"And what of you, Miri?" Hayla asked. "What takes you to the Traders' Market?"

A nervous giggle. "Burlon, again. The Polpethtira asked him if they could purchase a packet of our food for their journey home."

"Which ones are they?" Ingarra asked. "Were they at the reception?"

It was Gredin who answered. "Yes. The purple-skinned women who wear painted designs instead of clothing."

"With the baskets!"

"Yes." She glanced back. "Hayla, you should look at their baskets when Miri delivers the food packet. I don't know what the cost might be, but the baskets are light and sturdy and colorful. They would be a pleasing sight on a wall when they weren't in use."

"I will look," Hayla assured her. "It would be easier to justify the expense if an item is useful as well as pretty."

They walked in companionable silence for the next stretch of the corridor, and Ingarra saw with pleasure how the overhead lights glinted on Gredin's new outfit. It was fashioned from the material given by the Shodekekeen at the reception. The teal fabric bore delicate traceries of bronze thread that gleamed when light struck them.

She would have made the outfit sooner, since Gredin was short of clothing, but there had been a disagreement between Gredin and Burlon as to what sort of outfit it should be. From a practical point of view, Gredin wanted a duplicate of her travel outfit: pants, tunic, and jacket. But Burlon felt she should dress as befitted her position as First Speaker, and had suggested a floor-length gown.

As a compromise, Ingarra had crafted a one-piece, sleeveless garment, belted at the waist, with the bottom forming a pair of flared pantlegs. At rest, it looked like a gown. In motion, it gave Gredin freedom of movement. With the remaining material, Ingarra had made both a shawl and a fitted jacket with a high, formal neck that covered Gredin's throat, and long, flared sleeves that buttoned at the wrist. Part of the right sleeve was slit and seamed into an openwork trellis that revealed glimpses of First Speaker's hlette, where it embraced Gredin's upper arm.

Today, Gredin had left the top few buttons of the stiff collar undone. It gave the outfit an unexpectedly rakish air. In addition, Ingarra had interwoven Gredin's braids with several of the teal ribbons that had accompanied the Shodekekeen offering. If they crossed Burlon's path at the Traders' Market, Ingarra was confident he would approve of the impression Gredin made.

"We're nearly there," Gredin said. "Miri, Ingarra, I will act as your interpreter. Hayla, I am uncertain how much Tradetalk you know. If you wish to speak for yourself, I will stand aside. But if you need any assistance..."

"I will welcome your help if matters get beyond my comprehension."

"Very well. Everyone stay together. We will move as a group of four. If anything alarms you, tell me. And remember, say nothing of Venna's fate. It is not yet known, beyond ourselves and the Prett." Gredin stopped and turned to face them. "I do not doubt your discretion. I mean it only as a reminder, since there is no need to avoid the topic within the enclave."

"And yet everyone does avoid it," Miri said, as if the words pained her. "Some folk collapse, wailing, at the slightest mention of what has befallen us, while the rest stride about, full of energy and purpose, as if nothing were wrong at all..."

"Well, for the moment, striding is wiser," Ingarra said. "We have left the safety of the enclave behind and ventured forth on necessary business. To accomplish our errands, we will mingle with other races. I am unaccustomed to that, and appreciate having you three beside me. Today is a change in routine, a chance to experience new things. And we will keep one another safe." She turned to Gredin. "What happens first?"

"We go to the Polpethtira maartza so Miri can deliver her food packet and Hayla can look at their basketwork. Then we'll seek out the Shodekekeen maartza."

They arrived in front of a pair of huge metal doors which stood closed against them.

"This is the entrance to the Traders' Market," Gredin explained.

"Many here will be busy, hurrying from place to place. Some will be friendly. A few may frown or turn away, but they will offer you no harm. If you feel alarmed for any reason, say my name loudly and reach out to me with your private mind. I will deal with any situation that arises, and Prett security guards are here to see that nothing goes badly wrong. Are you ready to meet the Polpethtira? Their maartza is close to the entrance."

"We are ready."

To Ingarra's surprise, it was Hayla who said it, not Miri. In the days since Cirin's death, Hayla had been slack and subdued. People were ill at ease around her. They had all witnessed Cirin's death, through Sill's projected Memory of it, and it was difficult to know what to say about the shocking event. Ingarra considered Hayla's decision to accompany them to the Traders' Market to be a hopeful sign, since she could have stayed sequestered in her new 'nest' in K'lar's enclave. Better for her to be here, facing new sights and experiences.

Gredin did something to the panel and the huge doors slid open.

The Traders' Market was immense. Ingarra hesitated on the threshold, astonished by the Market's dimensions. It made the reception hall of the Vennan enclave seem tiny. And, while she had seen foreign guests on the night of the Trisectoriana, there had been no more than three individuals from any given race. Here, groups large and small wandered the broad aisles.

Gredin and Miri moved forward, projecting calm confidence, and Ingarra followed, not wanting to be separated from them in this unfamiliar place.

Two plump individuals with white hair passed, heading toward the Market doors. The two talked animatedly, but the sounds their mouths made were incomprehensible, like a babbling brook. Was it a language Gredin spoke? That seemed impossible, yet Gredin had spent long hours of her childhood with the Balamont Traders, listening to stories of this place and studying languages other than her own.

"Here we are," Gredin said, and guided them into a bright storefront.

Ingarra had no idea what purpose the objects on the shelves served but she recognized the colorful basketwork that held the items. The three Polpethtiran baskets brought as gifts to the reception had been spirited away for use in the kitchens, but not before Ingarra had admired them. And now she saw dozens of such baskets, in a wide range of sizes.

One of the Polpethtiran traders came toward them, a small, fine-boned woman whose skin was a deep, rich shade of purple. Her head was devoid of hair, but the curve of her scalp was decorated with intricate white designs. Coils and curves and tendrils covered the woman's neck and shoulders, her arms and hands and fingers. Her body, with its small, high breasts and lean belly, was equally adorned, as were her legs and feet.

Did the designs cover her back, as well? If so, Polpethtiran traders must help each other paint their designs, much as House members spent time braiding one another's hair, to achieve such an elaborate pattern. Did the paint smear when it rubbed against a bedmat, to be redone every morning, or was it impervious to smudges?

The little trader spoke to Gredin in a language Ingarra didn't recognize. Gredin responded and gestured toward Miri.

Beside Ingarra, Hayla murmured, "The Polpethtira is welcoming us… and Gredin is explaining that Miri is the kitchen Tender who prepared the food packet."

The Polpethtira looked at the substantial bundle Miri carried, then spoke again to Gredin, who nodded. With a smile that needed no translation, the woman drew her fingertip down her face from eye to chin in a gentle curve, then turned to look at Miri and repeated the gesture.

"She's thanking them," Hayla confirmed.

Miri said, "Gredin, explain to her that these things should be kept frozen until the day they want to eat them."

"Of course," Gredin said, and launched into sounds that meant nothing to Ingarra.

"Let's take a look around," Hayla suggested, and Ingarra followed her to where a cluster of baskets were displayed. Unlike the other baskets in the maartza, these were empty, artistically arranged on a countertop. Hayla lifted one and turned it to look at the bottom, then rotated it slowly. "They're much lighter than I expected," she said. "I don't know what they're made of, but the colors are lovely."

Ingarra looked down and gasped. "Such a beautiful carpet!"

Hayla said, on a wistful note, "Marvelous, but likely far too expensive for our purposes. The baskets, on the other hand…"

Ingarra realized that Hayla was probably right, but the notion was unwelcome. Admiring something and finding its price beyond her was a situation she had never encountered before. At home, the Common Market was a pleasurable place to wander, surveying goods produced by other Houses. If an item caught your eye and you sincerely desired it, you found an opportunity to meet with your Head of House, and the item invariably became yours. It stung deeply, to think the old ways were gone.

And Hayla was in an even more difficult position, tasked with finding items that could enhance all of the nests the Prett had newly provided. The carpet looked expensive. Without House funds to call upon the purchase of hundreds of such carpets was clearly impossible. Indeed, even that many baskets might amount to more expense than they dared to contemplate.

Of course, there was no need for every nest to be identically furnished, but who would decide what items went to which individuals? How could such matters be handled fairly within the community? How many furnishings could they afford, while, according to Gredin, Burlon still strove to ensure that they had sufficient food on their plates?

Ingarra felt tiny, one face in a vast sea of Vennans who all had needs, desires, worries. And now, within House Balamont, she was expected to confide her concerns to Tetralanna! Unter had been a kind man, never in a hurry, always willing to listen, inclined to think the best of folk and treat everyone kindly. But Tetralanna didn't like her, and she didn't like Tetralanna. Where did that leave her, now that Tetralanna had declared herself to be in charge?

She knew she could go directly to Gredin with her worries, but it horrified her to think of the weight of responsibility that now rested on her nifflin's young shoulders. In good conscience, how could she and Beda add their personal concerns to that load?

"I am going to ask her," Hayla said, with an air of bright determination.

Ingarra realized that Hayla had been talking for some time, and she had simply blocked the sense of it from her mind, intent on her own worries. That wouldn't do. "Your pardon," she said. "I was pondering something. What is it that you are going to ask?"

"No matter." Energy drained from Hayla's voice. "It was likely a foolish idea."

"No, tell me. Please. It was thoughtless of me to become distracted. I would very much like to hear what you are contemplating."

"Well, Gredin says the Polpethtira will journey home soon. It's why they want the food packet. I wondered if she could ask them about the price of the baskets, and how many they might bring when they return. There are fewer than a hundred baskets here, and nearly a thousand of us, and I'm uncertain how many they might agree to bring. But then I wondered whether they might be willing to sell all of the baskets here in their maartza, as a start, when they leave. That would be enough for each House to have some, and the initial cost would not be so great."

"Indeed, ask her," Ingarra said. "There is no harm – and no cost – in a simple question. And the baskets are as practical as they are lovely."

Hayla looked encouraged. "I want to take care how I spend the community's money, not knowing what hardships lie ahead, but bare metal nests do nothing to lift people's spirits. With the baskets, people can put them to use and enjoy a bright spot of color and craftsmanship, as well."

A glance showed Ingarra that Gredin and Miri had concluded their talk with the Polpethtiran trader. "Go and tell her your thoughts," Ingarra urged, and Hayla went to do so.

Left on her own, Ingarra strolled through the maartza, bemused by the contrast between the intricate, well-made baskets and the strange metal objects they held. *Griimoni* were a mystery to her, and it intrigued her that the Polpethtira had mastered such disparate skills.

They seemed a contradictory people. Uninterested in adorning their bodies with clothing, they still took time to cover themselves with painted designs. They communicated with one another silently, through hand gestures, yet were capable of speaking aloud to Gredin. Their skin was the dark purple of a voke berry, in contrast to the pale gold of Vennan skin. They seemed gentle and intelligent, the sort who could be good neighbors, even friends, if the Vennans lived on Tradepoint for any great length of time before the Travelers found New Venna.

Or perhaps that discovery would happen soon, and they would leave all of this strangeness behind, settling down to rebuild their lives under an open sky.

But that couldn't happen until Gredin permitted the Travelers to begin their search. And, as much as Ingarra longed for New Venna to be found, she couldn't fault Gredin for her caution. The community was not at peace. People like Beda seemed to have recovered from the initial shock and were acting largely as they used to, despite the underlying sadness that beset them all. But others were upset, arguing over trifles or bursting into tears. Some had no appetite, or spent their days in silence, ignoring concerned questions from their kin. She had even heard that some had taken to their beds and had to be coaxed and chivvied into coming to table for meals.

Beda said she mustn't let such things cause her distress, and pointed out that most folk were dealing bravely with circumstances. But she didn't have to look far to see individuals doing less well. Even the Needlecrafters working with her on the Sprygalian *timte* quilt were a cause for concern. Yesterday, Dabin te Indirin had pricked her finger so many times with the point of her needle that she required attention from a minor Healer. Imagine, a Needlecrafter pricking her finger! And Carbera te Torr cut several pattern pieces carelessly and stitched them into place so poorly that Ingarra had to remove and replace them. She'd waited until after he left the work session to do so, to avoid upsetting him further, but it made her wonder what the quality of his work would be when he returned. This quilt was an important Trade item. And they were short of material. Pieces inaccurately cut were a waste they could ill afford.

Still, people mattered more than things. She had no wish to hurt Carbera's pride. With a few meals and a night of sleep, he might rally. But she would sit close at hand, the next time he assisted with the project, and watch what he was doing, to head off future difficulties.

It was worrying. People's gyftes were an integral part of them. Other things might falter, but not their gyfte. Yet that was exactly what had happened to Dabin and Carbera.

Well, they had each lost their Chosen, on top of all their other woes. Ingarra would make allowances. But a person's gyfte was among their greatest solaces in life...

"Ingarra? Are you all right?"

It was Gredin's voice, as familiar as Beda's. Ingarra turned. "I'm fine," she said. "Are we ready to go on?"

Gredin nodded. "The Polpethtira are going to part with all of these baskets when they journey home tomorrow. They have offered them to Hayla at a small price, insisting it is only fair since the baskets have been used, and they say they'll have the baskets delivered to our warehouse. They will bring new baskets when they return, on the understanding that we will know by then how many more of our people would like to add one to their new living area – or, as you and Hayla call it, their 'nest.' And they seem delighted with the food packet Miri brought. So our business here is complete and we are ready to seek my friends at the Shodekekeen maartza."

Her words filled Ingarra with a thrill of anticipation. The lengths of Shodekekeen fabric she had worked with were astonishing in their quality and depth of color, and she was eager to see what else they might have to offer. There were days, as she and the other Needleworkers sewed on the Sprygalian *timte* quilt, that she felt a pang over their dwindling supply of thread and material, and found herself deeply in sympathy with Keegan te Fliss and his concern over his waning store of ink and paper. But she was luckier than he; the Shodekekeen maartza sounded like a trove of fabric, thread, and dyes that could be used by her gyfte. And now she would see it for herself, with permission from Gredin and Burlon to obtain whatever she might need.

Again, Gredin and Miri took the lead. This time, Miri's hands were empty, for she had delivered the precious packet of food to the Polpethtira. Hayla carried a single Polpethtiran basket. "They insisted I take one with me to show others at the enclave what is soon to come."

In front of them, Gredin and Miri stopped so abruptly that Ingarra nearly collided with them. Looking past Gredin's shoulder, Ingarra stifled a shriek of alarm.

Three Hesch stood side by side, blocking their path.

"Vennan!" the middle one said, its voice loud and hoarse.

In front of Ingarra, Gredin bowed her head in acknowledgment. "Nitikikani."

Ingarra remembered that name. This Hesch was the one who had leaned upon two others at the reception. Today, the Hesch walked without aid, gripping a black staff in one claw-like hand for support.

The other two Hesch clacked their bills. Ingarra was unsure what that meant, but it sounded ominous. She clutched Hayla's arm. "Where is Prett security?" she whispered.

"Hush." Hayla patted her hand. Did that mean the danger was less than Ingarra feared? Or did it mean that matters were very dangerous indeed?

As the Hesch spoke again, Hayla leaned close to murmur a translation so deftly in her ear that Ingarra had the sense of understanding the Tradetalk exchange.

"You same Vennan break bone," the center Hesch accused. "Wear firestone."

"Same," Gredin acknowledged.

More clacking of bills. The Hesch were tall creatures, their naked black heads clearly visible above Gredin and Miri.

"Judgment say you be go, many day past."

Gredin made no reply.

"You ignore Director, ignore Judgment. Stay Tradepoint. Walk hall. Dare come Market."

Gredin stood silent.

"Nitikikani complain Director. Vennan pay more Judgment." The Hesch raised a long, thin arm wrapped in a garment consisting of strips of black and green gauze, and pointed over their heads, back the way they had come. "You leave Market. You leave Tradepoint. Go!"

"Not so," Gredin said, sounding calm and firm. "Nitikikani want talk Director? Nitikikani go do. I talk Shodekekeen. *Then* leave Market."

Nitikikani emitted a sound that might almost have been a chuckle, and spoke in a voice grown suddenly soft, but containing a thread of threat that made Ingarra tremble. "Vennan much rich, eh? No care Judgment get more big? Pack bag soon, little Vennan. I talk Director, you go home. Other Vennan here be much mad, learn new Judgment you make happen."

"I hear." Gredin's tone was serene. "Now Hesch move. Shodekekeen maartza I go."

Ingarra's breath came in little snatches.

Then Gredin looked down and said, softly, "Foot better?"

Nitikikani made a harsh sound, then demanded, so loudly that Ingarra jumped, "Move!"

Gredin pulled Miri to the left, and Hayla drew Ingarra that way, as well. The three Hesch swept past and stalked off down the aisle with a final clack of their bills.

Miri began to cry.

Gredin embraced her. "I am sorry you had to stand so close while that went on." She patted Miri's back. "But it isn't wise for us to show our emotions so plainly. Can you calm yourself enough to meet with the Shodekekeen, or shall I take you back to the enclave?"

Miri shook her head. "I'll go on."

"I'll walk with her," Hayla said. "Lead the way with Ingarra."

Hayla passed her arm around Miri's shoulders, and Ingarra stepped up to walk beside Gredin, as she had done so often in the past.

"You were very brave," Ingarra said when they were all walking again.

"The Hesch like to tower over others, but they won't harm us, least of all here."

"Where were the guards when that Hesch was talking to you so harshly?"

"Oh, they were near," Gredin said. "I saw at least two, watching us. If I had called out, they would have aided us. But they know the Hesch well, and likely sensed that matters would go more smoothly if they didn't involve themselves. Much of what happens on Tradepoint is posturing. Traders need to do business, but no one wants to be perceived as weak." She sighed. "And Nitikikani is right. I *am* supposed to be gone. But I couldn't explain my continued presence without admitting what happened to Venna. So I encouraged him to carry his grievance to Wyve. It may force Wyve to invent a half-truth to explain my presence, but my wits could work no faster."

"And if the Director increases the fine?"

Gredin's smile was lopsided. "Wyve knows we aren't here by choice. I doubt he'll penalize us for something that can't be helped." She glanced behind. "Just a little farther, Miri. Then we'll–"

Something moved, drawing Ingarra's attention. She put her hand on Gredin's arm to halt her. A stream of small individuals spilled into the aisleway in front of them, moving quickly, chattering. As Ingarra and Gredin stumbled to a halt, with Hayla and Miri on their heels, indignant cries went up, although Ingarra's hasty warning had prevented any collision.

"Vennan!"

Gredin's voice sounded within her private mind. =These are Beng,= Gredin informed her silently. =They are pests, and angry with us. Stand very still. I will address them in Tradetalk and give you a sense of what we say to one another.=

"Silly Vennan!" one Beng proclaimed. "Walk while look over shoulder? Not smart."

Gredin stared down at the interlopers. "Beng walk sideways across aisle. Confuse? Lose way to Beng maartza? Want I ask security guard help you?" Her tone was solicitous, and she was smiling, but Ingarra felt even warier than she had when the Hesch shouted at them.

"No need Prett guard," a different Beng replied. "We be escort you."

"No," Gredin countered. "Vennan do Vennan business. Beng do Beng business."

"Vennan no order Beng. Beng go where Beng want go. No more Judgment say Beng keep away Vennan. Trader Market open everybody."

"True," Gredin said. "Beng free go where want. Vennan free go where want."

"True. Where Vennan want go?"

Gredin pointed ahead. "That way go. Where Beng want go?"

"Same."

Another unsettling smile from Gredin. "We walk together. You want lead?"

"No, no. We follow."

"Fine," she said, but her voice within Ingarra's mind added, =Hayla, lead us. Ingarra, take Miri's arm and walk behind Hayla. I will follow at the back. Move. Now.=

Their sudden adjustment of positions seemed to rattle the Beng, who fell away hastily to either side of the aisle.

=Walk briskly, Hayla,= Gredin directed. =I will direct you to the Shodekekeen maartza as we go. Once we are inside it, the Beng cannot enter. They are no danger, just an aggravation.=

Ingarra hooked her arm through Miri's and followed in Hayla's wake, glad Miri no longer wept. Trusting Gredin to walk between them and the Beng, Ingarra tried to stay calm.

Beng voices rang out, sometimes laughing, sometimes harsh. Gredin stopped translating, leaving Ingarra with no idea what they said. Whatever it was, Gredin made no reply.

They passed several maartzas, one open, the rest closed. Then Gredin's voice sounded in Ingarra's mind again. =Hayla, the next lighted maartza on the right belongs to the Shodekekeen. As soon as you reach it, go inside and walk straight toward the back of the shop. Miri, Ingarra, follow close behind her. I don't want the Beng to sneak in ahead of us. Once we enter, it is against Tradepoint rules for them to come in.=

It seemed to take a long time to reach the lighted maartza, but finally it was upon them. Hayla turned sharply to her right, lengthened her stride, and walked boldly into the Shodekekeen maartza. Ingarra hurried after her, holding firmly to Miri's arm. But she didn't begin to feel truly safe until she saw heard Gredin behind her call out, "Shamka?"

"Grrdin?" came the nasal reply, and Ingarra heard Miri gasp as a blue-furred Shodekekeen rose onto its hindmost pair of legs and, incongruously, crossed its frontmost paws in credible imitation of a Vennan greeting. Then it peered past them and growled, low in its throat, before making a more complicated mewling sound which Gredin translated silently as, =You bring Beng?=

To Ingarra's surprise, Gredin rendered the ensuing conversation between herself and the creature into mind speech, a kindness for which Ingarra was deeply grateful.

"They follow," Gredin explained to the trader. "Pester us. Talk, talk, talk."

Shamka dropped to all six legs and lumbered past the Vennans to the threshold of the maartza. "Go!" he shouted at the Beng, then threw back his head and roared.

Within moments, a Prett security guard arrived. "Trouble, trader?" the guard asked.

"See Beng run there? Bother customer. You make stay distant, yes? When customer done, I call, you walk customer out, get transport pod, yes?"

"Yes," the guard said, and took up a position directly outside of the maartza, speaking into his wristcom as he did so.

Looking reassured, the Shodekekeen turned his back on the entry and rejoined the Vennans. Looking to Gredin he asked, "One Gara?"

"Yes!" Gredin affirmed. "This one." She turned her smile on Ingarra, saying in Vennan, "And this is Shamka. He hoped to meet you at the reception, but that didn't happen. He is a great admirer of your gyfte." She spread her arms and spun slowly, for Shamka's benefit. "Reception fabric you give. Gara just Make. You like?"

A soft humming sound came from Shamka. "Good," he said at last.

"Much good." He extended a long, curved claw and flicked the hem of the short jacket. "All one?"

"No, this come off," Gredin said, suiting her actions to her words. "And, same fabric, Gara Make..." She shook her head. "Not know word. Like this." Stepping to one of the display ladders, she removed a length of fabric and draped it around her shoulders to indicate a shawl, then returned it carefully to its rung.

"Minui," Shamka supplied.

Gredin nodded thanks. "Same fabric, Gara Make *minui*. Look many way, same clothes."

"Clever Gara," Shamka said, and Gredin infused her translation with such sincerity that Ingarra blushed. "Why come? What need?" Shamka asked Gredin warmly.

"Gara need fabric, need…" She went through the motions of threading a needle.

"Seela," Shamka provided. "Gara make what?"

Gredin turned to Ingarra. "Show him the quilt," she encouraged.

Ingarra knelt and opened her carrybag. Taking out the quilt, she turned back the top corner of tan material she had used as a temporary backing. Inch by inch, she revealed the beginning of the lustrous red, purple and gold design.

Shamka crooned, sinking down onto all six feet, and came forward slowly until he was close enough to reach out and touch the fabric.

"Open on table? See all?" he asked and gestured toward the back of the maartza.

"I'll help you carry it," Gredin said, and slid her hands under one end of the expanse of fabric while Ingarra took the other.

The table at the back of the maartza was immense, its smooth metal gleaming beneath the overhead lights. Relieved that the surface was clean and dry, Ingarra unfolded the *timte* quilt to its full size. It wasn't finished, but the pattern had progressed far enough to show the color gradations she was working to achieve, and the spiraling patterns of piecework.

Again, Shamka crooned, and leaned to touch a single claw

unerringly to a piece of fabric Ingarra had salvaged from the left-over material of Gredin's scarlet gown.

"Shodekekeen," he said with evident satisfaction.

"Yes," Gredin confirmed. "Gara use big fabric, Make gown. Use small fabric, Make this."

"Many small fabric, make big. Clever. Gara need small fabric make this more?"

"Yes."

Ingarra nudged at Gredin's private mind. =And I need a big piece of fabric for backing.=

Gredin nodded. "Gara say need one piece big fabric, also. Replace this." And she turned back an edge of the quilt to show the tan material to which the pattern pieces were pinned.

"Yes," Shamka said with unexpected emphasis. "Bad color. I find good." He reached under the table and pulled out a misshapen sack with a drawstring at its neck. "Gara look here. Many small piece. Many color. Too small be use most thing. Any good Gara find, Gara take, use." He dropped it at Ingarra's feet and made his way back to the main portion of the maartza.

"A scrap bag?" Hayla ventured, once he was gone.

"I believe so," Gredin said. "And it sounds as if anything useful you find in it is yours, without cost. I'll make certain that I understood him correctly, once we know if there's anything in there useful for the project."

"What has he gone off to do now?" Miri asked.

"I believe he's searching for a better material to back Ingarra's quilt."

"Would he mind if Miri and I looked around," Hayla asked, "to let my eyes absorb all this color? I am so tired of grey." As soon as the words left her lips, she grimaced. "Your pardon. I mean no criticism of Tradepoint. We are fortunate to have found shelter here. But…"

Ingarra looked up from her perusal of the quilt. "Color Speaks to us," she said to Hayla. "It plays a role in our gyftes, yours and mine, and nourishes our spirit in a way that I suspect the Prett don't feel, or they couldn't be comfortable living as they do. The Prett are friends and protectors, but they are not Vennan. We likely have more in common with the Shodekekeen, despite the differences in appearance. Six legs and blue fur matter less than–"

"Gara!" Shamka reappeared, carrying four large bolts of cloth. Placing them on the table with great ceremony, he said, "You look. Say good, say bad, tell why. Help Shamka make good choice you." Then he unfurled fabric from the first bolt until it covered most of the table.

It seemed an odd choice. The material was black – not a color associated with new Chosens – and seemed to soak up the illumination from the overhead lights. Still, she doubted Shamka would make a careless choice, so she continued to look. She found, as her eyes adjusted, that it was like the night sky. The longer she looked, the more she saw. There were tiny flecks of color in the fabric: a flicker of red, a twinkle of gold, a whisper of purple, a flash of deep green.

Ingarra slid one hand beneath the fabric and ran the fingertips of her other hand over it, assessing weight and texture. The fabric, stroked in one direction, resisted slightly. Stroked the other way, it was like stroking the downy feathers of a water hen's fresh-hatched brood.

"Interesting," she said at last, sliding her hands free. "If this quilt were for me, I would be tempted. But Burlon wants it to be impressive, not subtle."

She left Gredin to translate as best she could, and waited to see the next possibility.

Almost before Gredin finished, Shamka had rewound the bolt, set the dark fabric aside, and spooled out another expanse of material for her to examine.

This second selection was a startling contrast to the first. Its background was as white as the snows at the mountain Holding, splashed at random intervals with bursts of vivid colors – reds, blues, purples, oranges – that might represent blossoms, each as large as Ingarra's finger-splayed hand. When she slid one hand beneath the fabric and caressed it with her other, she was entranced to find that it was soft to the touch.

"It has possibilities. Burlon would approve of the boldness and the intensity of colors. Its texture is pleasant and would add extra warmth to the quilt. Can we set this one aside, until I have seen the others and can compare them?"

Gredin translated. Shamka rewound the material and set the bolt at the end of the table. Then he lifted the third fabric and displayed it for Ingarra. The way it shimmered and caught the light put Ingarra in mind of the flamestone Gredin wore around her neck. If pressed to state what color the fabric was, Ingarra could not have given a single answer. It was… changeable. With every blink or breath, it altered. She began to see a picture in her mind: this fabric, overlain with a widely spaced pattern of thin black strips stretched diagonally across the quilt, giving the illusion that each diamond-shaped exposure of the fabric beneath was a separate jewel.

Tears brimmed in Ingarra's eyes. Surely this fabric must be priced beyond their means. But her gyfte wanted it.

Burlon would want it, as well. She had no doubt. But how serious had he been about purchasing whatever she needed? It would be terrible if she told the Shodekekeen merchant that she wanted it, and Burlon had to return and say there had been a terrible mistake.

=Why are you upset?= Gredin asked within her mind.

=This is the fabric it should be. But what if Burlon thinks it is too expensive after I have already purchased it?=

=Shall I tell you the very words he spoke to me, in council? He said, 'Whatever we spend, we'll profit many times over when I take the quilt to Sprygale.' If this is the proper material, be joyful, not sad. Shall I tell Shamka, or do you wish to examine the fourth fabric?=

It was a little frightening to take so bold a step, but her gyfte sang within her, free of doubt. =I have no need to see the fourth fabric. Tell Shamka, please, that this fabric is what I want. And I will need a length of the first fabric, as well, to form the lattice.=

=What lattice?=

=Oh, Gredin, I can hardly wait for you to see it. It will be astonishing!=

After that, their visit passed in a whirl. Shamka helped her match colors of thread – or *seela*, as she must learn to think of it – against the fabrics, ranging from black to scarlet to purple to gold. At home, thread came in little pots, the free end protruding through a small hole in the lid. Here, each color of thread came wound around a metal rod.

When Ingarra had selected all of her colors of *seela*, Shamka brought out a small metal case with a floral design etched into its cover. When he opened it, Ingarra saw that there were slots where the ends of the metal rods would rest, making a pretty display of her new supplies.

"Sit and go through the scrap bag," Gredin suggested. "Hayla and I are going to talk to Shamka about cloth panels for the doorway openings."

"I am delighted to do so," Ingarra said. Caught up in her gyfte-vision of the finished quilt, she had forgotten the bag of remnants Shamka had produced earlier. Now, with the Sprygalian quilt and her new lengths of fabric and the metal case of *seela* set safely aside, she pulled the scrap sack onto her lap and began to pull remnants out.

Miri soon came, helping Ingarra create three separate piles. The first, which grew at a surprising rate, were scraps in the color range she was using for the quilt. Even very small pieces would be of potential use, as she and the other Needleworkers pieced together a mosaic of color gradations in reds, purples, and gold.

The second pile, also large, consisted of prints and colors that had no place in her quilt but might be of use to Hayla in her project to beautify the nests. Hayla herself would have to decide which pieces to retain.

The final pile was for scraps of no interest, mostly drab colors. The community had no need of browns, grays, blacks, muddy greens. Life was dim enough already.

When they had emptied the sack and placed all of the scraps from the final pile back into it, there was still a large quantity of material on the table in the first and second piles. Ingarra worried that she was being greedy. Perhaps Shamka only meant his offer as a token kindness, expecting them to find two or three remnants to their liking while leaving the rest. =Nifflin?= she ventured, and explained her quandary to Gredin.

=I will ask,= came the reply and then, soon after, "No, you may take it all, if you wish. The sack is where they stuff scraps during their stay on Tradepoint. When they go home, they discard the sack. Shamka is pleased if you can use anything there.=

=Wonderful. I will take pieces for Hayla, as well. How is she faring on panels for the entryways?=

=Not well. There is much lovely fabric but she suspects the price is more than we dare spend. She wishes to confer with Burlon again before purchasing anything. If you and Miri are finished, join us. There are several things you should see.=

=Of course. We are coming.=

When she and Miri reached the main area of the shop, Gredin summoned her to a display by the wall. =Feel this,= she said, fingering the end of a bolt of gray-green fabric.

Ingarra approached it, dubious. The color was unappealing. It coordinated with nothing she was Making, and it would be a dreadful color on any Vennan. And the texture did nothing to improve her opinion. Neither soft nor rough, it had a sleek feel to it. "What drew you to this?" Ingarra asked, at a loss.

Gredin looked amused. "I know the color doesn't please the eye, but it is not meant to be seen. Shamka says it is popular because it keeps away the cold. Here. Wrap the end of it around your hand and hold onto it."

Willing to indulge her, Ingarra did so. "Now what?"

"Nothing. Just hold it for a short time while we talk. Have you found all that you need for the coat?"

Ingarra sighed heavily, her worries returning. "No."

"Shamka will show you where he keeps fabrics with only enough left for one or two projects. And he wishes to discuss whether you might sew a special garment for him. It is something the Thalken ordered, very delicate, and he is impressed by the quality of your work. If you take on the Thalken garment, your labor could be exchanged for supplies for the coat."

Ingarra's gyfte stirred within her at the thought. She longed to Make that coat. She could *see* it, yet she had begun to worry it was too ambitious, and too costly, however optimistic Burlon might feel. But if she could manage an exchange rather than a purchase…

"Tell Shamka I am very interested in hearing about the Thalken garment."

"Good. And how does your hand feel?"

"My hand?"

Gredin smiled. "Your hand that is wrapped in fabric."

Bemused, Ingarra said, "It feels… cozy. Much warmer than the rest of me."

"Indeed. That is this fabric's property. It is neither thick nor thin, and not a pretty color, but it captures body warmth and retains it. Might it do well, hidden between quilt and backing?"

"Or between a coat and its lining," Ingarra murmured. How wonderful if the quilt and coat could keep someone truly warm without thick padding between the layers! Would it not astonish the Sprygalians if the girl dressed prettily and was still cozy, despite the chill?

Looking at the dull-colored cloth, life was suddenly full of exciting possibilities.

"Can we talk to Shamka? And see the materials that are in short supply? And obtain enough of this lovely, lovely fabric to place a layer of it within both the coat and the quilt?"

Gredin beamed. "Of course. Come with me."

[21]

1537 OF 2000 ORBITS REMAINING: 33GREEN

Returning to the Traders' Market for the first time since his mortifying ejection from the Hesch maartza, Burlon felt just as he supposed Keegan felt when he sampled Prett grain at the Clinic – as if his insides were being turned sideways and squeezed.

Happily, he had no need to cross paths with the Hesch today.

Unhappily, he was on his way to Trade with the Beng, instead.

He had put the visit off for the better part of four days, telling himself that he needed time to regain his temper, and the Hesch might still relent. Then the shocking arrival of the Avilar Tradeteam had given him an excuse to hope that other teams might still arrive, and that he should be there to greet them. Moreover, he'd reasoned that his presence in the enclave was essential while Tetralanna and the other House volunteers still deluded themselves that they were House Heads forming a legitimate High Council, in direct defiance of the Power's instructions to Gredin te Balamont. It was a situation Gredin needed to correct without further delay, for it had been allowed to continue too long, as it was.

Last night, however, someone had made a wistfully critical comment about the Wilra grain that now appeared, in one form or another, at nearly every meal. And this morning, waking in the sweet security of Chenna's arms, he had admitted to himself that postponing his return to the Market was a craven personal weakness he was indulging at the community's expense.

So here he was at the Traders' Market entrance. He deliberately had not looked to see whether the Hesch maartza was open. He could not allow their presence or absence to dictate his actions. He was here for one purpose only: to dicker with the slippery Beng.

He reached the Beng maartza quickly, not letting himself browse along the way. When he reached it, he saw that no other traders were currently doing business there.

Go in, he commanded himself, and walked inside.

Three Beng were present, short, stocky figures, identically dressed in green coveralls, laughably small beside the mounded islands of bulging sacks. Burlon, having researched, knew that each mound was a different grain with its own characteristic flavor and texture.

Miri would be delighted.

He was unsure how to begin. No House had dealt with the Beng in recent memory. Still, Trade was Trade. And he had brought something special to coax the deal along, at need.

The three Beng exchanged glances, then turned their attention back to him. One Beng took a small step forward, grinning. "Vennan lost?"

It was a fair enough jibe, considering how many sectora had passed since a Vennan Trader had entered the Beng maartza. He managed a wry grin and gestured at the high-piled sacks. "Beng maybe lost, too. Stacks much high!"

"Good Beng grain. Many kind – stezzin, beek, faralat, doro, piprill. Bring Tradepoint some each. Beng proud. Good crop."

"Tell more," Burlon invited, to put them at their ease. "This Vennan know little. Want learn. You talk each kind, yes?"

If the Beng were surprised by his request, they hid it well. But then, all good traders did.

Huddling together, they talked amongst themselves, glancing up at him occasionally. Then they broke apart and nodded. "Vennan come sit. Beng talk grain."

They ushered him deeper into the maartza, maneuvering around several mountains of sacks. The arrangement seemed haphazard but, when they reached their destination, he realized that the staggered locations of the grain now screened him entirely from view of the public aisle.

They're not as silly as they try to appear, he reminded himself. *Keep your wits at hand.*

One Beng returned to the front of the maartza. The other two seated themselves on padded stools on one side of a table, gesturing for Burlon to seat himself on the other side.

The stool provided was the same size as theirs, reaching only to the middle of his shins, and the tabletop barely reached his knees.

The mismatch was obvious, which meant it was intentional, which in turn meant he had only two choices: accept their 'hospitality' as offered, or leave.

Burlon lowered himself onto the ridiculous little stool.

It occurred to him that the Beng always had to cope with the proportions of Tradepoint. Everywhere but in their maartza, enclave, and ship, the Beng faced out-sized surroundings. Did that account for their unending belligerence? The Thalken were even shorter… but the Thalken were ill-tempered, too. Maybe it was a protective stance. After all, you could make at least five Beng or a half a dozen Thalken out of one average-sized Prett. It must be unsettling.

At the start of any Trade, Burlon found it useful to consider what life was like for his current trading partners: their strengths, weaknesses, needs, and wants. This time, though, he was glad to end the exercise. There was no pleasure in imagining himself as a Beng.

"So." The Beng sat straight-backed on his stool, projecting a businesslike air. "What Vennan trader seek?"

"New grain, maybe. Vennan kitchen like try new taste."

The Beng nodded. "What taste now?"

Burlon looked at him, confused. "Say again."

"Beng many taste. Vennan want new taste. What Vennan old taste?"

Oh. Of course. "Wilra grain. D'limten."

The Beng's short nose wrinkled. "Loud taste."

The Wilra would have called the flavor 'bold,' or 'distinctive.' But he supposed 'loud' was a fair description, as grains went.

The Beng turned to his companion. "Stezzin, beek, faralat, piprill."

The second Beng scurried off.

"What Vennan kitchen want make?"

Burlon spread his hands. "Many thing."

"Name."

Tradetalk was not a language rich in food names since only certain classes of edible items were commonly sold. There were several words for 'grain' in Tradetalk, but none for 'bread.' Spices went by their name in the language of the race selling them. Fruits were a rarity, but jams and jellies were sometimes available. Milk was never for sale, but cheeses could occasionally be found. Meat was absent except in preserved forms. And the availability of all of it varied, depending on who was in port.

It left Burlon unsure how to respond. Then he thought of a solution. "You go reception Vennan enclave?"

A scowl. "No. Three only go."

"Those Beng talk you?"

A nod.

"Talk Vennan food?"

A vigorous nod.

"Vennan kitchen want make more."

That brought a glint to the Beng's eye.

The second Beng returned, carrying four miniature sacks.

Samples.

The first Beng said, "Piprill. Beek. Stezzin. Faralat."

"Piprill," Burlon repeated. "Taste loud? Soft? Use make what?"

"Piprill much soft taste. Do many thing. Put good with other thing."

A mild grain, versatile, without a distinctive flavor of its own. Miri would–

The second Beng pulled out a knife and flicked it open.

Burlon held very still, saying nothing.

At a gesture from the first Beng, the second used his glittering blade to slash the material of the first little bag as if it were the Shodekekeen's flimsy yellow paper. Tiny pellets cascaded onto the tabletop, reddish brown, rolling in all directions.

"Is what?" Burlon asked, unsettled by the quick slash of the knife and the resulting mess.

"Piprill. Thirsty grain. Put in pot. Put much water, cook. Piprill get big. Taste good. Or grind, make flour, use flour make–" He briefly pantomimed kneading and shaping a loaf. "Make hot, wait, make bake," he said, and went through the motions of cutting a slice.

Excited by what he'd heard, Burlon kept his expression neutral. Gesturing at the remaining three bags, he asked, "Beek?"

Again, the knife blade came down, cutting into the second bag.

This time, the grain was golden kernels, much larger than the tiny pellets of piprill.

"What beek make? How taste?"

"Cook long time hot water, eat in bowl. Is good."

The second Beng bounced, his expression gleeful. "Or make blow up!"

Burlon stared, alarmed.

"Good eat!" the second Beng insisted. "Make hot in pan. Small oil. No water." He placed three golden kernels on his palm. "Blow up, blow up, blow up!"

Burlon mentally removed beek from his potential purchases. "Stezzin?" he inquired.

The third bag, when split, yielded pale and dark grains, not kernels.

"Not like other. Hot water cook, eat. Make not hungry long time. Come two way. One way whisper taste, chew soft. Other way more chew, more taste. Both good."

"Make flour?"

The Beng looked doubtful. "Better just eat."

It sounded promising for meals, but Miri would want the ability to make flour for baking. Maybe half an order of piprill, and a quarter of an order each of the two types of stezzin…

Don't get ahead of the game, Burlon cautioned himself. "What say you faralat?"

The Beng slit the bag. “Seed. Cook, eat. Good friend other food, other taste – not fight.”

It was a relief to have choices. And what they didn’t buy this time, they could try next time. With a few staple grains, Miri could keep people safe from hunger.

Cautiously, Burlon began transitioning from listener to active Trader. “Good talk. Thank. I think on Beng word, talk my people. Maybe talk Beng tomorrow.”

The first Beng left his stool, gesturing for the second Beng to clear away the sample bags.

Burlon stiffened. *That* wasn’t what he had in mind. They were supposed to coax him to stay, maybe offer him a better deal if he purchased more than one type of grain. Instead, they acted as if they were in a hurry to see him go.

Staying put on his little stool, he said, mildly, “Leave those, please. Why no offer doro?” There were five types of grain in the maartza, and the Beng had only shown him four. Why?

The first Beng returned to his stool with an air of reluctance. “You say Vennan cook want new. You say you eat Wilra d’limten.”

Burlon nodded.

“Number five Beng grain doro. Loud taste. Not new. Beng think Vennan cook no want.” A measuring look. “Beng wrong? You want see doro?”

“No. Beng right. Think stezzin. Think piprill. Think maybe faralat now, maybe wait.”

“No want beek?”

Not wanting to give offense, Burlon said, “Think beek wait. Not understand beek blow up. Why blow up good?”

The first Beng said something to the second, who scurried away again.

Burlon watched him go, pondering his next step. After morning meal, he had consulted the information board regarding the Beng’s current visit. They were already into the yellow, leaving only ten days before they departed. Having arrived twenty days ahead of Vennans, their stay had been half over before the Vennans arrived.

Beng often lingered, delaying their departure as much as they could without incurring late-departure fines. Still, as they approached the final segment of their stay, they would be increasingly eager to trade as much of their cargo as possible. Otherwise, they would have to choose between carting it home again or leaving it in the Prett's care, which involved a storage fee and a percentage of any deal the Prett made for them in their absence.

The second Beng still hadn't returned. Rather than sit indefinitely, Burlon decided to prod matters. Catching the first Beng's attention, he said, "Vennan think take stezzin, piprill, faralat. If Vennan take, what Beng want? Vennan goods? Station credit?"

A strange sound reached his ears from the back of the Beng maartza. Repetitive yet random, the soft little noise puzzled him. An aroma reached his inquisitive nose: hot oil and… what? A wholesome smell, but he couldn't place it.

The first Beng's mouth twisted, conveying boredom. "Beng mostly done trade, this trip. Not need much. What Vennan got?"

He wanted to say, *Got jam*, knowing the Beng's fondness for sweets. But Gredin would be furious. They had reached an agreement about the jam and the honey, leaving only pickled relish, which wouldn't tempt a Beng.

"Vennan maartza not open yet, but I bring new things there tomorrow. You come see what Beng like."

The Beng sighed. "Today maybe. Tomorrow, grain maybe all sold."

Burlon's throat tightened, but he smiled. "You say good crop. Much grain you bring."

The Beng's grin was brazen. "Much grain Beng bring. Much grain Beng sell." He shrugged. "Bring more, next trip."

And how long would *that* take? Burlon swallowed against a flutter of panic. Yes, the Vennans' need for grain was long-term, but it was a short-term problem, as well. He'd already been turned away by the Hesch. He couldn't tell Miri that he'd failed with the Beng, as well…

The second Beng returned, carrying a bowl. Placing it on the tabletop, he gestured at Burlon. "You eat."

The Beng had no reputation for hospitality. Burlon looked at the bowl, curiosity warring with caution. It was filled with little white puffs. "Is called what, this?" he asked.

The second Beng laughed. "I tell you before!"

"Tell me again."

This seemed to amuse both Beng. "Is beek."

It clearly wasn't. He pointed at the golden kernels still littering the tabletop in front of the second bag. "Is beek."

The first Beng placed a kernel on his palm, then did the same with one of the small white puffs. Pointed at the kernel. "Is beek." Pointed at the white puff. "Is beek."

Burlon recalled their earlier words: *Make hot in pan. Small oil...* Hadn't he smelled hot oil, and then heard brief, muffled sounds, again and again and again.

Blow up, blow up, blow up!

Tradepoint was indeed full of wonders.

The second Beng picked up several white puffs and put them in his mouth, chewing with evident delight.

Rarely one to back away from a dare, Burlon did the same. The puffs crunched gently as he chewed them, releasing a mild, pleasant taste vaguely reminiscent of bread.

Perhaps he had been hasty, dismissing beek from consideration.

The first Beng claimed a handful of the blown-up beek, saying nothing, munching contentedly.

The act of chewing made Burlon remember what was stowed in his bag. "I thank. Beek good," he said. "I bring small thing for Beng." He reached into his bag and drew out a little packet, one he had put together after a somewhat heated discussion with Miri. Now, with care, he folded back the wrapping and set it on the tabletop.

A berry tart.

The second Beng's hand, which had been reaching for the bowl of beek, stopped in mid-air. The first Beng's gaze fixed on the tart.

After a tense moment, the second Beng withdrew its hand. The first Beng claimed the tart and ate it, in one enormous bite. "Much good," it said, crumbs falling from its juice-purpled lips.

Miri would have winced.

The second Beng picked up the bowl of beek and headed for the back of the maartza.

Now we get down to business, Burlon thought.

The first Beng, still chewing the mouthful of tart, gazed at him. Then it swallowed and said, "Vennan come Beng maartza, talk nice, bring Vennan tart like Beng friend. Why? Beng no friend Vennan. Why talk nice? Why bring tart? What Vennan want?"

Burlon said, "Want piprill. Want stezzin. Want faralat. Want beek."

"Why? Bad crop Venna, this year?"

"Good crop," Burlon said. It was true. But now all of it, along with the rest of their world, was gone. "Told Beng. Vennan cook want new. Want try different."

The Beng regarded him, its tongue flicking out to clean berry juice from its thin lips.

Burlon waited.

"Big noise, other day," said the Beng.

Burlon waited.

"Hesch much angry. Much loud."

Scrapes! Don't you Beng ever miss anything?

"Is true Hesch call Prett guard, Prett guard walk Vennan out?"

Burlon nodded.

"You Vennan they walk?"

There was no point in denying it. "Yes."

"Why you fight Hesch?"

"No fight Hesch," Burlon said, alarmed to think such a rumor was circulating.

"No? Heard yes."

"No fight. Hesch talk loud only. No fight. No touch."

The Beng looked disappointed. "Ah. So, why loud talk? Why guard take Vennan out?"

Patience, Burlon. "Beng already know. Other Vennan step foot Nitikikani. Judgment. Hesch much mad."

"Judgment." The Beng made a sour face and spat.

Oh, this is not going well.

The globule of spit was swirled with purple from the berry juices. It glistened on the tabletop, perilously close to where Burlon sat.

He ignored it.

Sometimes, as a Trader, you had to take a bold approach. He did so now, schooling his expression to bland neutrality. "Bad judgment," he said, with mental apologies to Wyve. "Accident. Vennan no want hurt Nitikikani. Beng not at Market doorway. Beng inside Market, not see, not know Nitikikani hurt."

The Beng glowered.

"No can change Judgment. But..."

The Beng pursed its lips. Finally, it said, "But?"

Burlon disliked the course he'd decided to take, but the community needed grain.

"Vennan sorry see Beng caught in Judgment."

The Beng made a skeptical sound, as well it might.

"No can fight Judgment. But can buy Beng grain."

Cool disinterest from the Beng.

Time to step over the slippery edge. "Buy Beng grain, maybe pay extra, help make up Judgment on Beng."

The Beng gave him a sidelong look. "Prett take piece whatever Vennan pay."

Burlon shrugged. "Prett own Tradepoint. Take piece every sale always."

The Beng's gaze grew crafty. "Maybe Vennan pay grain price, then give Beng gift. Prett no take piece of gift."

A bribe, paid secretly, with the express intention of cutting the Prett out of the deal? Burlon shook his head in firm negation. "No want Prett enemy. Vennan no break trade rule."

"Afraid Prett?" the Beng sneered.

Burlon gestured around them. "Prett own floor. Ceiling. Walls. Lights. Heat. Air. Yes. Vennan afraid Prett, no want Prett enemy."

"Too bad." The Beng rose abruptly from its stool.

Stubbornly, Burlon stayed seated. "Vennan come talk maybe Trade, maybe sale."

"Sale." The Beng spoke the word with harsh emphasis. "Vennan no give gift Beng? Vennan want pay station credit?"

Burlon nodded with misgiving. It wouldn't be this simple. He could sense it. He'd thought the Hesch were mad? Not compared to the animosity rising off this Beng in waves.

But it would be all right. The current price of Beng grain was steep but tolerable. He could afford to pay in station credits – this time. Before the Beng's next visit, he'd try to work out some other source, in addition to Wilra grain. In the meantime, they had goods in the warehouse to compensate for the credits he spent, and would soon be Making more.

"Station credit," Burlon affirmed. "Want understand cost Beng grain."

The Beng removed a techpad from its coveralls. "Different grain, different price."

Not unexpected. Burlon nodded. "What grain least, what grain most?"

"Beek least. Piprill most."

"Piprill sack price," he requested, pointing at the techpad.

The Beng punched buttons. "Best price sack piprill." He held out the techpad.

Burlon knew what number to expect. Instead, this price was nearly double that amount.

It was a tactic. Calmly, Burlon erased the number and entered one that was roughly half of the proper price. Bit by bit, they would haggle until they met in the middle at a fair price, or perhaps a little higher. Given the Beng's current temper, Burlon could live with that. He handed the techpad back across the table.

The Beng glanced at the screen, erased Burlon's proposed price, entered a new number, and set the techpad on the tabletop, far enough away that Burlon had to lean to grasp it. A petty move but, again, Burlon could live with it. He picked up the techpad, sat back, and consulted it.

The Beng's new number was higher than its opening price had been.

That left Burlon in a quandary. Should he reduce own his bid, in response, or raise it to something more closely resembling the fair price, to indicate his willingness? He didn't want a contest of wills. He needed the grain. He was willing to pay a fair price for it. He just wasn't willing to pay a wildly inflated amount to soothe the Beng's offended pride.

With what he hoped looked like a decisive nod, he entered a number midway between his first bid and the Beng's first bid, and flipped the techpad back onto the tabletop.

The Beng's arms were much shorter. It had to hike its stool closer to the table to reach the techpad. After glancing at the number Burlon had written, the Beng made a guttural sound and muttered something under its breath. Then it snatched up the techpad, erased the screen, jabbed in a new entry, and dropped the techpad pad onto the tabletop directly in front of itself.

This time, to reach it, Burlon would have to half-rise from his stool and lean forward across the table, under the Beng's scrutiny. He did so, but he made no attempt to look down at the screen until he had reseated himself.

The Beng's quote was now twice what its opening price had been.

In a flat voice oddly devoid of rancor, the Beng asked, "Vennan stupid?"

Burlon could feel the grain slipping away. There was no point in losing his temper; the Beng controlled the situation. Instead, he offered a wry smile. "Most time, no. Today, maybe."

"What I tell you when start?" the Beng asked.

Burlon searched his memory. "You say 'Best price sack piprill.'"

"Yes. But you no believe. Clever Vennan think stupid Beng no mean what say. Offer insult price. Offend Beng. Penalty for that. Beng raise price. Let Vennan try again. Again, Vennan no believe Beng. Offend Beng. More penalty." It held out its hand for the techpad. "Give. Offer gone."

"But–"

"No piprill. I save, sell polite customer. Give."

Feeling ill, Burlon handed the techpad back. He would try again on another day, closer to the Beng's departure date… But could the Beng possibly be telling the truth? Did Beng allow no leeway for negotiation on their prices? *Had* he offended the Beng with his counteroffer? Or were the Beng playing with him, exacting revenge by mocking his attempt to Trade with them?

The Beng pressed buttons on the techpad and held it out. "Best price sack stezzin."

And that put Burlon on the spot. Having fumbled his chance at the piprill, his options with the stezzin were limited. If he tried to counter the price on the techpad, the Beng might claim offense again, and remove the stezzin from consideration. But could he afford to accept the Beng's price, as presented? It was a double question – could he afford whatever price was printed there, and could he afford to set the precedent of blindly accepting Beng prices?

Could he afford not to?

Swallowing hard, he reached across the table to take the techpad from the Beng's hand.

For the barest moment, the Beng retained its grip, then allowed the techpad to pass into Burlon's possession. It was a taunting move, that instant of resistance. A very Beng move. It reminded Burlon to tread carefully as he attempted to deal with them. He shifted on the little stool, letting himself settle before he looked down at the screen.

The 'best price' for a sack of stezzin was nearly as high as the piprill had been.

Fair or unfair, that was the price. Accept it or go back to the enclave empty-handed.

Instead of saying yes or no to the price, he asked, "How many sack stezzin Beng offer?"

"How many Vennan want?"

He might as well be bold. "Four hundred sack."

The Beng's gaze flickered. "Need check," it admitted. "Maybe got. If not, close."

Burlon waved his hand. "Better you wait. We talk faralat, talk beek. Maybe Beng need check those, too." He leaned forward and offered the techpad, its number unchanged. "You show best price sack faralat now, yes?"

It was like playing pletkin, moving a piece forward on the board and waiting to see how your opponent would react. Advance and retreat, probe and recoil… or press ahead, and hope the speed and daring of your approach would win the day. He was asking for the sack price of faralat without explicitly accepting or rejecting the sack price for stezzin, although his voiced interest in four hundred sacks of stezzin *could* be taken as acceptance.

As expected, the Beng price for faralat was only marginally less than their price for stezzin. But that meant he could count on the price of beek to be lower still. *Beek least. Piprill most.* That's what the Beng had told him. And even a small reduction in price became significant when you talked about hundreds of sacks.

Burlon handed the techpad back. "Best price sack beek?"

Again, the Beng entered a number.

Again, the techpad changed hands.

The beek was priced more steeply than Burlon had hoped, but that was how things were. This was proving to be an expensive day, but he would deliver both quantity and variety to the Vennan kitchens. The grain would fill the plates of hungry Vennans and improve morale.

Now that he had seen all three prices, he gave the Beng an affirmative nod and returned the techpad for the final time. "Vennan buy stezzin, faralat, beek. Four hundred sack each. Beng check, see what got. If not got four hundred one kind, Vennan maybe buy more other kind. Want twelve hundred sack, unless..."

"Unless?"

There was no harm in trying. "Unless Beng take Vennan apology, offer some sacks piprill Vennan buy, too."

"No piprill." The Beng rose. "You wait. I check stezzin, faralat, beek."

"I wait," he conceded.

When the Beng left, Burlon stood up, stretching. Dratted little stool. Dratted little Beng.

But it would be worth it when he saw smiling faces at tonight's evening meal.

Burlon paced, eager to conclude the transaction and return to the Vennan enclave to share the good news. They could always earn more station credits. They couldn't do without food. On this day, in this circumstance, the Beng purchase was a result he could tolerate.

But where were they? How long did it take to check a few inventory numbers?

Tonight, he would tell Chenna how the Beng described the taste of d'limten grain as 'loud.' It would amuse her…

"Vennan?"

He looked around but saw no one.

"Vennan." This time, the tone was sharper.

"Where Beng?" he asked when another survey of the room showed him no one.

"Here!"

"Here!"

"Here!"

The three shouts were nearly simultaneous as all three Beng popped into view, each from a different location. Burlon jumped, in spite of himself, and the Beng laughed.

It wasn't funny but Burlon feigned a chuckle. Humor was a tricky issue between one race and another. Without social context, the nuances were lost, making it hard to know whether a joke was well-intentioned. There was no point in taking offense. He needed the Beng's good will, at least until they got the contract signed and the grain safely transferred.

"So, you check numbers?" he asked a Beng coming from the rear of the maartza.

"No, *I* check numbers," said the one who stood off to his left.

So much for telling them apart. Or had the first Beng delegated the task to the second? No matter. "What numbers you find?" he inquired.

"Enough stezzin. Enough beek. Faralat twenty bag short. Want be twenty short or want add ten stezzin, ten beek?"

"Add."

"Contract?"

"Contract."

Contracts on Tradepoint, like conversations, required finding a middle ground both races could accommodate. The Prett's standard electronic contract form was used, presented in Prettian and the languages of the two sides of the agreement. The Director's office updated the contract form from time to time. Vennans, not fond of using *griimoni*, traditionally let the other party in the transaction pull up the contract form on their techpad.

And that, Burlon realized, had probably been the delay. Many sectora had passed since Beng and Vennans entered into a deal together, Wyve had probably needed to transmit copies of the updated contract blanks in the Beng/Vennan format.

Most of the contract was pre-printed, with generous spaces left for description of the goods being purchased, the price agreed upon, the delivery date and details, and the identifying marks of the two principal traders. The contract, completed on the techpad, was submitted to Wyve's office, where it would be held in the Director's active file until the terms of the contract had been fulfilled to both parties' satisfaction. At that point, payment was channeled through the Director's office, where a percentage of the price was diverted into Tradepoint's coffers.

Sitting at the table, the Beng made a quick amendment, then passed the techpad over.

Sinking onto the little stool, Burlon ran his gaze over the familiar contract form, ignoring the pre-printed portions; he dealt with them often and knew what each paragraph said. His saved his attention for the details the Beng had filled in. In 'Description of Goods Purchased,' the number of sacks had been corrected from 400/400/400 to 410/380/410, to make up for the shortage of faralat. As a result of the difference in price between one grain variety and another, and the last-minute adjustment from faralat to stezzin and beek, the total price in station credits differed from the original figure. Seeing that large a total written out was daunting, but Burlon had known it would be high. Other than that, everything appeared to be…

Wait.

He stabbed a finger at the line specifying the delivery date. "Why contract say plus ten day? Vennan pay today. Vennan take grain today."

"No."

The flat negative sparked his temper but he kept his voice level. "Explain. Why Beng need ten day?"

The Beng looked puzzled, as if the answer should be apparent to him. Well, it wasn't. He wanted that grain *now*, not ten days from now. If the Beng were going to fight him on that, he at least deserved to know why, scab it.

The Beng sighed. "Vennan no have ship."

"Right. Vennan no have ship. Why matter? Have warehouse."

The Beng shook its head. "Warehouse *inside* Tradepoint. Beng ship *outside* Tradepoint."

"So?"

"Beng leave Tradepoint, ten day. Load items on ship, bring items off ship. Hard work. Not do twice. Load, unload, all happen ten day, not now."

Cuts. He should have conferred with some race that dealt regularly with the Beng. Was it normal that the Beng only off-loaded cargo on their day of departure? Or was this a sly move to make things as inconvenient as possible for the Vennans?

Stay calm. Think.

Turning, Burlon gestured at the mounded grain sacks behind him. "So Vennan take these sack now, rest of sack ten day when Beng go."

The Beng broke into raucous laughter.

Fuming, Burlon waited them out, then asked, "What funny?"

The first Beng shook his head in apparent pity. "You think Beng stupid? You think, each time come Tradepoint, Beng drag many heavy sack, pile in maartza, unpile when go home, drag back to ship?"

Burlon had assumed exactly that. "Not so?"

That set off another round of laughter. "Maybe Vennan like sweat. Beng no."

Burlon scowled, still not understanding the reason for their mirth. "So Beng do what? Leave old grain here maartza display?"

They found that hilarious, as well.

Finally, when their laughter had worn down to snuffling chuckles, the first Beng said, “You want take sack? Go take sack.” And it pointed to the nearest mound.

Well, Beng were much smaller than Vennans. They would find the weight of a sack of grain more of a burden. If they wanted him to supply the muscle power, he was willing. Rising from the stool, he walked over, took a firm, two-handed grip on the top bag, tugged… and found that it weighed almost nothing. There was no shifting of contents within the bag, as he would have expected kernels of grain to do. Although the bag kept its shape, it had almost no weight.

The Beng were now practically weeping with laughter.

“Foam,” one of them wheezed, patting the cushion on its stool. “Like chair, like bed. Make look like many sack grain. Not want maartza look empty. Not good business. But not need sweat. Bring maartza little sack each time, like show you. Not big sack.”

The small sample bags the Beng had sliced open for his inspection were real. But the rest of the apparent bounty stacked around him was all illusion.

There would be no Beng grain for evening meal. Not tonight. Not for ten more days, if the Beng had their way. Burlon replaced the big bag on its stack and returned to the table.

“Ten day,” the Beng repeated. “Offload all, ten day.”

“No. Bring most, ten day. Bring some now.”

The Beng shook its head. “Offload all, ten day. Tell Vennan cook be patient.”

Bruise it, he couldn’t go back to the enclave with nothing. “I take sample bags.”

A negligent shrug. “Rip. Grain fall out.”

“I take all sample bag Beng have in maartza. Stezzin. Faralat. Beek.” That might at least allow Miri and her kitchen Tenders to begin to experiment with each of the new grains.

“No!” the Beng said, its tone obstinate. “Beng here ten more day. Need sample bag for customer.” He gestured at the techpad. “No more time waste. You sign contract or no?”

Burlon pointed at the table. “Take *these* sample bag. Stezzin. Faralat. Beek.”

Grins. “Bag rip. Vennan leave path in corridor,” they teased slyly. “Messy. Prett not like.”

“I put in pocket. No mess.”

An airy wave of the hand. “Vennan want? Vennan take – *after* sign contract.”

“Fine,” Burlon said, his voice guttural. Clinging to the shreds of his temper, he punched in his Trader’s code and pressed the pad of his thumb to the screen until the little techpad beeped in recognition. Then he passed the *griimoni* over to the Beng, who did the same. A pair of numbers flashed on the screen: authorization codes for the contract, one for him, one for the Beng. Burlon committed his to memory, long accustomed to doing so.

When the second Beng reached to push the sample bags toward him, Burlon said, “No touch. I do.” Let them think him rude. He didn’t care. Right now, he resented every lost grain and kernel, and he wasn’t about to let a clumsy Beng compound the problem. Tipping the bag of stezzin back so that the rip was uppermost, he rested his forefinger along the gap and urged the fibers on the two sides of the cut to join and merge. Then he tucked the bag deep into his pocket and repeated the process with the bag of faralat and the bag of beek. Given a moment of privacy, he could have Fetched the spilled grains into their respective bags, but there was no privacy to be had in the Beng maartza. Better just to get the sample bags with their remaining grains to the Vennan enclave.

With the third bag safely in his pocket, he forced himself to cross his palms to the Beng and offer a small nod. “Contract good. Grain ten day.”

“Contract good,” said the first Beng, and added, grinning, “Berry tart good, too.”

Swallowing the urge to say something highly impolitic, Burlon turned on his heel and, maneuvering between the stacked sacks of useless foam, strode out of the Beng maartza.

[22]

1511 OF 2000 ORBITS REMAINING: 10BLUE

After the previous day's clashes with the Hesch and the Beng, Gredin supposed she should have been grateful for a safe return to the Vennan enclave. Instead, when the Prett transport pod dropped them at the entrance, she'd been strangely reluctant to go inside. Abroad in the corridors of Tradepoint, she felt alert and alive, ready to face whatever challenges came her way. It was the enclave itself that had become the source of all her worries and woes. She wasn't sure which was worse – people who expected her to fix their problem with a snap of her fingers or people who wanted to manage every decision themselves, expecting her to scuttle into a corner and become invisible.

This morning was little better, She felt like a seedling that had been pulled up, its roots exposed to sun and wind, withering for lack of water…

Stop that, she told herself. *You are among friends and kinsmen. The Power graced you with its touch. You are still alive, and you have a purpose. Serve it.*

But she was weary. Today's early conference with Wyve and Figg had been exhausting, and now, without respite, she needed to meet with Burlon, Miri, Keegan, and Sill.

Greeting them, she saw that Burlon looked energetic, even if his eyelids were heavy – unsurprising when he devoted days to the community and nights to his new Chosen. He and Chenna were only halfway through their dydanin, and she envied them; she had barely completed her own dydanin with Dreff before journeying to Tradepoint and losing him to Venna's destruction.

Sill seemed alert, though she appeared worn. She was one of only two survivors with gyfte of Memory, and the community had been calling on both of them constantly to Harvest memories of lost loved ones. Steeped in the use of her gyfte, and fresh from a night with her Chosen, Sill was in formidable Balance, making Gredin grateful for her calm steadiness.

Keegan, too, had been managing surprisingly well, despite his full days. While busy with interviewing others, constructing his lists, and reporting for Binn's daily food challenges, which continued to make him ill, he still managed to look energetic and rested on most mornings.

But today his chair sat empty.

=Keegan?=

His response to her mind touch was immediate. =I am unavoidably detained. Begin without me,= he requested, and the sense of him was gone again.

It wasn't like Keegan te be abrupt *or* late. No doubt he would explain when he arrived.

That left Miri. Yesterday's upsets at the Traders' Market had shaken her. She still looked nervous, as if a Hesch might burst through the door at any moment. Well, a return to routine would likely ease her mind. With that hope, Gredin said, "Keegan is delayed and asks that we carry on. Sill, if you would begin?"

Sill nodded. "Certainly, but I have little to tell. A steady stream of people are coming to me and to Vik with their memories, but many still cannot Focus sufficiently for a Harvest. We assure them they can return another day, when they feel steadier, but we are both worried. Every day that such a Harvest is postponed, their memory becomes more diffuse. Still, warning them of that would only distress them further. We can only remain available and hope for the best."

Gredin shook her head, troubled by the image Sill's words conjured.

Normally, Keegan would have spoken next. His absence moved them to Burlon. "Since Keegan is delayed, tell us of your day, Burlon."

"I spent the morning in the warehouse, sorting items to be moved to the maartza. If you still feel you need to inspect my choices before they leave the warehouse, you'll need to come with me and look, after our meeting." His wording was polite, but his gaze and tone conveyed an air of challenge.

"I will come," she assured him. "Your plan is to open our maartza today?"

"Yes, as soon as we can manage it, once you view the goods. People are beginning to comment, at the Market. When a race is present on Tradepoint, the assumption is that they will do business. I have fielded inquiries, as have some of the other Traders, as to why our maartza remains closed and it is difficult to know what public statement to make."

"I understand," Gredin said, repressing a flicker of annoyance at his implication that *she* was the cause of the delay. "You and I will resolve the matter of our various warehouse goods as quickly as possible, this morning."

"Can we at least agree to sell items if we still possess the ability to Make more of them?"

"Not precisely," she said, and saw Burlon's look darken. "If there are items in the warehouse that you wish to sell, and we possess the skills and materials to Make more, I would rather see us Make more and sell *those*, rather than the ones presently in the warehouse."

"Why? What possible difference is there?"

She was shocked by his question, and she let it show. "The creations of those who are now lost to us, made from Vennan materials, should be cherished within the community. We will never see their like again."

Burlon looked belligerent. "We prize objects over the needs of our living community?"

"No," Gredin countered sharply. "We consider each decision carefully, instead of being so frightened by today that we give no thought to our future."

Burlon's hot gaze clashed with hers.

He was not altogether wrong. Neither was she.

Into that silence, Sill asked, "And how did you spend the rest of your day?"

"With the Beng," Burlon replied, all expression draining from his face. He looked down at the table, then up again, this time directing his gaze to Miri. "They showed me a variety of grains. I ruled one out as being too similar to the d'limten grain we obtain from the Wilra, but I've made arrangements for the other types. They will be off-loaded and delivered to us when the Beng leave Tradepoint, nine days from now."

"Nine days?" Miri repeated, sounding dismayed. "It can come no sooner?"

"No."

"If we could obtain even one bag now, I could–"

Burlon's face grew red. "If Kendar's Traders think they can strike a better deal, let them try."

Miri shook her head. "No. Your pardon, Burlon. I only… No."

A sharp rebuke rose to Gredin's tongue, but Burlon spoke again before she could utter it. "I am sorry, Miri. Dealing with the Beng is never pleasant, but that does not excuse me for addressing you so. I did all I could to persuade the Beng to hasten the delivery, but they refused. I should not let my frustration spill over onto you."

Miri nodded. "I understand. Truly. I also regret how easily my emotions brim over, these days."

"It is a difficult time for all," Gredin said. "But yesterday was not without its triumphs. Have you calmed enough to talk about the Polpethtira, Miri, or shall we come back to you?"

"I can talk now," Miri said, and even managed to meet Burlon's gaze as she added, "I packed a bundle of food for the five Polpethtiran crew members to take on their journey home, as you had arranged. I tried to be generous, as you asked, but… may I offer a suggestion?"

"Of course," Burlon said.

"You told me there were five of them, and that was helpful. But if you strike such a bargain again, can you ask how many days their journey will be, and whether our food packet replaces their own food or simply augments it? The Polpethtira seemed quite excited by the packet I delivered, and so I think they felt that they received good value from us. But it was mostly guesswork on my part."

"I'm glad they seemed pleased," Burlon said. "And certainly, if we undertake another such Trade, I will gather far more details for you. May I ask you a question or two?"

Miri nodded, her eyes wary.

"It cannot be an easy matter," Burlon began, "deciding how much food to prepare at each meal for our large community. Now that we have eliminated the snack at mid-morning and late-day, I know the other kitchen Tenders take care to provide enough at our meals for everyone to feel satisfied. But I have sat at table and watched some folk pick at their food, or ignore it entirely, or eat one item and leave the rest. What becomes of the food they don't eat?"

"It depends. Some can be Cleansed and saved for use in another form at a later meal. Some cannot."

"At evening meal, yesterday, you served small, individual d'limten loaves. I found mine quite tasty, but some tablemates left theirs untouched. What became of those?"

Miri sighed. "We packed them away and froze them. Perhaps we will grate them into crumbs, or slice them into little cubes and brown them, to sprinkle onto a soup or stew…"

"Or you could give them to me."

"Pardon?" Miri asked, sounding as startled as Gredin felt. What did Burlon want with leftover d'limten loaves?

"I am determined to reopen the Vennan maartza. And while our community may have wearied somewhat of the taste of d'limten grain, other people on Tradepoint have not eaten anything fresh-baked since they left their home world. If Miri is willing, I could take whatever leftover food there may be, after each meal, and offer it for a price at our maartza."

"Sell our food?" Gredin asked. "That hardly seems wise."

"Sell our *unwanted* food," Burlon clarified. "Food that has been presented at table and returned to the kitchens. After each meal, we could take whatever is left and offer it at the maartza. If no one there purchases it, I can bring it back to Miri. But I don't think that will be the case. I think other traders on the station will be as eager for what Miri and her kitchen Tenders prepare as our guests were at the reception."

"But that was party food," Miri protested. "Fancy things."

"You underrate your gyfte," Burlon said. "Everything you and the other Tenders create is excellent. And if I am wrong, and there is no interest in such things at the Traders' Market, we have ventured nothing. I only intend to offer what has already been prepared for our meals. If there is nothing left over, we offer nothing. If a little of this and a little of that is available, that is what we put out for sale. And if perfectly worthy items like the d'limten loaves are largely ignored at our own tables, the maartza will offer all that are left." His gaze gleamed, and his voice took on new energy. "Traders will learn they must come to the Vennan maartza often, if they wish to be there when such things are presented for sale. If they miss them, they can try again, later in the day. And, since they are at our maartza, they might as well see what else we are offering." He leaned forward in his enthusiasm. "They will pay well for the food they want. A dozen small d'limten loaves might bring in enough station credits for us to purchase a number of other things we need. I suggest we try. Gredin? What do you think of the idea?"

Gredin's thoughts whirled.

When she didn't immediately reply, Burlon looked across the table. "What do you think, Sill? Miri? Does my plan make sense to you?"

Miri looked as confused as she was feeling. Gredin switched her gaze to Sill's calm face. "Yes, Sill. What are your thoughts on the matter?"

Sill smiled. "I see no risk in trying. We already have the maartza, once Burlon has opened it again. We already have the food, so long as he only takes what was rejected at table. If he takes surplus that the kitchen Tenders have prepared, it caused no additional work for them, and uses no supplies not already committed to the meal. I assume we need no permission from the Prett about discontinuing such food sales if we change our minds. Is that correct?"

"That is correct," Burlon assured them all. "I will, however, mention it to Wyve first, to be certain there is no difficulty I have overlooked… if the rest of you approve."

Gredin shrugged. "I find no fault with the plan. But the kitchen is Miri's province."

Before Miri could respond, Burlon added, "If she wishes, Miri could come to the maartza to oversee displaying the food and keeping it the proper temperature."

After their encounters with the Hesch and the Beng, Gredin expected Miri to reject the suggestion. Instead, Miri asked, "Might Hayla accompany me? She speaks fair Tradetalk, and it would give me companionship when there were no customers."

"Ask her," Burlon said. "It would be good for her, if she'll do it."

"As I understand what you propose," Miri said to him, "it wouldn't interfere with my meal preparation times. We'd only be taking things down to the Market after meals, and only staying until whatever we took is sold."

"Exactly."

"Then I would like to try doing that," Miri said, and shot a shy look at Gredin. "If everyone else agrees."

The tenor of the morning meeting, which had teetered on tears and disappointment over the Beng delivery date, was suddenly bright with optimism. Gredin was savoring the change when Burlon looked to her and asked, "How did matters go with the Shodekekeen?"

She could simply answer his question, which would perpetuate the group's good mood. Or she could enlighten him about what had happened as they passed between the Polpethtiran maartza and that of the Shodekekeen. The first option was tempting, but the Traders' Market was Burlon's territory; he needed to be kept current on what occurred there.

"Matters with the Shodekekeen went well, but we had some encounters along the way."

Burlon's manner became instantly grave. "Who did you meet?"

"Nitikikani and two of his companions."

"Did he say anything?"

"Yes. He wanted to be certain that he recognized me. He said I was on Tradepoint in violation of the Judgment, and demanded that I leave."

"To which you replied…?"

"That I had business with the Shodekekeen."

Burlon shook his head. "I'm sure *that* was a popular response."

"He threatened to go to Wyve and demand a new Judgment. I said he was free to do so."

"All of this happened yesterday and I'm only hearing about it now?"

"My apologies. Other matters intruded, and I forgot."

"Forgot you had a confrontation with the Hesch in the middle of the Traders' Market? That seems unlikely."

"It may seem more likely when you learn that our next encounter was with the Beng."

Burlon went very still. "Tell me."

"There isn't much to tell. A group of Beng ran out into our path, trying to provoke an incident. We stopped in time to avoid contact and remained calm. They followed us to the Shodekekeen maartza, making rude remarks. We ignored them. Once we were inside, Shamka ran them off. When we finished our business, Prett security escorted us out of the Market and brought us back to the enclave in a transport pod, at Shamka's request."

"Bleeding Beng," Burlon said, his tone bitter.

"I wish you had been with us," Gredin continued, "but not because of them. I wish you had been there to see Ingarra and Shamka putting their heads together on your project. The Sprygalian quilt is going to be astonishing."

He brightened. "She found what she needed?"

"Definitely. She could scarcely wait to return to the enclave and begin working again. And Shamka asked her to take on a special project for him, once the quilt and coat for Sprygale are done. The Thalken–"

The door to the room opened, and Keegan hurried in as if being pursued, his usual air of calm gone. "Sorry to be late but the House volunteers – the High Council, as they call themselves – convened an urgent meeting. I thought we should know what they were saying."

"I'm grateful that you are a member of that group since you're House Fliss's volunteer," Sill confessed. "While we all want to stay abreast of their opinions, I hope it doesn't place you in a conflicted position."

"As House Fliss's volunteer, you are a member of that group," Sill observed, "which puts you in a somewhat conflicted position."

"Conflicted? Not at all," Keegan said. "Anyone with eyes and ears knows that my loyalty is to Gredin."

"And theirs is not?" Burlon asked.

Gredin flinched at the blunt question, and yet she was grateful to have the matter addressed directly.

Just as bluntly, Keegan replied, "Their loyalties are divided. Of our surviving Houses, Gredin has the support of Vell, of the triad of Avilar, Calidane, Kendar, and, of course, of House Fliss. Three other Houses – Darius, Shelahn, and Torr – are undecided."

"Which means," Burlon said harshly, "that we are opposed by Bentain, Indirin, K'lar, Laith… and Balamont." He shook his head. "My former and current House oppose the actions I take, as does Gredin's own House. Sill's House is undecided. Congratulations, Keegan. Only you and Miri have your House's approval for your presence here."

"We have the Power's approval," Gredin reminded him. But it stung to know she lacked the backing of her own House. Or perhaps that only meant she lacked Tetralanna's backing, as she had already known. Certainly Beda and Ingarra didn't stand against her. How many others within the House felt the same but were voiceless under Tetralanna's leadership? "Sit down, Keegan. Have you eaten? What purpose was this meeting of theirs intended to serve?"

But he didn't sit. Standing stiffly behind his chair, he said, "They want me to bring First Traveler's hlette to them."

Burlon surged to his feet. "What?!"

But he had heard. They all had heard.

"They announced the meeting to me while Gredin was still at Wyve's office," Keegan explained. "Most of them aren't usually awake at that hour, so I thought perhaps something alarming had happened. I didn't expect it to take long enough to make me late here. But they were in an uproar when I got there. I thought Edin te K'lar might strike someone, and most of the others were ranged against her. When I asked what the difficulty was, Edin turned to me and demanded that I..." He slid an apologetic glance toward Burlon. "What she said was, 'I want Cirin's hlette, and I want it now.' And then the others all started talking again."

"Sit down," Gredin urged again. "You, too, Burlon. Let's discuss this quietly." Once both men were seated, she asked, "Why were they shouting at Edin te K'lar?"

"They dispute ownership of the hlette," Keegan explained. "When First Speaker's hlette abandoned Tetralanna and came to you, both of you were of House Balamont, and were the only two Speakers in the delegation. But there are many Travelers, from many different Houses."

"Are there Travelers here from House K'lar?"

"One," Burlon said. "Doboro te K'lar."

"Then what am I missing?" she asked. "Cirin was First Traveler for House K'lar and wore that House's hlette." She looked to Burlon. "Now that he is gone, doesn't the hlette pass to Doboro, by default?"

Burlon heaved a long sigh. "Perhaps."

"*Perhaps*?"

Looking troubled, Burlon said, "We have spoken, for days now, about *community*. We have told the Houses that items in their individual warehouses no longer belong to them alone but are the joint property of all of the survivors, to be used for the benefit of the community."

"What does that have to do with the hlette?"

Keegan said, "At home, every House had a hlette for each of its major gyftes, to be worn by the individual in that House whose gyfte was greatest. Thirty-three hlettes for each of the major gyftes. Now, nearly all of those hlettes have been lost. We only have four – Sill's hlette for First of Memory, Salderon's for First Healer, Gredin's for First Speaker, and the hlette that was Cirin's for First Traveler. Are we to assume that nine of our remaining thirteen Houses will never again possess a hlette of any kind? What if a child is born into one of those Houses, and that child possesses a gyfte for Speaking that surpasses even yours, Gredin? Would you continue to claim the hlette, because it was created by House Balamont? Or would the hlette be worn by that more gyfted individual, even though they were not of your House?"

It was a dizzying question.

"But they're being stupid," Burlon said.

Gredin stared at him, and saw the others do the same.

He returned her stare directly. "*You* know," he said.

"What do I know?"

Burlon shook his head, the picture of impatience. "Think back to the night you acquired the hlette. I was there. I saw what happened. Was the matter settled by discussion? By debate?"

"No…"

"No," he affirmed. "The hlette is an object of Power. It knows where it belongs."

"And where is that?" she demanded. "To Doboro, as House K'lar's only remaining Traveler? Or to whichever surviving Traveler is most gyfted, regardless of their House?"

"Why ask me? I have no idea, nor do they. Given the chance, the hlette will show everyone where it belongs, just as your hlette showed us on the night it left Tetralanna and came to you. Anyone who thinks they can dictate where it belongs is being foolish."

"You will have your chance to tell them so," Keegan said.

"Pardon?"

"You should be hearing from your House, any time now. All Travelers are being summoned to the meeting so that the matter can be settled – over Edin te K'lar's vehement objections. And, according to *their* plans, I am to bring the hlette."

"And what are *your* plans?" Gredin asked.

"I would not presume to take possession of an object of Power. I am hoping, since it is in your hands for safe keeping, that you agree that finding the proper individual to wear it is wise, and that you will bring it to where the Travelers assemble."

Gredin found herself smiling. "Which, I imagine, is the very last place where Tetralanna and the others will wish to find me."

"*Some* others, perhaps," Keegan replied. "Shall we surprise them?"

"Yes. But where?"

Burlon said, "Indeed, where? Palla te Laith has not seen fit to invite me." He raised one eyebrow. "An oversight, I'm certain."

Poor Burlon. His new House seemed determined to make him feel unwelcome. Gredin wondered again if she had misconstrued the Power's intent when she insisted that Chenna and Burlon select a single House for their allegiance. But there was little to be done about it, at this point. When they emerged from their dydanin and took up formal residence within House Laith, perhaps matters would become clearer.

At this moment, there was the matter of First Traveler's hlette to settle. Excusing herself, she went into the room where she slept, opened her bag and carefully removed Cirin's hlette.

The sight of it froze her where she stood, so perfect was its form. Her own hlette warmed on her arm as if in recognition. Through the grace of First Traveler's hlette, Cirin had managed to Travel the River back to them despite the wounds draining his lifeblood away. And now this same hlette would grace the arm of a Traveler who might find New Venna.

"Gredin?" Keegan stood in the doorway, watching her with concern. "Are you all right?"

"I am well," she assured him, and it felt more true than it had in days. Was contact with a second hlette strengthening her? No matter. It was not hers to keep. Turning, she joined Keegan, and saw that the others were standing, as well. All except for…

"Where is Miri?"

"She has gone back to the kitchens to experiment with the samples of Beng grain. There was no reason for her to meet with the House representatives and the Travelers. Sill will formally observe the passing of First Traveler's hlette. Burlon is coming because all Travelers are required to attend. I go as representative for House Fliss. And you..."

"I go because it will annoy Tetralanna, and because I wish to see the hlette find its new home." She looked to Burlon. "Any guess as to who it will claim?"

"Not Doboro te K'lar," he declared dourly, "unless it is constrained to stay within its original House. I have rarely encountered a less adventurous Traveler than Doboro. Given his way, he would only have journeyed between Venna and Tradepoint, never varying his route. As to who it *might* be..." He opened the door, and they stepped into the connecting corridor that led to the reception hall. "The Power might select Yohn te Avilar, now that he is back with us."

"How is the Avilar Tradeteam settling in?" Gredin asked with a pang of conscience. "I intended to ask Miri if she had spoken with Plithik te Kendar since the Team's return."

Burlon shrugged. "Plithik is a Traveler, so we shall see her shortly. Where are we headed?"

Keegan pointed diagonally across the reception hall. "Over there. Now that House Balamont has moved into their new sleeping quarters, their former sleep space is serving a variety of uses. It looks quite different, with that maze of cloth dividers gone."

Gredin noticed other people walking in that direction. "Are they Travelers, Burlon?"

He nodded. "Many of them. We have fifty-one Travelers left, as best as I can figure it. Does that agree with your lists?" he asked Keegan.

"Yes. There were fifty, then we lost one, and gained two with the return of the Avilar Tradeteam." He said it in a preoccupied way, as if looking inward to consult his lists. Only when he had finished his reply did he color and say, "Your pardon, Burlon. That sounded callous. Cirin was far more to us than just a number on a list."

Burlon nodded, saying nothing.

When they passed through the door, Gredin saw that the area had indeed been transformed. It was now a rather large room, empty except for two long tables placed end to end, with stools on the far side to accommodate the thirteen House volunteers. Most of those stools were already occupied by the individuals Gredin had introduced to the community. Only two places were vacant. One, at the end of the nearer table, was likely intended for Keegan. The other, at the very center, no doubt had been claimed by–

Tetralanna's voice broke through the buzz of conversation. "Travelers, identify yourself to your Heads of House and form a line in front of them. This need not take long if you listen and cooperate. Keegan te Fliss? Good. Bring First Traveler's hlette to me and take your place, please. We wish to begin."

Keegan turned to Gredin. "Are you willing to come forward with me?"

"Of course," Gredin said. "But be warned – I don't intend to hand First Traveler's hlette to anyone but a Traveler."

"Then hand it to me," Burlon said. "They already think me stubborn beyond all reason. I might as well affirm their view."

"That I can willingly do," Gredin said, and placed the hlette on Burlon's broad palm. "And now, having done so, there is no reason for me to go forward. I'll wait with Sill." Perhaps, if she and Sill remained silent, they could go unnoticed as the drama of First Traveler's hlette played out.

But Gredin sensed the moment when Tetralanna's attention fixed upon her, as Burlon and Keegan threaded their way through the Travelers who were sorting themselves out by House. The frowning woman walked a straight line through the crowd to confront Gredin. "What are *you* doing here?" she demanded.

"Sill and I are observing."

"Sill is welcome. You are not," Tetralanna announced. "Why should you expect to be admitted here? You certainly made it clear that I was unwelcome at *your* little meeting, the other day. As you'll recall, Burlon threatened to carry me out if I didn't leave voluntarily." She looked to Gredin's left. "Sill, your gyfte serves a purpose." Her gaze flicked back to Gredin. "But you will leave so that we can attend to the business at hand."

Gredin hesitated. She wanted to escape from Tetralanna's presence, but something warned her that obeying Tetralanna's command would set a dangerous precedent. Instead, she said, "I handed First Traveler's hlette to Burlon. He is walking to the table with it now."

Her words ignored Tetralanna's command but added the powerful distraction of the hlette's whereabouts. As she had hoped would happen, Tetralanna turned, searching the crowd avidly as she made her way back toward the front of the room.

Gredin felt a pang of guilt but Burlon was quite capable of dealing with Tetralanna. Gredin slipped back and joined Sill, near the wall.

Sill murmured, "Deflection will not serve, in the end. You must disabuse Tetralanna and the others of this ridiculous claim to be Heads of House. It confuses and upsets the community."

Gredin sighed. "I know, but…"

"Attention!" At the front of the room, Tetralanna's voice was strident. "Welcome to our Travelers. We have requested your presence here to determine which of you is First Traveler."

"We *know* the identity of First Traveler, where the hlette is concerned," an angry voice contradicted. "It is House K'lar's hlette, and its proper possessor is Doboro te K'lar."

A murmur of comment ran through the room.

"Thank you, Edin," Tetralanna said, "for clarifying House K'lar's stance. If that is indeed the case, our meeting will be short. But some hold a different opinion. It is best to settle the matter so that no Traveler is in doubt. And it does no harm. If Doboro is destined to wear the hlette, none will be able to take it from him. Agreed?"

Edin te K'lar looked as if she longed to challenge that assertion, but she said nothing.

"Very well then. Doboro te K'lar, please come forward."

He did so.

"Bare your arm," Tetralanna directed.

After a moment's hesitation, Doboro removed his shirt.

Tetralanna looked out over the room. “Burlon te Bentain, bring forward the hlette.”

“Burlon te *Laith*,” came the correction from deep in the crowd.

Tetralanna’s mouth tightened in annoyance. “Burlon te Laith,” she said, as if the name tasted unpleasant. “Bring the hlette forward. Now.”

Burlon took his time, weaving his way through the assembled Travelers.

As soon as he was within reach, Tetralanna snatched the hlette from his hand and offered it to Doboro. “Place this hlette upon your arm, Doboro te K’lar, since your House claims that it is yours by right.”

He did so.

“Edin te K’lar, you are content?”

“I am content for the hlette to stay precisely where it is, upon Doboro’s arm,” she replied.

“That is for the Power to decide. Travelers, form a circle.”

Raggedly, they did as she asked.

“Doboro, stand in the center. Is any Traveler absent?”

It was Keegan who replied. “No. All fifty-one are present.”

“Then we will begin.” She pointed at Yohn te Avilar. “You are most recently returned to us, by the Power’s grace. Let us begin with you and progress around the circle.”

“What would you have me do?”

“Approach Doboro te K’lar. Place your hand upon the hlette and see if it wishes to come to you. The rest of us will stand witness. If it resists, return to your place in the circle, and the next Traveler can come forward.”

“That seems clear enough.” Yohn walked toward where Doboro stood waiting.

Remembering Burlon’s prediction that Yohn was a likely candidate for the hlette, Gredin held her breath. Perhaps this meeting would be very short indeed.

Reaching the center of the circle, Yohn crossed his palms and inclined his head to Doboro in a respectful bow. “Your pardon,” he said quietly, and reached out to place his hand upon the hlette. His fingers gripped it, and he gave a slight tug.

The hlao did not move.

"My thanks," Yohn said, and retreated.

It set the tone for all that followed. Each Traveler approached, greeted Doboro respectfully, and thanked him when their effort failed. It made Gredin realize how few of them she knew. Most of the men and women coming forward were unknown to her, although Sill recognized a fair number, identifying them to her by name and House in turn.

Burlon was the last. When his turn came, he bowed to Doboro, asked his pardon before reaching out to touch the hlette, and gave it the ritual tug.

The hlette slid down Doboro's arm and off, into Burlon's hand.

Both Doboro and Burlon fell back a pace, their faces twin mirrors of shock.

Edin te K'lar rose from her place, scowling, but Doboro simply crossed his palms, inclined his head in respect, and walked away, leaving Burlon alone in the center of the circle.

"And so the Power makes its choice," Sill murmured.

Burlon looked dazed, but the other Travelers surged forward to congratulate him.

"Wait!" It was Tetralanna's voice, but it was thin and shrill, lacking all command. Ignoring her, the Travelers pressed in, voicing their pleasure at the outcome. For a second time since Venna's destruction, Burlon had been singled out by the Power, first as Chenna's Chosen, and now as First Traveler. Both incidents broke with the old ways: his Chosen was from another House, as was the hlette. But, in both cases, the will of the Power was clear.

Looking more stricken than elated, Burlon made his way through the crowd, murmuring thanks and apologies to them. Then, reaching the door, he left the room.

"Where is he going?" Sill asked. "To tell Chenna?"

Gredin sighed. "I suspect he has gone to break the news to Hayla."

[23]

1509 OF 2000 ORBITS REMAINING: 12YELLOW

In the metal nest provided for her by the Prett, Hayla sat cross-legged on the foam sleeping mat, surrounded by Polpethtiran baskets full of colorful fabric scraps. Behind her, a luminth glowed so brightly off the metal walls that she had to squint against the glare, but it was either that or sit in darkness. Something ailed the dratted luminth. She'd have to ask Cirin to–

No.

She could never again ask anything of Cirin.

Count, she told herself sternly, and picked up the nearest stack of scraps.

For days, she had puzzled over how to cover the sleeping nest doorways so as to provide both privacy and identification. There were nearly seven hundred doorways, and she needed an affordable solution. Moreover, many of the scraps were irregular in shape.

But an idea had come to her, last night. Faced with too many entries and not enough fabric, she would fill the remaining space with air.

Today, she had set to work, sorting scraps, cutting up panels from the old sleeping quarters, measuring the entryway of her nest, then starting to sew. It was hardly even sewing, in one sense. Certainly, she had no need to trouble anyone with Ingarra's gyfte for Needlework. What Hayla undertook was simple enough for a child to do…

Except that there were no children. Not a single Vennan child still existed. Even if the people here managed to survive and persevere, there would always be the missing faces of those whose hlaos had never had the chance to unfurl…

And she was crying again.

Disgusted with herself, Hayla threw a handful of scraps at the entryway.

"Should I come back later?" Burlon asked, picking a strip of blue cloth from his shoulder.

"No. Come in."

"Are you trying to blind us both?" he asked.

"No. Something's wrong with the luminth. I can't–"

The glare softened to a glow. "There. Is that better?"

She made herself inhale. "Yes. What did you do to make it work properly?"

"Nothing unusual. I just drained some of the energy out of it."

"Don't be ridiculous. That's what I did, and it shut itself down completely. It would either flare like the sun or give no light at all, nothing in-between."

He made no comment.

Reaching out, Hayla patted the foam pad. "Sit. Move those things aside."

"You're upset. I could return at a better time."

"Lately, I'm always upset. So, stay."

"All right." He dropped down beside her. "But I came to tell you something that might upset you more." He gave her a lopsided grin. "Do you suppose you can just bundle it all into one big upset and get it over with?"

"Perfect. What is this upsetting thing you've come to tell me?"

He leaned his shoulder against hers. "Strangely, I have inherited Cirin's hlette."

The news stole her breath away.

Burlon sighed. "It didn't seem right, wearing it under my shirt and not telling you."

"You're wearing it *now*? But I thought that Doboro… I mean, it's K'lar's hlette," she said defensively. Still, she knew Burlon far better than she knew Doboro, and so would likely see him – and the hlette – far more often, which would be a comfort… wouldn't it? But still… "It's K'lar's hlette," she said, again.

"It seems to think otherwise," Burlon said. "The Travelers assembled, and Doboro put on the hlette. When the other Travelers went up and touched it, it stayed put. But when I reached out to it… Well, it just fell away from his arm, and I knew it was mine."

"But you're not K'lar."

"No, I'm not. That doesn't seem to matter anymore."

Understanding dawned. "Like your Choosing."

He nodded.

"Such a rule-breaker," she said, but she couldn't make it sound stern.

He glanced at her warily. "You're not angry?"

She considered. "Uncertain. Oddly glad. But not unhappy. He would be pleased, don't you think?"

"I don't know. Would he?"

"Well, he was never much impressed by Doboro." A fresh thought struck her. "Does this mean you'll be in charge of the search for New Venna?"

He looked uncertain for a moment, then thoughtful. "I certainly hope so."

The possibility frightened her, but there was little to be gained by saying so. Traveling the River was one of Burlon's major gyftes, perhaps even greater than his gyfte for Trade, if First Traveler's hlette was a reliable indicator. As a gyfted Traveler, it was inevitable that he would want to seek their new home, just as Cirin would have wanted to.

Cirin had lost his life as a result of his Travels, but that would not deter Burlon. Gyftes called to those who bore them. Some gyftes were gentle, like her own for Tending. Through it, she enriched any surroundings in which she sheltered. But the gyfte of Traveling the River was wayward and jealous, a gyfte that separated those who possessed it from Chosen, from kinsmen, from House. It put their very lives at risk. But, since gyftes were given by the Power, they had to be exercised fully in order for that person to find peace and Balance.

"We're going to reopen the maartza today," Burlon said.

Hayla was strangely cheered that the presence of First Traveler's hlette upon his arm hadn't distracted him entirely from his other major gyfte.

"At least, we're going to reopen it if I can persuade Gredin to let us sell anything."

"What business is it of Gredin's?"

Burlon groaned. "Of late, everything is Gredin's business."

"Perhaps that's what happens when the Power Speaks to someone."

"Perhaps. I just wish she would adopt a stance and stick to it. Often, she is bold and fearless. Other times, she shrinks from making any decision for fear she might offend someone."

"All of this is new to her. She is doing her best to find her way."

"Perhaps. Or perhaps she has undertaken more than she can handle and is afraid to admit it. She worries me, Hayla. People are widely divided in their opinion of her. They are taking sides. Entire Houses are taking sides. How can that be good for us?"

Hayla thought back on her visit to the Traders' Market in Gredin's company. "She dealt steadily with the Hesch and the Beng when they confronted her. The Polpethtira clearly like her, as do the Shodekekeen and the Prett. If other races have less difficulty with her than her own community, that may be more a criticism of us than of her."

"What are you saying?"

"People fear change, and an immense change has landed upon us. It is unsatisfying to have no one to blame, and people dare not blame the Power itself, so they blame Gredin. Her House has not rallied to support her. What better target for their fears and criticisms?"

"Edin would not be happy to hear those opinions," Burlon warned.

Hayla waved away his caution. "Edin calls herself Head of House but that does not make it so. Someone was sought to listen to House needs. With little else to occupy her, she volunteered. No mention was made of a new Head of House. Was it not the same in Laith?"

"I don't know," Burlon admitted. "Chenna and I weren't paying attention. But I suspect it was much the same. I'll ask Chenna what she knows of Palla te Laith, but she lived primarily at one of Laith's Holdings, tending hives, and knows few of Laith's survivors. The Trisectoriana attracted some people but held no interest for many others. And that's a problem because Keegan te Fliss has been interviewing people, creating lists… and it appears we are missing some of the gyftes."

"What do you mean? How can a gyfte go missing?"

Burlon shook his head. "Well, we have only two Speakers in the entire enclave. Of major Healers, we have one. As to Facilitators, we have none. And no major Builders. And there may be other gyftes that are no longer represented. We can hope a child will be born with one of the missing gyftes… but how do we train them, with no one to act as Tutor or Mentor?" He shrugged. "We will just have to wait, and trust in the Power."

"And you are so very good at waiting," Hayla said, her tone droll.

"I *am* good at waiting when it serves my purpose," Burlon protested. He gestured at the stacks of scraps. "What is all of this mess, if I may ask?"

"It isn't a mess. It's a door."

"You jest."

"Only a little. Now that the Prett have stacked up these nests for our use, we have more doorways than we have material to cover them. The floor-level nests will require a normal curtain to protect against passing gazes, but we don't need anything that complete for the upper levels. Instead, we can take the scraps from the Shodekekeen, cut up some of the panels from the old sleeping quarters, and sew the pieces onto a webwork of strips, with spaces left here and there between the pieces. Do you see what I mean?"

"Not entirely," he admitted, "but clearly you do. Proceed with your plan. If Ingarra has Needleworkers who aren't needed for the quilt, they could help you. And if you need more fabric or thread, let me know. This will benefit everyone in the community. We'll make sure you have whatever you need, within reason."

"Whose permission are you giving me?" she asked, pleased but cautious. "That of the High Council? Or are you speaking for Gredin?"

"For Gredin," he said. "There *is* no High Council, just a gathering of House volunteers whose ambitions outpace their authority."

"Oh? And what authority do you and Gredin's group have?"

"The Power chose Gredin, and Gredin chose us," Burlon answered without hesitation. "It is a level of authority the others would do well to respect."

"And if they don't?"

"They will find themselves at odds with the Power's intent." There was no bluster in his tone, just a quiet gravity that impressed her. It struck her that Tetralanna and the others should reconsider before defying Burlon in his present mood, or they might face a more formidable battle for leadership of the community than they anticipated.

[24]

1341 OF 2000 ORBITS REMAINING: 30GREEN

Wyve wanted to see him.

Wyve wanted to see *him*, not Gredin.

Why? Should he consult with her first? He could try to reach her private mind…

But what was the point of that when he had no idea what was on Wyve's mind? For all he knew, the Director wanted to consult with him about some matter of Trade that had nothing to do with Gredin.

No. He would go to Wyve first, and talk to Gredin afterward, if it turned out that there was any need to do so.

The message had reached Burlon at the Traders' Market during one of his first stints at the newly reopened Vennan maartza, delivered by a Prett security guard. Burlon knew from experience that questioning a security guard on an errand from the Director was a waste of energy; he didn't even try. He just turned to Trafin te Calidane, who was manning the maartza with him. "Wyve wants me."

"Go. I'll manage here."

"Ellis can fill in, unless you want someone from your Team."

"No, Shoal and Mistilan aren't adjusting well to the losses. Ellis will do fine."

Burlon agreed with his assessment. Trafin, Shoal, and Mistilan were members of the Tradeteam that had arrived mere days ago, and the news of Venna's destruction and the deaths of their kinsmen was still raw. And for Shoal and Mistilan te Avilar, who were Chosens, those deaths included their two young daughters, who had been at home on Venna with their Guides.

So much sorrow. So much loss.

Pushing emotion aside, he reached out to Ellis. Using private mind seemed to have become easier since he'd acquired the hlette. =Are you free?= he asked. =I need to see the Director, and I don't want Trafin coping alone at the maartza.=

=I'll come immediately,= Ellis assured him, then asked, =You aren't in trouble, are you?=

=I don't think so.= The possibility hadn't occurred to him. =A Trade matter, more likely.=

But her question weighed on him as he bid farewell to Trafin and left the Market. Was this about his embarrassment at the Hesch maartza? If so, he had no need to apologize. He had made polite contact with them. It wasn't his fault they'd blown the matter out of proportion and called security. He'd left at the guard's request, so likely it wasn't about the incident.

But what else could it be?

Burlon reached the Director's office feeling unsettled and a bit resentful. He had always had a friendly relationship with Wyve and Figg, and visits to their office had been pleasurable. He disliked this ache in his middle. Scab it, he had no cause to feel ill at ease… and yet he did.

When he was admitted to the Director's office, Wyve was alone. Burlon had thought Figg might be there, but apparently it was too early for the overlap that occurred at shift change. "Good day," Burlon said courteously in Prettian, and came to a halt just inside the door, unsure how formal to be.

But the Director smiled and waved him to a bench. "Sit. Thank you for coming. I thought it might benefit your community if you and I spoke directly."

That was ambiguous. "Certainly," Burlon said, and took a seat.

"You were at your maartza?"

It was a pointless question; Wyve would already know the answer from his security guard. But Burlon said, "Yes, we decided it was past time to open it again."

"I hear business has been brisk," Wyve said, with what might be a twinkle in his eye.

Reassured, Burlon grinned. "Yes, it has gotten rather lively. I mentioned, the other day, that we might open a small food stall in the maartza. Just left-over items, really. Things our kitchen Tenders prepared that ended up not being needed. Rather than waste them, we tried offering them for sale at the maartza."

"And caused quite a commotion," Wyve said, but without censure in his tone.

"Perhaps we underestimated how hungry the other traders were for fresh-baked goods."

"So your experiment is a success. But, by nature of its success, it is causing difficulties for Security. I have a solution to propose, it you are open to hearing it."

"Of course."

"Positioning your little food stall inside the Vennan maartza causes difficulties, since only one race at a time can join you there. Some awaiting their turn only wish to purchase a food item. Others seek a legitimate trade discussion – which can, or course, take much longer. As a result, people accumulate in the aisle outside of your maartza, impeding foot traffic and growing quarrelsome when the delay stretches."

"I am sorry if–"

Wyve waved his hand. "The fault is not yours. But we need a better solution. I suggest we place a small tent beside the entrance to your maartza, in the common area. Your kitchen folk can sell from there, separating trade from food purchases. It should alleviate the congestion. Does that sound acceptable?"

Burlon sighed. "You wish me to say yes, but there are matters to consider. Our kitchen Tenders are not Traders. Tradepoint is new to them. They are unused to individuals who aren't Vennan. Inside the maartza, the other Traders and I can oversee what goes on, answer questions that arise, allay their worries and confusion…"

"Then assign a trader to the new food tent, in addition to your kitchen people."

"That is also a problem. There are few of us left."

"Then a traveler, perhaps. Your travelers are fluent in Tradetalk, and I'm told that the food you offer has an assigned price, no bargaining. Your traders will be close by, inside the maartza, and I will assign a guard to keep the waiting customers orderly. Will that suffice?"

It did cover his concerns rather thoroughly. "Yes. We can try that."

"Good. That brings us to the matter of your travelers."

"In what way?" Burlon asked, disquieted. What concern could Wyve possibly have with the Travelers?

"Since your travelers are available to help with the food stall, Gredin must still be withholding permission for them to leave Tradepoint. How do you feel about that?"

It seemed disloyal to voice his reservations to Wyve. "Travelers always want to Travel," he said, deciding not to mention his inheritance of First Traveler's hlette. "Why do you ask?"

"The delay is causing difficulties with the Vokastra," Wyve admitted glumly.

Burlon felt the day darken. "What difficulty?"

"The usual. They are anxious about the geddel crystals."

"But we haven't yet reached the next delivery date."

"So I remind them. But the destruction of your world has shaken their confidence in your continued ability to maintain the supply schedule. If there is a way to make this next delivery slightly in advance of schedule, it would go far toward putting their worries to rest."

"I understand," Burlon said. And he did, all too well. Vennan tenancy on Tradepoint rested on the generosity of the Vokastra, and the generosity of the Vokastra rested on their belief that the Vennans could and would uphold their end of the geddel crystal agreement. At the time of the last delivery, it had merely been a Trade that kept House Bentain happily solvent. Now, the Vennan community's very security depended on timely delivery of geddel crystals to the Prett.

"I am confident that you understand. I cannot say the same for Gredin. I have raised this subject several times, but her grasp of the Vokastra's position seems… imperfect."

"She is unfamiliar with Prettig and its government," Burlon agreed. Reluctant, but knowing it was what Wyve wanted, he added, "I will approach her and explain it again."

"Also," Wyve said, "the Market guards have heard grumbling about Gredin, of late."

That didn't sound good. "Grumbling?"

"About her continued presence on Tradepoint. Apparently Nitikikani even made some threat to her about requesting a new Judgment, since she is in violation of that portion of the first one. He hasn't followed through, but I suggest that Gredin make herself less identifiable."

"Less…? You once said all Vennans looked alike, aside from being men or women."

Wyve shook his head. "Only one wears a flamestone around her neck. It seems to have caught Nitikikani's eye. He called it a 'firestone,' according to the guard."

Burlon grimaced. "I've warned her about it before. It seems I need to do so again."

"It would be wise. For now, I'll let you get on with your day. As to the food stall, by tomorrow morning I will have a small tent in place next to the Vennan maartza. You will alert your kitchen workers to the change in location? And arrange for a traveler to assist them?"

"Yes." He rose, crossed his palms, bowed his head. "My thanks. An efficient solution."

"It is a time for trying new things," Wyve said, his expression sober, his tone intense. "Be assured that I wish you and your people well in all of your endeavors."

Burlon didn't doubt his sincerity. He only wished the Vokastra shared the sentiment.

[25]

1339 OF 2000 ORBITS REMAINING: 32PURPLE

Gredin paced her room, waiting for the next arrival.

Meeting with twelve House volunteers should have been far more efficient than listening to hundreds of grief-stricken individuals. But it was just a different sort of impossible task.

The five most hostile volunteers seemed to delight in referring to themselves as 'Head of House' in her presence, despite her even-tempered and persistent reference to them as volunteers. They brought her long lists of complaints – sometimes from specific members of their House, but more often from themselves. They criticized how slowly things improved. They refused to adopt the Prettian system of dividing the day into identifiable fragments, then complained when they came unannounced to talk to her and found her occupied. They made it clear they disliked, distrusted, and disrespected her. Whichever House they represented, *it* was the most neglected and inconvenienced, and the neglect and inconvenience was, in their opinion, intentional on Gredin's part. The names of those Houses formed a dismal chant when she let her worries overtake her: *Bentain, Indirin, K'lar, Laith and Balamont.*

It drained her energy to deal daily with five individuals who thought so ill of her. And the worst of the five was Tetralanna, who seemed to draw strength and pleasure from contradicting her at every turn. The former First Speaker made it clear she knew the remaining members of House Balamont well and understood their needs personally, while Gredin knew them little better than she knew the members of any other House. The subtle implication beneath Tetralanna's demands was that Gredin should protect Balamont's members more aggressively because they were her kinsmen. All talk of 'community' rolled off of Tetralanna, unabsorbed.

Dealing with the three neutral Houses was a different sort of strain. Gredin had made naïve assumptions in her early days on Tradepoint. But if she could not persuade those like Tetralanna to her side, she would at least have to seek common cause with the undecided Houses. Sill advocated as best she could within House Torr, but House Darius and House Shelahn had to be informed of the reasoning for each choice Gredin made, and why the choices were to everyone's advantage. She took care, meeting with the volunteers from Darius and Shelahn, to listen attentively to their concerns and to be frank about the likelihood of their requests being met. If something was beyond her influence or impossible to obtain, she said so and explained why. She would make no promise she could not keep. Instead, she strove to impress Fennin te Shelahn and Amata te Darius with her honesty and reliability. Amata, a quiet woman, was hard to read, but Fennin, who had looked bored at first, now seemed to be warming to Gredin's candor.

Of the Houses that supported her, the triad of representatives from the Houses of Avilar, Calidane and Kendar were still uplifted by the arrival of the five members thought to have been lost forever, and her talks with Sulian te Avilar, Mallar te Calidane, and Lillig te Kendar were among her least stressful encounters. House Fliss was Keegan; he and she needed no separate, formal meeting. That left only House Vell, represented by Nunellin. To Gredin's relief, Nunellin was organized and cheerful. In time, she might even become that rarest of things: a new friend.

But Gredin's last visitor would be Rig te Indirin, inflated by his own self-importance. Still, he *was* the last House volunteer of the day, and she tried to take heart from that. As soon as Rig had come and gone, she would ask Miri to provide her with a d'limten roll, rather than wait for evening meal. She would then retreat to her room. To her bedmat. To her rest. To the oblivion of sleep, she hoped. She could not seem to get rested, no matter how long she spent abed. Mornings continued to test her will, with the importance of her meeting with Wyve and Figg counterbalanced by her foam sleep pad and warm covers…

A signal from the door sounded. Rig te Indirin? Why had he not simply announced himself to her private mind as he usually did, eschewing any use of Prett *griimoni*?

She triggered the door to open… and found Burlon on her doorstep, looking cross.

Well, *she* felt cross, too. "Come in. But Rig te Indirin is due soon, so we may be interrupted."

"Then I'll be brief," he said. "I've come for permission to leave for Sprygale."

Shocked, she said, "No. Not yet. We'll discuss it when your dydanin has ended."

"Wyve doesn't want to wait that long, and we shouldn't ask him to. I can be there and back in three days' time."

She felt a flicker of panic. "Your dydanin is already only half of what it should properly be, with your days given over to the community. What will your new House think if you run off to another world now? Indeed, what will Chenna think?"

She expected him to argue. It was what Burlon did when someone opposed him. Instead, he shrugged and said, "In that case, I'll need to give Wyve the geddel crystals from your dress."

She stared at him in bewilderment. "From my…?" And then, horrified, she remembered. "No," she said, her voice thin and strange even to her ears. "That wasn't a serious offer."

"Actually, it was. And the Vokastra are entirely serious."

Tears blurred her vision. She needed a logical argument to refute his demand. Instead, she heard herself say, "It is the dress I wore on the night Dreff and I became Chosens."

"Then keep it," Burlon said, "and grant me permission to make the trip to Sprygale."

"No! You need to stay here."

"Then give me the dress. The choice is yours. But decide you must, on one or the other."

She felt as if she were spinning this way and that, unable to accept either alternative. But Burlon would have no patience with that. He would insist or, worse, take the decision into his own hands. She had to select one of his solutions to satisfy Wyve. And, if she *had* to make a choice, the answer was clear. One alternative served a precious memory; the other served the community as a whole.

"I will get the dress," she said, and turned away to do so.

Behind her, he said, "I'll take it to Ingarra. She'll remove them carefully, without harming the dress. Once I bring new crystals from Sprygale, she can restore the dress."

You don't understand, she wanted to wail. *These are the crystals Dreff admired. These are the crystals that made me feel beautiful, that night. These are…*

But Dreff was gone, never to return. Once these crystals were gone, she had no need of replacements. They wouldn't be the same. Nothing would ever be the same.

Her hands shook as she handed the dress to Burlon. "Take it." When he opened his mouth, she said. "Excuse me. I must prepare for Rig te Indirin. I will see you in the morning."

He sighed and said, "And about that flamestone… Stop wearing it, except here in the enclave. It singles you out to the Hesch. And it's a temptation to people like the Beng. Wear it when you're here but not in public areas. The corridors. Wyve's office. The Traders' Market.

It's worth a great deal. If times get tight, we may have to Trade it for food."

Gredin couldn't quite stifle a sob at the very suggestion of such a thing.

Burlon continued as if he hadn't heard. "So don't put it at risk. If you think you might forget, better to stop wearing it altogether, for the time being."

Saying nothing more, he turned and walked away.

The door closed behind him.

Shaking, Gredin wrapped her arms around herself and paced the room, trying to shut Burlon's words away in some distant corner of her mind. She would not, *would no*t let Rig te Indirin see her with tears on her cheeks.

Slowly, she was able to force herself to a state of calm. When Rig made his presence felt within her mind, she triggered the door to open and crossed her palms. "Good day to you, Rig te Indirin," she said, in the same cool tone he always used when addressing her. "Come. Sit. Let us attend to matters. How fares your House?"

[26]

1029 OF 2000 ORBITS REMAINING: 42ORANGE

For six days, Burlon wavered between resentment and remorse. At morning meetings, Gredin appeared calm but discussed nothing beyond the day's agenda. She treated him no more brusquely than she treated the others, but she was the last to arrive at the morning meeting – a difficult feat, since they met in her chambers – and the first to leave when the meeting concluded. Burlon worried that their clash over the geddel crystals was the reason.

Ingarra had done as he asked, regarding the dress, although he had been reluctant to draw her away from work on the Sprygalian *timte* quilt and the accompanying coat. When he'd handed the dress to her and explained what he needed and why, she made no objection but her mouth had compressed into an unhappy little line. He supposed, on reflection, that removing the artfully placed crystals was as offensive to her gyfte as it would be for him if someone demanded he renege on a Trade he had successfully negotiated.

Stab it, he'd rather have gone to Sprygale. Gredin could have kept her dress as it was, and Ingarra could have avoided the distasteful task. But Gredin hadn't given him that option.

Removed from the dress, the crystals made a paltry pile compared to the Sprygale shipments he routinely brought, and he had been forced to go to Hayla, too, and ask for the geddel crystals from Cirin's House sash. The request appalled her, and matters grew even touchier because she had turned the ceremonial outfit over to Edin te K'lar, days before. When Burlon sought Edin out, the resulting conversation had been deeply unpleasant. Had Hayla not intervened, he might have left that confrontation empty handed. As it was, he'd had to take the sash to Ingarra and ask the further favor of removing those crystals, since he dared not risk damaging them or the sash.

He'd taken the crystals to Wyve the next day, a temporary appeasement to the Vokastra.

Wyve's reaction had been less enthusiastic than he'd hoped. Many of the ornamental crystals were smaller than those the Prett normally used for industrial purposes. They would have to be ground smaller still to remove the tiny piercing by which each crystal had been sewn to the garment it decorated.

And now, despite the expense of upsetting Gredin, Hayla, and Ingarra with his demands, even that thin cushion of 'extra' was used up. If the Vokastra made more demands before the delivery date, or if Gredin resisted having him make the trip to Sprygale when that date arrived, he would have nothing to offer.

Was this how the future would be, with necessity driving him into deals where neither side came away satisfied? The prospect sickened him, too sour a thought to have in his mind as he joined Chenna in their borrowed room for the night. She deserved a loving, eager mate, not a man who had to be coaxed from the bleakness of his mood.

Movement was the best remedy for dark thoughts. He would walk a final circuit of the reception hall before he went to his Chosen.

Evening meal was done, and the kitchen Tenders had cleared everything away. Most of the bare tables had been folded and stacked, less from necessity than because of the exercise that doing so afforded. No one had enough chances for activity within their day. Sill and Gredin had made preliminary arrangements for an evening dance to be held, but when word of it had reached the House volunteers, a group of them had thrown themselves into a righteous rage, claiming it was disrespectful to dance so soon after the deaths of their loved ones.

That protest had taken place here in the reception hall, in plain view of the community, with more and more people wandering over to voice an opinion, and more and more people becoming upset as they argued vehemently on one side or the other. Finally, Sill had felt the need to soothe everyone's mood with a Memory of snowfall at Torr's mountain Holding, each flake floating down from the sky with slow grace.

And the issue of the dance had been set aside for later discussion.

That sort of clash was becoming common. When House volunteers took a stand counter to Gredin's, they were ruthless about winning their point, even if it meant agitating everyone.

It wasn't a tactic Gredin was willing to employ. He had to grant, even when he was most frustrated by her, that her instincts always swung toward protecting the community...

A blinking light over the exit doors caught his eye. *42orange* was about to give way to *43purple*. The end of evening. The beginning of night. Prett divided each day into fifty segments, and each segment into five color-named portions. Vennans didn't really divide time, not rigidly. There was past, present, and future. There was yesterday, today, and tomorrow. There was a moment, or a while. There was soon, and later. For vaster stretches, there was 'long and long.' It had always worked fine for them.

Oddly, though, their notion of what constituted a day and a night in the constant artificial illumination of Tradepoint was a comfortably close fit with the Prett's concept of the same. Some races were less fortunate, and had to limit their activities to a shorter cycle in order not to exhaust themselves. The F'lala would drop right off to sleep, chin on chest, if they were kept up too long. The Chibi were like torches made of straw: a brief, bright flare of activity, and then nothing more until they had rested.

In Trading, it was important to know such things about the other races. Otherwise, drowsiness could be mistaken for disinterest. But races like the Beng and the Hesch revealed as little about themselves as they could manage, choosing confusion and caution over candor.

In fairness, he supposed Vennan Traders could be accused of

adopting similar tactics. People on Tradepoint didn't know that Vennans could Send, or Fetch, or even do simple things like keeping a plate of food warm throughout a meal so that the last bite was as tasty as the first. And he certainly didn't want other races to know how vulnerable Vennans were to breaks in their skin. A scratch, a cut, a puncture wound, however minor, left a Vennan weak and dizzy, or even nauseous, depending on the state of their Balance. It was why minor Healers were so valued; their modest gyfte could set such problems to rights in a matter of minutes. Without them…

A new light flashed on the board – an arrival symbol.

Someone was docking.

Burlon cut diagonally across the reception hall, hurrying to see who had come. He tried to keep his gaze fixed only on the symbol, but he couldn't wipe out his awareness that the Vennan rotation allowance, now at *1029/2000*, appeared in green. Several days ago, the reassuring blue numerals had switched color, and now the countback monitor was a constant reminder that they had exhausted nearly half of their permitted stay. Days were slipping through their fingers, unused, while Gredin insisted that no Traveler leave Tradepoint. Why couldn't he make her see sense? At this rate, she was going to 'protect' them right into a second disaster.

Reaching the display, he saw the symbol, a blue oval in a purple oval: the Rodorno.

The Rodorno! He had eagerly awaited their arrival. Now, though, he was filled with conflicting emotions: relief, worry, reluctance, happiness, dread…

He closed his eyes and calmed his thoughts, reaching out to Chenna. =My love?=

=Burlon. I am in our chamber, awaiting you.=

=And I, regrettably, am delayed. The Rodorno have arrived. I must meet with them. I cannot say how long our conference may take. Sleep, and I will wake you when I return.=

There was a long moment of startled silence before her reply reached him. =It is your gyfte to know how such matters must be handled. I will welcome you when you return.= And the sweetness of their contact faded from his mind.

It was unfair. Already, he spent his days apart from her. Now his duties were infringing on their nights. And he couldn't stay with her longer, tomorrow morning; Gredin and the others would expect him at their meeting over morning meal.

There had never been such a disjointed dydanin.

But his bond with Chenna was deep and true. They would make it through this troubled time, knowing that they would spend the rest of their lives together. Events were strange and unsettling, but a better future was promised to them.

Holding to that belief, Burlon left the enclave.

One of the benefits of the extended quarters the Prett had equipped for the Vennans was that an entire corridor section was now theirs. As a result, the bio-mist chambers at the entrances to the four original enclaves had all been deactivated, replaced by a single chamber where their corridor connected to the public areas of Tradepoint. Even Tetralanna and the crankiest of her fellow House volunteers had conceded their pleasure at being able to pass from one House's area to another without undergoing the bio-mist treatment.

As a result, except for Gredin's comings and goings, the chamber was now mainly used by Traders – or Miri and her kitchen Tenders – on their way to the Vennan maartza.

At this odd hour, Burlon was alone as he underwent the process. Released into the public corridor, he strode to the corner and pressed his hand against the screen.

"Where want go?" the mechanized voice asked.

"Want Rodorno. Where dock?"

"Purple. Go purple," the voice replied. A map of Tradepoint appeared on the screen. "Look floor." Purple lights flickered between the floor tiles. "Go purple. Rodorno dock."

It would be quite a hike to the docking station assigned to the Rodorno. But he'd wanted exercise, hadn't he?

He made his way along the corridors, following the purple path, trying not to think ahead. The Rodorno were friends. This was a reunion, not a Trading mission. Business could wait.

He was actually presuming a bit on that friendship. Arrival at Tradepoint was a busy time. It would have been considerate to give the Rodorno a night to settle before he approached them. But idle gossip ran rampant on the station. And where matters pertained to Cirin's return to the Source, or Wyve's Judgment, or his own all-too-public eviction from the Hesch maartza, *he* wanted to be the one to deliver the news.

By the time he reached their enclave entrance, his breathing had quickened and he felt warm and loose. He pressed the keypad and said into the panel, "Burlon te Bentain."

But that wasn't right. He was Burlon te Laith now. Guiltily, he looked up and down the hallway, relieved to find it empty. What would his former kinsmen in House Bentain think, if they had heard him? What would his new kinsmen in House Laith think?

What would Chenna think?

He hadn't meant anything by it. He hadn't. It was just habit. Until seventeen days ago, he had lived his life as Burlon te Bentain. It was what he had always said. And it was how the Rodorno knew him.

Two cross-corridors distant, a troupe of Beng clattered by, talking loudly to one another, pushing and shoving as they walked. Burlon stood still, unwilling to draw their attention. The memory of negotiating with them rankled every time he ate a mouthful of the Wilra's d'limten grain. And he'd *still* have to wait another–

He froze.

What day was this?

It seemed inconceivable that he, a Trader, had lost track of how many days he'd been on Tradepoint. But he had never been here so long, or under such circumstances. Was this the eighteenth day or the nineteenth?

Darting a glance at the closed doors to the Rodorno bio-mist chamber, he wondered how much time had passed since he announced his name. Not much, surely. One of them would have to leave whatever unloading task was assigned to them, walk to the chamber, key it to begin, wait while the mist cycled…

He had time.

Burlon sprinted to the closest corner and pressed his hand against the screen.

"Where want go?" came the inquiry.

"Want information."

"What want know?"

"Want know how many day Vennan Tradeteam on Tradepoint."

"Twenty."

Twenty. *This* was the delivery day for the Beng grain!

"Want check status cargo Beng grain to Vennan warehouse."

"No delivery this day."

"Same status yesterday?"

"No Beng grain to Vennan warehouse past one hundred day. Check older record?"

"No. Want know Beng delivery other warehouses past ten day."

"No Beng delivery any warehouse past ten day."

"How many orbit-hour remain Beng visit?"

"Seven. Stay expire *forty-nineyellow*."

So, the Beng were postponing the off-loading of cargo until their final hours before departure. Nothing unusual about that. Likely he would rise, tomorrow morning, to find the Beng grain had been processed by the Prett and deposited in the Vennan warehouse while he slept.

Down the corridor, the doors of the Rodorno antechamber opened.

Burlon sprinted back, raising a hand in greeting when a plump Rodornon face appeared in the opening. It looked the wrong way first, then toward him. An enormous smile formed at the sight of Burlon, then faded to surprise, and then to concern as he came closer.

The Rodorno were empaths, highly sensitized to the emotions of others, even when those others weren't Rodornon. By the time Burlon reached the open doorway to the antechamber, the Rodorno awaiting him looked as if Burlon's appearance distressed him. "You come in," it urged. "You come, stay, talk."

At close quarters, Burlon was sometimes able to tell one Rodorno from another. He ventured a name now, relatively certain he was right. "Di-gul?"

"Yes!" The smile made a brief reappearance, fading again as the outer door closed and bio-mist descended. The Rodorno were always pleased when a Trader recognized one of them as an individual, and Burlon was more adept at it than most. The normal height for a Rodorno seemed to be shoulder-high to a Vennan, and their bodies carried a comfortable layer of natural padding, despite their strength and dexterity. Their faces were nearly round, and their eyes were their largest features, followed by the rounded ears that sat atop their heads. Short, silver fur covered all of their visible skin, with the exception of their nose tips and the palms and long fingers of their hands, where the skin was a silvery pink. What might exist beneath their utilitarian jumpsuits was anyone's guess; Burlon had never seen a Rodorno who was not decked out in a jumpsuit of grey or blue or brown, with soft boots covering their feet and ankles before vanishing into their pantlegs.

Di-gul peered at him through the mist. "Cirin no here to come with?"

He had known they would ask; he and Cirin came together to visit the Rodorno whenever their visits to Tradepoint coincided. But he was unprepared for the painful stab of loss that pierced him, and the worry on Di-gul's face. "No," he said, and could manage no more.

They stood together in silence while the mist finished its cycle and cleared. Then the inner doors opened, and Di-gul ushered him into the Rodornon enclave.

He expected everyone to be busy with arrival tasks. Instead, he found them standing in a line, waiting silently to welcome him. There were no smiles or spoken greetings, just the somber regard of seven sets of lambent eyes, and the attentive tilt of seven sets of ears.

After a moment, one of the Rodorno broke from the line and approached. Heavier set than the rest, with a bit more white than silver in the fur, this was the head of the Rodorno Tradeteam and captain of their ship, a female Burlon knew well.

He crossed his palms and inclined his head. "Artett Abna-gul."

"Burlon te Bentain," she replied, and extended her hand.

Burlon wished he could refuse. Proximity amplified Rodornon empathy, and physical touch intensified it even further. But he hadn't come here to insult them. He'd known that hiding his pain would be impossible. And so he permitted Artett Abna-gul to wrap her long, dexterous fingers around his. "Come," she said after a moment, and tugged gently on his hand.

They walked through the enclave, moving between crates of trade-goods that had been off-loaded before his arrival. He assumed she was taking him to the little suite of rooms analogous to those Gredin and Keegan occupied at the Vennan enclave, since that area included a small office with a desk and stools. But it quickly became apparent they were headed in a different direction. "Where go?" he asked.

"Ship."

It would not be the first time he had boarded the Rodornon ship, but the occasions had been few and usually cargo-related. "Why?" he asked, not so much in protest as in confusion.

She cast him a knowing look. "Kippi."

A bark of laughter escaped him. *Kippi* was Rodornon brandy, and he could use a bracing sip. Willingly, he followed Artett Abna-gul through a double set of doors, down a curving hallway, through another sequence of doors, and onto the Rodornon ship. Unlike his previous visits, they didn't enter the cargo hold. Instead, Artett Abna-gul took him down a narrow passage that widened out into a large, round room.

The place looked cozy. Less metal. More cloth. *This must be where they relax*, he thought, and saw that the floor's center, sunken and padded, formed a welcoming hollow.

Footsteps sounded behind him.

Burlon looked over his shoulder. Members of the crew assembled, singly and in pairs, until the entire group was present.

Artett Abna-gul opened a storage locker and brought out a slender blue bottle.

Kippi.

Then she selected two small glasses. "Sit, Burlon. Crew sit, too."

The only place to sit was the padded well in the center of the room. Burlon stepped down into it, then waited to see whether he was expected to sit on the rim or down in the well itself.

Di-gul jumped down and sat on the padded floor, leaned his back against the upholstery and gestured for Burlon to do the same.

Different races, different customs. It was usually wisest to mimic the hosts. With a nod, Burlon settled himself on the floor and leaned back. Other crew members followed, taking places around the circle. Artett Abna-gul handed the *kippi* bottle down to one of them, and the glasses to another, before seating herself on the upper rim and sliding into the hollow. Then she pointed imperiously at the Rodorno at Burlon's right, who slid over. Artett Abna-gul settled herself into the space the man had vacated.

It was a tight squeeze. They sat hip to hip, shoulder to shoulder, with Burlon snugged between Di-gul and Artett Abna-gul, his head somewhat higher than any of the Rodorno.

Softly, the chant began. "*Chin-bah, chin-bah, chin-bah, chin-bah...*" It translated, somewhat imperfectly, to 'game' or 'challenge,' and prefaced any round of drinking Burlon had experienced with the Rodorno. In the warmth of the hollow, he waited to see what the rules of tonight's drinking game would be.

Artett Abna-gul held up her hand and the chant ceased.

"No chin-bah," she announced. "Tonight, dok-watorn." Her dark gaze ensnared Burlon's. "Dok-watorn woes for our ears only. Stay in circle. Stay private."

It wasn't a word Burlon knew, but the faces of the crew became instantly solemn. "Dok-watorn," they echoed softly.

"Pardon," Burlon said. "Not know *dok-watorn.* Artett Abna-gul explain more?"

She nodded, but said, "Kippi first."

The two empty glasses passed from hand to hand in opposite directions until one of them reached Burlon and the other reached Artett Abna-gul. The bottle followed, unopened until it reached Di-gul, who unstopped it and poured a drizzle of *kippi* into Burlon's glass.

Artett Abna-gul tapped Burlon's empty hand and placed the other glass in it.

Di-gul poured another drizzle, barely enough to cover the bottom of the glass.

"Dok-watorn, dok-watorn!" cried Artett Abna-gul.

The others took up the cry. "Dok-watorn, dok-watorn!"

At her gesture, silence fell. She hummed a doleful melody, then sang, "Burlon heavy cargo bear, dok-watorn, dok-watorn!"

Nods from around the circle, and a whispered chant of "Dok-watorn, dok-watorn."

Di-gul nudged Burlon and whispered, "Drink both."

Burlon was caught off guard by the instruction, but he had never known a Rodorno to tease or make a joke, least of all at someone else's expense. Glad that each glass held only a tiny amount of liquor, Burlon swallowed the contents of the first glass, then the second.

Artett Abna-gul hummed, then sang, "Burlon carry it alone? Dok-watorn, dok-watorn."

The whispered chant of "Dok-watorn, dok-watorn" began again.

Di-gul poured into both glasses, then took one of them from Burlon's hand and passed it to his left. It progressed halfway around the circle before a Rodorno raised the glass in the air and sang, "Tay-gul ask you, name a woe. Dok-watorn, dok-watorn."

Again, a subtle nudge from Di-gul, who whispered, "Name something that troubles you. Say dok-watorn, dok-watorn. Then drink."

Burlon winced. All gazes were trained upon him, their big, dark eyes soft with concern. This was clearly a ritual, and they respected him enough to include him in it. He struggled to find words, then felt Artett Abna-gul's hand come lightly to rest on his shoulder.

It gave him the courage to say, in rhythm with their chant, "Cirin te K'lar is dead. *Dok-watorn, dok-watorn.*"

A collective gasp. The Rodorno had long been on the friendliest of terms with Cirin.

Burlon lifted his glass and drank.

Halfway around the circle, Tay-gul stood. "Cirin te K'lar is dead. Dok-watorn, dok-watorn. Share the burden Burlon bears. Dok-watorn, dok-watorn." He, too, drained his glass, walked across the circle, and placed the empty glass in Burlon's free hand. Then he bowed his head and backed across the circle to reclaim his place.

Di-gul added more *kippi* to both glasses, claimed one from him, and stood up. "Di-gul ask you, name a joy. Dok-watorn. Dok-watorn."

Burlon gathered his thoughts, choosing his wording as they chanted. Then he responded, "Burlon find his life-long mate. *Dok-watorn, dok-watorn*." And drank.

Smiles on every face in the circle. Beside him, Di-gul responded: "Burlon finds his life-long mate. Dok-watorn, dok-watorn. Share the joy that Burlon wears. Dok-watorn, dok-watorn."

Artett Abna-gul's hand tightened on Burlon's shoulder. "Again. There is more woe."

Di-gul poured *kippi* into both glasses and sent one around the circle in the other direction.

Almost at once, a Rodorno claimed it and stood. "Lor-gul ask him, name the woe. Dok-watorn, dok-watorn."

With the second swallow of *kippi* still warm in his throat, Burlon felt compelled to bare the reasons for his pain to these friends who had gathered to support him. "Home-world Venna is destroyed. *Dok-watorn, dok-watorn*."

They stared at him in horror.

Burlon lifted the glass and drank.

Lor-gul chanted, "Home-world Venna is destroyed. Dok-watorn, dok-watorn. Share the burden Burlon bears. Dok-watorn, dok-watorn." He drained his glass and took the few steps necessary to return the empty glass to Burlon's free hand. Then, as Tay-gul had done, he bowed his head and, with it still bowed, reclaimed his place.

Artett Abna-gul said, hoarsely, out of rhythm with the chant, "No joy can balance such a loss. There are only lesser woes. Name them to us, so we might help you bear their weight."

Di-gul poured *kippi* into both glasses and sent one around the circle.

A female Rodorno claimed the glass and stood, her fur a shinier plush than that of her male crewmates. "Er-gul ask him, name a woe. Dok-watorn, dok-watorn."

It was as good a time as any to inform them of the change in his identity. "I no longer am Bentain. *Dok-watorn, dok-watorn*," he said, and drank.

This time, he read confusion on their faces. Names were closely attended to, on Tradepoint. These Rodorno knew him not just as Burlon but as Burlon te Bentain. They would see a change of title as significant, even if they didn't comprehend the reason behind it.

Er-gul chanted, "He no longer is Bentain. Dok-watorn, dok-watorn. Share the burden Burlon bears. Dok-watorn, dok-watorn." She drained her glass and crossed the circle to return the empty glass to Burlon's free hand. Then she bowed her head and returned to her place.

"Again," said Artett Abna-gul.

Di-gul poured more *kippi* into the glasses and passed one.

A Rodorno rose. "Shen-gul ask him, name the woe. Dok-watorn, dok-watorn."

Burlon replied, "New House, Laith, is stranger-filled. *Dok-watorn, dok-watorn*," and drank, noticing that his bottom lip was growing numb.

"New House, Laith, is stranger-filled. Dok-watorn, dok-watorn," Shen-gul repeated. "Share the burden Burlon bears. Dok-watorn, dok-watorn." He, too, drank, and brought his emptied cup to Burlon.

At Artett Abna-gul's implacable 'Again,' the ritual persisted for another four rounds. On the first of them, Burlon heard himself say, "Gredin rules, but she is young. *Dok-watorn, dok-watorn*." For the second, "Travelers not allowed to leave. *Dok-watorn, dok-watorn.*" For the third, "Hesch and Beng oppose us now. *Dok-watorn, dok-watorn*." And the fourth, "Prett Vokastra wish us gone. *Dok-watorn, dok-watorn.*"

Each time, a different Rodorno rose to repeat the woe and drink with him before returning the emptied glass to his hand. On the final round, when he named the Vokastra as a woe, it was Artett Abna-gul herself who rose to drink it down with him.

Casting his thoughts back over the ritual, it seemed to Burlon that

Di-gul had poured with an increasingly heavy hand as they progressed. Perhaps that was why his eyes refused to focus, and his hearing faded in and out of acuity. He had tipped sideways, and something soft was under his cheek – Artett Abna-gul's forearm? Voices around him murmured soothingly but the words made no sense. But he was warm, drowsy, surrounded by friends. Nothing was expected of him. No harm would befall him. He was safe. He was…

[27]

1028 OF 2000 ORBITS REMAINING: 43GREEN

"I can't! I just can't!"

Ingarra heard Miri's voice, shrill in distress, as she walked past the entry to the kitchens. Concerned, she stepped inside, looking for her friend.

"And who are *you*?" a man with a fraying braid demanded, coming to confront her.

Ingarra smiled at him. "I've come seeking Miri te Kendar," she said and, seeing his expression darken, improvised. "Gredin's asking for her, if she can be spared for a short while."

"She can be spared permanently, as far as I'm concerned."

That didn't sound promising but Ingarra didn't let her smile waver. "How very obliging of you. I'll be waiting, just outside, whenever she's ready," she said, and retreated.

Miri came out almost immediately, her cheeks chalky, her eyes damp and bloodshot.

Ingarra pretended not to notice. "Oh, good," she said. "Give me your hand." And, grasping Miri's chill fingers in her warm ones, she Sent them both to Gredin's quarters.

She wasn't supposed to Send. But she and Beda kept each other in fine Balance, and both Gredin and Keegan kept their shared suite tidy.

It would have been cruel to subject poor Miri to a lengthy walk past the idle gossips who spent their evenings in the reception hall.

Miri looked around the room. "Where is Gredin?"

"I have no idea."

Miri's shock melted into grudging amusement. "You told Horbil te K'lar an untruth?"

"Well, it sounded as if one more minute in that kitchen would have you either sobbing or doing violence to someone. Better to bring you to a place with privacy and no sharp knives."

That coaxed a wisp of a smile onto Miri's face. "I won't resort to violence, I promise."

"I'd rather not see you driven to tears, either. A difficult evening?"

"A difficult evening," Miri conceded, wilting. "A difficult time. A difficult life, and it's getting worse, not better. I don't know how much longer Horbil will tolerate me in the kitchens, truly I don't. Food is far too scarce to risk having me there, burning this and spilling that. Tonight, it was one of my tasks to place a tray of raised d'limten rolls in the cooler, and I dropped the tray. The rolls ended up as flattened blobs of dough on the floor. It meant hours of wasted work, as d'limten flour is slow to rise, and the incident tried Horbil's patience past the breaking point." She shook her head, a portrait of despair. "I suppose I should just stop trying… but sometimes I still manage to get things right, and those times bring me the only joy I can find in these dark days. How can I walk away from that? It would feel like turning my back on the Power itself!" Miri shivered. "Still, if I can't be sure of doing things right, I'll have to shut down the food stall at the maartza."

Judging that Miri needed answers even more than sympathy, Ingarra pondered the problem. What Miri said about the food supply seemed true, judging by all of the 'normal' things that had vanished in these first difficult weeks on Tradepoint. No more besk. No abundance at table, just a small helping that appeared on your plate, whether you wanted it or not. No extra helping of a food you favored. No mid-morning or late-day snack…

Miri touched Ingarra's sleeve. "Actually, I *do* need to talk to

Gredin, if we can arrange it." She shivered. "I'm very much afraid I know what's wrong with me."

"You're desperately unhappy that's all," Ingarra said staunchly. "Too sad to Focus properly."

"There is a sorrow that ails all of us," Miri agreed. "But some, like you, are dealing with it far better than others, like me. And if I'm right about why… Oh, Ingarra, if I'm right, then there will be worse times ahead for the community, and I don't know how we'll weather it, truly I don't. So I must find Gredin. To tell her. To warn her. Because she's going to be one of those most in danger."

[28]

1027 OF 2000 ORBITS REMAINING: 45BLUE

Figg reviewed the Day Report filed by station security, then checked the chronorb. In five hours or less, the Beng would leave the station, headed for home. Life on Tradepoint was always calmer when the Beng were gone. And the Rodorno had docked, earlier in the evening. They were a welcome addition, sensitive to nuance, wishing to offend no one. Getting rid of the Beng and gaining the Rodorno was a good trade, in her opinion. Now if the Hesch would just get past their boycott of the Vennans, who had entirely enough trouble on their hands…

Vibration under her feet – the floor mat, announcing someone's approach.

Moments later, Gredin te Balamont appeared in the doorway, dressed in the handsome teal and bronze outfit she had had fashioned from material gifted by the Shodekekeen.

"You're up late," Figg observed. "Is everything all right?"

"No."

Not the answer she'd anticipated, nor the one she wanted to hear. "I'm sorry to hear that. Come in. Have a seat. Tell me what I can do to help."

Gredin took a hesitant step into the room, peering at her surroundings as if she hadn't spent time in this room every morning for the past twenty days. She was pale and her eyes were bright with unshed tears.

"Are you injured?" Figg asked, rising in concern.

"No."

"Unwell?" Reaching the girl, Figg put a steadying arm around her and guided her forward, not to the benches but to the chair where Wyve usually sat, hoping that its back and arms would prevent the young Vennan from simply sliding to the floor. Then, returning to her own chair, she swiveled to face her visitor. "Are you unwell?" she asked again, speaking with slow emphasis.

"No." Gredin put a hand over her eyes. "Well, yes. But not in the way you mean."

"Have you consulted one of your healers?" Figg asked, cursing the fact that the Prett Clinic still knew so little about Vennan physiology.

Slowly, Gredin shook her head. "A Healer cannot help me. Nothing can help me. That's why I came to see you now, before I decline any more. To tell you that, soon, you and Wyve will have to meet with someone else. I won't be in charge much longer."

Figg recoiled. "Are you dying?"

"No. That would be… simpler. Kinder for the community. But no. I am not dying."

Figg slid her chair closer and captured Gredin's hands in her own. "Look at me. Listen to me. None of this is making sense. You have put yourself to the effort of coming here. Now explain to me what is happening. Can you begin at the beginning and help me understand?"

Gredin sat motionless, saying nothing.

"Should I call Burlon?" Figg asked, her concern increasing.

Gredin shook her head. "I can't find him. I tried, before I came here."

Figg squeezed the girl's lax fingers. "Someone else, then? Sill? Keegan?"

"No. Just… give me a moment. Let me gather my thoughts. This has been a shock…"

"*What* has been a shock?"

Gredin leaned her head against the high chairback and, with a visible effort, met Figg's gaze. "Your pardon. I will do as you suggest and begin at the beginning. Miri te Kendar sought me out, earlier tonight. You know Miri?"

"I have heard you and Wyve speak of her, in our meetings. I know of the recent popularity of her food stall at your maartza."

"Yes. She is our most gyfted kitchen Tender. Well, she came to my rooms, tonight, deeply distressed. She told me about a member of her House, a woman named Ulm te Kendar. Ulm's Chosen returned to the Source, long and long ago, due to an injury he received while working at a remote Kendar Holding. He could not reach a Healer quickly enough, and he died. Ulm was left to carry on without her Chosen..." Gredin closed her eyes.

"Would you like a drink of water?" Figg asked. "Perhaps you should rest. You can tell me this story of Miri's later."

Gredin's eyelids lifted. "No," she said firmly, "I do not need water. And no, I cannot tell you this story later. You need to know it now."

"Very well. But what purpose is served by the tale of one more Vennan whose loved one has been lost, in the face of so many deaths?"

"I am trying to tell you," Gredin said, her tone weary.

Figg resigned herself to patience. "Then I will listen. You were speaking of Ulm."

"Yes. Ulm, without her Chosen. I know of no one in House Balamont whose Chosen returned to the Source, and Ulm is the only one Miri knows of, in all of House Kendar. It was very sad... but then it became more than sad. It became troubling. Ulm did not regain her spirits, and she began to make small errors when she exercised her gyfte. Ulm was a Grower, and the plants in her care began to die – not from neglect, for she was a devoted Grower, but from being given too much or too little water, or too much or too little direct sunlight, or a dozen other situations where her judgment of what her plants required went awry. It was horrible for her. And then the troubles worsened. She made the same wrong judgments when heating or cooling her food, and frequently burned her tongue. Sending herself from her balcony down into the garden, she injured her foot by misjudging the distance and landing with too much force. Eventually, it reached a point where she could not do the simplest things for herself. She could not even convert her own waste, or Fetch herself a cool drink from the kitchens. One of her kinsmen had to be with her constantly, to keep her safe. She lost all Control of her gyfte, so that the sight of plants made her weep, for she felt she had failed them. She grew sadder and sadder, more helpless than a small child. With no ability to employ even the most minor gyfte, she felt estranged from the Power, and knew that she was a burden to her House."

"What finally happened to her?"

Gredin looked bewildered by the question. "Happened? Nothing. She was still in that state twenty days ago, when Venna was destroyed. Of all who perished on that day, perhaps only Ulm felt a measure of relief when her life ended. But that is not why I told you her pitiable tale."

"Why, then?"

"Because, preparing this evening's meal, Miri salted the stew three times. It was barely edible. And after the meal, when she reheated a cup of roin tea for herself and took a sip from it, she burned her tongue."

"Oh dear. I am so sorry. But why do Miri's troubles concern you? With a good night's sleep, she will no doubt feel better tomorrow."

"That won't happen. Weren't you listening?"

Chagrined, Figg reviewed the tale. "Ah. You believe these lapses of judgement were caused by Miri's grief?"

"No. We are all grieving, to one degree or another, and yet the entire community has not fallen into chaos. Many manage to maintain their Balance, and some have even regained full control of their gyftes."

"Then I am confused," Figg admitted. "What is different about Miri and Ulm?"

"The loss of their Chosen," Gredin replied.

Figg felt as if they were talking in circles, addressing the same issue but failing to connect. "The death of a Chosen is mourned differently from other deaths?"

"You talk as if death and mourning are common occurrences," Gredin protested.

"As they are," Figg said gently. "We all die, eventually."

"No. Not true."

Figg felt her ears prickle, as they did when she unexpectedly stumbled on a new piece of data. "Explain. You cannot mean that Vennans never die. I witnessed Cirin te K'lar's death."

Gredin's blue eyes were deep pools of sadness. "Cirin died of his injuries. That is always a risk. But, aside from such a mischance, we are born by the Power's grace, and we live our lives in service to our gyftes."

"Until…?"

Gredin looked at her blankly.

"Until old age or illness overtakes you, and your life ends," Figg suggested.

"No. Unless we suffer an injury too great to Heal, our lives do not end. Well, our lives *did* not end until Venna itself ended, taking with it the lives of all who were there."

Figg stared at the girl. "Your lives do not end?"

"No."

Ridiculous, she wanted to say. But then she recalled Cirin te K'lar's youthful vigor and appearance as he prepared to celebrate the three-hundredth anniversary of his first arrival on Tradepoint. Even if she dismissed the idea of a race that simply didn't die, objective evidence made it clear that they had a life span beyond anything previously documented by the Prett.

Small wonder they were staggered, now, by the loss of most of their population. They had no real experience with grief.

Wyve and I should offer counseling. We Prett have plenty of experience with death.

But none of that cleared up this confusion she had stumbled upon regarding Miri and Ulm. Figg folded her hands, putting aside Gredin's claims of immortality for the moment, to discuss later with Wyve. "Tell me again about Miri. Use simple words and be patient with me. Sometimes, between races, these concepts are difficult to make clear. Help me understand."

Gredin looked troubled by the request, but she nodded. "What do you want to know?"

Figg gave serious consideration to the question. "You say everyone has now lost many people they love, so why are you more worried about Miri than about the others?"

"Because her Chosen died."

Figg mulled over that response. "So… Miri has more difficulties because she lost the person she loved the most?"

"No."

"Explain, then, why she is having more troubles."

"Because her Chosen has died."

And around they went again. "Tell me in a different way," Figg entreated.

Gredin reached up to toy with one of her long braids. "Every morning, once I have spoken with you and Wyve, I return to the enclave for a different meeting, one where I talk with Burlon, Miri, Sill, and Keegan. A sort of… council. There are five of us, and we all lost many House members – mothers and fathers, brothers and sisters, Guides and Tutors and Mentors, kinsmen more experienced than many of us are and kinsmen who were still younglings. All gone. But beyond that, for this talk you and I are trying to have, you could say there are three ways of being."

"Go on."

"Burlon and Sill have Chosens here with them on Tradepoint. That is one way of being."

"All right. I understand that."

"Keegan is different. He has not yet found his Chosen. He could not lose her because he had never found her. That is yet to come, in his life. A second way of being."

"He has never had a mate," Figg amplified. "I see."

"And Miri and I are alike. We had our Chosens, but now our Chosens have returned to the Source. That is the third way of being."

Figg nodded.

"For the first way of being, like Burlon and Sill, they can turn to their Chosens for solace as they mourn, and their Chosens restore their Balance – the Traders say that you call this *dorada* in Prettian. Keegan must rely on friends for solace, as he is the only survivor of his House, but he is able to attend to his own Balance since he is Unchosen. But Miri and I... well, kinsmen and friends offer what solace they can, as we all mourn, but no one can help us restore our Balance, and so it is draining slowly from us, day by day, until at last we will be left as helpless as Ulm."

"Wait." Figg rubbed her face briskly with both hands, using the physical abrasion to counteract the lulling rhythm of Gredin's words. Something important was being said here, something she still did not entirely grasp. "I do not understand why your traders say that 'dorada' and 'balance' mean the same thing. When I lose my dorada – my 'balance' – I fall over. But that isn't what you mean, is it?"

"No. If it were that, we could simply sit down and carry on with our duties and our lives. In Vennan, there is another word. Hlinga. It is the energy that fills our vessels and keeps us in Balance. When it ebbs, it must be restored."

Figg sighed. "I think perhaps dorada was never the best term for your traders to have used. I need more words. Different words. Talk to me more about *hlinga*. What purpose does it serve in your life?"

Gredin's eyes widened. "It is everything."

"That doesn't really help," Figg informed her wryly. "Be more specific."

Gredin sat quietly for a minute, then said, "It is how we walk in rhythm with the Power. When all is well, our hlinga fills us and makes everything easy. Effortless, even. It is like swimming with the tide. We are supported and strengthened, carried in the direction we desire. At those times, it feels as if it has always been so, and always will be so, and we are content. Happy. Fulfilled. How we are meant to be." She smiled, looking wistful. "Just now, listening to my own words, I doubt whether anyone in the community is totally in Balance. We are too saddened by all we have lost. But some are much improved. Those who have their Chosens or are Unchosen are recovering most quickly.

Those who lack their Chosen… Well, they cannot progress. They can only fall farther and farther from Balance, and will never experience it again."

They were now approaching the heart of the matter, Figg believed, and yet she still could not connect all of the threads to make a coherent pattern. "You speak of people like yourself and Miri, yes?"

Gredin nodded. "Miri says in House Kendar, they referred to Ulm as bereft."

"And you're saying that people like the two of you can never regain your balance and replenish your *hlinga*? That you will never again walk in rhythm with the Power? Just because your mate died? Gredin, how can that be? I think… Forgive me. I am going to say some things and ask some questions that may offend or disturb you, and for that I am genuinely sorry, but I'm not willing to step aside and let you label yourself and others in your community as hopeless or lost or condemned."

"You are fierce in our defense," Gredin said, "but nothing you do can change this."

"Perhaps not. But you haven't convinced me of that yet."

Gredin lifted one hand and let it fall to her lap. "Then say your thoughts and ask your questions. I know you mean well by us. I do not think you will offend or disturb me."

Don't be too certain, Figg thought, and began. "Are we talking about emotion? Are you telling me that your love for your Chosen was so deep, so central to your life and sense of well-being, that you must now pine away without him? We have certain animals on Prettig that mate for life – they take only one mate, and if that mate dies, they do not ever choose another. Are Vennans like that?"

"No. And no. And yes."

Figg stiffened in confusion. "What do you mean?"

"You asked me two things and stated another."

"So… we are not talking about emotion? You will not be destroyed by your sadness?"

"No. I am deeply saddened that my Chosen is dead, but that is not what I came here to tell you, tonight. It makes me weep, but it is not what will undo me."

Figg considered her third utterance, the one to which Gredin had said yes. "But you are telling me that Vennans do not replace their Chosen, if that individual dies."

"Of course not. How could we? Our Chosens are selected for us by the Power."

Normally, talk of 'the power' made Figg's teeth ache in their sockets. This time, however, she tried to consider Gredin's information objectively. "The power selects this 'chosen' for you… and so the loss of that chosen interferes with your ability to 'walk in rhythm with the power'? Is that right?"

Gredin nodded. "The Choosing ceremony unites us, and our first mating alters us, attuning one to the other. We are meant to be together always. But Ulm lost her Chosen, and Miri tells me that Ulm's hlinga faded and faded until no vestige of her Balance was left to her and she was unable to exercise any of her gyftes."

"And you're afraid that will happen to you, now? And to Miri?"

"And to every other member of the community whose Chosen is gone."

As always when matters seemed dire, Figg reached for data. "How many people are we talking about? How many surviving Vennans lost their Chosens when your world died?"

"I don't know numbers. I know people. But Keegan has been creating lists, and he says that one of every three is now without a Chosen."

A third of the remaining population. And there were roughly a thousand Vennans in the enclave, so that meant roughly three hundred afflicted individuals. The figure made Figg's last meal move uneasily in her stomach. A thousand survivors had already been too small a number for viable diversity in the gene pool. And now Gredin was telling her that a third of *them* had lost their partners?

As a people, in the long run, the Vennans were doomed. And in the short run… Well, in the short run, Ulm's tale shifted from one woman's sad story to an entire people's tragedy.

"Tell me more about Ulm," she requested. "How quickly did she begin to decline?"

Gredin shook her head. "I don't know. I can ask Miri for more details when she is calmer. Tonight, she could barely talk through her tears. But we already see the early signs."

"What sort of signs?"

Gredin's shoulders sagged. "This morning, a member of House Calidane injured himself when he Sent down from his sleep nest, which was four levels up. Such a thing – to Send from the front platform of his nest down onto the visible floor below – should be no difficulty at all. He was not distracted. He simply misjudged the distance. Figg, we do not misjudge such distances. But he did, and his ankle was injured, and a minor Healer had to be summoned."

"Four levels up? He could have been badly hurt," Figg protested. "We'll have staircases installed as quickly as possible." She eyed Gredin. "This is a man who has lost his chosen?"

"Yes. But there will be no need for staircases. This morning, when we thought it was an isolated problem, we arranged for one of his kinsmen to assist him. Now that we understand the cause of the difficulty, and how wide-spread it soon will be, all of those whose Chosens died will be moved to ground-level nests."

Figg frowned. "And you mentioned that Miri had burned her tongue…"

"And over-salted the stew. Days ago, Ingarra mentioned that some Needleworker had accidentally pierced her fingertip with a sewing needle. If I inquire, I am sure we will find that she, too, suffered the loss of her Chosen. These are small things, but they are not usual. I fear we will soon see many more such instances, and their severity will increase."

"Until…?"

"Until every member of the community who has lost their Chosen is eventually shorn of their gyftes, large and small, and must be attended constantly for their own safety. They will be unable to Fetch distant belongings, unable to Convert their waste, unable to Send, unable to use their private mind for conversation, and, worst of all, they will be unable to exercise the gyfte that gives the most meaning to their lives. For like Ulm, they – we – are bereft. To lose both their Chosen *and* their gyfte is a cruel blow. And to know, due to that double lack, that they will never again experience true Balance, never know the uplift of spirit that comes from pleasing the Power…" She put her hand over mouth, pressing hard, as if to stop a flow of words that had become unbearable.

Unsure how to comfort her, Figg did what she did best: she brought reason to bear on the problem. "Can you explain to me," she asked, keeping her voice low, "*why* this happens? You say it isn't grief. Is it loneliness? Isolation? If this person was intended to be your life-mate, is it the lack of their companionship and support that causes this downward spiral?"

Incredulity transformed Gredin's features. "No. Nothing like that."

"Then what essential thing is it that your life lacks, with your chosen gone?"

An odd expression came over Gredin's face, a look that seemed to be formed at least in part of pity. "I know little about your people," she said. "Perhaps the needs of Prett are different from the needs of Vennans. But when a Vennan finds their Chosen, and the two make a life together, they mate. Their bodies… join."

"Sex," Figg confirmed, but saw that the word meant nothing to Gredin. "Yes, Prett do this, as well. It is how we make our children."

"Oh!" Gredin looked skeptical and faintly amused. "It is not the same, for us. Vennans have very few children. Sometimes two in all our years, or only one. Sometimes none at all. But mating is a different matter. Chosens mate every night, often several times in a night, and during our midday rest, as well. It brings us great joy and it restores our hlinga."

Figg considered describing the intricacies of ovulation and fertility cycles, and the many other factors that accounted for why not every coitus resulted in a pregnancy… and decided it was a futile effort. She could only speak to Prettian anatomy; she had no idea how much of that would apply to Vennans. Better not to challenge Gredin's statements, at least for the time being. Instead, she focused on Gredin's final assertion. "Did you just say that mating with your chosen restores your *hlinga*?"

All amusement drained from Gredin's face, replaced by a look of bleak despair. "Yes. Without our Chosen, hlinga ebbs and Balance soon begins to fade. At home, that was rarely a difficulty, but those Chosens with a gyfte for Traveling the River, or who Traded on distant worlds, took great care not to stay away too long, for their own sake and for the well-being of their Chosen. But now, when so many Chosens have returned to the Source, we who were their mates have no such recourse. We will fade, and our gyftes will drift beyond our reach, leaving us… empty. Bereft."

"Because you don't have your chosen to mate with," Figg said. "That is what you mean, yes? I have understood you correctly?"

"Yes."

A bubble of excitement rose up within Figg, but she tamped it down, not quite ready to believe. Surely, if the solution were this simple, Gredin would have seen it for herself…

But maybe not.

Carefully, Figg asked her next question, needing to confirm each piece of information as she moved forward. "You say it was a man who injured himself, this morning, trying to send himself down to the floor, yes?"

"Yes. A member of House Calidane."

"So men and women both suffer from this loss of *hlinga*? And both men and women within your community have lost their Chosens?"

"Yes," Gredin said, leaning back slackly in her chair.

The bubble of excitement rose again. Scarcely able to contain it, Figg said, "Then it seems to me that the members of your community need to help one another."

"We have been. We will. But it is going to be a terrible burden on the community when so many of us begin to need daily care…"

"That isn't the kind of help I'm talking about. Gredin, let me ask you again, so that I am certain that I understand. Mating with their chosen restores a person's *hlinga*, yes?"

A weary nod.

"And you have approximately three hundred men and women, like you and Miri and this poor man from House Calidane, who have now lost their chosens?"

"Yes. I have already *told* you this," Gredin said, frustration flickering in her gaze.

Figg leaned forward and took Gredin's hands in her own. "Then *help* each other," she said again. "Your chosens are gone, never to return. That is tragic. But losing your gyftes would be tragic, as well. Don't let it happen."

"We cannot prevent it!"

"Of course you can."

"We cannot."

"You can – by mating. You said so, yourself. Mating would restore your *hlinga*."

Gredin tried to wrench her hands free, her face contorted with tears. "Dreff is dead!"

"But the man from House Calidane is not."

Gredin stared at her, then shook her head. "You don't understand."

"Then explain it to me. After listening to what you have told me, this seems like the obvious solution. It benefits everyone."

"No. Figg, Vennans mate only with their Chosens."

The words were spoken with such utter conviction, and such an absence of outrage or anger, that Figg's confidence faltered. "Why?" she persisted. "Are you physically incapable of mating with another?"

Gredin looked bewildered by the question. "We only ever mate with our Chosens. It has always been that way. The Power finds your perfect mate for you, and the two of you are together forevermore."

"But now you *aren't*. And neither is Miri. And neither is the man from House Calidane. And neither are hundreds of other Vennans who feel their purposeful lives slipping from their grasp." She leaned toward Gredin, meeting her gaze with fresh determination. "You are telling me that if your people have never done a thing, that they never can. I disagree."

Gredin shook her head from side to side, slowly, then forcefully. "Dreff is my Chosen."

"Forgive me, Gredin, but Dreff is dead. He would never willingly have left you, I am sure, but events overtook him, and now he is gone. Forevermore. And you are faced with a crisis that could ruin your community. Did the power not instruct you to lead them, and to keep them safe?"

"I cannot. Not now. Not from this new threat."

"Is the power stupid? Is it cruel?"

"No!"

"Does it ask impossible things of you? Did it tell you to find a way to save Venna?"

"No."

"No," Figg agreed. "It asked you to protect the survivors. If your power is neither stupid nor cruel, then do not assume that what it asks of you now is impossible." She patted Gredin's knee. "You had a life on Venna. All of you did. It was a good life, and your laws and traditions worked well for you. I say this because, in all of our dealings with Vennans, we Prett have found you to be a peaceful, fair-minded, cultured people. But where are you now?"

Gredin looked up at her in silence.

"Tell me. Are you still on Venna?"

A slow shake of the head.

"No," Figg agreed. "Will you ever be on Venna again?"

"No," Gredin whispered.

"Then perhaps the laws and traditions you revere cannot serve you well, in this strange new future you face. Are you willing to consider the possibility of change? Of new ways?"

Indignation. "I have done little but argue in favor of new ways since we lost our world, however reluctant the community is to hear my words."

"Then there is hope," Figg said, and sat back.

Silence. Then, reluctantly, "How?"

Patiently, Figg laid out the logic again, as if she were assembling the necessary pieces of a machine. "In order to be healthy and to exercise their gyftes, Vennans require balance."

A nod.

"Vennans who have found their chosen need to mate in order to restore their *hlinga*."

A nod.

"Vennans who lose their chosen have no way to restore their *hlinga* when it ebbs, with the eventual result that they lose their balance and can no longer exercise their gifts."

A shiver and a nod.

"In the past, this was a very rare occurrence. But now, because of the destruction of your world, this fate has befallen a third of your community. If nothing is done to help them–"

"There *is* no way to help them!"

Figg waved her to silence. "Eventually, if nothing is done to help them, they will lose control of their gifts, and someone will need to stay with them constantly to attend to their needs. Doing that will place a heavy burden on the remainder of your community."

Gredin blinked, and a single tear traced a meandering path down her cheek.

"Are we agreed," Figg asked, "that this would be a terrible tragedy, both for those afflicted and for those whose lot it becomes to look after them?"

Another tear, and a sharp bob of Gredin's head.

"Then don't let it happen."

Gredin cast her a look of wounded reproach. "There is no way to stop it!"

"I say that there is. I say, at the very least, that there is a way for you to try, if you have the courage. You tell me that Vennans mate only with their chosens. What you *mean* is that Vennans have *only* ever mated with their chosens. And that was fine, and lovely, and right, so long as chosens lived together forever. But that life is gone now, for far too many of you. And so I look at what you tell me – that mating with your chosen restores your *hlinga* – and I add to that your acknowledgment that Vennans have only ever mated with their chosens… and it leads me to believe you may still be able to restore your *hlinga* and regain your balance through mating, even if that mating can no longer be with your chosen."

Gredin regarded her with something akin to horror.

Figg sighed. "Both men and women have lost their chosens. So both stand to gain – or regain – a great deal. Has your power forbidden you to mate with one who is not your chosen?"

"No. But Chosens find true happiness only in one another. Why would we look elsewhere?"

"And before you find your chosen? Does no one ever grow impatient or lonely, and seek pleasure with another, when physical maturity is new and spirits are reckless?"

"No," Gredin said flatly. Then she added, with a candor that startled Figg, "We simply pleasure ourselves to restore our hlinga and maintain our Balance until our Chosen becomes known to us."

Figg pondered that for a moment. At the Vennan reception, she had been surprised to see how airy and revealing their party clothing was, in comparison with the traders' usual garb. Thinking about it afterwards, she had wondered whether it indicated that Vennans might be a rather lusty race, within the privacy of their own enclave. Now she began to think it was a sign of just the opposite; this was a race with a moral code so strictly regularized that there was no risk in displaying their bodies, because no Vennan would contravene the social order.

But for them to survive, they might have to do precisely that.

"It would seem there is now a different need. Those who have not yet found their chosen, or who still have their chosen with them, can proceed as usual, and no harm will come to them. But for those of you who are garamog, a new time has come upon you, with new demands."

"*Garamog*?"

"Shorn of your mate, your 'chosen.' *Bereft* as you named it. The garamog can either cling to old ways and follow Miri's relative down into misery and decline… or they can be brave, and rally, and seek their own redemption."

"By…" Gredin's mouth twitched. "…doing this thing."

Equivocations were no kindness. "By mating with each other, garamog to garamog."

"We don't know that it would work."

"We don't know that it wouldn't."

Gredin hung her head. “I can’t ask it of them. They are so sad and worn down already, longing for home and familiar ways. How can I ask them to do this unheard-of thing, when it might bring them no benefit at all? How can I ask them to leap into darkness?”

Slowly, gently, Figg reached out and placed the tip of her finger under Gredin’s chin, raising it until she could meet her troubled gaze. “By leaping first, yourself.”

Gredin shrank from her touch. “Oh, Figg,” she whispered, “I couldn’t.”

“Then we will never know if it might have saved you all.”

Lips trembling, eyes shiny with new tears, Gredin said, “But I don’t *want* to.”

And then, to Figg’s utter bafflement, she laughed.

It wasn’t much of a laugh, and it didn’t last long, but it drained the worst of the misery from Gredin’s face. Taking a fresh breath, she said, “I used to say exactly that when Beda and Ingarra told me it was time to Send home from the Ocean Holding, when I stood no higher than your knee.” A shaky sigh. “They are not the words one expects to hear from First Speaker, entrusted by the Power with the safety of her people. I ask your pardon. You are doing your best to help, and I am digging my heels into the sand and refusing to leave the beach.” She took a wavering breath. “But I am no longer a child, with the luxury of whining.”

Figg withdrew her touch, content to watch Gredin think. The solution, if it *was* a solution, rested entirely in Gredin’s hands. As logical as the plan sounded to Figg, she had to acknowledge that Gredin had a right to feel deeply reluctant to become an active participant in it. And it wasn’t something Gredin could undertake alone. If she found the nerve to proceed, she would have to find a partner, a man who had lost his chosen, one who could be trusted to keep the matter private if the attempt gained them nothing, and who would be willing to take part because of… what? Civic responsibility? Fear of the loss of his gifts? Curiosity? Simple animal hunger?

A surge of protectiveness rose in Figg. She wanted the Vennans to prosper, but not at Gredin’s expense. How damaging might she find the experience, if it did nothing to restore her *hlinga*? And yet, if it did succeed, how daunting would it be for her to stand before the entire community and promote a plan so directly opposed to how Vennans had always lived their lives?

Gredin scooted forward in her chair. “You are a good friend, Figg. I thank you for your thoughts. Yours is not an answer that would ever have come to my mind, but it is worthy of serious thought.” She got to her feet. “I will return to my room and think on all you have said. And we will see each other at tomorrow morning’s meeting.”

“I will call a transport pod for you.”

“No. Please don’t. I need to think, and walking is good for that. Again, my thanks.”

With that, she crossed her palms, bowed her head, and made her way out of the office, leaving Figg to wonder, with a frown, whether she had just found a path to salvation for the Vennans or had done them more harm than good.

[29]

1024 OF 2000 ORBITS REMAINING: 46PURPLE

The public corridor was long and empty, and the glaring blue-white overhead lights made Gredin's eyes sting. She half-closed them, concentrating on the flooring panels directly in front of her, trying to ease the throbbing in her head.

What a day. Many of her meetings with the House volunteers had been maddening wastes of time. And the mere sight of Burlon at the morning meeting had made her flinch, though she ought to be over it, by now. She understood why he had needed the geddel crystals, but the loss still made her want to wail, every time she saw him. It made no sense…

A memory of Miri's voice rose suddenly in her mind: *Ulm became terribly emotional. The littlest thing could set her off, like the House not having the kind of berries she fancied at morning meal, or someone in a hurry not making a point of smiling at her before they left the table – the sort of minor things everyone encounters and simply moves beyond... She couldn't get past such things. She would dwell on them, and worry, and weep...*

Was Burlon's demand for the geddel crystals still troubling her because she was bereft? Was she showing other signs, as well, that she hadn't known to attribute to their proper cause?

Miri had been forlorn, even before the incident with the stew. And what of Tetralanna? Her Chosen, Elander, had left on a Trading mission even before Tetralanna came to Tradepoint. She'd had longer for her hlinga to fade. Did it account for her outbursts and flashes of temper?

A new thought struck Gredin. Were some of the House volunteers also bereft? Might that account for their increasing hostility and outrageous demands?

If so, their attitudes would get steadily worse, not better, unless…

No. No! She didn't want to think about Figg's words until she was back in her own room, with the door firmly closed. It was too threatening. Too unsettling. Too impossible.

But she had better hope it *wasn't* impossible. And she might well have to ask the Houses to select new volunteers if their current representatives were among the bereft…

At which point Tetralanna might rise and demand that Gredin herself step down, as well, since Dreff had returned to the Source. That would sound fair and reasonable. Had she not gone to Figg's office, just now, and said it herself? *Soon, you and Wyve will have to meet with someone else. I won't be in charge much longer.*

But stepping aside was not what the Power demanded of her.

Did that mean that Figg's outrageous suggestion would work? Or was there some third answer – neither surrender nor rebellion – that she had not yet discovered?

Oh, how she wished she could collapse into bed and plunge into sleep, confident that the Power would come and make the path clear. But that third visitation had been the last, and so here she was, her hlinga eroding, trying to discern what she was meant to do.

If she did nothing, she abandoned herself to Ulm's fate. Worse, she dragged a third of the community with her, and threw them on the mercy of the other two-thirds. Finding New Venna would be a tainted victory if much of the community that went there was crippled beyond repair.

But the alternative…

Figg, not being Vennan, didn't understand the impact of what she suggested. How could Figg expect her to–

No. Figg expected nothing. Figg explored. Figg questioned. Figg suggested. Wasn't that the very reason for going to talk to Figg? Figg was *other*. Figg could examine the difficulty with an objectivity Gredin could never achieve. And so she had bundled up her woes, carried them to Figg, and laid them out to be examined.

Figg had listened, and questioned, and considered.

And then Figg had suggested.

It was no fault of Figg's that Gredin found the suggestion horrifying.

Think calmly, she commanded herself, but her thoughts went skipping and plunging, careening as her stones sometimes did when she dropped them from a height onto a hard surface. Sternly, she attended only to the rhythmic impact of her slippers on the metal flooring. *One... two... three... four...*

By the count of fifty, feeling steadier, she considered the problem confronting her.

Since Gredin's matings with Dreff had enhanced her hlinga throughout their dydanin, Figg believed Gredin might be able to reverse her current fall from Balance by mating, as well. But Dreff was dead, and so any mating she undertook must be with someone else whose Chosen had returned to the Source. If it worked, it would save them both from Ulm te Kendar's fate.

And if it did not?

Then she would have done a terrible thing to no purpose. If it became known, Tetralanna would harass her mercilessly, as would the other like-minded members of the community.

But if it did work, there was no question of 'if' it would become known. She would have to *make* it known to the entire community, and make them understand that every individual who had lost their Chosen needed to do the same. And wouldn't *that* be–

Her foot came down on something, tripping her, and she tumbled forward with a gasp, banging knee and forehead and shoulder against the cold, hard flooring as she fell and rolled, coming up hard against the wall. Half-stunned, she struggled to lift her head as a blur of green appeared, inches from her face.

"Stupid Vennan!" a Beng hissed. "No look where walk. Cause hurt. Cause fall."

A groan – not her own. At least, she didn't think it was.

"Lazy stupid! Get up. Help Beng you hurt!"

"What?"

A chorus of Beng voices rose to mock her. "What? What? What?"

The Beng looming over her nudged her shoulder sharply with the toe of his boot. "You big. We small. You help Beng, maybe we no file Judgment on you."

"Judgment?"

Hands tugged at her wrist, pushed at her shoulder, her hip.

"Lazy Vennan no pretend. Get up!" one voice insisted loudly, while others muttered, "Hurry, hurry, hurry…"

More hands pulling and pushing. She was still sprawled, sliding on the sleek metal floor, propelled sideways, the fabric of her jacket and pants affording no friction as she tried to resist. Then she heard the sound of doors parting.

A Beng chanted, "One, some, ALL," and Gredin cried out as hands pushed at her in unison, jolting her farther.

Doors sliding closed. Then a smell like tongue-peppers: a bio-mist chamber.

"Quick!" several Beng urged, and fingers plucked at her jacket, trying to open it. Someone grabbed her face, pinching hard, turning her so that her field of vision was filled with the sight of a pair of angry eyes. "You try send Beng home poor, make big trouble for Beng. Ha! We fix good. We take necklace! Only fair. You owe Beng. We take from you, make equal."

They wrenched at her jacket, and she heard a button pop loose and bounce on the metal floor. Then mist-moistened air touched her neck as the jacket halves were pulled aside.

Hot fingers touched her skin, scrabbling. Searching.

Not finding.

"No necklace."

Exclamations of distress, anger, panic.

Someone tugged at a trailing end of her hlao. "We take this?"

A hand gripped the sleeve that covered her upper arm. "Armband she wear reception bigger. Gold."

"Ha! Take both!"

Hands tumbled her, jerking her head to and fro, and yanking at the jacket in an uncoordinated effort to strip it off. At last, the Beng succeeded in pulling it away, and she heard a little crooning sound of admiration as First Speaker's hlette was revealed. They seized it and tried to drag it down but it stayed stubbornly in place, as did her hlao. Fingernails gouged her skin as they tried to pry both items loose, without success. Then, hands gripped her. A Beng leaned close, brandishing something silver and shiny.

"Good knife," he said. "Much sharp. Blood make arm slippery, armband slide off good. You want me cut?"

"No!"

"Then take off band and ribbon, give to Beng. That way, no need cut."

"No!"

Another Beng muttered, "Mist gone soon. Already late. Hurry!"

Gredin cried out as the tip of the wicked little blade broke the skin of her upper arm, then prodded at her forehead. Dizziness surged through her, swamping her senses. Pain and nausea blurred what was happening. Beng voices echoed, overlapping each other, until one shrill voice cut through the rest, hoarse with rage. "Not go home with nothing!"

Her head was tugged sideways, and someone pulled at one of her braids.

A new pain began. It was duller than before, but it went on and on, and her head banged repeatedly against the metal deck.

The hissing stopped.

The smell of tongue-peppers faded.

She heard the sound of door panels gliding.

A savage tug caused her head to bounce painfully.

Vicious laughter.

Muttered comments.

A final pair of hands patted at her, searching.

For what?

For pockets.

Her pouch was in one of her pants pockets. The pouch that held her stones. Her last fragments of Venna.

"No!" Gredin screamed, and lashed out, her fingers arched like talons. She struck something soft – skin? – and clawed at it, provoking an answering scream from someone else.

"Crazy Vennan," a Beng wailed, and kicked her thigh with a force that made her cry out.

Hurried footsteps.

The sound of door panels again.

Then silence. She was alone in the chamber.

But they might come back.

Rolling onto her stomach, she tried to rise to her hands and knees.

Dizziness flattened her, and her stomach roiled. Remembering Keegan's first day at the Clinic, Gredin managed to brace her hands on the floor and raise her face a few inches above the decking before remnants of her evening meal spewed out between her slack lips. Horrified, she pushed away from the mess until her trembling arms gave out.

Shivering and panting, she considered her plight. Her body was rebelling, far more quickly than when the Hesch's claws punctured her skin. Gredin made no attempt to look at her upper arm, where the hlette still clung securely. She didn't want to see what damage the Beng's knife had done there.

She needed a Healer.

She needed to get far away from this place, before the Beng came back.

She needed the room to stop spinning.

Focus, she told herself. *Reach out to someone. Contact Burlon. Or Beda. Someone.*

But it was like telling herself to fly – impossible.

Then do something else! You can't stay here. It isn't safe.

She dragged herself toward the door that would take her back into the public corridor.

Halfway there, she realized her jacket was still where the Beng had pulled it off of her in their pursuit of the hlette, but she didn't dare go back for it. She would just have to ask Ingarra to make her another one....

When she reached the antechamber doors, she peered up at the control panel. It looked impossibly far away, and the buttons swam in her vision What would happen if she pressed the wrong one? Would the inner doors open, exposing her again to the Beng?

She wouldn't take the risk. Instead, she pressed her body tightly against the cool doors, closed her eyes, and envisioned the public corridor that lay just beyond. Blue-white lights. Metal floor panels. Metal walls...

And she Sent.

It was only a matter of inches – from one side of the doors to the other – but the effort made her retch. When she could finally squint through the glare and see that she was, indeed, in the spacious public corridor, she wept with relief.

But it was only the first step. Her next goal was the nearest corridor intersection. The direction didn't matter. She was already lost, or she would never have found herself outside the Beng enclave. Walking in a cloud of worry when she left Figg's office, she must have wandered past the corner where she meant to turn.

Well, done was done. None of that mattered now. She just needed a corner. Any corner.

It was a slow, demoralizing process. She couldn't stand, couldn't crawl on hands and knees, could only drag herself forward, using each new floor seam to mark her progress. Each time the effort seemed too great, the distance too far, she found new strength in her fear that the doorway behind would open, releasing a group of angry Beng to drag her back.

She would not let that happen. Would not... But when she reached the corner, she faced the same difficulty as in the antechamber: the control panel was far above where she sprawled.

This time, she had to reach it.

On her first attempt, she collapsed, retching.

On her second attempt, she made it partway up, but then her foot slipped, and she fell back to the floor, fighting tears of frustration.

For her third attempt, she removed her slippers. The bare soles of her feet found better purchase on the cold metal, and she thought she would succeed. Instead, dizziness overtook her, and she awoke, some unknowable time later, sprawled on the corridor floor.

That made her angry. With anger for fuel, she swarmed up the wall, spots blurring her vision, and slapped her palm against the panel before collapsing again.

"Where want go?" the mechanized voice asked.

Forcing words past dry lips, she croaked, "Prett security. Hurry. Need Prett security."

"Prett security call. Stay this place, you. Prett security reach you soon."

Looking down the long corridor, Gredin saw something move. As it neared, she realized it was a transport pod, speeding toward her at a faster rate than she had ever seen one go.

She stayed as she was, although it was impolite not to rise to greet them. In moments, the pod halted next to her. The guards tumbled out, then hesitated before approaching her as if she were a broken-winged bird they were anxious not to frighten.

Raising her head, Gredin said in Prettian, "I am lost. Can you help me?"

Then the spots returned, and she knew no more.

FROM THE PUBLISHER

Thank you for reading *Aftershock,* book two of *The Tradepoint Saga.*

We hope you enjoyed it as much as we enjoyed bringing it to you. We just wanted to take a moment to encourage you to review the book on Amazon and Goodreads. Every review helps further the author's reach and, ultimately, helps them continue writing fantastic books for us all to enjoy.

If you liked this book, check out the rest of our catalogue at www.aethonbooks.com. To sign up to receive a FREE collection from some of our best authors as well as updates regarding all new releases, visit www.aethonbooks.com/sign-up.

JOIN THE STREET TEAM! Get advanced copies of all our books, plus other free stuff and help us put out hit after hit.

SEARCH ON FACEBOOK:
AETHON STREET TEAM

APPENDIX

VENNAN HOUSE NAMES:

Vennan Houses are extended families (much like Scottish clans). A Vennan's full name consists of his personal name and House name, linked by the word 'te' (basically 'of'). Therefore, **Gredin te Balamont** means **Gredin of the House of Balamont**. The thirteen Vennan Houses represented on Tradepoint in *The Tradepoint Saga* books are (in alphabetical order):

House Avilar
House Darius
House Laith
House Balamont
House Fliss
House Shelahn
House Bentain
House Indirin
House Torr
House Calidane
House Kendar

House Vell
House K'lar

RACES PRESENT ON TRADEPOINT IN *AFTERSHOCK:*

The tradeteams of twenty-three different races do business on Tradepoint, but only a fraction of them are present there during the events of *AFTERSHOCK*. In alphabetical order, they are:

Beng — Short and sly, they all dress and look alike
F'lala — Mild-mannered and stocky, with cloud-like white hair
Hesch — A tall, intimidating, bird-like race, unnervingly interested in Gredin
Mamora — Benign but malodorous, a race trading primarily in spices
Polpethtira — Purple-skinned female tradeteams, tech specialists
Prett — This large, burly race owns and operates Tradepoint
Rodorno — Emotional empaths, solid allies of the Vennans
Thalken — Small, fragile, haughty, and artistic
Vennan — A delegation of 937 Vennans who came to attend the Trisectoriana

TELLING TIME ON TRADEPOINT:

Tradepoint is owned and operated by the Prett, and the time designations used on Tradepoint are based on Tradepoint's orbits around the planet of Prettig. The Prett themselves keep very accurate time, down to fractions of a second, but Tradepoint uses simplified time units for the convenience of the many different races who do business there.

- A day/night cycle is divided into fifty hours.
- An hour equals one Tradepoint orbit around the planet of Prettig.
- The hours in a day are numbered 1 through 50.
- Each hour is divided into five equal segments, designated by a progression of colors: purple, blue, green, yellow, and orange.
- Therefore, a meeting may be scheduled to begin at 23blue.

PRETTIAN TERMS FOR BLOCKS OF TIME:

Sect — A day (50 hours)
Sector — A month (40 days)
Sectora — A year (400 days)
Sectoria — A century (100 years)

FOR PRONUNCIATION OF ALIEN WORDS, GO TO: www.jjblacklocke.com

ALSO IN THE SERIES

REFUGE

AFTERSHOCK

THE BEREFT

ACKNOWLEDGMENTS

REFUGE and AFTERSHOCK would not have been possible without the comments, counsel, and real-world assistance of the following individuals:

• Matt Bialer, literary agent, who examined the REFUGE manuscript in its very earliest iteration when he put himself up for bid in the Worldbuilders charity auction, several years ago. Thanks, Matt, for your time and generous advice!

• Brett Hiorns, beta reader extraordinaire, who read a later version of the manuscript when *he* put himself up for bid in the Worldbuilders charity auction, the very next year. His feedback was both insightful and encouraging.

• Anne Tibbets, author and literary agent, who took the gangly, overlong manuscript under her wing, advised some judicious cuts to move the opening along faster, brain-stormed the title REFUGE, and agreed to represent the project.

• Tory Hunter, whose detailed manuscript critiques and encouraging pep talks have been equally valuable. (Don't ever go out of business, @PartyFreckle. You're needed!)

• Denice Domke, aka my Person, who kept reminding me of my dreams and encouraging me to continue trying to grab that brass ring whenever life threw me a curve ball. A good part of my joy belongs to her.

• Suzanne Barrett Nesmith, the best beta-listener ever, whose warm enthusiasm and encouragement made forward progress a pleasure and a joy.

• And special thanks to our team at Aethon Books: Rhett Bruno and Steve Beaulieu at the helm, Paul Simpson editing, Kate Reading narrating our audiobooks, and cover artist Tom Edwards. It took a group effort to bring *The Tradepoint Saga* into the world.

ABOUT THE AUTHOR

Born in the South and raised in the Midwest, J.J. Blacklocke wears many hats, with skills as diverse as public speaking, catering, teaching, and business administration. *The Tradepoint Saga,* which began with *REFUGE* and continues here in *AFTERSHOCK,* is the result of a private fascination with Vennans and the adventures forced upon them by a twist of fate.

For more about the Vennans and Tradepoint, visit the website: www.jjblacklocke.com.

www.ingramcontent.com/pod-product-compliance
Lightning Source LLC
Chambersburg PA
CBHW030351310726
48979CB00001B/256

* 9 7 8 1 9 4 9 8 9 0 7 3 0 *